BIG AND LITTLE SATAN

WHO WILL TAKE THE EVIL ROAD TO EXIT THEIR GRAVE?

BIG AND LITTLE SATAN

WHO WILL TAKE THE EVIL

ROAD TO EXIT THEIR GRAVE?

DIRTY DESERT INN
CEMETERY

6159

SHAWN L. BAILEY

This book is a work of fictional names, characters, places, and incidents that are the product of the Author's imagination or are used fictitiously any resemblance to actual events, locations or persons living or dead is simply coincidence.

PALMETTO
PUBLISHING
Charleston, SC
www.PalmettoPublishing.com

BIG AND LITTLE SATAN
Copyright © 2024 by SHAWN L. BAILEY

First Edition

Paperback ISBN: 979-8-8229-3895-3
eBook ISBN: 979-8-8229-3896-0

THIS BOOK IS DEDICATED TO:

First and foremost, I want to dedicate this book to my Lord and Savior, Jesus Christ. Thank you for your patience, guidance, direction and calling upon me to be used by you in a time of need for your children to be saved. Thank you for never leaving me nor forsaking me and for the precious gift you've given me to write books and minister your word. All that I do is for you.

I also want to dedicate this book to Benny L. Bailey, Ronald R. Arnold, Mary L. Bell, Don Watkins, Mrs. Sarah Watkins, Mrs. Jean, Dirty Red, City D, Ira Watkins and to my beautiful Queens Lavonna Bailey and Shavanna Star.

Mark A Bailey, I want to thank you Bro for being such an awesome person in my life. Always encouraging me to a better me, being a role model and my hero. Life is not the same without you in it, but I know we'll meet again. This book is especially for you. Keep encouraging me, I know your signs. I love you King 4life.

Lavonna Patterson, I want to thank you for giving me the most precious gift that any man can share in life; unfortunately God called her home too soon. But my love for you all will always remain in my heart. You are a phenomenal woman. Bishop Alexis Thomas. Benjamin Austin, I want to thank you Ben for every moment shared with you in life. We done it like Kings supposed to do it. Keeping them ten toes down to the ground for our riches. I'll see you soon, my brother, in our Father's Kingdom. Love you 4life. Bro RIP.

May you all rest in peace and thanks for such wonderful moments' times spent. Until we meet again, I love y'all 4life.

ACKNOWLEDGMENTS

To all my real mighty men and women followers. I'm going to acknowledge all of the haters across the world first. When it is God's plan it can't be stopped. Through my trials and tribulations, I had to find God in order to find myself in purpose. The word of God prepares the person of God, for the purpose God has chosen for them. So, thank you Lord for your patience and time that you invested in remolding and reshaping me into this new beginning and journey in the urban book world. There is no me without you. All Glory be to God.

To the person that gave me a strong encouragement to never stop writing stories. Kevin Sumpter, I pray you get to read what you inspired to be released on the world. Sometimes it takes raw and uncut criticism to get your point across. You said that if I ever stop writing, that I was stupid. Well, I am forty-three books deed with no sleep and can't stop and won't stop, until I leave my crown on the urban industry. May God bless you and may you prosper in all you do.

To my favorite lady in the whole world, Mary Arnold. I want to thank you mama for always being by my side when I needed you, and for setting a powerful example as to what being a go getter and leader should be. They said it takes a village to raise a child, well you proved them wrong because all you did was, be a phenomenal woman in the village and never giving up on your children. Thank you, beautiful lady for your prayers over my life, God heard you. Look at me now. Ditto!

To all my baby mama's. Thanks for sharing and blessing me with Kings and Queens to carry on my legacy. I want to give a special thanks to Kayla Lonnie for taking life chances and always being there when I needed you. Your love and respect for me runs deeper than the eyes can see. You're a unique and special individual and I crown you with much love and respect. To Cheryl Williams, you're in your own class. All my life you have sacrificed for me unconditionally and believed in me like no other. You have laid your life effortlessly on the line many times for me. Trusting and believing in everything I've done. You have been the cement to building my legacy through the good, bad, and ugly you kept me shinning. My love is unconditional for you and I'm always wishing prosperity and blessings over your life. Much love and respect to you all.

To my beautiful Queens, I love y'all until my last breath to breathe unconditionally. Y'all the purest diamonds of them all (a black diamond).

BIG AND LITTLE SATAN

To my Kings, I see me in each one of you, so I know the laughing hyenas ain't safe in the jungle, keep 'em ten toes down to the ground for your riches. I love you, Bailey Boys.

To my brothers and sisters, Regina, Rodina, Mark and Duke, we spent more time on the playground with Satan then with each other. God only gives us borrowed time in this world. Life is too short with all the bullshit, but y'all all know that it wasn't nothing but love and respect on mine. I cherish all gifts from God. We should have been a family of strength. Strength comes through exercise. Proverbs 24:10 say…if you faint in the day of adversary your strength is small.

Kimberly G, I want to thank you for always showing up in my life at the right times and making sacrifices to keep me on top. You will always have a special place in my heart. Keep shinning cause the real stars never came out until you touched down. Much love and respect 4life.

To my ride or die chick, every sense I sprinkled this ism on you, you been right by my side. Thank you for always believing in me and never turning your back on your king. Ms. Rayanna, you are what every man needs to experience in life. Lyfe Jennings say, when the wheel stops spinning, you didn't. 4Life, I'll always love you.

Lisa Griffin, I want to thank you for believing in me when I was counted out and everyone else jumped ship on me. There wasn't no time, pain or suffering that you wasn't willing to endure to prove your loyalty to me. You are a Queen of Queens in my heart and eyes. There are not just Kings that are crowned, Queens get crowned too and your loyalty is secured in the biggest vault of them all, my heart. Love you beautiful. Keep letting God direct our steps.

To my spiritual brothers from another mother. I want to thank Die Ru, Pitt's, Rocky, Devron, Darius, Slick Rick & Valentine. For y'all pens and time hearing these chapters given negative and positive criticism encouraging me to pursue God's gift in me. These hard times that we shared, too shall pass…"We in here baby"

To all my international cross country go getters stay tying up the highway whether going or coming just make it count. Sucker ducking ain't easy. It's more serpents in the game trying to trick Eve to bring down Adam. Here's a toast to the next BBB adventure. If I got to tell you what those B's stand for, then look in the rearview mirror cause you in a real one's way.

To all my grandbabies it's time that grandpa passed the torch because I know that each and every one of you will wear the Bailey crown well. Each diamond represents each and every one of you. I love yall and carry on this legacy. As Proverbs 22:6 say, "Train up a child in the way he should go and when he is old, he will not depart from it."

First off, I would like to thank Loyalty Graphics for helping to bring my vision of the cover to life. I want to give a special thanks to all the models for helping me produce such a wonderful book

BIG AND LITTLE SATAN

cover. Young Mac Fresh, Antwain Tyler, Sania Gilbert, Elizabeth Mercy, Ebony Write, Kelly Preston, and Naomi Washington thank you all again.

To all my readers, I didn't come into the industry to tell stories, I came to teach throughout my stories. I'm trying to reach the teachable readers. 1 Corinthians 14:38, but if anyone is ignorant let him be ignorant. I want to leave y'all with a spiritual nugget-there comes a time when we are to stop attempting to reach or instruct those who choose to be ignorant. When someone chooses not to be teachable, move on to another. When people say that they will, and continually do not, leave them alone. When a spouse, friend, or family member repeatedly makes promises and repeatedly breaks them, do not count on them any longer. Be a friend. Give folks opportunity; but eventually, if they continue in their own devise leave them to those devises. We cannot keep on feeding bad habits. There will always be people who will not change. There will be people who will choose to remain in their lost state. When we continually give them our time and energy, we rob those who are willing to change and better their lives. There is a time when anyone who is ignorant is to be left in their ignorance. My loyal readers, always look for the teachable. I welcome you all to the Roll'z Roy$$ of $tory Telling. Let's ride.

SHAWN L BAILEY

OF STORY TELLING

ROLL'Z

ROY$$

TO MY KINGS AND QUEENS THAT ARE INCARCERATED, DON'T LET THIS TIME DEFEAT YOU. YOUR
BODY IS ONLY AWARDED TO THE STATE, BUT WE ARE CREATED IN GOD'S IMAGE SO YOUR MIND
BELONGS TO GOD. USE YOUR MIND AND TIME WISELY AND BECOME WHO GOD SAY YOU ARE AND
NOT OTHERS
"THAT YOUR FAITH MIGHT NOT REST IN THE WISDOM OF MEN BUT IN THE POWER OF GOD."
1st CORINTHIANS 2:5

ABOUT THE AUTHOR

Shawn L. Bailey was born in Chicago, Illinois and was raised on the Southside at a time where he witnessed crimes, drug addictions, and deaths on a normal basis. His mother had him in 1967 and she was a single parent. He almost lost his life at the age of 6 years old. He was trapped in an apartment fire on 79th Troop but God had a much bigger plan for him. Shawn became a legendary gentleman of leisure throughout his lifetime. God later called him to Minister his Word. He was ordained October 3rd, 2019, where he was blessed with the gift that would leave his mark in the Urban Book industry for times to come. Some people say that he has a way to change someone's life, others have called him a prophet. But after reading his book you'll know him as The Roll'z Roy$$ of $torytelling.

TABLE OF CONTENTS

CHAPTER ONE

THE SWEET TASTE OF FREEDOM

I t was 2012, 10:36 in the morning. This was a day that Marquan never thought would come. He sat there in R and R, which was Roll-up and Release. He was waiting on Sergeant Edgemyor to come and sign his release papers.

That was the only thing holding Marquan in that fucked up prison. Marquan had just served 12 years and 7 months on a 15-year prison sentence, behind a female that snitched on him, and his partner. The only problem was he was sleeping next to her every day and taking care of her.

After the raid on his home in Chandler, Arizona, the cops confiscated two gallons of water and twenty-five kilos in the bust. Water on the streets of Phoenix, Az was known as Lovly or Sherman. But to the cops and lab techs, the drug was known to them as P.C.P after coming back tested.

"Hey Serg!" Marquan head quickly turned looking in Sergeant Edgemyor's direction, "Well what do you know? My how time flies. Looks like you're about to leave us Mr. Burton." Marquan put a half ass smile on his face, "Yea!" I can finally put this hell hole behind me. "Hold up Burton! How dare you talk about the Residence Inn like that. Man, you must want to stay here." Naw, Naw! Partna, I'm good on that. Ok! Ok! I take all that back. The Serg and Marquan busted up laughing.

"Ok Burton! Let's get cha out of here. Booking Number? 60208. Your mom's maiden name? Sheila Housemoore. Where were you born? N.Y.C New York; New York City baby boy! You headed back there? I still gotta take y'all bullshit a few more months before I can completely get my life back. Well, I wish you well, Mr. Burton. You made some bad choices, but you're not a bad guy. Thanks, Serg. Man, now get me the fuck out of here. The Sergeant handed him his two-hundred-dollar gate money and two photos. One was him surrounded by a group of guys at a nightclub. The other one was a female bent over in front of him holding money in both hands.

Sergeant Edgemyor seen many guys go crazy, behind Dear John letters, but the look on Marquan's face, told him that she hurt him deeply in a different type of way. The two veins that popped up in Marquan's neck after looking at the picture almost made Sergeant Edgemyor want to say; "Burton we'll save your bunk for you, because you'll be back soon." But he held those words and released him.

BIG AND LITTLE SATAN

Marquan came walking out of Florence State Prison in the City of Florence, Arizona. He took in a deep breath of fresh air and raised up his 24-inch arms on his medium built frame body. Marquan stood 5'10" with a physique that men and women would die for. The men because they would want to impress the ladies. While the women would want to invade every muscle on his body.

Marquan had brown skin with deep dimples on his cheeks. He kept a unique style haircut. Marquan looked a lot like a young Denzel Washington, but with a muscle fitness style body. The nurse weighed him before he left the prison. He was 239 pounds, but not with one ounce of fat on his body.

Marquan looked around for his ride and saw nobody was there. His man Supreme promised that his sister, and a nice dime piece for him would be waiting. Just as he turned back to look at the prison, that he never wanted to see again, he heard Marquan! Marquan! Marquan! The two most, sexiest women that he had saw in a long time was headed in his direction. Snooty was running full speed in his direction. Hey bro! She jumped into his arms.

Marquan couldn't believe that this was Sabrina, Supremes' baby sister. "Damn! Man, look at you! Girl! Look at you! Bro, you about to be driving the slut buckets crazy out here. Snooty grabbed Marquan's arm, "Damn" What you been lifting, the prison?

It hadn't been since 1999 the last time Marquan had seen Sabrina. She had to be about twelve years old. Now Sabrina was about to turn twenty-five, and was showing every woman, men were falling for on T.V. The Kardashians, J-Lo's, and Cardi B's can take a back seat to Sabrina. Marquan begins to look past her now focusing on the eye candy approaching them, "Hey Snooty damn! Y'all didn't tell me Dada working with all of this. 'Snooty?' 'Snooty?', Oh is that what people calling you now Sabrina? Sabrina and Marquan extended their arms, to better take in each other's physique. "Oh Girl," I'm so sorry, this my other brother Marquan. Marquan, this is SoSo.

SoSo had the biggest smile on her face, but the whole time, Marquan was wishing that Sabrina wasn't referring to him as her brother. Apart of him was wanting to take Sabrina down right there in the prison parking lot. SoSo extended her hand, "Hello Marquan!" So, what does the SoSo stand for? So So sexy? That even put a bigger smile on her face. 'Naw, I'm just SoSo that bitch, that the next bitch can't be.

Sabrina rolled her eyes at SoSo's comment and grabbed Marquan's hand. Come on man let's shake this spot. While walking to the car, Marquan couldn't do nothing but take in Sabrina big ass. While at the same time, telling his emotions and countenance to change. Before Sabrina noticed that he wasn't seeing a little sister figure behind her, SoSo was staring him down in the same way that he was watching Sabrina.

Sabrina started dialing on her cell phone and moments later said, "He right here bro! looking like the Incredible Hulk." 'Here man! She passed Marquan the phone and he was about to say

BIG AND LITTLE SATAN

hello, but Supreme S550 Mercedes Benz triple white on 22-inch Sprewell's silenced Marquan's words." What? What? Hell naw Sis, tell me Supreme aint shitting on the town like this? Man! That man got all type of toys at home.

Marquan finally spoke on the phone as Sabrina chirped the alarm. Chirp, Chirp. What's up my concrete? Supreme spoke first. Still solid like cement baby boy! He was telling Supreme that he was still ready to walk the pavement side by side with him for their riches. That was a childhood thing that they would say to each other.

Man, I see you sitting like new money on the pavement Supreme? SoSo was opening the back door on the driver's side for Marquan. He was so deep into their conversation to even prepare for what was about to happen next. SoSo closed the door and headed to what Marquan thought was the front passenger seat. But the back door opened, and she sat down and closed the door. Sabrina started the car, and they left Florence Prison and headed toward the freeway back to Phoenix. Just as Sabrina got on the highway, SoSo raised up the middle armrest. She took in Marquan's body for a moment. Then she helped herself to pulling back the black sweatpants he was wearing.

Before Marquan could even resist or stop her, SoSo took control of his penis and start giving him head. "Ummm damn!" Marquan almost started talking in tongues to Supreme. It didn't take long for Supreme to realize that now SoSo was in full control of their conversation. Hey Hommie, enjoy the ride home. I'll see ya when you get here. Not responding at all he reached Sabina her phone back slowly.

But to Marquan's surprise, him and Sabrina eyes locked on each other. The whole ride back, Marquan was looking at Sabrina and wishing that it was her who was giving him head in that back seat. Sabrina drove and watched SoSo take long deep strokes on Marquan's penis but couldn't believe that so much of him hadn't even been touched. It seemed like his penis grew and got longer.

Marquan was now starting to get more turned on by Sabrina watching. Then he was enjoying SoSo give him head while her ass shook back and forth. Sabrina and Marquan both almost at the same time made a silent promise to themselves. "I'm fucking him." "I'm fucking the shit out of her first chance that I get." Almost at the same time they gave each other a devilish smile.

While pulling up to the two story two car garage home in Mesa, Arizona, Marquan watched as the garage door slowly opened. His eyes went from the extravagant home to SoSo. She was still being SoSo that bitch! Sabrina pulled into the garage and hit the button closing it behind her. This was the first time that SoSo even came up for breath. To Marquan's surprise she hadn't even spilled a drop of semen on those new seats. SoSo wiped her mouth and smiled at Marquan. I hope you enjoyed it as much as I did. She reached over and kissed his cheek then exited the vehicle with Sabrina. "Bye Sweetie cum again."

BIG AND LITTLE SATAN

Marquan wanted to exit the vehicle but even as great of shape that he was in, SoSo had become the kryptonite to his superpowers. SoSo is creole and black with straight silky black hair. Tall and built much like Khloe Kardashian. But her apple bottom shape came naturally from her black side of the family. She has smooth caramel skin, that's flawless with high cheek bones. Her full lips and attractive gray eyes would easily win you over, just like her physique.

It was as if she left you mesmerized after looking into your eyes. Let me just say that it ain't to many men have told her no before. SoSo, twenty-six and extremely heartless to anything the average women care about. SoSo and Snooty aren't best friends. They were only business associates, but only when Supreme put them together to handle his business. Marquan, get your drained ass out that car boy! What, your main man don't get no love? Marquan knew that voice anywhere and it put life back into his body. He jumped up and ran to pick Supreme up, but Supreme side stepped him and threw up a hard open hand. "Wow!" Hold on big boy. You ain't about to be shaking me up like no rag doll. They both laughed and embraced into a brotherly hug. Man, look at you! "Naw Supreme; Look at you," living it up man. Now upon entering the house, Marquan could see that the home was just as extravagant on the inside. Damn Supreme, looks like the dope game been treating you real good? "Nope player" Same hustler but I'm holding a different poker hand. "What?" Don't trip we will holla later, but let's get you situated first my guy.

Marquan was eating an apple the next time that he saw SoSo enter the room. That pink sweat suit that she was wearing showed off her curves. But nothing like the two-piece turquoise lingerie set with a pair of black high heels that she was now wearing in the kitchen. Hello Dada, Supreme was doing what Marquan was doing, taking in the sexy attire SoSo wore. Hey baby! I'm sure you met my man, Marquan? Sure, Dada I did. I'm laureated to have met them both.

Marquan heard SoSo say, them both and at the same time they all busted up laughing. SoSo have ass fluffing up out those panties, like a fresh batch of pancakes. Damn boy, you a lucky man Supreme. Marquan couldn't hold back the suspense any longer. Supreme you really having it your way out here. What's the secret? But just as those words left his mouth, the side door open and one beautiful woman after the next entered the kitchen carrying grocery bags.

Supreme just sat there and smiled as his girls made Marquan's mouth fly open. Ms. GeeGee led the way. Hi Dada! Oh, this must be your friend you talked about. GeeGee put her bags down and popped SoSo on the ass. "Ouch!" that hurt girl! "Ummm yea bitch! That's quality beef right there; Supreme approved, ain't it Dada?

Marquan was looking at Supreme like Damn! What is this boy doing, pimping? All four of Supreme girls started introducing themselves. Hello, I'm GeeGee. I'm Glory. I'm Ecstasy. I'm Persia, nice to meet you. Oh Dada, look what I got you. The last to walk through the door was Supreme baby mama. Hello, I'm Stigma. After hearing her name, Marquan looked at Supreme with a supercilious look. He knew what Stigma name stood for. A puncture made with a sharp instrument. He noted to himself to watch her.

Supreme overlooked Marquan's reaction and started opening the bag of Oreos that GeeGee gave him. Man, you still eating Oreos. They both laughed remembering all the bags of Oreos they shared selling drugs together. To Marquan's surprise, Persia was white with blond hair and blue eyes. She could easily put you in the mind of Paris Hilton. She didn't have that traffic stopping body, but her long attractive legs and beautiful smile 34/30/32-inch backside. You know typical white girl suffering from Assital. That means no-ass-at-tall.

GeeGee was your hood, raised on soul food, sexy chocolate black female. She was twenty-nine with a body, and a woman of many hair styles. She built like Serena Williams, but she favors Ciara, with her slim face, and high cheek bones. Glory was the drop dead, ten of the bunch. It looked like God perfectly made her. The Commodores sang about Glory. The song was Brick House, and her measurements is 36/24/36 with that young Ashanti Babyface and lips. Glory 5'9", but everything sits on her in all the right places on her body. Ecstasy was an Amber Rose but with a face like Kylie Jenner, naturally straight black hair that stops at the crack of her ass. She Samoan and black on her mother side of the family, but her dad is Caucasian. When Ecstasy enters a room to most people, it would seem like time had completely stopped. Her 40 DD and 31-inch waist took to a 40-inch backside. That said, this seat is mine and taken bitch!

Ecstasy stands 6 ft without heels and 6.3 in heels like an Amazon. Which is what Supreme calls her most of the time. Stigma is the baby of the bunch. She had just turned twenty-two and small but very, very, explosive like dynamite. Stigma 5.1, 38/29/34 with long bowlegs and a gap to die for. She is another one who loves changing her hair styles with colors. Stigma, Latino and Chinese with soft cocoa butter skin and tight eyes. Stigma is also the mother of Isaiah Supreme Washington Jr.

Supreme came walking down the stairs dressed in a pair of black jeans and a black, white, and gold Versace shirt with black Versace shoes. Supreme looks a lot like Drake the Rapper. But with a more muscular physique and he keeps his hair in designer braids. Supreme also is creole and black, his hair also long black and silky. He like a magnet to women, when entering a room. He 5'10" and enjoys working out. And when he not lifting weights, you can easily find Supreme reloading clips into different guns and assault weapons.

Supreme found Marquan enjoying the PlayStation and basketball game. "Boy, you don't know nothing about that." What team you got? He had chosen the New York Nets and was playing against the Miami Heat. Even though he has Carmelo Anthony, The Miami Heat and LeBron were serving him up 47 to 24. But Marquan was just starting to learn the game.

Man, you got a lifetime to play that shit. Let's get you fresh and pushing something nice bro. Supreme unzipped a black bag and tossed a stack of hundred-dollar bills. "Here Family." Now let's go spend some of that Ba'Dussy pleasure. That's what Supreme always called money.

Marquan thumbed through the stack and counted $50,000 in cash. Damn bro this me? Naw! Shit! Unless you want to give me half of it back. Then I'll spend half. Your ass know how I spend money. Quick, fast, and in a hurry just like I make it. They both laughed. But Marquan laid that controller down and stood up fast. Come on then let's go player.

$ $ $ $ $

Hours later Supreme and Marquan were walking through the New Mall they built on Baseline (Arizona Mills Mall) and the Freeway carrying over ten bags of clothes. Marquan was also taking in the New Mall that wasn't there when he went to prison. He was enjoying him and Supreme doing it big again. That it reminded him of the old times they had.

After leaving the mall, Supreme started taking Marquan to different car lots to find him a vehicle to push. Marquan was mesmerized by all the different types of extravagant vehicles that lined the car lots. He appeared to be like a kid in a candy store. Supreme broke his attention, Man, you love my Mercedes Benz so much, let's go by my man's lot and see what he got posted up on his lot. Cool, let's get there. Supreme took Marquan to Scottsdale Road and before Supreme could turn up into the car lot good, it was like love at first sight. Dame Supreme! What's right there Preme? It was a 2009 Cadillac EXT Truck. Burgundy with peanut butter interior. Supreme said, "Man is you crazy?" You want a Cadillac Truck over a Mercedes Benz, Marquan, Damn my dude! Your ass has been locked up too long.

Before Supreme could even stop his vehicle good, Marquan was already jumping out Supreme Benz. Supreme started laughing happy to see Marquan home. He knew life was about to be good all over again. Having his right-hand man beside him all over again.

Supreme know Marquan very well, so he headed toward the office to go and make the deal with his dealership buddy Hason. Hason! Hey! What's up my friend? How's the Mercedes? It's no trouble, is it? "Nope my friend," I just brung you a customer with a pocket full of money. Oh! I like that. Hason started rubbing his two hands together, already smelling the money. Marquan was already sold on the truck. But when Hason showed him the four T. Vs in the headrest and the one popped out of the console.

Marquan went crazy. "Hell Yea, Preme!" This me right here baby! He felt like he would own the flyest truck in the whole world. Marquan didn't have a driver's license. So Supreme called Stigma

BIG AND LITTLE SATAN

to come put the truck in her name. Supreme had his baby mama put the truck in her name. Damn Dada another one? "Naw, this for my man." Stigma rolled her eyes and pulled off in her Benz. Supreme knew that it wouldn't be long before Marquan went and got his credentials straight.

Marquan followed behind Supreme in his New Cadillac EXT truck, showing all thirty-two teeth. Without even having to tell Supreme, he took Marquan to Circles Records on Central. Supreme already knew just how much Marquan loved his music. Plus, the truck already has a nice stereo system somebody already had installed.

It was starting to get dark outside, Supreme and Marquan had went stunting through the town just like old times. Marquan stops by his mother's house to visit his family. He gave his mother twenty-five-hundred-dollar bills just getting out of prison a few hours earlier. She tried her best to beg him to stay home. But that fast money and life had already given him that fever of street life.

$ $ $ $ $

Back at Supremes house after eating a nice soul food cooked meal, Supreme told Marquan to put back on his sweat suit and come take a ride with them. Not expecting anything negative, Marquan quickly got dressed. Supreme, Marquan, Ecstasy, and Stigma all jumped into a black-on-black Dodge Magnum with dark tinted windows and drove off. Ecstasy was driving with Stigma in the passenger seat. No music was even playing, pure quietness. Supreme and Ecstasy was talking, then he looked at Stigma.

Ok! Baby Girls! Y'all know the drill, just like we always do. "In and Out." Okay Dada! They both responded at the same time. What's up Supreme? You got some type of funk with somebody? Naw fam we good. Just back me up on this, Marquan. Supreme reached into the center console in between them. He removed a 40-cal pistol and a 9mm Glock and handed the Glock to Marquan. Boy! You still know how to use one of these, don't you? But before Marquan could even answer, Ecstasy said, "Dada! We're here." Ecstasy pulled two houses back and turned off their lights. She and Stigma exited the vehicle and made their way up the sidewalk, switching in their two pretty, custom dresses, walking, holding their purses real close to their bodies. Before Marquan could even ask what's going on, Supreme hit Marquan's arm, Let's go! Just watch my back, Marquan. They exited the vehicle, and the lights were flashing off and on, two houses down.

When Supreme and Marquan entered the house, the two females already had their weapons drawn on the man and his family. The white dude had already pissed his pants and was crying. What's going on? Please! Please! Don't hurt my family. I'll give y'all whatever you want. Just don't kill us, pleaseee!

Supreme said, "Well if you'll give us whatever we want, then why haven't you sent that money to Miami?" The man's eyes got real big. No! No! I told Harry that I'll need a little more time. Well sorry buddy your time seems to have expired.

Supreme, Ecstasy, and Stigma opened fire up on the whole family. Pow! Pow! Pow! Boom! Boom! Boom! But while they were emptying slugs into the family, they got an unwanted surprise from another man that was also in the home. He started shooting at Supreme, but Marquan was already pumping slugs into the man's body. Each bullet found a resting place in the man's forehead, chest, and stomach. Supreme looked at Marquan like damn, you saved my life bro.

In record timing they all were exiting the house and headed back towards the Dodge Magnum. Ecstasy exited the neighborhood calmly and slowly. Man! Man Supreme! What the fuck just happened back there? What just happened? Supreme, what did I just do?

Marquan was spazzing out. What the fuck did we just do, Supreme? Supreme called Ecstasy name and before Marquan could realize what was happening the Dodge Magnum was being pulled over on the side of the road. Stigma held a 9mm Glock to his chest, just like the one he just murdered the man with. Supreme grabbed Marquan by the arm. Calm the fuck down nigga. And I'm only going to say it once. He mean mugged Marquan. Marquan looked at Supreme sideways. Now Nigga! What's your fucking problem? Marquan started to get loud, but he noticed the motion of Stigma and changed the tune of his voice.

Man, I just got out of prison, from doing 12 fucking years and seven months. I still got to go see my parole officer Monday morning and I've already killed somebody. What the fuck am I going to do now, Supreme?

Well let's see, you just got out of prison this morning and you got your dick sucked by my bitchhh. You've been on a mad shopping spree getting fly. You bought a $30,000 dollar Cadillac EXT truck. Gave your mother $2500 cash and gave your sister and little brother money. Well, what you about to do right now is stop acting like a little bitch! You about to pull yourself together and let's get this money nigga!

Man, why you didn't just tell me first what was up? So, I'd know what to expect? "Well Fam," this ain't a tell all first job. It's a do all first job. To see just where we stand. And right now, Marquan, it doesn't look like we standing too good on the concrete, or are we? Marquan didn't speak too fast. He knew the very next wrong word could cost him his life.

Marquan thought about his mother, sister, and little brother. Oh! Plus, you just made some more paper to get your own place and put money into that new truck sitting in front of my crib. Marquan if we got a problem here, then it's best that the truck is already in my girl's name. No problem there, right? Marquan stared at him. Right? Supreme spoke again. "So, are you in or out?"

Marquan took a deep breath and finally smiled at Supreme, what the fuck you think nigga? I'm in for life Preme. You should already know that. "We until the concrete crack."

BIG AND LITTLE SATAN

Supreme held out his hand for his 9mm Glock back. Just as Marquan returned the gun, Supreme nodded his head at Ecstasy and she hit the lights and drove away. "We good?" We good! Supreme and Marquan shook hands, and they hugged each other. "Marquan! Bro don't ever make me question the concrete that we walk on again. Supreme gave him that look, letting him know that he ducked the grave tonight look.

CHAPTER TWO
FAMILY TIME

After returning back to Supreme house, the small dispute that Supreme, Marquan, and Stigma had in the car, Stigma wasn't feeling good about Marquan and clearly suggested to Supreme that it probably would have been at their best interest to say goodbye. Stigma even offered to solve the problem personally herself before it came back to haunt them.

Stigma had never but once saw Supreme show any weak affection towards anybody or anything. The only time that she witnessed something like that was the day that she gave birth to their son Isaiah Supreme Washington Jr. Now here it was time to kill, and that same emotional affection came into his eyes. The very moment that she was about to leave Marquan brains splattered across that back seat.

The look in Supreme eyes told her that, if she would have pulled that trigger, then she may have left Supreme's brains back there also. That sent a hurt and cold feeling through Stigma body.

BIG AND LITTLE SATAN

Stigma wasn't in love with Supreme, but she did love her son and that left her to be loyal to his father. The interaction with all the other women wasn't to please Supreme. It was more adventurous to her sexual desires.

Stigma sexually felt that men and women both brought her to boredom. But when she put them together, somehow, they put a spark to her flame. Supreme and Stigma rode in silence on the way to their home, where they share a home with little Isaiah and their live-in nanny Ms. Bergess. GeeGee, Glory, Ecstasy, and Persia, they all live in the same house in Chandler, Arizona. While SoSo stayed in a condominium in Tempe. She had bought her condo years before she even met Supreme.

The house in Chandler is where they all meet and spend time together. Mostly for business or sexual desires. Stigma always referred to the Chandler house as Hell. In fact, that was the home that she called Supreme Satan at. Stigma said that the house was hotter than the Arizona sun and Supreme abandoned the cross there. So that's the same place that God left him shipwrecked.

Ms. Bergess isn't just Supreme and Stigma nanny. This is the same woman that raised Valorie Ong. Stigma's real birth name. Ms. Bergess lived next door to Stigma and her mother, Adonis. After about two and a half months, Adonis never returned home, and the school sent the Phoenix police to get Stigma. Ms. Bergess fought the juvenile court system a year and three months to get Valorie Ann Ong back.

$ $ $ $ $

The next day came and life for little Isaiah was just as normal as any other kid living in Scottsdale. He actually was luckier than most kids his age. Because he still has both of his parents. Isaiah was knocking on the double door of his parents' bedroom. "Dad!" "Dad!" Wake up Dad! It's Saturday, dad. Are we still going? Are we dad? After knocking on their door two more hard times the bedroom door flew open.

"Boy!" What is your problem son? Oh, good morning mom. Hi! Where's my dad? Stigma smiled and stepped to the side. She pointed at Supreme still sound asleep. Little Isaiah rushed past his mother to go wake up his dad. "Wow!" Like that son? Mama don't get no love. He quickly ran over and kissed his mama.

Running back to Supreme, "Dad?" "Dad?" Wake up! Wake up dad. Supreme turned over quickly putting a smile on his face. His son was Supremes' whole world. Ahh little man! What are you all so excited for this early in the morning? Remember dad! Our shoes, our shoes! They came out today dad! Get up! So that we can be the first ones to buy them first dad. Michael Jordan was to release a new pair of Jordans today. Supreme always spoiled Isaiah with everything that came out first. Xbox, PlayStation games, shoes, you name it.

Isaiah isn't like your normal nine-year-old kid. He's very book smart. His nanny been teaching him since he could first read. So Supreme always reward him, not just with materialistic things but also with his love and time.

BIG AND LITTLE SATAN

Ok! Ok! Son, you go have Ms. Bergess make us some breakfast and I'll start getting dressed. She already making breakfast dad. That's who told me to wake you up. Gee thanks Ms. Bergess, he said under his breath. Ok son, I'm getting up. Isaiah ran out the room with the biggest smile on his face.

Oh! Little man says get up and you get right up Dada. If I tell you to get up your butt just lay there. Stigma made a sad face and crossed her arms. You told me to get it up, and didn't it rise up for you last night? Stigma walked over to the bed and grabbed his penis and started smiling. He always listens to me, but you don't Dada. They kissed and Supreme welcomed her to join him in the shower. Hell, forget that shower, I want some Jordans too!

Come on dad! Get up dad! Stigma said it imitating their son. Supreme started laughing. Man, you're just a hater. Stigma got on her knees across the bed. Come on dad! Dad! Supreme slapped her on the butt and headed to the shower.

Ms. Bergess has the whole house smelling good with bacon, eggs, sausages, grits, waffles, and fresh squeezed orange juice. Ms. Bergess is a high yellow heavy set older woman in her seventies. Fat eatable cheeks with smooth pretty skin. Her hair is long, thick, and black like she an Indian woman.

Hey Ma! Good morning Ms. Bergess. Oh, good morning baby! Hey Preme. That's what Ms. Bergess always called him. Y'all take a seat and let me fix these plates. That son of y'alls was up bright and early this morning. Complaining about some tennis shoes. He says,

Nanna! Nanna! Wake my dad up so that we can go and buy my J's. His J's is all that he been talking about for the past three days. Child! Please go buy that boy some J's. They all busted up laughing. Where is he at mama? You know that boy, child. He ate two bowls of cereal and ran to that room to play video games, child.

$ $ $ $ $

Ms. Housemoore stood over Marquan watching him in spurts. Yelling out different things in his dream. She is a God-fearing woman and know the behavior of someone acting out like her son. Ms. Housemoore knew that he was either fighting off something, someone, or demons. She was staring at Marquan strangely when he woke up. "Mama!" What are you doing? He jumped up. Why you just standing there watching me? Ms. Housemoore just stood there and said nothing. She wouldn't allow him, being startled to take her out of the prayer that she was in. Mama! Mama!

Ms. Housemoore sat down at the edge of the bed then looked up at her son. Marquan, you just got out of prison yesterday. Boy! How could you be so stupid? What are you getting yourself into now, Marquan? Tears began to roll down her face. Now for the first time, Marquan noticed the pain that he was causing her. Marquan bent down on one knee and reached for her hands. Mama, I'm fine. You don't have to worry about me. I'll never leave y'all alone again. I promise you that. That made her cry even more, hearing those words.

BIG AND LITTLE SATAN

Marquan, I go to work every day. I've been doing it for the last 12 years you been gone to provide for this family. Son, nine out of them 12 years, I've been driving that same car. That you got blocked in, with the devil's gift that he bribed you with. God makes a way out of no-way for us in this house. I've been waiting twelve years, seven months and one day, for you to bring your black ass in this house. "Boy, then the first thing that you do is bring Satan and destruction to my home." Marquan knew that she meant Supreme and his Cadillac truck.

His mother reached into her bra and removed the $2500 dollars that he gave her. Here boy! Take this fire, I don't need the devil's money son, and you don't either. Don't allow the devil to destroy our home and lives again, son. We love you, Marquan. You have a family who cares. Marquan's eyes begin to fill up with tears. It was at that moment that he realized that he had sold his soul to the devil last night.

Ms. Housemoore put her son's chin in her hands, and she looked him right in the eyes. Marquan, what did you mean when you said, what have I done Supreme? Marquan realized that what he had encountered reflected on him so badly. That he must have repeated part of him and Supremes conversation in his sleep.

Marquan removed her hand, "Mama, I didn't mean nothing that I can't fix." Hearing them words, Ms. Housemoore knew that it would be just a matter of time, that once again in her life that she would lose Marquan to the streets. They both were quickly interrupted by a knock on the door. Hey Bro! Mama! What's the matter? Why are you crying? Marquan's sister walked into the room and detected that something was wrong.

Ms. Housemoore lied not wanting to upset her daughter. She wiped away her tears. All girl, ain't nothing wrong baby. I'm just happy that your brother is home and now I got all my kids. Whitney still gave them a suspicious look. Then she kissed her mom and then Marquan. Boy! Don't be stressing my mama out no more. We have been dealing with her crying and missing you for 12 years. Marquan don't make me kick your butt about my mama boy!

What? What? Marquan grabbed Whitney and started tickling her. Stop boy, stop! Mama! You gone do what girl? Ms. Housemoore walked out of the room to gather herself.

Marquan, here son take this money and y'all run to the store for me. Ms. Housemoore was in the kitchen trying to finish making the potato salad for the church BBQ that they were having at the park. Give me the list mama, I got you. Ms. Housemoore removed a fifty-dollar bill from her purse. Then she gave Marquan a look that sent chills through his body. "Ok mama" He smiled and took the money and list. Come on Whit! She ran and grabbed her shoes. Bro wait, wait! I'm coming. Say mama, do you got a couple of stamps and a few envelopes? Whitney, grab your brother a couple of stamps and envelopes off my dresser. Ok mama.

Boy, what do you need stamps and envelopes for? You are at home now Marquan. I want to look out for Twan and Chris. You know I can't forget about them mama. Yea I saw Twan mother at the light yesterday. But we couldn't talk thou. She was just yelling that she knew that I was happy cause you were coming home.

Marquan how that baby holding up in there? Mama, you know how hardheaded Rocky is. When does he get out? He got six more years, but I ain't playing with you boy! You better get yourself together first, talking about you got the hommie. Ms. Housemoore rolled her eyes at Marquan.

Looking back over her shoulders, don't think we ain't going to talk later. So, you can make up all the lies that you want to. You're going to tell me where that expensive truck came from Marquan.

$ $ $ $ $

Whitney took Marquan to the Fry's by their house on Camelback Road. Marquan parked his truck right in front of the store. Boy! What are you doing? You can't park like this! It's not 1999 Marquan. They will tow this nice truck. Park right there! We can still see your truck bro.

Marquan was hesitant but decided to park right. Marquan and Whitney were play fighting, until he stopped walking and just watched as some female body sashayed across the pavement. Whitney missed whatever it was he was watching or quickly got his attention. But she saw what it was upon entering the store. Because the female even caught Whitney's attention.

"Yea!" She is cute bro, but I think Ole Boy is about to beat you to her. Another man shopping was already following the attractive young lady that was catching everyone's attention with that provocative walk. Whitney is an extremely outgoing female herself. If you knew her, she is the one that's the life of the party. She gives great conversation and always asks intellectual questions. Ever since she turned eighteen, grown men would always approach her, even at times when she was shopping with Ms. Housemoore. She'd always threaten to kill them about her baby, who looks like the singer Rihanna.

Marquan laid back and watched as the attractive female turned down ole boy pretty fast. So that made him hesitant to approach her too fast. But all that would quickly change at the checkout counter. It was a man separating them and Marquan couldn't do nothing but stare. "Damn she beautiful."

But surprisingly the female spoke to Marquan first. "Hello!" Your girl hair is pretty. Who done that? Whitney started laughing, girl that's my brother but thank you. My mother done my hair. Hey, do she got a shop girl, or did you get that home care love? They smiled at each other and laughed. Knowing that the home care love is a female inside joke. Marquan said, Sexy! Beautiful as you are, I'll make sure she braids your hair and I'll pay for it.

Thanks for the compliment, but sorry, I pay my own way sweetie. Trust me handsome, "God do provide." Almost at the same time Marquan and Whitney said 'Ooh Wee! My mother would definitely love you then. All three of them laughed at their comment.

BIG AND LITTLE SATAN

Whitney asked her, "Girl, what church do you go to?" Pilgrim Rest Church, Bishop Alex Thomas. Oh! We been to that church before. That's on the Eastside of town, right? Yes. Marquan took another shot at her. Can you give me your name and number? I'll be sure to call you. I mean have my mother call you. That's cool. I don't mind you trying to holla, but God is my man and you got to go through him to get to me, honey.

The female realized that she forgot something else important, so she waited for the cashier to get it. By the time the female came walking out the store, Marquan was following behind her with his truck. I'm sorry, Marquan started telling her while leaning out the window. But you got to excuse my truck, it's got its own mind and attracted to beautiful things.

'Well find it a thing Sweetie, cause I'm a woman". Have a blessed day. She hit the remote button and her Lexus Gs 400 chirped. Marquan stopped and jumped out of his truck. Whitney was shaking her head. AYE! Beautiful Lady, I meant you no harm. I'm not trying to run game at all. I just feel like we can complete each other's world. She smiled.

I'm not sure what world you're in but my world is with God. Besides, we both know that most men don't have time for him. Their minds are mostly on money, women, and sex, right? But mostly sex. So, I can't help you, Sweetie! She started her car. Aye I never got your name. Besides that, Sweetieee! You never invited me to church. So how am I ever going to get to have a relationship with the Father or daughter? That quickly got her attention. "What Christian wouldn't invite someone to Christ?

Ok Man, I see that you're real persistent. You don't give up do you? She grabbed a pen and started writing her number on her receipt. Here stalker man. She started laughing at her own comment. Don't be having your women calling my phone. Besides, where is your woman?

Marquan looked at the receipt. "Emoni" Emoni, look in that mirror right there. He pointed to her rearview mirror. Emoni looked into the mirror, Marquan pointed. There she go! There go my woman right there. Emoni couldn't do nothing but smile. Yea! Whatever man, you're crazy. Maybe we'll have to just see about all that. Now stop holding me hostage and move your truck.

Marquan was about to leave Fry's and almost forgot about his two friends. Come on Whitney, we've got to go back in the store. Why? I forgot to grab the money orders. Marquan came back holding two money orders and told Whitney to fill them out. To who, boy? To Antwan Simmons and Christian Anderson. They both were $200 dollar money orders. He filled out the two envelopes, that was an address that Marquan could never forget. He placed their booking numbers on the money orders. Hey Whitney! Where can I, and in mid-sentence he spotted a mailbox. Marquan jumped out of his truck, remembering all the days of missing commissary.

He gave Rocky and Slow Drag his word, that they wouldn't experience no more of them days. At least not as long as, he was free.

BIG AND LITTLE SATAN

He made a note to himself that the next time he was in a store to grab a camera to send them pictures of him and his Cadillac truck.

Marquan's mind went back to Emoni, and he knew that the two of them would be in most of those pictures. In his mind he was already making future plans for him and Emoni to be together and have kids.

After Marquan and Whitney took Ms. Housemoore her groceries, Marquan decided to take Whitney and his little brother Jacob shopping. They went to the Spectrum Mall on Bethany Home Road. Besides Supreme told Marquan to buy a cell phone and call him later with the number.

Before he left Supreme, he gave Marquan another $25,000 for that work that they put in. But Marquan didn't know that Supreme really collected $300,000 for the job. The job paid $50,000 a head and they left six bodies behind.

Marquan and Whitney have the same dad, but Jacob was by another contributor that planted his seed and kept on traveling. Even thou Marquan knew that his mother wouldn't accept his gift, he bought Ms. Housemoore a $5,000 dollar tennis bracelet from Daniel Jeweler's. He didn't let Whitney or Jacob see him buy it. Besides, they were too busy going through the thousand dollars a piece that he gave them to spend.

Jacob is twelve years old. He was born right after Marquan went to prison. Ms. Housemoore always said that was God's way of blessing her for losing Marquan. Marquan and Jacob's relationship developed over prison visits and phone calls. Now Marquan was happy that he was there in his life.

After leaving the Spectrum Mall, they were putting their shopping bags in Marquan's truck. Jacob said, AYE bro, can I drive? Whitney snapped, Hell Nall! You can't drive boy. Y'all ain't about to kill me!

Marquan said, come around on this side little bro. Whitney started fussing at the both of them. Marquan, you can't let that boy drive this truck. Are you crazy? You don't even got your license, Marquan.

Jacob jumped up in Marquan's lap to steer the truck. Marquan, mama gone kill y'all! Why? You go tell, Whitney? You know that I hate snitches sis. Don't tell me that you one of them, too! Whitney took a deep breath and was really upset. But she chose not to say nothing. Marquan said, Wait bro! Let me drive to the other side of the mall. I saw a lot of open space over there. Jacob was smiling at Whitney from ear to ear. Just as Marquan got where there weren't that many cars, he allowed Jacob to take the steering wheel.

For a minute, Jacob was handling the truck pretty good. But the adrenaline and excitement made Jacob want to go faster. He stepped on Marquan shoe, go faster bro. The power under the Cadillac truck responded to the pressure. The truck speeded up and Jacob have full control of the wheel. Whitney started screaming and hollering. "We about to crash"! They were headed straight into a bunch of parked cars that was parked in front of the Walmart that's next to the mall.

BIG AND LITTLE SATAN

But in just a nick of time, Marquan overpowered the steering wheel from Jacob. He almost ran straight into a Ford Expedition. 'Boy lookout, Whitney shouted! She slapped Jacob right upside his head. Jacob started crying. Marquan swiftly maneuvered the Cadillac truck around the Expedition. Marquan stopped the truck and took a deep breath. "Whooo!" Whitney started yelling at Jacob. "Boy! What's wrong with you"? Are you stupid? You almost killed us fool!

Jacob started crying harder. Hey! Hey! It's okay Whitney. And don't you never let me hear you call him stupid again. That was my fault. Stop crying little bro. It's okay. It's okay, chill. I see you got your mama's driving skills.

That made Jacob and Whitney laugh. We need to work on this some other time. Yea! But not with me up in this truck. Marquan realized where they were at. Hey, wait I believe that I can fix this problem.

$ $ $ $ $

Hours later…Those tears that Jacob had rolling down his face was now the biggest smile you could ever see on a kids face. Marquan had taken him into Walmart and bought him a PlayStation 3, five video games, plus all the accessories to the PlayStation game. Marquan even made sure that he had his own steering wheel to go to his racing game. Whitney thought about their mother and knew that she was going to have a cow. But hell; what could she really say about anything? She couldn't afford to buy them things like this.

Ms. Housemoore always told her kids to let God provide for them. Whitney felt that from where her and Jacob sat right now that God was doing a fantastic job providing for them right now. Whitney was playing with Jacob on the way back to Marquan's truck. Hey! Hey! Excuse me handsome. Marquan, Whitney, and Jacob all turned around to see who was trying to get their attention. Handsome, can I go home with y'all too? Or are you already spoken for?

Marquan really didn't know how to respond. He wasn't used to females being so forward, 'before he got locked up, the men usually approach women'; the way she was approaching him in front of Whitney and Jacob. But now Marquan could see that times have changed.

When a female felt that she can see a future or happiness in a man, they get bold and don't allow their future to walk away. Then there's females that are looking to be pampered. So, they see a man with money as a sugar daddy or trick. That will make them pursue that guy.

Marquan took in her beauty and couldn't believe that she was coming at him so boldly. Once again, he thought about SoSo and it made him get an erection. Excuse me sexy, but do I know you from somewhere? Nope! But you can get to know me if you're not already taken. Whitney knew that the female was thirsty and was

BIG AND LITTLE SATAN

just jocking Marquan's truck and money. Bro let's go! Her ass just thirsty for your money.

The female rolled her eyes at Whitney. Oh, Miss lady, I'm so sorry is that your man? Marquan turned around and snapped at Whitney. Aye, you need to stay in a little girl's place. Go put your brother's stuff in the truck. I'll be with y'all in a minute. Whitney was embarrassed and the female laughed in Whitney's face. Whitney said under her breath, "Fine with me. Be stupid then with her ugly self. Come on boy!"

I'm sorry about my sister's behavior. I'm Marquan and you, sexy lady? She smiled, I'm Angelica but everybody calls me Star at the Strip Club. Oh, you a stripper? Yea! Why is that a problem? Naw! No. We all got to make a living somehow, right?

An hour and a half had gone by. Marquan and Star were so into each other that they forgot Whitney and Jacob was sitting in his truck. Whitney blew the horn taking them out of their moment of laughter. Marquan and Star exchanged numbers and made plans to see each other later. Marquan got his first phone call on his new cell phone, which made Whitney laugh at him now because he didn't know how to answer the phone.

He kept saying hello, hello. Marquan was now looking at Whitney for help. She snatched the phone out of his hand and push send. Hello! Now Marquan was feeling embarrassed the way Whitney felt. Whitney passed him the phone back. Here boy! It's your little hot box girlfriend. Whitney already knew that she would be seeing more of Star. She rolled her eyes and thought to herself. Why was boys and men so stupid behind women?

CHAPTER THREE

TWO FOR ONE

arquan had gotten the address to Satan Dolls Strip Club on Indian School Road from Star. One problem that he didn't have was finding a place in Phoenix. He knows his way around Phoenix like the back of his hand. Marquan pulled up to the strip club a little after midnight. The crowd that was trying to get into the club was checking out his truck. Upon trying to enter the club, Marquan ran into a slight problem. He forgot that he didn't have no identification. So, he found himself left in that embarrassing position again. "Damn! My ID."

The bouncers knew just about everybody that regularly came to the club. They weren't about to chance it with Marquan. He could easily be a cop or someone trying to close the club. I'm sorry buddy, but you must have identification to come in the club.

Just as Marquan was about to turn away, Star had been also watching out for Marquan and she was stepping out to tell the bouncers to look out for him. Hi baby! Star came walking up behind Big Chub just as Marquan was about to leave. Star, is this your guest? Do you know this Kat? Yea man! That's my daddy, right there! Star grabbed Marquan by the hand and led him into the club. Big Chub moved to the side and allowed Marquan to enter.

Star was so attractive and sexy, that Marquan's head and chest went up high. But no matter what direction that Marquan turned to; each female was just as attractive as the next. But Star stood in her own lane over all the other females.

Her 5'9" frame and high yellow complexion almost past her off as a white woman. Her green eyes and 40 DD, 31-inch waist and 44-inch backside, spoke its own language to most men and their wallets. You could set a 40-ounce bottle on Star's ass and the bottle wouldn't move.

Watching Star muddle off her Tina Turner legs in that white Teddy lingerie, it seems like Victoria Secret had made it right on her body. Her hair was blond with a few burgundy streaks that went past her shoulders.

Star asked Marquan, 'Baby, what will you have to drink"? He looked her straight into her eyes and said, You, Pretty Lady, before the night is over. That made Star get hot in all her secret places.

Star led Marquan to a table and sat him down. The D.J played Suga Free, "Get Cha Money, Why You Bull Shittin". Star began to let her body do things that Marquan didn't even know a body could do. Star popped and wiggled her ass, now drawing a major crowd around them. She got on her hands and put both legs on each one of Marquan's shoulders. Then she shook her ass to the beat. Marquan head followed Star's ass and Sugar Free music. By the time she finished, the whole club was whistling and shouting, "Star!" Star! Star! Marquan was smiling and laughing. He has never experienced the strip club life before.

When a woman would have done all that Star let Marquan see her do. Marquan felt that he would have been having sex, then would be ready to sleep for hours. Marquan was feeling like he already had a sexual encounter with Star and they ain't touched each other yet.

Marquan didn't know what that experience was, but he did know that he wanted more of it. Star had to leave Marquan, because it was time for her next performance, and she had to make it backstage. Before leaving him, she made sure that he was comfortable. Star kissed Marquan on the lips and promised to return soon.

$ $ $ $ $

The D.J announced the next dancer to the stage. Ladies and Gentlemen, our next dancer is so hot and flexible with her body. That I have to go change my boxer after all of her performances. Let's give a warm welcome to Snooty with that exotic booty.

Rick Ross, "Money make me cum," came on and all the fellas rushed the stage, making it rain on snooty. She came on stage in a nude two-piece booty short set and three-inch stiletto high heels.

Bouncing and popping her ass like she owned the stage. Marquan was so into admiring the club and taking in all the dancers. That he hadn't even noticed the name when the D.J announced her.

Marquan did notice that whoever was on the stage they were setting off fireworks for the fellas. All types of bills were going up in the air and landing on the stage. Marquan had just downed a glass of Hennessy at Star's request, and it was making him more comfortable.

Just as Marquan stood up, the waitress came and handed him another drink. Plus, a napkin with a phone number on it. It said call me, Spicy! The waitress pointed at the female who sent the number and drink. She smiled at Marquan while shaking her ass on a customer face. Marquan held up her number and let her see him place it in his pocket. She blew a kiss and turned around to complete her dance.

Marquan made his way over to the stage to interact to see what all the excitement was about. When he finally made his way through the crowd, Marquan almost stopped breathing. His glass of Hennessy went straight to the floor. Bam! He couldn't believe that the dancer was Snooty, Sabrina, Supreme baby sister. Now he understood what all the fuss was about. He couldn't blame none of the guys, because she had done the same thing to him, the moment that he first laid eyes on Snooty.

He was stuck right in that spot watching her as she danced. He was so mesmerized by Snooty presence every time that he laid eyes on her.

BIG AND LITTLE SATAN

Iz U by Nelly came on next. Snooty started working the whole stage and that's when she spotted Marquan. The same man that couldn't escape her mind the moment he walked out that prison.

Snooty wanted so badly to stop dancing and run into Marquan's arms. But her heart told her that she'd never want to let him go. Plus, that was something hurting inside her. That she knew that Supreme wouldn't ever allow that to happen.

Snooty kept working the stage but never took her eyes off of Marquan. Now she started scanning the crowd to see where Supreme was seated. Also wondering why Supreme brought Marquan there to her place of business. Supreme knew Snooty was a stripper and at times disapproved of it. But somehow overcame it with the help of Stigma assuring Supreme that it was all business. They both finally locked eyes with each other. It seemed that every time they were in each other's company, this is what they done. Just stared into each other's eyes.

Their eyes seem to do all of their talking for them. Snooty ran and jumped on the pole and let her mind invade Marquan in every way. Snooty was even shocking herself. Because she started doing things on the pole that nobody else had done before. After finishing her set, Snooty blew Marquan a kiss and he caught it.

Marquan placed her kiss on his private part to her surprise. Snooty placed her hand over her mouth. Now she knew that it wasn't just her, that wanted him and his love, but it was also him too who wanted hers.

Snooty came out from the back looking for Marquan like the police tasks force on a drug bust. She was feeling like the police do when it came to pursuing a criminal. The perpetrator isn't getting away from her, nope! Not this time, Mr. Burton. That was the thought on her mind. Hey Marquan! Snooty still tried to play it cool. Like Marquan was her brother and was in the family. Where's Supreme?

Marquan wasn't trying to hear that Supreme my brother bullshit. When Snooty tried to hug Marquan in a friendly way, Marquan pulled her close to him and started passionately kissing Snooty. She didn't reject the kiss. She just allowed her body to go limp.

Marquan allowed his hands to explore her body parts. Her ass was nice and soft but with the right firmness to it. The only problem of them interlocking into a kiss wouldn't be Supreme at that moment.

Star has just taken to the stage. She was dancing to Stupid Ho by Nicki Minaj. Just as Star started to get into her rhythm, she spotted Snooty with her arms around Marquan. They were interlocked in a passionate kiss. Star temper exploded inside of her, and that song couldn't end fast enough for her. That special pink outfit that she bought to dance in for Marquan, he never even saw the lace bra and panty set. He was too busy taking up Snooty space. Finally, after interlocking lips with Snooty, Marquan finally saw the burning eyes that were cutting him and Snooty in half.

BIG AND LITTLE SATAN

"Oh shit!" He thought to himself, Man I fucked up. I blew it, damn! Star exited the stage and headed straight towards them. Star pushed Snooty so hard that she and Marquan almost fell down. But Marquan caught Snooty. "Bitchhh!" who do you think you is, kissing all on my man?

Snooty was looking at her and Marquan with disbelief and confusion. "Bitch!" Have you bumped your head or something? Your Man! Your Man! This man just got out of prison, a couple days ago and this my brother, bitch!

Snooty finally realized how stupid she sounded. After almost sucking Marquan tongue out of his mouth, Snooty was so mad and embarrassed that she slapped Star and they started throwing blows. It took Marquan, Big Chub, and three customers to break them up.

Titties was out and hair was all over the floor. After Marquan explained the whole situation to them both, they both were standing there waiting to see who Marquan would choose to be with.

Marquan remembered while he was in prison, he spent time with a veteran pimp named Worship. Pimping Worship told Marquan one day while talking about his lifestyle, he said; Marquan, Ho's choose pimps. It's not a pimp's job to choose a female. That's a disposition for her to make if he's worth her tears, pain, and money. Because after she makes that decision, all her time belongs to him.

Money is time and time is spent getting a pimp's money, young blood. Marquan knew that he wasn't a pimp. But he also remembered Worship saying. Even if a woman was a square or prostitute, that a real woman wouldn't never walk away from a man that she saw her father in.

Say peep this Snooty and Star. He looked them both right in the eyes, I'm not trying to hurt either one of you. I've been locked up 12 years and 7 months. Star's eyes opened up wide because she didn't know anything about Marquan in prison. The whole time I've been dreaming, thinking, and contemplating on putting a spectacular team and future together. That I can see us all winning in it together. Ladies, I'm not religious or anything, but while I was serving time, my beautiful mother use to send me scriptures. There's a couple of them that I remember rather good. Ecclesiastes 4:9 say, "Two are better than one, because they have a good reward for their labor". Snooty and Star looked at each other.

Marquan quoted another scripture. Genesis 2:18 say, "It is not good for man to be alone". Now that's the word of God ladies. So, if there's anyone standing here don't see themselves in my future, I won't hold you up any longer. You're free to walk away.

Snooty and Star could see how serious Marquan was and knew that he wasn't running game. He just meant every word that he said. They reached out and hugged each other. Star said, well I guess that were family 'bitch" because I ain't going nowhere.

Snooty kissed Star on the same cheek that she slapped her on. "I'm really sorry for slapping you, and I ain't going nowhere either bitch! They both turned to Marquan and hugged him. Snooty said, "Daddy let's see just where that future takes us".

Big Chub spoke up, "Okay fuck all this bullshit, right now" I'm y'all daddy and let's get back to work! Y'all know y'all gotta answer to Big Mike about all this bullshit in his club. Snooty and Star said almost at the same time, Yea trust us "we know." They both kissed Marquan on each cheek and went back to taking table dances. Big Chub stood there holding somebody's hair, looking at Marquan.

$$\$ \; \$ \; \$ \; \$ \; \$$$

Come on in and make y'all selves comfortable. I guess my home is y'all home tonight. Marquan and Snooty both were impressed with Star's layout in her home. She has her condominium plushed out like a high-class Presidential Suite at M.G.M or Treasure Island in Las Vegas.

Baby, would you like anything to drink? Naw! I'm good right now. Your place is really nice baby. Thank you. Star smiled. Snooty what about you, are you thirsty? Nope! She joined in with Marquan. Your place is really nice Star. But you can show me where the bathroom shower is at. Yea daddy! We have been dancing. Can you excuse us? He nodded his head. Star turned on some music and they disappeared into the back room.

Marquan sat there and couldn't believe that the life he wanted was starting to shape up so fast. Marquan happy moment, quickly turned into a dark sad unhappy moment. It seems that every time that he sat still and wasn't doing anything. Marquan could see the face of the man that he pumped bullet slugs into his body. Marquan could see the expression on the man's face, every time one of the bullets entered him and found a resting place. Boom! Boom! Marquan jumped as Snooty touched his arm. She didn't think too much of it being where he just came from. Whenever Supreme talked about Marquan, he also told Snooty about prison experiences that Marquan could encounter being there in prison.

Marquan opened his eyes and the volume on the music went up. "Be about your Doe," by Mac Dre and Cognito came on. Star started the lap dance off. She was wearing a burnt orange pair of booty shorts and a matching top with three-inch heels. Marquan sat up and took in his private show. He slapped Star ass and told her to pop it harder. Snooty switched off dancing to Bitch by E40 and Too Short. Snooty dropped down to her knees and unzipped Marquan's pants. Then she removed his already erected penis.

Star kneeled down next to Snooty. They took turns helping each other give Marquan bomb head. They undressed each other and Marquan. They both grabbed a hand and the three-some continued in Star's round spinning bed.

CHAPTER FOUR
WHO YOU ARE

E cstasy spent around in her office chair. Okay ladies it's all done. She had just split up 2.5 million dollars, that Supreme told her to put in their accounts. Each one of them received 500 thousand in their offshore accounts.

Supreme, Stigma, Ecstasy, Glory, Persia, and GeeGee, their all-professional hitman's. They all are trained murderers and are incredibly good at what they do. Ecstasy, GeeGee and Persia all started out being hitmen for an unknown Rich man whom they thought was from China. Ecstasy was married to a hitman that wind up forcing her into the lifestyle, which later brung her two best friends into the game. The man that ecstasy was married to, she truly didn't feel like, that she even knew her husband true and real birth name. He kept too many different identification cards for her to truly know who Aubrey Yang was. At least that's the last name Ecstasy changed her last name to the day they got married.

She was born Elizabeth Maje Swaziski. But after taking all the lavish trips around the world, Ecstasy became Elizabeth Maje Yang in Paris France. Aubrey had her whole family fly out from Seattle to Paris France. The men that were at their wedding acting like his family members, ecstasy later learned that they to where also hitmen for the same man.

Still to this day, Ecstasy only knows their boss as Papa Jack. Ecstasy, GeeGee, and Persia where all roommates going to the University of Arizona. They were all piecing together change to buy them lunch at Taco Bell when Ecstasy first met Aubrey.

He was standing behind them in line patiently waiting to place his order. He was a very well-dressed man with shinny shoes. The girls were forty-eight cents short from buying their food. Damn! Come on girls dig deep into those purses. "We're short forty-eight cents, Ecstasy said as they all filled around for change."

Aubrey said ladies, I'm so sorry please excuse me. He stepped up to the cashier, I'm so sorry. Will you forgive my bad manners? I was on an important business phone call. They're with me. We would love to have three of every meal that's on the board. Also, two beef tacos and four, "What are we drinking ladies"? Coke, Pepsi, Mountain Dew, What?

GeeGee said Pepsi will be just fine! Thank you, Sir. But no thank you, we'll manage. Girl, what's your problem? If he is willing to treat us, then let him. GeeGee was looking at Ecstasy like she had lost her hunger mind.

BIG AND LITTLE SATAN

No ladies please, I insist and I'm not taking no for an answer. The cashier stood there confused. So, do I ring that order up or what? GeeGee and Aubrey said yes! He told the cashier; Ma'am I'll take those two-beef taco's and one Pepsi separately. GeeGee said, well sir if you're going to treat us to lunch, then you can at least be a gentleman, Right ladies? Ecstasy and Persia smiled but embarrassed, said yea that's right. While eating lunch, Ecstasy kept noticing Aubrey pay more attention to a man eating his lunch. Ecstasy thought to herself, Damn! What a waste of such a handsome man. Now Ecstasy was more than sure that Aubrey was a gay man.

The whole time they ate lunch together Aubrey did seem to show Ecstasy more attention by looking into her eyes. He really wasn't paying GeeGee and Persia to much attention. It was really like him, and Ecstasy were having lunch together, while he pursue his gay lover a few tables over from them.

Because Aubrey only asked questions seeming to only show an interest in Ecstasy. He only asked Ecstasy her name and was she married? My name is Elizabeth and no I'm single. What about you? I'm Aubrey and yes, I'm single also. Ecstasy thought, that's only until you introduce yourself to the guy sitting a few tables over.

After Ecstasy gave Aubrey her number, he never would give up asking to see her. Ecstasy figured the two of them at the Taco Bell didn't work out. After finally giving in to one dinner with the help of GeeGee, Ecstasy found herself more attracted to Aubrey than she could imagine. After dinner, Ecstasy couldn't see herself living without Aubrey.

He spoiled her daily. Taking her to expensive restaurants to eat meals that she couldn't even pronounce. But it wasn't until they were in Dallas, Texas; that's when Ecstasy learned that all her outing around the world with Aubrey wasn't just him being such a romantic guy.

$ $ $ $ $

Their second anniversary was coming up soon and they sat enjoying a steak dinner. They were discussing how to spend it together. Ecstasy wanted badly to return back to the place they wedded in Paris France. But angerly Aubrey insisted that they spend it in New York City. Ecstasy started to watch Aubrey more closely. Because even though he'd take her to nice places, somehow while dining he'd always excuse himself to go to the bathroom for long periods of time. Ecstasy even once offered to take him to go see a doctor for what she thought was an overactive bladder problem.

But Aubrey would always laugh and would refuse to see a doctor. Ecstasy reached across the table and was trying to feed Aubrey. But just like all the other restaurants outings, from the first time she met him back in Taco Bell in Arizona. Aubrey seemed extremely interested in the two men that sat in the corner of the Steak House Restaurant. Ecstasy watched her husband closely and before he could even get his words out, Ecstasy said, "Go ahead honey I'll excuse you. Bathroom break, right?"

They both gave each other the most uncomfortable stare. But Aubrey was about to lose the two men. Yea! Bathroom break! Ecstasy smiled as he stood up and left their table. Only this time, Aubrey done something that he had never done before. He accidentally left his cell phone on the table. Almost two hours had passed and still no sign of Aubrey. Ecstasy asked the waitress to call her a cab. She paid their bill and returned back to the hotel.

After falling asleep and waiting for her husband, Ecstasy was being woken up by her husband's cell phone ringing. Ecstasy never answered his cell phone under his instructions. She thought to herself that it has to be Aubrey calling. She picked it up on the fifth ring. Hello honey, where are you?

Ecstasy listened and never spoke a word. She just was blown away by the whole conversation, by a man name Papa Jack. Ecstasy cried after the call because she had just learned that she has lost the only man she ever loved, her husband. Also, learning that for the last two years she spent with him that he was a hit man.

After Papa Jack gave her an address and told her that it was a black mustang sitting in the parking lot. He told her that she would find everything that she needed in the car. Before hanging up the phone, Papa Jack told Ecstasy to check the center console.

Ecstasy sat on the bed crying but kept staring at the address in her hand. The cell phone started ringing again. Hello, that mustang will be gone in ten minutes, Mrs. Yang. With you in it or without you. It won't return and this phone won't exist anymore.

Seven minutes had passed, and Ecstasy was looking out the window. She saw the mustang sitting there with no one else around it. Ecstasy looked at her Rolex that Aubrey bought her for her Birthday. Two and a half minutes left. Ecstasy grabbed her purse and the cell phone and rushed out the door. She ran toward the mustang and opened the door fast. An old gentleman seems to be rushing towards the car also.

Ecstasy reached the car first just a few seconds before he did. The man didn't say nothing, nor did he even look in her direction. She opened the door and sat down quickly locking the doors. Ecstasy looked in the rearview mirror and the old man wasn't there. She quickly turned around looking in every direction. But it was as if the man never passed her in the parking lot. He was gone without a trace of ever being there.

The keys were already in the ignition. Ecstasy's heart was beating fast, Damn! She closed her eyes and started the mustang. It started right up. She opened her eyes, then looked at the address. Ok! I'm still alive.

Ecstasy entered the address into the G.P.S system. Forty minutes later she was approaching a home with plenty of land. Almost forgetting to, she opened the center console. There was a gun and a yellow envelope.

BIG AND LITTLE SATAN

Ecstasy stopped the car, errrr! It jacked knifed and came to a complete stop. Her heart started beating fast. But all that quickly changed when Ecstasy saw all that money in the envelope. It was $250,000 in cash plus inside was a blank title to the mustang.

$ $ $ $ $

Ecstasy slowly closed the door with the rag that she removed from the home. She left the man that killed Aubrey with two bullets in his chest and one in his temple and one where his heart use to beat. He was dead even before his body hit the floor.

Knock, knock, knock! Hello, can I help you? Ma'am are you lost? Yea I'm sorry for coming on your property, but I seem to be having car trouble, may I call for some help? He couldn't seem to take his eyes off of Ecstasy breast. She made sure they were very revealing to him. Oh! Sure, come right this way. She closed the door behind her and when he turned to hand her his phone, Pow, Pow! Pow! Pow! Papa Jack said hello Bitch!

$ $ $ $ $

Ecstasy pulled into the airport at Dallas International and waited for GeeGee and Persia's plane to arrive. They all went on a mad shopping spree and then drove back to Arizona in Ecstasy new mustang. She told them everything about her and Aubrey mysterious marriage. Girl, so you mean to tell us that Aubrey wasn't gay.

Ecstasy slapped GeeGee arm playfully. Girl! Hell, Nall stupid. He wasn't gay.

If he was gay, then his ass killed all of his lovers. They all started laughing. Well hell, you are lucky, at least he didn't try to kill your ass. Girl, men kill men that tamper with their pussy. If they killed the pussy then who's going to be around to fuck and suck them, Persia said? Shit another bitch, they kill bitches too. They all busted up laughing. "Oh, Oh girl! Tell us about this Papa Jack guy?"

CHAPTER FIVE
LOCK IT DOWN

Rocky was sitting in the bathroom stall with a Plus XL magazine, trying to get himself to cum for Ms. Dutches Love. Their main XL model featured on the cover of XL Magazine. He was talking to her. Come on baby with your big thick sexy ass. Damn! You fine girl! Come on Come here! Don't you run from me Dutches? You know you want this dick! That's right! That's who I am. Say my name. Say daddy's name say it! Scream my name daddy, Rocky killing this juicy pussy.

Boom! Boom! Boom! Rocky's heart almost jumped out of his chest. But he didn't drop that XL magazine startled or not. Nigga, bring your nasty ass out that bathroom jacking off to them fat ass pigs.

Boy your ass is sick. You sick Rocky. All shut up punk! Ain't nobody in here jacking off. I'm using the bathroom. He quickly closed the book. But not before he could take another look at Dutches Love eating pizza with sauce falling onto her breast.

Aye! Fuck you Slow Drag. I'm bustin' your head to the white meat just as soon as I get through wiping my ass punk. Don't you mean to say that you bustin' your head to the pink meat on them fat bitches? Slow Drag busted up laughing. Nasty ass niggaaa.

Man, check out this trick ass nigga. He was talking to Lazy Eye, a crip from the southside of Phoenix, who have just walked into the bathroom. Lazy don't listen to that fool. A nigga can't even shit in peace around him cuz. What's up Young Lazy? Man, y'all better strap up. What? Looks like something about to pop off with the Mexicans.

Rocky jumped up and tucked his XL magazine behind his back. Then he pulled his shirt down to cover it. Rocky flushed the toilet like he used it and walked out calmly. But he still was mad at Slow Drag for busting in on him and Dutches Love sexual encounter. Man, what did you just say Lazy? He reached out to shake Lazy Eye hand. Cuz, wash your hands?

Yea dirty dick ass Nigga. Awe fuck you Drag. He took a playful jab at his face. Then at Lazy Eye but he ran backwards trying not to be touched. Rocky started washing his hands.

Aye hommie, on the serious tip. Something about to pop off on the yard. Everybody getting they banggers. What happened Lazy Eye? Due Dirty, Black Money, and Sleepy all smashed one of Alex, Riders. What? Hell Nall Drag, let's get to the yard. Grab them thangs hommie.

Rocky got so excited that he forgot that he still has his XL magazine on him. Just as soon as Rocky, Slow Drag, and Lazy Eye hit the yard, the riot popped off. The blacks and Mexicans were swinging, punching, and stabbing everything that wasn't their race. Rocky and Slow Drag got back-to-back, the same way they would if Marquan was there. They both were holding their own business down. Anybody that got close was taking some powerful blows to the face and body. Watch out Lazy? A dude was running a homemade shank into Lazy Eye body. He stuck him twice, but Lazy kept on fighting.

Rocky and Slow Drag have some Mexican guy playing soccer with his head. They were kicking him back and forth to each other. Both sides were giving and taking punches. There were all types of homemade weapons being used. All the white inmate prisoners were trying their best to stay out of the mayhem.

The prison alarm sounded off. Now the guards came running, carrying night sticks, riot gear and cans of mace. They were trying to take back control of the prison in Florence. The fights have gotten so out of control. That by the time they made it into the yard, there was lifeless bodies already slumped over on the yard.

An hour and twenty minutes later, by the time they sprayed mace and took down the inmates who wouldn't stop fighting, there were five white sheets being placed over five inmates, who didn't make it out the mayhem. Twenty-eight prisoners were needing major medical attention at a hospital. One inmate was being air-vac off the yard to the nearest hospital.

The Warden was yelling at guards ordering a complete lock down on the whole prison. He was storming the prison in rage, fussing at different officers. Get their asses locked down and I mean lock'em down, now!

CHAPTER SIX

DON'T BLOCK YOUR BLESSINGS

Marquan was riding on the passenger side falling asleep. At least that's what he was hoping to do before he saw his parole officer. Ms. Housemoore was taking him to see his parole officer for the first time. He didn't want to drive his Cadillac truck and take a chance for the parole officer to see it.

When Marquan was in prison, he always heard the guys talk about the mistakes they made to violate their parole. Driving without a license or buying expensive things showing off. Marquan wanted to appear to be broke and broken by the system.

He wanted to keep the white man off of his ass. His paperwork said to report to a Mr. McKinnon in Suite B at the parole office. Marquan came pretty close to not going to see his parole officer at all. In his mind he was feeling like just as soon as he walked into the building that they would come and take him back into custody for what happened when he got out. Marquan could see them surrounding the building and taking him back to prison. Right in front of Ms. Housemoore and that would have hurt him more than her.

"Marquan Burton", you're under arrest for the murders of and they would start naming honkies that Marquan didn't even know himself. But after he called and gave Supreme his cell phone number they spoke about him visiting his parole officer. Supreme told Marquan that nothing came up on the news about an earthquake in California. That's what they would always say about the concrete breaking up under their feet. That meant that things would be coming apart on their pavement.

Hearing that made Marquan get a little more comfortable to visit his parole officer. Supreme told him to touch down with him after their visit. So that he'd know that Marquan was straight. Marquan was so happy to finally make it to the parole office.

Because Ms. Housemoore was starting to act like she was his parole officer, she started asking Marquan a million questions. Who is that? What is this and where did that come from? Mama Damn! Can you give me a break, is what Marquan kept saying to all of her questions.

Hello! Would you please take your belt off and place everything that's in your pockets into a bucket? Thank you, Sir. Ma'am, right this way. It was a fat black security guard who was checking everybody as they entered.

BIG AND LITTLE SATAN

Marquan went and stood in line so that he could go to one of the windows to check in to his parole officer. Plus, that forty-dollar money order needed to be turned in for his visit. After about thirty-five minutes, a short red neck white dude came to the door.

"Marquan Burton! Marquan raised his hand, and the parole officer waved him over to come to him. Ms. Housemoore tried to go back with Marquan. But she was stopped at the door. Ma'am, you're his mother, right? "Yes". Okay fine. But I'll just see him right now. I'll come to your home soon, then we'll get to talk then.

Ms. Housemoore said okay! They already came once to make sure that he was able to go there. Right this way Mr. Burton. Marquan extended his hand in a friendly manner. But the parole officer turned and headed to his office.

Have a seat Mr. Burton. His parole officer went over all of the conditions of his parole. Then told Marquan what he expects from him on parole. Whom he can and can't be around while on parole.

Now Marquan was starting to give his parole officer the same look that he was giving Ms. Housemoore on the way to the parole office. After Marquan signed and initialed all of his parole papers, his parole officer finally extended his hand towards Marquan.

Mr. Burton, you only have a short time on parole. Let's get through this without me having to place these back on you. He placed a pair of handcuffs on the table which made Marquan look at the door and embraced himself. I'm sure your mother, brother, and sister will be disappointed in you. So, keep it clean and go find a job. No more drug dealing, Mr. Burton. He and Marquan shook hands.

He gave him copies of his parole papers and told Marquan that he needed to report once a month. He also let him know that he will be out to their home, so make sure that you find a real job that pays a paycheck. They said their goodbyes and he allowed Marquan to leave. No more drug dealing! They both laughed. Gotcha, you don't have to worry about that.

Marquan left his office feeling like parole wouldn't be so bad after all. How was he, son? I know he told you to stay out of trouble. Yea mama he did. Let's go old lady and find something to eat, I'm starving.

Ms. Housemoore didn't move from where she was sitting. Come on mama! You didn't answer me, Marquan. Well, are you going to stay out of trouble? Yea mama! They told me that I need to find a job, then he walked away laughing. Me find a job, yea right! He said that under his breath so that Ms. Housemoore didn't hear him.

Marquan knew just how to get her off of his back. Walking to the car he said, Hey mama! What boy! What are you mad at me for? Because you are hardheaded and don't listen to nobody. They sat in her car and Marquan kissed her cheek. Don't worry mama. I know y'all love me and don't want nothing to happen to me. I love y'all too mama, and I won't never ever leave y'all again. I promise you that. Okay! You can trust me.

BIG AND LITTLE SATAN

Hey by the way, I met this girl, and she invited me to church. I think that I'll take her offer. Thank you, Jesus! Hallelujah! That's what you need Marquan. Jesus! He'll give you a good God-fearing woman that will keep you on a righteous path.

Mama, she was asking Whitney about you. Why was she asking about me boy? Who is she? Her name is Emoni. That's a pretty name. She saw Whitney's hair and complimented you on your work. "Hell, I ain't doing nobody's hair." Shoot! I hate having to do hers.

What church does she attend? Mama, you know I don't know nothing about no church names. Whitney knew the name thou. She told Emoni that y'all been there before. Umm! Maybe you can invite her over for dinner one day, Marquan thought to himself. Trust and believe me, you're going to meet this one real soon.

Even though Marquan had just had major fun with Snooty and Star, Marquan mind was strongly on Emoni. He reminded himself to call her and the Stripper Spicy that sent her number to me. So, she must want to be team Marquan. He laughed at his thought.

Boy! You losing your mind or something? What's so funny? You mama, you!

$ $ $ $ $

Marquan sat in the driveway in his truck waiting for Emoni to answer. Hello! A soft voice spoke. Hello wifey. What are you doing? Excuse me! I'm sorry! But you must have dialed the wrong number. I told you that God is my husband. They both started laughing.

Their conversation was going smoothly to Marquan's surprise. She and Marquan learned that neither of them has kids. Emoni told Marquan that she had just gotten out of an abusive relationship. Also, that's why she was so in love with God. Because he was the only one that seemed to never hurt her.

She told Marquan that she lost her parents to a drunk driver coming home from church. Emoni told Marquan that she never blamed God for taking her parents away. Emoni said, her pastor's wife helped her get a strong relationship with God.

It had been six years since her parents died, and she said that she still attends their church. Emoni works at the Native New Yorker in Tempe. That's where she meets a lot of men that sponsors her lifestyle. Emoni herself have worked at a few strip clubs before taking her job.

That's how she paid off the Lexus GS 400 that she drives. One day a car lot owner came into her job with a few of his friends and Emoni was their waitress. The man felt that she treated all of them respectfully. So, he left her a two-hundred-dollar tip.

Emoni got off thirty minutes early before the man left the Native New Yorker. While sitting at the bus stop, Emoni kept hearing a horn blow, but she was so use to men blowing at her. This seemed like another day for her leaving the restaurant. Men would pull right up to the bus stop and offer to date her for money. Holding either their money in their hand or penis. Emoni would just walk away until they left the bus stop. After cussing a few of them out, she learned that it only turned them on more. Randy was a heavy-set white man, and really was married. He was just trying to sale Emoni a car for work.

He loved her outgoing spirit and loved how she found a way to tell her customers about how great God is to us. Hey Emoni! It's me, Randy. He was driving a brand-new Jaguar. Even though that, they just got through talking in the restaurant. To Emoni he still was just some stranger.

Now she was starting to think that he only gave her a two-hundred-dollar tip, to give himself an open invitation to a date. To Emoni he was just another customer, and her shift was over. "Bye"! Take it easy, bring your wife next time that you come.

She was trying to remind him that he had a wife and children. Because he had even showed Emoni their pictures. But she knew that most tricks were sick and disrespectful like that.

When it comes to sex, they will forget who their mothers are. Hey Emoni! Why are you taking the bus? Cause I don't own a nice pretty car like yours. What type of car is that? It's a Jaguar! "Wow" Okay baller! Take it easy. Have a blessed day. Once again trying to dismiss him.

Hey, maybe I can help you out Emoni. Ok! Here we go with all the bullshit. Here you go, Emoni, take my card. I'm a car salesman remember. Emoni just remembered that he did say that he owned a dealership in Scottsdale.

Emoni got up and walked over to his car, but while they were talking, her bus drove by because nobody was there. Damn! I missed my bus. I'm so sorry, can I offer you a ride home? I don't take rides from strangers Randy. Hey, I won't hurt you, besides I'm on camera in the restaurant and you got my business card.

Here look at my driver's license. I'm harmless. Ok! I trust you, Randy; besides I'm covered with the blood of Jesus. That made Randy smile to hear her say that. Emoni see; that's what I love most about you. He jumped out and went and opened the door like a gentleman. To Emoni's surprise, Randy didn't try anything. He only took her straight home.

$ $ $ $ $

Two months later, Emoni was at Randy's car lot. He allowed her to put down two thousand dollars on a Lexus GS 400 with no credit. After Randy wrote up her paperwork and Emoni signed them, he gave her the keys and said, Emoni the Holy Spirit told me to tell you that now you don't have to wait on rides for church. Also, there won't be no more missing buses, being late for work anymore. He smiled, but Emoni wasn't smiling or laughing. She was now giving him a strange look.

"How in the hell do you know that I wait on rides to go to church"? What have you been doing all this time; watching me, Randy? Is that why you wanted to give me a ride home?

BIG AND LITTLE SATAN

Randy laughed. Then he pulled out his desk drawer and handed Emoni one of his cards. It said, The House of God Ministry Church. Emoni looked at the rest of the card. Pastor Randy Westley and First Lady Monica Westley.

You're a pastor Randy? Emoni turned around and looked back at her car. She couldn't control the tears that were running down her face. She placed her hands over her face. "You're a Pastor"! 'THANK YOU, JESUS" The words slowly came out of her mouth.

Pastor Randy invited Emoni to their church and she invited him to Pilgrim Rest Church. Right to this day they both still attend each other's church. Pastor Randy and Emoni became good friends.

CHAPTER SEVEN

I AIN'T NO SNITCH

E moni finally agreed to take in a movie with Marquan since it was her day off. Marquan made sure not to be late when he went to pick Emoni up. She told Marquan that she would be ready at 7:30 pm and he was knocking at her door at 7:29. Emoni looked at the clock and smiled. Most men that promise to pick you up at 7:30 normally show up at 9:30 or not at all.

Emoni opened the door wearing a pencil dress, that showed off every curve on her body. Her dress was the same color as Marquan's Cadillac truck. Her opened toe sandals showed off her French Tip pedicure.

Emoni put her hair in loose spiro curls which accommodated her few freckles that's on her cheeks. When Emoni smiled, she showed off a perfect pair of white teeth. Emoni 36/26/38 bumper, made her sexy beautiful thick legs, make you want to explore them. She is just one inch shorter than Marquan.

BIG AND LITTLE SATAN

Marquan stepped back when she opened the door. "Wow", wifey look at you! "Boy stop it". Emoni turned red from blushing, taking in Marquan's compliment.

"Well Sir", you're looking mighty handsome yourself there! When Supreme took Marquan shopping, he took him into a store that he normally shops at and got Marquan right. Marquan was wearing a designer dress shirt with multiple colors in it with his black slacks and black dress shoes.

"Here Beautiful"! These are for you. He handed her 24 single long stem red roses. Emoni tried to fight back the tears, but she couldn't. This was her first date that any man had brought her flowers. "Hey Beautiful, come on Sexy don't cry". This is nothing compared to what you deserve. Hearing Marquan say that made Emoni cry harder.

Now she wasn't chastising herself so much about accepting his offer to the movies. She reached up and kissed him on his cheek, Thank you Marquan. You already made my evening with you special. Now you've got to come in for a minute so that I can fix my face.

"I know you don't want no ugly woman riding with you, right"! Lady, ain't shit-He grabbed his mouth, "Oops," I'm so sorry. I didn't mean to cuss. Man, you do not have to apologize to me. "Marquan, everybody cusses every now and then". Hell, if you piss me off tonight, you might hear a few cuss words from me. They both started laughing.

Emoni's apartment wasn't nothing like Stars condominium. But Marquan could tell that she took pride in what she had. Everything was clean, smelling good, and neatly in order. Sweetie, make yourself comfortable. I'll be right back. I don't listen to much worldly music, but maybe you'll like this. Emoni grabbed the remote and pushed play.

"Do I speak for the world" by Gerald LeVert came on. After hearing the first song, Marquan was hooked. By the time Emoni returned, Marquan was standing there swaying back and forth. Oh! I see that you do like my type of music. "Yea" that's nice. Who is that? That's my man when God ain't in my Spirit. I love me some Gerald LeVert. "Who"? Gerald LeVert! You don't know who he is? Nope!

That's Eddie LeVert son from the O'Jays. You do know who the O'Jays is right? Yea, my mother use to play them a lot before she got all into church. Ok! I thought so. Well since you're hooked now, I guess my man can go on our little date with us. Marquan laughed, and she popped his C.D out. Here, treat him in the same way you treat me.

Marquan laughed. He started reading the back of the case on the way to his truck. Now Emoni was falling in love with the C.D all over again. Because Marquan surround sound made LeVert speak another language to her ears.

They went to the movie theater outside Spectrum Mall on 19th Ave. Marquan allowed Emoni to pick the movie and she laid in his

BIG AND LITTLE SATAN

arms throughout the whole movie. Marquan didn't know it, but Emoni was feeling him just as much as he was her.

Emoni's body was starting to sexually arouse, but there wasn't no way that she would reveal that to him. Not on a first date. Marquan also wasn't trying to do anything to push Emoni away. So, he was on his best gentleman behavior.

After the movie, they just sat in his truck listening to Gerald LeVert's CD and talked. Sharing their both past lifestyles. Marquan got so comfortable with Emoni that he told her the truth about getting out of prison four days ago.

But to Marquan's surprise, Emoni didn't make up any excuse to go inside her house. She just sat there and listened. Emoni told Marquan about her stripper lifestyle and her abusive drug dealer boyfriend. How he spoiled her into being his showoff dime piece to his family and friends.

Emoni learned by being his punching bag, that he really was an immature, self-centered, jealous control freak. One of the guys that he copped drugs from, wanted Emoni just as bad as Tone did. One day Tone took Emoni with him to meet Omar to buy two kilos of cocaine.

Emoni and Tone already knew that Omar wanted Emoni by the little comments that he would say when he saw her. When they pulled into Omar's neighborhood, Tone smiled at Emoni and said, "Baby look around you, this is why I do what I do for us". One day Emoni, I'm going to buy you a home just like these ones.

Emoni was smiling. She was dressed in all white Gucci jeans and shoes. Omar house still have the for-sale sign posted up in the yard. It was a two story, triple garage, swimming pool, jacuzzi and a wet bar. The marble floor and cabinet counter tops really told how expensive the home was.

Omar opened the garage and had Tone to park next to a Porsche 911. Tone's boxers got more wet than Emoni panties did seeing the home and Porsche 911. Omar closed the garage door. "Damn my dude, you about to buy this crib"?

Omar looked at Emoni, Yea! I already did that partna. "Who whip is this you pushing"? I ain't never saw you pushing this in the neighborhood Omar. Yea I know. Y'all come on in. Emoni was about to follow Omar into the house. But she had to stop and wait for Tone to stop fantasizing over Omar's home and Porsche 911. Tone shook his head and finally took Emoni into the house. Omar told Emoni, Aye you can peep out the rest of the house while me and Tone handle some business.

Emoni looked at Tone waiting for his approval and not Omar's. Yeah Baby, you can get use to this type of living anyways, because we about to buy one soon ourselves.

Emoni started walking around the house and Tone followed Omar into the room with the wet bar. There wasn't anywhere to sit. The whole house was empty.

Omar placed two brown square packages on the wet bar and a scale. Each package weighed 2.2 pounds and that let Tone know that it was all there. He put a smile on his face thinking about the money that the cocaine would bring in.

Tone was counting money, placing it in stacks when Emoni returned. Wow Omar! Your home is beautiful! So, you really like it, Emoni? No! I love this house. Great! Omar reached into his pocket and had two sets of keys. He walked over to Emoni.

Here, these are the keys to this house and a set to that Porsche 911 sitting in the garage. There yours Emoni if you're ready to leave this broke ass nigga! Emoni and Tone mouth opened almost at the same time. "What nigga!" Have you lost your fucking mind, Omar?

Emoni was so shocked that she didn't know how to respond to Omar's bold offer. Tone slung his money on the bar. Man, what the fuck wrong with you? You're just going to get at my girl in my face? Omar never even looked at Tone. He kept his eyes focused on Emoni.

Emoni, you don't have to take no more abuse from this sucker. "Just tell me that you want to stay, and all this bullshit ends right now". Tone grabbed the two kilos. Your bred all there. Here take it. He pushed a few stacks towards Omar. Man, we out of here. Open your shit up. "Come on baby." Omar, you do know that you just fucked up some good business.

Omar put his hand up in between Tone and Emoni. He blocked her from leaving with Tone. Omar said, partna I don't give a damn about losing your business. But losing her, I do care about.

Omar and Tone gave each other that are you ready to die stare. Emoni! You never gave me an answer to what I asked you.

Tone is a normal size guy, dark with a well-manicured beard, and short wavey hair. He is 5'8, two hundred and twenty pounds and not too in shape. Omar looks a lot like Suge Knight and they are around the same size except he has long dreadlocks.

I'm very flattered Omar. But you know that Tone is my man. I'm good with my relationship. Emoni walked around Omar and stood by Tone. Omar stared at Emoni, "Hey sexy, whenever you get ready to upgrade my offer still stands. I'll be right here. He mean mugged Tone. Omar stepped to the side and allowed them to leave his house.

Marquan looked at Emoni "Damn!" Why didn't you just stay? It sounded like the Omar dude was ready to change your life. To be that bold in front of your man. Well to be honest and truthful. I really didn't know Omar like that. I knew of him from the streets. But money don't move my heart.

Marquan, love do. "But hell, you're right. I should have stayed with Omar." Because that man took me home and beat the shit out of me for that. Marquan said, "Damn Emoni." Where did you meet that fool at? The Strip Club!

He came to my job, and I danced for him. You know just a few lap dances. He always came back to the club, but he wouldn't allow nobody but me to dance for him. Plus, he tipped me much more than the dances cost. I just kinda fell for him and his smooth talking. Emoni put her head down.

BIG AND LITTLE SATAN

Marquan lifted her head up. "One day he beat me for two days. Just because we went to the phone company to pay my bill. "The worker said hello to me, and I spoke back". That man took me home and tied me up like he was a fucking cowboy. He beat my ass for two days straight, Marquan.

I didn't look at or talk to men for years. What! Baby, are you serious? Yep! I'll show you the pictures. They put him in jail for that. Marquan set-up in his seat. Because one thing he hates no matter what, is a snitch.

Oh, so you had him put in jail. Nope! He got his own self put in jail. My neighbors kept knocking on my door asking to see me. They must have heard him beating me through the walls. They didn't call the police until the next day though.

That made me want to beat their asses more than I want to see him go to jail. Marquan busted up laughing. Girl you crazy. Fuck that shit! I'm dead serious. Marquan looked at her because she cussed. They came and took him to jail and me to the hospital.

But when it was time to go to court, Marquan I didn't go. "Those detectives were made at my ass". They act like they wanted to lock me up. But I ain't no snitch, Marquan. I know better. I placed my own self in that situation. The first time he hurt me I should have left his ass or cut his throat!

Marquan sat back in his seat, grateful to hear her say that. Marquan walked her to the door and kissed Emoni then left like a gentleman. He called her cell phone. Hey baby! You left your CD.

It's in good hands, that means you have to come back to return it. Click!

CHAPTER EIGHT

A DATE WITH DEATH

Today was a day that Marquan was so much avoiding and didn't want to come. He was on his way to Supremes to catch a plane flight to Sin City, Las Vegas, Nevada. Marquan pulled into the driveway and Supreme was out front watering the grass talking to GeeGee.

Aye, what's up Preme. Marquan tried to put on the most, straight face that he could. This was Supreme and Marquan first time seeing each other since Marquan got out of prison and they left a whole family soaking in blood.

What's up baby boy! How that Cadillac holding up? You sure look good pushing it. Man, I love it. Hey GeeGee. Hello Marquan. That's pretty. I love the color on that truck. Thanks!

Supreme cut the water off and they all headed into the house. Marquan said damn, something sure smells good. Oh' Glory and Ecstasy are whipping up some Mexican food for everybody. You hungry? You know that I'm always down to eat, Preme.

Stigma and Persia were watching a film that have something to do with their next job, that they were about to fly to Las Vegas and handle. Supreme made sure that he kept a close eye on Stigma and Marquan when they saw each other.

Marquan walked into the living room. Hello ladies! He greeted Stigma and Persia in a humble manner. Oh! Hey, what's up dude. Stigma looked up and spoke before Persia could say hi. Hey Marquan. Persia finally spoke. Minutes later...GeeGee, Glory, and Ecstasy came into the room. They started passing out plates full with different Mexican foods. Supreme had everybody pay close attention to the DVD that they were watching of the Caesars Palace Hotel.

After the DVD ended, everyone asked questions and gave their opinion as to what they saw. Supreme answered each question and agreed or disagreed to any opinion valid or nonvalid.

After the DVD was over, he put in another tape showing the Treasure Island Hotel. They all learned that the two men that they were about to pay a little visit to, were business partners. But they always check into two different Hotels. That was to keep their two noisy wives from interacting in their business.

Mr. Ravitz's wife always wanted to know all of his business. Supreme told them that the Ravitz' would be the family checking into the Treasure Island Hotel. Mr. Ohanian and his family would be checking into the Caesar Palace Hotel. Both families' always get joined rooms at the Hotel.

BIG AND LITTLE SATAN

Marquan wanted to know why the families got joined rooms, if it's only the men and their wives. Without any type of care or concern on Supreme face. He said, I'm told that this is their family vacation that their taking.

Marquan put a serious look on his face. So, you mean to tell me that there will be kids involved? Supreme looked at everyone "All I know is that there will be business involved and that's why we'll be there. So, make sure that we do just that, "handle business"!

Is there anyone here that feel like they can't handle business? Then speak up now. Persia said, I don't know about y'all. That made Marquan's heart stop beating so fast to hear one of Supreme girls speak up. Instead of it being him who looked like the weak one. Persia kept talking...

I don't know about y'all, but I sure can use two more of these enchiladas. Marquan took his hand and placed it over his face, Damn! GeeGee joined in, hey fix me two of them tacos while y'all going into the kitchen.

Marquan's heart dropped to the floor. He couldn't believe what he's gotten himself into. There was no turning back now. When Supreme pointed to each person. Each one of his girls said, ain't no problem here Dada! When Supreme pointed to Marquan, his heart wanted to say, I'm out of here. But his life easily said there's no problem here either.

Flight 218 was boarding at 6:45 at Southwest Airlines. Supreme, Marquan, Stigma, Ecstasy, Glory, Persia and Gee-Gee all boarded the plane. They all have different seats on the plane. They didn't so much as talk or look at each other on the plane. They all took different taxi cabs to their rooms.

Supreme rented a charco gray Dodge Magnum and Glory rented a black Cadillac DTS sedan. After they all checked into their rooms, they all showered and just relaxed until they received Supremes call. He'd always call and let the phone ring three times then he'd hang up. No one was to leave their rooms under no circumstances.

The Ravitz and the Ohanian's weren't do to arrive into Las Vegas until the next day at 12:00 noon. Supreme spent his time studying those DVDs that they all have a copy of. Before they left their rooms, Supreme ordered for the DVDs to be destroyed.

Marquan was in his room stressing like an expecting father in delivery that's about to have a baby for his first time. Persia was enjoying her new sex toy that she brought on the trip. She was laying ass hole naked watching porn that was showing at the hotel.

Stigma was reading a book on real estate. She always keeps telling Supreme how much that she wanted to go into real estate. GeeGee was at the MGM playing the slot machines. Supreme already knew that taking them to Las Vegas and them not gambling, that GeeGee wouldn't be the one that would listen to him.

Supreme knew that they wouldn't be handling business until tomorrow, so that's why he didn't keep a close eye on her. He knew GeeGee was great at what she do. She ain't never failed him or the girls when handling a job. Ecstasy was drinking a glass of Champagne, relaxing in the hot tub watching Wendy Williams talk about everybody in the whole world.

Glory was trying on her waitress outfit. Making sure her gun didn't show or wouldn't fall while moving around. Supreme knew that the only way the girls would fit in, in Las Vegas was to make sure their waitress outfits mixed in with the rest of the waitresses. It would be hard to tell if they worked at the Hotel or not. Daily, so many people are hired to start in new positions in the Hotels.

Supreme needed them to be employed there for just a few hours. Besides, the hotel wouldn't even have to pay them for their services.

$ $ $ $ $

Supreme was sitting in the lobby reading a newspaper and drinking a cup of coffee. He raised his head when he heard the lady say, "Welcome back Mr. Ohanian, we have your rooms ready, sir!"

The man's wife stood next to him. She was a red head fat woman who was putting a hurtin' on a small pair of high heels. Supreme couldn't do nothing but laugh at the sight of her in those shoes. A short red-headed fat little girl was hitting her brother while Mr. Ohanian was trying to check into the hotel. Mom! Tell Penny to stop hitting me. I'm not hitting him mom. He hit me first. She separated them by putting them on each side of her. So that put them at a nice distance away from each other. Okay kids! Both of you stop it at this once. Mr. Ohanian looked back at his children and his son hid his face in his mother's leg. Marquan and another man walked up in their bell hop outfits. Marquan glanced over at Supreme.

Hey, excuse me, can you grab their bags and show them to their suite? The guy with Marquan grabbed their bags, but Marquan told him that he'll show them to their suite. Marquan gathered Mr. and Mrs. Bielec bags, showing a big smile. Right this way, ma'am, sir.

Excuse me ma'am, Marquan and Mr. Ohanian looked right at each other. Mrs. Ohanian stepped back holding the kids by their shoulders and allowed Marquan to pass. Another bell hop showed Mr. and Mrs. Ohanian to their suite. When Marquan was on his way back downstairs, Marquan and Mr. and Mrs. Ohanian family passed right by each other.

But only this time Mr. Ohanian nodded his head at Marquan. Marquan nodded back. But he slowed down just to make sure that they didn't change suites. The bellhop opened rooms 619 and 620. Marquan watched as they entered their suites.

All at the same time, the Ravitz were checking in at Treasure Island. Ecstasy was standing right behind them in a two-piece business suit acting like she was checking in also. It was really busy at the counter, so nobody was really paying any attention to her.

Mr. Ravitz stood next to his two daughters that appeared to be about eight and twelve years old. His wife was holding a newborn baby in her arm. She was tall, blond and had blue eyes. Ecstasy shook her head as she watched her kiss and bond with her child. Some lady approached them, "all honey, look at him, ain't he so handsome?" She was talking to her husband who was also at the counter checking in, may I? Mrs. Ravitz removed his blanket so that the lady could see their son. "All look at you little one", how old is he mommy?

He'll be three months tomorrow. Girl good luck, my baby days are over. But you'll never know what might happen in Las Vegas. Both ladies smiled, then they waved goodbye to each other. The baby started crying. Honey he must be wet. Do you have our room yet?

Moments later… a bell hop was taking the Ravitz towards the elevator to their rooms. After the elevator closed it opened right back up, Ecstasy stepped inside just as the bellhop pushed the eight button for the eighth floor.

Oh! I'm so sorry, shall I catch the next elevator? The bell hop said, oh ma'am what floor are you on? Ecstasy already saw the number eight lit up. I believe I'm on the 8th floor. Oh good! We're headed to that floor also. Ok thanks. Ecstasy gave him a gentle smile.

Mr. Ravitz were trying to cut his eyes at Ecstasy ass but one of his kids interrupted that by asking when they are going to Circus Circus. The door opened and Ecstasy stepped off first. Unfortunately, they all started walking right behind her. Oh shit! Y'all would come this way.

They almost followed her to the end of the hall, but suddenly they stopped and found their room. But Mr. Ravitz was trying to see what room Ecstasy was staying in. Being that he noticed that she was all alone. Maybe he'd run into her without his wife and kids. They stopped at room 824 and 825.

Ecstasy stopped in front of room 832 and started fumbling through her purse looking hard like she couldn't find her room key. Mr. Ravitz didn't take his eyes off of her. Now he just kept watching her. The bellhop opened their doors then handed Mr. Ravitz his keys.

The bell hop grabbed their bags and took them into their suites. Mr. Ravitz's wife and kids rushed into their suites. Ecstasy still hadn't entered any of the rooms yet. Mr. Ravitz was handing the bellhop a tip. Thank you, Sir! If there's anything that I can do, please don't mind calling me back.

Ecstasy knew that Mr. Ravitz was watching so she called the bellhop over. Umm excuse me sir, can you please give me a hand? Yes ma'am! Sir, will that be all? Mr. Ravitz smiled at Ecstasy, and she smiled back. That's all, thank you. Mr. Ravitz finally walked into his room and closed the door.

Just as the bellhop walked up to Ecstasy, ma'am is you having trouble with your key? No! I'm fine now thank you and she walked off and left him standing there. He watched Ecstasy thick ass, as she walked down the hall.

BIG AND LITTLE SATAN

Stigma, GeeGee, Glory, and Persia phones all started to ring. After the third ring the phones stop ringing. They all exited their rooms wearing waitress uniforms. GeeGee and Glory went to the Treasure Island. Stigma and Persia headed to the Caesars Palace Hotel. They all found the kitchen area and walked into the Casino kitchen ready to work. It was a fat white man that was ordering everybody around. Just as he saw GeeGee and Glory walk into the kitchen. Let's go ladies, clock in, we're super behind. Let's go! Let's go, we have no time to waste.

Stigma and Persia ran into a slight problem. The head lady wanted to know what day they started working there. She also wanted to see their health cards. The woman took the fake names that they gave her, and she headed into her office. You ladies have a seat, I'll be right back.

Just as Stigma and Persia were about to get up and walk out, the lady came back with their name tags. Hey here y'all go. You're Judy, right? Stigma said Yes. Here put this on your uniform. Mindy, here's yours.

Mr. Holland don't never tell me shit, but until the last minute. He makes my ass hurt sometimes. I couldn't get in touch with him. I'll have to try him back later. Ellie! Yes ma'am. You train them two, until I can find out what the hell is going on around here. Right now, I need a nap. She walked away, fussing and cussing to herself.

At 1:48 pm, Supreme nodded at Ecstasy as to say, Is it the same rooms? She nodded her head yes twice. That meant it was all good.

Ecstasy exited the dining area. At 2:15, Supreme gave the same nod to Stigma and she nodded back twice. Supreme got up and left the restaurant.

At 2:45, he entered the restaurant at the Treasure Island and GeeGee was getting chewed out by some fat white man. Supreme smiled and nodded at GeeGee and she nodded back twice. Supreme turned and left the restaurant.

It was 4:20, and Glory and GeeGee were pushing food carts to room 824 and 825 in the Treasure Island Hotel. While at the same time, Stigma, Persia, and Marquan were coming down the hall at Caesars Palace Hotel. Headed to room 619 and 620, GeeGee, Glory, Marquan, Persia, and Stigma all knocked on all four doors at the same time. They all have their watches set at the same time, 4:30 on the dot.

Knock, knock, knock, knock, bam, bam, bam, bam! Each door begins to open up one after the next. Room Service! Before Mrs. Ohanian or her daughter could ask her husband or dad about the food, GeeGee and Glory were pushing the food trays into their rooms.

Mr. Ravitz and his wife were answering both doors at the same time. Mrs. Ravitz was next door in the room with her kids. "Room service"! Before the Ravitz could even ask each other about room service,

Stigma, Persia, and the bellhop Marquan were pushing food trays into their room. Where would you like the food? Persia drew her weapon first. Papa Jack said hello! Mr. Ravitz couldn't believe that he was hearing that name.

Persia put a bullet right in the center of his forehead. She fired again putting a slug in his body. A little smoke came from the barrel of her silencer. Mrs. Ravitz started to scream but Marquan silenced her real quick with a few bullets straight to the heart. Pow! Pow! The two little girls held each other and also were beginning to scream. Stigma popped off again killing both of them. Pow! Pow! Pow! Pow!

Marquan looked at them, come on let's go! Let's get out of here! Persia said wait! Dada said that everybody must go. She walked over to the baby that was lying in a baby seat wrapped up "Pow" now let's go, Marquan. He closed his eyes and turned to walk out the door.

GeeGee told Mr. Ohanian, Papa Jack said hello! He tried to run, Pow! Pow! Pow! She pumped three bullets into his back and leg. Then walked up on him again while he laid there, Pow! Putting a bullet into the back of his head.

Glory already had put his wife, son, and daughter down. Pow! Pow! Pow! Pow! Pow! Pow! Pow! All up close head shots. GeeGee and Glory came walking out of the Treasure Island Hotel looking like nothing had ever happened. Ecstasy pulled up in the Cadillac DTS Sedan and they jumped in the car and Ecstasy drove away.

$ $ $ $ $

Stigma, Persia, and Marquan exited the Caesars Palace Hotel and Supreme pulled up in the Dodge Magnum. He too also calmly drove away as if nothing ever happened. They headed straight to the airport and returned their rental cars. Then they took cabs to the rooms and removed their bags. Then headed back to the airport. But this time they were boarding a plane to California to finish handling business.

Excuse me Sir, would you like something to drink? Supreme looked the white girl up and down then said, No thank you. I'm traveling on business.

CHAPTER NINE
HELD HOSTAGE

E cstasy had her eyes closed tight, while gripping both arm-rests. The landing was a little rough coming in from Las Vegas headed to California. Supreme already knew which one out of the five girl's hated flying was Ecstasy. But the type of work that they do sometimes allows them to have to be in different parts of the world, anytime and at any spur of the moment.

Ladies and gentlemen! My sincere apologies to everyone for such a rough landing. But hey! Look on the bright side, we're all here safe, right? You could hear everyone on the plane commenting and complaining about the pilot's comment. Well, welcome to sunny California, the weather is lovely today. It's 79 degrees, but here, unfortunately nothing like the hot city we just left.

"Gentlemen! I hear that the beaches are packed with plenty of beautiful women." Thank you all for flying with us on Dela Airlines. "Have a wonderful stay in sunny California."

Supreme already had two D.T.S Cadillacs waiting for them at Avis rental car. One was white and the other one was black. They begin loading their bags into the trunk of the rental cars. Supreme drove the white D.T.S and Marquan drove the black one. Supreme couldn't wait to visit his favorite Soul Food restaurant that he always went to every time that he would vacation or do business in California. Plus, it was an easy restaurant to go to coming out of LAX airport. He'd always come out of the airport and kept traveling east up Century Boulevard. Supreme would always laugh, watching all the prostitutes chasing that Ba'dussy.

Supreme got caught at a red light. He was pointing at the restaurant, that was just across the light on Century and Western. The light turned green and just as Supreme was about to cross the intersection, a blue Chevy Super Sport Impala came inches from slamming right into Supreme. He slammed on his brakes Errrrr!

Now Supreme and Marquan could hear a rattle of bullets. Pow! Pow! Pow! Pow! Boom! Boom! Pow! Pow! Pow! Pow! Pow! Boom! Stigma and Persia all ducked down in the cars. Persia was lying across the back seat. Marquan, GeeGee, Glory, and Ecstasy all was doing the same thing. They ducked down also breathing hard and looking around. Right at that moment, they were all thinking the same thing. Damn! Here we all go and got caught slipping. Nobody had a weapon to return fire to save their lives.

Papa Jack always made sure that their weapons were already waiting in their hotel rooms. He'd always have the weapons they killed with dismantled and melted after a job. Supreme said, "Fuck this shit! I ain't going out like this and just sit here waiting to die." He popped his head back up and was getting ready to drive off. That's when he realized that the ambush wasn't for them. The car full of gang bangers with blue rags wrapped around their heads was banging on some blood gang members. The bangers were hanging out of an old school Suburban shooting at an old school Caprice Impala full of bloods. They were following the blue Chevy Super Sport Impala that passed by first shooting.

Supreme sat up. Ok! Ok! "It's all good! It's all good!" "We good ladies." Stigma and Persia sat up and was looking around like some smokers on crack. Supreme smiled at them, "Hey ladies, welcome to Cali." Marquan had peeped the same thing that Supreme has saw. After the light turned green again, Marquan followed Supreme into the small parking lot next to the Soul Food restaurant.

They exited their vehicles hugging each other. Now happy that it wasn't them for the first time getting gunned down. They all were experiencing the same feeling that people experienced when they came for them. Glory said, "Damn bitch! Fuck all this shit! I need to go to their bathroom, to make sure that I didn't shit on myself." Everyone busted up laughing. Stigma said, "Girl don't feel bad, I need to check my panties to." They all headed into the restaurant that said Bertha Soul Food restaurant on the side of the building.

Supreme and Marquan sat at the same table. They started discussing making some changes. They wanted weapons available upon them arriving in any state to handle business. The owner came out to pay his respect to Supreme, after he noticed that Supreme was there in the restaurant.

"What's up Supreme?" Man, I thought that you moved on your Island some damn where. "Man look at you, where you been boy?" Supreme stood to greet his long-time friend. Supreme didn't waste no time asking about his wife. She always took good care of Supreme. "Shit she ain't divorce my ass yet." We still riding it out. She is back there fussing at somebody, I'm sure. It ain't my ass so I stay out the way. Gone back there, I'm more than sure that she'll be glad to see you, Supreme.

One by one they all were taking deep breaths trying to relax and get control of their thoughts. They were all so full that all of them just wanted a bed and to sleep until the next day. "Aye man, just like always, the food here was delicious!" They ate smothered steaks, pork chops, oxtails, fried chicken, and all types of side dishes. Bertha's Soul Food restaurant is known for their famous Cabbage, Candy Yams, Greens, Sweet Corn on the Cob, and mixed vegetables with different meats in it. Almost at the same time, they all downed the last of their Kool-Aid and fresh squeezed Lemonades.

Supreme cell phone started ringing. He pulled it from his waist and looked at it. "All damn!" Y'all give me a minute. He asked the owners to excuse him a minute, I have an important call. The owner waved him off as Supreme was exiting the restaurant. Now Marquan, Stigma, Ecstasy, Persia, Glory, and GeeGee all were thanking the owner for enjoying the great food that they had just ate at their restaurant. "The food was remarkable!" I ain't been this full in a long time. Trust me when I say that we'll be back again. Marquan was telling the owners as he was paying for their bill. The owner told Marquan that it was nice meeting them and to tell Supreme not to stay away too long.

$ $ $ $ $

Supreme was now headed towards Hollywood. Papa Jack told him that they were to check in at the Metropolitan Hotel on Sunset Boulevard. They have four big, nice rooms facing the Sunset strip. The Metropolitan Hotel was an all-glass building that had underground parking. Just as they entered the first room, like always, Supreme lifted the mattress and all the weapons that they were wishing that they had earlier were all laying there neatly in a roll. They all grabbed their weapon of choice and started checking them for any flaws.

Supreme had over 30 different photos, that he started passing around the room. The two brothers that they were there to put ten feet down in the ground was in each picture.

Marquan got the first photo. "Damn!" What was their mother feeding them? Now Stigma and GeeGee were looking at the photo. "Shit, you can't be serious." They asses are going to eat the bullets. Supreme raised up a 357-magnum clip and removed a bullet. They asses won't be eating these. The twins were born in 1980 to Alicia Humphrey and Joseph Grimes. But everyone knew the twins in the California streets as Big Mozzie and 40 Whop. They themselves were also two notorious killers.

Big Mozzie stands 6'5", 345 lbs of 95% muscle. Ever since him and 40 Whop got out of Y.A, for serving time for attempted murder for beating a man close to death at the age of 13, Big Mozzie and 40 Whop started lifting weights, after Big Mozzie fell in love with an IFBB pro league Hall of Famer name Shawn Ray, after he tied Arnold Schwarzenegger for seven Olympian titles in 1990.

Back then the twins were just ten years old. His brother 40 Whop is 6'4", 360 lbs with just as less fat on his body as Big Mozzie. When they were younger, everybody called them the Jefferson twins, because the older they got, they started looking like George Jefferson from the show The Jeffersons from the early 70's sitcom. Plus, their hair in the middle was missing, just like Mr. Jeffersons.

But they kept their bodies in tip top shape and that's what made everyone fear them in their neighborhood. They also have them mean tempers to trigger off their muscles. The twins didn't have any problem solving a problem that they came up against. The twins weren't your hanging out on the corners or selling drugs and gang banging dudes.

Big Mozzie and 40 Whop were very educated men. That also helped shape their minds in a way that they handled business dai-

BIG AND LITTLE SATAN

ly and shaped their bodies. Big Mozzie could just about convince anybody to finance anything that he took an interest in.

The twin's mother Alicia loves her two boys. She is the neighborhood beautician, and she kept every female, player, and pimp looking their flyest in the streets, except her two boys. All she could do was cut the rest of their hair that didn't grow. Nobody would ever be caught being disrespectful in her shop. Her man Joseph was much worser than her two sons. Alicia always told her customers that her two sons got their tempers from Joseph, their daddy.

Big Mozzie and 40 Whop owned a Car Wash, Used Car Lot, and a Clothing store that everybody in the neighborhood shopped at. They were known for putting their money back in the neighborhood. The only thing that separated the two brothers was, Big Mozzie is married with two kids, and he has a daughter and son. On the other hand, 40 Whop didn't have any kids. But he was a nymphomaniac when it came to having sex with women. When it comes to having sex, 40 Whop has to have two or multiple women at the same time. Big Mozzie always drives expensive vehicles. His brother owned expensive vehicles also, but he normally drives his 64 convertible Chey Impala, candy blue sitting on 13'7" Dayton rims. Big Mozzie got tired of all the police attention that his triple white 64 convertible Chevy used to cause him. So, he kept it business and drove either his Porsche 911, Mercedes Benz, or Bentley G.T Coupe convertible. The twins always had money, but lately they have been doing it big time.

Big Mozzie and his wife had just opened a Sea Food restaurant in Hollywood. They named it The Red Sea Food restaurant. That's where Supreme, Marquan, and Persia were sitting across the street from, watching with two 357 magnums and a Desert Eagle 40 caliber to end the twin's world. Supreme only have two names on his list and that was Derrick and Donald Grimes. A.K.A Big Mozzie and 40 Whop, the twins.

Supreme and Marquan thought that their food must be great because they had been watching for the last five hours, and the restaurant stayed packed. Even the inside of the restaurant was full of customers dining in. Supreme was just about to call Stigma, GeeGee, Ecstasy, and Glory to change shifts to watch the restaurant. The girls were posted up at the twins clothing store. But Supreme wanted to go by their Car Wash before it closed. It was deep in L.A in the neighborhood, which was going to be a problem because the twins keep a lot of gang members around the Car Wash.

Ever since Supreme had arrived in Los Angles, him searching for the twins had turned out to be no sign of them. Supreme knew that it was getting late, and someone has to close their Car Wash. Just as Supreme reached for his cell phone to call the girls, Marquan said, "Supreme look dog." It was a blue 64 candy blue convertible Chevy pulling up in front of the Sea Food restaurant. It was the same vehicle that Supreme was showing in the photo's back at the hotel.

BIG AND LITTLE SATAN

Supreme gripped the handle of his 357, while Marquan and Persia checked their weapons. 40 Whop came walking around the corner with a light skinned female with blue hair and blonde streaks in it. "Damn, that Nigger look bigger in person, Marquan commented." Persia said, "Dada you gone have to empty the clip on him because a few of them bullets he gone eat." Marquan started laughing. Supreme said, "If that boy eats these bullets and don't die, I'm going to leave him alone and let him live to tell the story." That means that it ain't that nigga's time to die. Marquan and Persia open up their doors ready to handle business. Wait! Wait! Not right now, not here. Marquan and Persia looked at each other. Let's follow him. It's too many witnesses that can give us up, and who knows what type of camera system they have. They both closed their doors but looked at Supreme crazy. They want to catch 40 Whop off guard.

Supreme hit Marquan leg, "Look," what did I tell you, just as I expected. 40 Whop was walking behind the female popping her on her fat ass, as she switched hard back to his car. She was carrying two plastic take out bags in one hand and another bag and a Styrofoam cup in the other hand. "Stop!" "Stop!" 40. You could hear her playfully yelling out to 40 Whop.

Three minutes later the Blue Chevy came pulling out of the restaurant headed east on Hollywood Boulevard. Supreme allowed a few cars to get in between them and jumped right behind the convertible in the same lane. 40 Whop was bobbing his head to Rick Ross "Don't G's get to go to heaven." 40 Whop made a right turn headed to Sunset Boulevard and when he made it to Sunset, he made a right turn. The next time Supreme came to a complete stop, was right behind 40 Whop bumper. Because the vehicle that was in between them got in the next lane and that put Supreme right behind them. "Shit!" Supreme knew that 40 Whop could easily be looking him right in the face.

But to Supreme's surprise, just as he was about to change lanes, 40 Whop came to a complete stop and put on his turn signal turning into the Dunes Hotel. Supreme didn't want to draw any attention to himself, so he kept on going straight. After 40 Whop turned into the hotel, Supreme busted a U-turn and pulled over next to the hotel. Supreme turned around and looked back at Persia, put that bitch ass nigga to sleep and I'll be waiting for you. Supreme pointed pass the Dunes hotel closer to the gas station by the 101 freeway.

Persia tucked her weapon behind her back and slid out of the car. When she entered the hotel, 40 Whop and the female was just starting to walk up the stairs. Persia put a pep in her step and took two stairs at a time coming up from the opposite side. 40 Whop was walking on one end of the hotel and Persia was now facing them from the other side. 40 Whop quickly took notice of the attractive woman, that was headed in their direction.

The female was in between them, just as they were about to walk up on each other. 40 Whop said, "Hey what's up sexy lady?"

BIG AND LITTLE SATAN

Persia said, Papa Jack said and before she could complete her sentence she reached for her gun. But just as 40 Whop heard the name Papa Jack, he was already jumping over the rail and when Persia came up with the gun it was just her and the girl standing there screaming. The girl kept screaming. 40 Whop had jumped and landed on the hood of an F150 Ford Truck.

He rolled over to the ground, just as Persia started putting bullet holes into the hood of the truck. Pow! Pow! Pow! Pow! The female dropped their food and started running towards the stairway. Persia said, "Fuck, Shit, I missed that prick." Now she was trying to exit the hotel herself. Persia didn't care too much about the girl because she wasn't on the contract to die. Just as Persia was passing by the hotel office, the owner like a fool was yelling at Persia while she still had her gun in her hand. Hey! Hey! I'm calling the police. Persia ran fast as she could, heading towards Supreme and she jumped into the back seat, "let's go!" Supreme headed straight for the 101 freeway to blend in with the rest of the vehicles.

"Did you get him?" Supreme wasted no time asking that question. No Dada, I missed him. "Fuck!" No Dada, I'm sorry. Supreme started slapping the dashboard. "What, you missed him?" What the hell happened? How did you miss that mother fucker? Persia started to give Supreme play by play as to what happened. After hearing what had happened, Supreme said, "Shit!" I guess that nigga ain't just got the Incredible Hulk in his ass, he got Superman in his ass too. All at once, they all busted up laughing. Damn Persia, you should have split his shit. Now he is about to alert his twin, that they got a hit out on them.

A week later, Supreme was hotter than a dope fiend needing a fix with no money. So that Jones won't be leaving no time soon, nor will Supreme's attitude. He had rented another car and everybody was moving in every direction in California looking for Big Mozzie and 40 Whop. It was as if they had disappeared off the face of the earth. Supreme wanted them so bad, that he had started to allow the girls to enter their establishments, which turned out to be a great call.

Stigma, Persia, GeeGee, and Glory all pulled up into the Car Wash. Stigma was driving the black D.T.S Cadillac. They all have on booty shorts and high heels trying to draw all attention their way. Just as soon as they jumped out of the car like Tupac say, "All eyes on me." All the Ballers, Gang Bangers and Tricks that was at the Car Wash was rubbing their penises and shooting their best shot.

"Hey baby!" "What's up girl!" Damn y'all sexy as fuck. How can a brother get to spoil you? Damn you know you can be wifey? Fuck all of that, they say it ain't tricking if you got it. "I'm super trick a dick, what's up?" He was holding two handfuls of money and smiling. One dude after another, popped their lines at Supreme's girls. The girls just followed Stigma's lead and kept smiling and just stayed conversating amongst themselves.

Twenty minutes into taking up all the attention at the Car Wash, a candy apple pussy pink truck came flying into the Car

BIG AND LITTLE SATAN

Wash. The music was rattling the windows, "Me Ho" was bumping by Plies. Everybody turned to watch as the bomb shells exited the truck. On the passenger side, a gorgeous thick blond, white girl stepped out the truck. The truck was sitting on 24-inch rims, so when she jumped out, that fat ass just bounced like a Spalding basketball. She looked a lot like Iggy Azalea but with much bigger breasts.

The two back doors opened up and a female from the Dominican Republic stepped out with long sexy legs and a body to do back flips for. Her skin was so pretty and smooth that it looked like she was made by a computer. She has long wavey auburn hair, 38DD, 28 waist and a 40-inch bubble butt. The other female was from Columbia. She grew up in a little town not too far from Bogota called Anserma Caldas. She stood 5'9 with a schoolteacher haircut, Brazen color skin, 38 (28) 40 rock me tonight back side. This female was jumping out to open the driver's door. Stigma was expecting some fly looking pimp to step out the truck to flex his pimp game in front of everybody. But it looked like The Bratt twin from Chicago.

When the female stepped out with her hair long in twisted up designer braids. She quickly got everyone's attention, even Stigma, GeeGee, Persia, and Glory. She stood 5'8 with a hard banging body and a pretty face. But her dress style was more like a swagged out crip gang banger. Her 501's and white T-shirt have an ironed crease down the middle of her shirt. Her j's have a pink fat lace and she was rocking a pink bandana over her face. Everybody watched as she exited her vehicle and the three ladies followed right behind her. Persia said, "will you look at this little hot fire engine bitch?" The female was very cocky and loud. "Aye, yo little Spanky, what's up cuz?"

Aye make sure y'all get my whip straight and better not shit come up missing out of my shit! The female already has her eyes locked on Glory. Her perfect figure had drawn her right to her the moment she saw Glory. The female walked up on Glory and whispered something in her ear. Glory was about to say something smart back, but one of the guys washing the cars called her. Hey Sunni, your brother on the phone. She popped Glory on the ass and ran to grab the phone. The three females walked behind her to catch up. Stigma was hitting Persia. "Aye bitch! Did I hear old boy right?" Did he call dyke bitch the twin's sister?

Before Sunni could return back from her phone call, Stigma told the girls, hey let's play along with this bitch game, y'all act like we dyke bitches too. Right now, everybody belongs to me. We got to get next to this pussy sucking ass bitch. Sunni came back with a big smile on her face. Aye, so what pimp do I got to call and serve about your sexy ass? You fit just perfect in my family ma. Won't she Mumu? The Columbia female smiled and said yea! I'd love to have fun with her daddy. Stigma said, "Aye home girl, I ain't no hater but the next time you put your hand on my bitch ass, we gone cause a much better excitement then your entrance."

BIG AND LITTLE SATAN

What! What! Oh, this fine little dime belongs to you? Yea, all three of them belong to me and I wouldn't mine putting Cinderella in my stable. Spicy, wouldn't you love to have that pink toe in our bed? Stigma called Glory, Spicy. GeeGee, Glory, and Persia all spoke up and joined in on the conversation. White girl ain't you ready for something Spicy like you? The white girl smiled but stayed close to Sunni. Ok little mama I ain't tripping off no black bitch no way. It's been ten years' since I've ate some Cat Fish, can't you see that? She white, she Columbia, and she from the Dominican Republican baby girl. But we can really see what it do tho, if you down for the toss-up.

Sweetie, the only thing I'm about to toss up, is a bag full of money after I'm through handling my business. It looks like you have got too much time on your hands. Me, I'm sending a bitch to get something for her time, so if you see something that you paying for, then you can get as handsy as you like sweetie. If you into just tasting any type of pussy, then you can reach in between your own legs and taste Catfish. Stigma came off so hard that it made all six of the females laugh at Sunni. "Say little momma, I see we got off on the wrong foot." Hey, no disrespect about yo bitch, she just sexy that's all. Sunni said that looking Glory right in the eyes. Hey, if you decide to change your mind we can stay in touch and maybe get some money together. Stigma and Sunni exchanged numbers before they left the Car Wash.

$ $ $ $ $

Supreme, Marquan and the girls were all eating at the Denny's restaurant, and they were filling Supreme in on the twin's dyke sister. Turned out that after their little encounter at the car wash, Sunni had invited them to a lesbian night club in Hollywood, called The Wet Tub Night Club. It was a private gay club for men and women on different nights. Tuesday was lesbian's night, and it was only Sunday. Supreme realized that he was just going to have to have patience and wait them out. The only way that Supreme and the girls were going to get close to Big Mozzie and 40 Whop, was to have their own sister lead them right to them.

Monday morning Supreme, Marquan, Stigma, GeeGee, Ecstasy, Glory and Persia all went shopping at Playmates on Hollywood boulevard and purchased some sexy lingerie. Besides Stigma had planned to bring Ecstasy along with them. Making it appear to Sunni like she has pulled another girl in her stable. Just to impress Sunni even more than she already has. Stigma knew that Sunni had taken the bait because while they were shopping Stigma's cell phone was ringing.

Hello, Ms. Bad Bitch. Who diss? Oh, so I see that you forgot about me already. Your beautiful ass been on my mind ever since you left my brother's car wash. Stigma said, don't you mean that your mind been on Spicy ass. "Girl! I knew that you were a shot caller just like me." I just used her to get to you. Stigma was saying under her breath, "bitch don't you mean that I used her to take life from your brother's?" Oh yeah, is that right? Sweetie, you do know that I ain't one of them weak bitches that you're used to, right? Baby trust and believe that, if I thought that you were a weak bitch, I damn sure wouldn't be calling you right now. Baby girl, can you imagine the type of lifestyle that we would be living if we were on the same team? Stigma said, "Sweetie I don't do teams." That shit is for a nigga with bitches. I'm a boss and I put teams together to play for me. I damn sure don't join teams.

Sunni said, "Well I do see that you head strong and that just make me want you even that much more." So, does this mean that I won't be seeing you Tuesday night? "Naw!" That's not what that means. Because I'm curious to see what else Cali has got to offer me. Besides this new young tender that I just pulled yesterday. "What?" You knocked another bitch? "Yep!" So, what that make y'all? A tall can from a six pack? Yep! Damn y'all having fun or you at your paper. Damn I just met you and you already in my business and pockets. Honey, I do see you are used to lollypop type of bitches. Don't nothing lick on me or check my finances unless I allow it to.

Sunni said, "Baby girl if you ever allowed that to happen, trust me sexy lady, it will definitely be you and me forever then. Stigma responded by saying, "I'm not expecting to live forever so that's why I'm making me happy right now." But I'll see you Tuesday night and let's see what that day holds before you look into a future that you can't see. Click! Stigma hung up before Sunni could respond back.

Stigma knew just how to lead Sunni along, just long enough to get what she wanted. Then Sunni would soon learn that I'm not that bitch to play with. Stigma smiled at her own thought. Stigma walked over to Supreme, Dada don't they know that I'm that bitch that left Charlotte in her own web? Supreme kissed Stigma. Sounds like that bait is in the mouth of the fish. Hooked dyke style Dada.

$ $ $ $ $

Supreme, Marquan and the girls were back chilling in their hotel rooms. Everybody was on their cell phones, either checking on loved ones or paying an unpaid bill. Stigma had called Ms. Bergess to check on their son and Ms. Bergess told Stigma that her son asked her a question, that she felt that either Stigma or Supreme should be the ones to answer it. Stigma put her cell phone on her loudspeaker because Supreme was missing little Isaiah.

"Isaiah!" Yes Nanna. Your mom and dad are on the phone for you. Ok Nanna. Little Isaiah came running into the room so fast, that he knocked over Ms. Bergess glass of hot tea. "Hello mom where's dad?" Boy! Now look what you have done. Oh, I'm sorry Nanna. Hello son, what happened? Nothing mom! He was still apologizing to Ms. Bergess. Boy don't nothing mom me, what just happened? I got it boy, just talk to your parents. Mom, I knocked over Nanna cup, running to the phone. Boy, be careful son. I am, mom. Where's my dad?

BIG AND LITTLE SATAN

Stigma loved her son dearly, but she hated it when he only asked for Supreme. Supreme had a big smile on his face. He was listening to how excited Isaiah got when he heard his voice. Hey champ! Hey dad, where are you? When are you coming home? Stigma spoke up with a sad face. Well, what about your mom son? No mom I miss you too, but…He got real quiet. Isaiah was trying to gather his thoughts. He didn't want to hurt his mom's feelings. "Mom, I meant, when are y'all coming home?"

"Yeah, sure okay Isaiah!" I'm going to remember all this when your dad gets on your little butt. Don't come running to me. Here, you want your dad, here he go Isaiah. Stigma threw her cell phone next to Supreme on the bed. "Champ, see you made your mom mad." Stigma was standing there with her face frowned up and arms folded looking at Supreme. All mom don't be mad at me. You know that I love you more than anybody. You're my mom. Stigma smiled and licked her tongue out at Supreme. I love you too son, and we'll be home real soon.

"Isaiah, if you're asleep when we get home, I'll come in and give you a kiss." Mom! Supreme said, "Ok Champ!" I'll let that go for now, since what I just heard made your mom smile. Man, give me my phone, you can't be trying to turn my son against me. Stigma snatched her phone. So, what's all this I hear you asking your Nanna? What mom? What are you talking about? Ms. Bergess said, ask your parents, what you asked me at breakfast. "Oh!" "Oh!" I know now, mom. I asked Nanna that if something ever happens to you and dad, Mom what's going to happen to me? Stigma looked at Supreme and tears rolled down her face. She couldn't even talk.

$ $ $ $ $

Marquan had called Snooty and Star. They both had told him that he needed to come home. Because they were badly missing him. They also told Marquan that they had made a lot of money at the strip club. Between the two of them, they had stacked close to $20,000 dollars. Marquan let them know that he was missing them also. That he had purchased them a lot of dancing gear from Play Mates in Hollywood. They both had promised Marquan that they would model it for him first before anybody. Marquan was happy to hear that, Snooty and Star were starting to get close to each other. This time with him away, would solve a lot of their problems before they could even get started. At least they would realize that they were one big happy family.

The conversation was going good, until she asked Marquan the question that almost made him stop breathing. "So, Daddy!" Did you tell my brother about us yet? Just hearing those words, it made Marquan vision him and Supreme pulling guns on each other. Pow! Pow! Pow! Boom! Those gun shots snapped Marquan back into their conversation. Nope baby I ain't hit him with that yet. Maybe at the right time, maybe we both can tell him. That was a time that both of them knew would never be a right time.

BIG AND LITTLE SATAN

Marquan finally called the woman that was continually on his mind. Emoni was excited to hear Marquan's voice. She even made him laugh when she said, okay let me know that you know where home is. I thought that you chose my man over me. She was talking about her Gerald Levert CD she left in his truck. I'll admit that he sings great and all, but the truth is, you the only one that do something to my heart Emoni. That made Emoni happy to hear him say that to her. Because before he had made the call, her heart didn't know how to feel about Marquan. Emoni thought that she had run Marquan away about the stories that she told him about her ex-boyfriend Tone. Emoni said, so tell me something. What's up sexy lady? When do you think that I'll see you and Levert again? Marquan told Emoni that he was away on business, and she didn't even question him about it. All she said was, baby be careful and come back home to me safe, so that we can finish what we started. "Oh, and before you go, Levert can't go nowhere else with us, he be keeping you away too long."

Marquan was laughing so hard that tears started forming up in his eyes. Girl you are crazy ain't no CD done kept me from you. "But ok sexy, next time just me and you." No Levert ok? You had better call me just as soon as you get back. Ok, Ok I will. Bye sexy. Bye baby.

Supreme was on the phone with SoSo, she was house sitting at the house in Chandler until Supreme came back. SoSo wasn't a Hit man. She was just around to do whatever Supreme needed her to do. She got her own Condo and was a 911 operator. Plus, SoSo kept Supreme up on a lot of police info that he needed to stay up on. SoSo was actually turned on to Supreme through Stigma. Their threesomes turn into SoSo being a part of their family and criminal activities. In fact, all of Supreme girls has explored SoSo sexy body. Even Supreme's sister Snooty, but they don't think Supreme know. But Supreme have sent them to draw men out for him too many times. Supreme know that the only way that men would be attracted to two women would be to experience them together.

$$\$ \ \$ \ \$ \ \$ \ \$$$

Stigma, GeeGee, Glory, Ecstasy, and Persia were all dressed up looking like Barbie Dolls wearing high end lingerie. They all were in the black D.T.S headed to The Wet Tub nightclub. They were going to meet Sunni and hoping that she would lead them to her brothers. They also had heavy artillery in the trunk to shut down the whole night club. The club was packed with every type of confused person that would follow the devil into every type of sin the night was about to offer. While Stigma was trying to find a parking spot in the parking lot, they had witnessed more sexual encounters in that lot then someone would experience watching a triple X porn film.

The thing about those that follow Satan, when they come out at night is, right at that moment in their life nothing or no one matters to them. Almost anything and everything goes into their body. Drugs, liquor, sex from men and women, tongues, titties, penises, vaginas and even bullets wind up entering their bodies before the night end. It's like Dracula meeting the Serpent and their waiting to see who puts the most poison into your body or who sucks the most blood out of you.

Stigma could have sworn that she was looking at Dracula and a Serpent. Because the female that was laying back on a car have on so much make-up that she looked just like Dracula. While the woman that was in between her legs was trying to push her tongue through her uterus. She was moving her head and body like she was a snake.

They all took a deep beath. Ladies come on, let's go see what our mothers and grandmothers ran from after slavery. Glory busted up laughing. "Shit not my mother, hell we might bump into her ass up in the club." Everybody started laughing. Every type of female had pushed up on Stigma, Persia, Ecstasy, Glory, and Gee-Gee. Right about now they have no idea as to what was what anymore. Ecstasy said damn! Shit, what do women complain about men for? Shit Bitch! It looks like to me; they asses is the messy one's. They are about to go home and act like they are good mothers and wives. These whores make me want to go home and sew up my own pussy! Damn for reals!

Stigma and the girls finally made their way into the club, and Sunni was sitting in V.I.P with her three girls. They were popping big bottles of champaign. "Hey!" Ladies, look what the cat's meow,

meow, meow drug into the club. Sunni stood up to greet Stigma and the girls. She hugged Stigma letting her hand invade her ass, and Stigma grabbed her hand. "Excuse me." I told you once already that, only I'm the one who allows somebody to park at this mansion. Sunni stepped back and held her hands in the air. "Excuse me Ms. Lady, my bad."

Hey, let's just have some fun, ain't that what we all came to do? Stigma quickly lost the attitude after the look that GeeGee gave her. She didn't want them to blow getting next to Big Mozzie and 40 Whop again. Even Persia was looking at her, saying come on don't fuck it up like I did. "Will you ladies join us in a glass of champaign?" Stigma thought that maybe the Champaign might relax her. "Sure!" Ladies, come on up and join us.

After about five bottles of Don P and a few blunts of some of California's High Dro, Stigma, Persia, Glory, Ecstasy and GeeGee all was in a comfortable state of mind and was partying. The DJ put on California Love by Dr. Dre and Tupac and the club went up. Stigma and her girls were freaking Sunni girls on the dance floor. Stigma and the girls didn't know it, but every bottle of Champaign that they popped open, it was ecstasy pills being dropped into every bottle. Every hand that touched them felt like a firebomb exploding into their bodies. Sunni had even went in for a kiss on Stigma and without her realizing it, she had returned the kiss and was seeming to enjoy it more than Sunni did.

BIG AND LITTLE SATAN

The club was closing. It was four in the morning, and nobody wanted the club to end. So, Sunni invited everybody back to her place. She has a nice home in Carson, California and that's where the party continued. After more blunts and drinks were passed around, everybody started undressing each other. Nicki Minaj, "sex in the lounge" was playing loud throughout the home. Sunni, Stigma, and Glory all headed to her bedroom. Mumu was already laying across the bed naked waiting on Sunni.

GeeGee, Ecstasy, and the Dominican Republican Choicy all went into another bedroom. Persia and Chelsea from Columbia were already taking each other's body temperatures with their tongues in another room. Sunni got up and stepped out the room, but minutes later returned with a 357 magnum in her hand. Pow! She shot the gun in the ceiling. "Bitches get the fuck up right now, before my pussy be the last thing that y'all taste in the world." Persia, and GeeGee were being led into the room at gun point. "Ok Bitches!" Y'all got one time to come out with the fucking truth or I'm going to start killing you trick ass bitches one at a time. Stigma spoke up first. "Wait!" "Wait!" What's wrong sweetie? Oh, now I'm your sweetie, you punk bitch.

I want to know, who in the fuck sent y'all to kill my brother's. Stigma eyes opened up the size of someone who has just seen a ghost. "Bitch a few days ago, some bitch popped up from out of town taking shots at my brother." Then you Bitches pop up at the Car Wash and don't nobody know shit about y'all. Did you think that we sleeping like that in Cali bitch? You think I'm slow or something? Sunni walked up to Glory and slapped the shit out of her. Bam! See, your sexy ass should have joined me when I tried to give you a chance to. Now you are about to die with these tricks. Glory was looking at Sunni like she wanted to blow her head off with her own gun.

"Ok Ms. Smarter than me ass bitch!" She put the gun up to Glory head, "Who in the fuck sent y'all to kill my brothers? Tears started rolling down Stigma face. Who do I say sent us, what do I say to this crazy bitch? "Papa Jack sent us!" Persia, Ecstasy, Glory and GeeGee all looked at Stigma. They couldn't believe that Stigma have just gave his name up to Sunni. "Oh, one more thing. Who the smartest and baddest bitch in this house?" Sunni kissed Stigma on the lips. You are. She said it in a real low tone of voice. What? You are. "You damn right bitch, I am and don't you ever forget it.

Sunni looked at all of them. "Which one of you fags shot at my brother?" I'm going to wait and give him the honor to do what y'all couldn't do. Then I'm going to take the privilege in sending each one of y'all back to wherever the fuck y'all came from. I believe that every mother should get the honors to bury their child when they leave this hell hole. Sunni walked over to her nightstand and picked up her cell phone.

She waited patiently to hear 40 Whop voice come in over the line. "Aye bro! Yeah, y'all was right, some cat name Papa Jack." Right, I know, that's the only reason her bitch ass still living cause she told me the truth. Glory was so happy that Stigma didn't lie because they didn't have no idea that Sunni knew who they were. "Ok! Ok!" bro, I'll be waiting on y'all. "Fuck all that, we family." Just hurry up before I kill this bitch myself.

Sunni mind went into rage and anger. Because she started slapping the shit out of Stigma, Ecstasy, GeeGee, Glory, and Persia. But she was doing Stigma the worst out of the five girls. She looked at her swap meet diamond watch and realized that her brother's ain't come yet. It was now 7 o'clock in the morning and now Sunni started to point her gun at them and was pacing back and forth. "Bitch!" If my brother's ain't here in the next 30 minutes, I'm just going to smoke all you tricks. Just as Sunni said that a knock came at the door. You tricks lucky, but not really. Because if my brother recognizes anyone of y'all asses, it's on and poppin.

"Mumu if anyone of these tricks move, let they asses eat them bullets." Sunni walked out of the room and went to answer the door. Big Mozzie and 40 Whop walked into the house and 40 Whop closed the door behind them but didn't think to lock it. He was too excited to see the faces of the females that Sunni held hostage in her bedroom. Big Mozzie nor 40 Whop knew if the females knew why they were there to kill them. This hit wasn't about Papa Jack personally. Big Mozzie and 40 Whop had talked a friend of Papa Jack out of three million for some diamonds. After leaving with the diamonds, Papa Jack's friend learned that they had switched the diamonds out for fake one's,

Then to top that off, they had the man pistol whipped and robbed. Papa Jack's friend Mr. Kushner got shot in the left eye and faked being dead to save his life. After the men left, he drove himself to the hospital. That's when he contacted Papa Jack to have a hit put out on the twins.

Big Mozzie, 40 Whop, and Sunni were all walking down the hallway. But nobody even noticed that the front door was slowly being opened. Just as they entered the room, 40 Whop started looking at each female real carefully. After looking at all of them, he went right back to Persia. He was about to say that he thought it was her but he wasn't sure. Persia hair was now short and was a different color. Plus, his sexual problem was starting to overpower his mind.

He was starting to get more turned on, by all the naked women that was standing in the room. He started all over again checking their faces one at a time. "Man, what the fuck bro, is it any of them or not?" Big Mozzie started getting pissed off, he knew that his brother has a sex problem and right about now. He wanted to take his penis out his pants and start fucking the shit out of all of them. 40 Whop walked back up to Persia again and he stopped. He closed his eyes and tried to relive that moment. But that was the worsest thing that he could have ever done. Because Persia would be the last person, he'd ever see in life again. Pow! Supreme put a bullet right in the back of his head. Pow! Pow! He put two more bullets in 40 Whop body to finish the job.

BIG AND LITTLE SATAN

The only person that was about to react to the gunshots was Mumu, because Sunni had taken her from her brother, and they became lovers. But just as soon as she reacted, Marquan had already put a bullet right in her throat. "Bitch, drop it or die with your brother." Marquan was telling that to Sunni because she was the only one still holding a weapon. Choicy had gotten too relaxed, because Chelsea held her gun on them while Sunni went and answered the door. She had laid her gun down on the nightstand.

Supreme was now pointing his gun at Big Mozzie. "Hey big fella, you're hard to catch up with." Thanks. He looked at Sunni. Man, if it wasn't for your sister, I don't know how I would have found your big ass. Just as he said that his temper went from a calm state to a mad man. Supreme noticed Stigma face, "Bitch ass nigga you hurt my woman?" Supreme let off a shot in Big Mozzie leg. Pow! Awwwwwe! "Man, what the fuck?" Ok man, your bitch ass already know what I'm here for, did you bring that money? Stigma was collecting Sunni and Choicy weapons while all along with a blood smile because Sunni was beating the shit out of her before Supreme and Marquan walked into the house. "Wait brother, you don't have to kill us." I can get that three million and three more for ya, if you spare me my life.

"How about it brother?" Ok big man, where's the money?" Man, all I got to do is make a call to my wife and she can have that money here in one hour. Supreme looked at Marquan and then Stigma. "Who in the fuck did that shit to your face?" Ms. Smart ass bitch right here. Stigma walked over to Sunni with a 357 magnum and slapped the shit out of her. Blood shot out of Sunni mouth, along with a few teeth. Awwwwe! Sunni hit the floor and held her mouth, now looking up at Stigma. "So now, let me hear you tell us all who the smartest bitch in the room now." You are baby. I'm so sorry. Right bitch, I am and yes, you're a sorry bitch. Pow! Stigma puts a bullet right in Sunni forehead. She fell over like a sack of potatoes.

Big Mozzie started crying uncontrollably and Choicy joined him. She even held Sunni leg crying. "Baby, I love you!" I love you so much Sunni. Supreme said, "Nigga you about to join her, if that bitch doesn't get here with that paper." Where's the fucking money? I'm not lying man. It's in my safe at home. What's the number to the safe? 26 to the right, 9 to the left, and 19 right after going around once. Supreme knew that it had to be some type of major cash, because Big Mozzie dropped his head right after he said it. Damn! Does your wife know that number? Nope! Just me. "Ok, I'll tell you what. GeeGee find some paper and a pen.

Just as soon as everyone heard Supreme call GeeGee name, they knew that nobody would be left living in that room but them. GeeGee returned back in the room, holding a pen and paper that she got out the kitchen. Here Dada! Put the address and safe number on that paper, and I'm going to make this clear to you one time. If my man doesn't return with that bread; you, your wife, kids, and these bitches all dying today. "Do I make myself clear?" Big Mozzie

BIG AND LITTLE SATAN

said yes. He tossed the pen and paper over to Big Mozzie. After catching it, Big Mozzie looked at Supreme, "No games brother." No games. So, how do I know that you ain't still going to kill us after you ger the money? Well, here's how you know, I'm a man of my word. I was sent to kill you and I been here ten days. "Your brother laying right there and you are next if you bullshitting me."

Big Mozzie started writing fast. Here! He gave Supreme the paper. "So, what's your wife's name?" Big Mozzie took a deep breath, Nefessa. Big Mozzie put his head down, he knew that he should have just joined his brother and sister. Instead of sending them to kill his family too. Supreme sent Marquan and Glory to pick up the money. Almost two and a half hours had passed, but Marquan came walking through the door with the money. He walked over to Supreme and whispered something in his ear. Then he pushed Nafessa next to Big Mozzie.

Supreme said, "Ok!" It seems that we have a problem, my brother. It seems that we had agreed on six million, but you seem to be three and a half million short. Big Mozzie said, "wait my brother." I got the rest, but you got to take me to it. Supreme said, "Ok I'll tell you what's about to happen now. Nafessa started crying, because she knew that they were about to die. Big Mozzie started hugging his wife and was trying to calm her down. Supreme pushed the clip out of his gun, leaving only the bullet that was in the chamber.

Supreme whispered something in Marquan's ear and pointed his gun at Nefessa's head. She started screaming. No! No! Wait, please don't kill me. I ain't done anything to hurt nobody. I got my two kids to raise, please don't take their mother away from them. Please! Please!!! Supreme said, Aye calm down. I'm not going to kill you ma'am. Come here, it's ok, come here. Nefessa went over walking towards Supreme and was shaking like a bad motor in a car. "Sir please don't kill me. Please!!!!!!! "Please don't hurt me." Supreme laid the gun down on the top of Sunni dresser drawer then he stepped back. Ma'am I'm not going to kill him. I want you to do it, for him having you brought here. "What type of man would include his family in such bullshit?" Nafessa was shaking scared to death, but she was listening to what Supreme had just said. Supreme asked Marquan for the paper that he had given him before he left. He laid the paper next to the gun, and asked Nafessa, "who's handwriting is that?"

Nafessa picked up the paper and saw their address on it in her husband's handwriting. Tears started rolling down her face, and she slowly picked up the gun. Big Mozzie was now begging and pleading with the mother of his kids and wife to spare his life. "Nafessa, this me honey, your husband and kids' father. Pow! Nafessa had closed her eyes and she pulled the trigger putting a bullet right in his heart. Then she dropped the gun, right at her feet. Supreme looked at Marquan and Stigma, and they made everybody jump and pop harder than they did back at the club. Big Mozzie, 40 Whop, Sunni, Choicy, Mumu, Chelsea, and Nafessa all laid their dead.

CHAPTER TEN
IN TOO DEEP

Marquan was following Supreme in a different rental car. They were on the highway headed back to Phoenix. Supreme knew that there wasn't any way that he'd take a chance coming back through the airport carrying that type of cash. It was a five-hour drive going back to Phoenix from California. They all were riding back in silence. Stigma's son's words kept on playing back over and over again in her head. "Mom, if something happens to you and dad, what's going to happen to me?"

Stigma didn't want Supreme to see the tears that were rolling down her face. So, she turned her head and looked out the window on the ride back. Funny thing was, Supreme was riding thinking about the same thing. He knew that if he and Marquan hadn't followed them from the time they left the hotel, that he would be taking that ride back to Phoenix by himself. Then what could he say to their son about his mom. "Son your mama not coming home, because I sent her to die." Tears swelled up in Supreme's eyes, but he wouldn't allow them to fall. He quickly turned his head and wiped them away.

GeeGee, Persia, Ecstasy, Glory, and Marquan too, all where all in deep thought. Even though they all knew what it was that they were about to do beforehand. Somehow, no matter the outcome or the money, it always made them relive the moments when they took another human being's life away. But they all were in too deep to turn back now. It would be either them or the person that they came for and they all knew that it couldn't be them.

$ $ $ $ $

Supreme had already placed a call to Papa Jack, letting him know where the keys were to the Cadillac that he was driving now. So, that he could recover some of the money that the twins took from his friend. He never told Papa Jack about the million and some change that he kept for him and his crew. Papa Jack seems more excited to hear that the twins were six feet deep, then to hear about any money. Mr. Kushner might be happy to know that they recovered some of his money, but Papa Jack didn't seem to care.

Supreme and Marquan had parked the car with the money in it and were headed back to the house in Scottsdale to split up the money. Supreme knew that Stigma wouldn't want to stay at the house, so he stopped to check her into The Hospitality Suite for a week. It wasn't home, but there wasn't no way in the world that he was about to allow little Isaiah to see his mother's face looking like that.

Stigma and Supreme had a big argument about her going home and letting their son see her face looking like that. But when it was all said and done, she knew that Supreme was right and was protecting their son's feelings. She knew that bruises in time can heal, and pain will eventually go away. But memories last a lifetime, and that's what Supreme didn't want to happen to little Isaiah.

Him having memories of his mother beautiful face looking beat up, would definitely leave him scared for many years to come. After staying a day at The Hospitality Suite, Supreme and Stigma both decided that it would be best that Supreme went home to be with Isaiah. Him not seeing his mom was one thing, but him not seeing either one of them would be a problem. Besides, Stigma knew how much little Isaiah loved his dad. That made them both come to an agreement, that Supreme should go home and be with their son. Stigma told Supreme that she'll be fine in the room.

CHAPTER ELEVEN

THIRST TRAPPER

Marquan walked into the strip club and found him a seat at the bar. Snooty and Star both have customers and wanted to badly walk away and go see Marquan. But their last little problem that they had in the club with each other, the owner Mike placed both of them on probation in the club for six months. He told them no being late, or no more problems or they'll be looking for new jobs. Spicy also had her eyes on Marquan, but he had not noticed her yet.

It was her turn to dance on the stage, so the D.J announced her. Ladies and gentlemen let's give a warm welcome to the sexy lady Spicy. Marquan had just bought a drink and turned around after hearing her name. To see just what Spicy was working with. Spicy was wearing a red see through body suit. With clear plastic hearts over her nipples and vagina, allowing all flesh to be seen. Marquan wasn't about to go make it rain on Spicy, when he already has the two baddest strippers in the club.

BIG AND LITTLE SATAN

Spicy had someone remix a Snoop Dogg classic with her name being said instead of Snoop Dogg's name. The D.J played, "who am I, what's my motherfucking name." The club was yelling, Spicy! Spicy! Who! What's my motherfucking name? Spicy! Spicy! Spicy was working the stage, she looked like she had just walked out of heaven. Her 44-inch booty was clapping harder then a pair of hands. She moved swiftly across the stage on her knees, bouncing and popping her ass like a professional stripper. Then she turned into an Olympic Gymnastic on the stripper pole. The crowd and dancer cheered her on. "Go Spicy, Go Spicy, Go Spicy, shake that ass girl."

Marquan told himself that he was about to have a problem out of Spicy. He was reliving a conversation that he had with a pimp named Worship back at the prison. "Say young Prince." That's what Worship would call Marquan, when he would try to check him about hanging with Rocky and Slow Drag. "Young Prince, you need to shake them marks, they going to keep you stuck in prison with all that foolishness." Worship was always popping that pimp game at Marquan, because he saw something in Marquan.

Prince, the type of women that you going to be letting choose you, is Thirst Trappers. "Do you know what a Thirst Trapper is young Prince?" Marquan shook his head confused. "Nope I don't Pimpin." A Thirst Trapper is a pretty little tender, that's going to try and trap you with her vagina. She go be at your bread, but she gone use her vagina to lock your feelings in her. She gone be showing you off to her family and friends. In the same way that a pimp shows off a fresh young tender turned out to other pimps in the game. But in the end young Prince, you got to be careful of them type of bad seeds. They can run off everything that's good for you because she ain't family oriented. Them type of snakes want everything for themselves.

"They ain't going to work towards shit and they will eventually tear down everything that you build up." Just to keep you on their level, and out the way of a real woman getting to you. If they can't have you to themselves, then they will eventually turn on you. I let one of them Thirst Trappers get up in my game, young Prince. That's why I'm in prison now. Them I love you's really mean, "Nigga I love you as long as you want just me, but as soon as you don't, I'll be the biggest bitch, that you'll ever know. Young Prince, let me tell you something, the only way that you'll get rid of a snake is to cut the head off completely. "Then they will die."

Marquan was staring at Spicy and was thinking to himself that Spicy might just be the same type of woman that Pimpin Worship was talking about. Marquan was starting to like bold type of women and Spicy seemed to want to do things in secrecy. Snooty and Star finally got to get the hug and kiss that they wanted.

"Well, hello handsome!" Snooty looked at Star. "Bitch ain't are daddy handsome?" Marquan has on a two-piece silk black pants suit and a pair of black and gold Murray Gators. He was starting to step up his dressing style from going shopping with Supreme a lot. Marquan decided to test Pimpin Worship theory. Spicy was walking by and Marquan grabbed her by the hand. "Hey sexy you asked me to call you, so I'm calling right now." What's up with you? Spicy acted like she had never even seen Marquan before. Oh, excuse me, what you trying to get a lap dance? Ain't these your girls?

Nall bitch, my daddy doesn't want no dance. He must have thought that your punk ass wanted to win. Since you around here sliding phone numbers and shit. Marquan had already asked Snooty and Star what was up with Spicy. Naw, no thank you. I'm cool, I don't share my man with nobody. Spicy pulled her hand back from Marquan and then walked away giving him that I want you look. Star said, daddy fuck that funky bitch. She doesn't get our type of money no way. You don't need her, she needs you, but not as much as we do. They both kissed Marquan and asked him, daddy is you coming home with us tonight or are you still handling your business? Marquan pulled them both in close to him. I've already been to both of y'all cribs already and y'all is my business. Just tell me where and when and I'm there. Snooty said, "How about my house then, after work." Marquan stood up, and downed his drink and sat it on the table. I wouldn't miss spending time with y'all for nothing in this world.

CHAPTER TWELVE
LAST IMPRESSION

Marquan pulled out the strip club and before he could make it to the light, red and blue lights were lightening him up. Whoop, Whoop Whoop! Fuck! Marquan was starting to sweat like two WWF wrestlers. Marquan pulled over. "Hello Sir." Did I do something wrong? First off, I'm not a sir. Yes, you did do something wrong. You switched lanes without using your turn signal. "Driver's license, registration, and insurance please.

Marquan reached into his center console to grab the paperwork to his truck. Marquan gave the paperwork to the female officer. Sir, have you had anything to drink tonight? Before he could even answer her, she said, "So did you enjoy yourself in the club tonight?" Just as Marquan was about to answer her question and beg her not to take him to jail. A call came in over her radio. The officer started listening to the call. Here Sir, make sure you use your turn signal next time. Yes ma'am! Be safe and have a good night. She took off running back to her vehicle. She turned on her siren, went around Marquan and speeded off to her call. Marquan looked up and said a prayer. "God, yes I owe you one."

Marquan was telling himself that he got to get his license before he get behind the wheel again. Next time might not be a close call. That also reminded him that the truck wasn't even in his name so it really wasn't his truck. Here he was about to go back to prison on a violation that everybody always got caught up on. Driving with no license or either suspended one's. Marquan turned around and went back to the club. He just realized that, if she searched that truck, he'd have more bigger problems then some driver's license. He has his 40 caliber in the truck also.

Marquan sat in his truck with his eyes closed and was thinking about everything that happened since being released. He was trying to convince himself that he needed to slow down. Because he was definitely moving too damn fast for his own good. He has Snooty and Star who seemed to really care a lot about him. Then there was his mother, brother, and sister, who he couldn't never let down again. Then there was Emoni, who he was catching feelings for. He didn't want to hurt her because he felt that she had been through enough shit already. That knock at his window, what Marquan didn't know was a knock that was about to change his life forever.

Tap, tap, tap, tap, tap. Marquan thought that he was dreaming, but he opened his eyes anyway. "Hello handsome man, are you waiting on me?" They told me that my ride was here. Marquan sat up quickly. "Sexy and whom might I be picking up?" Hello, I'm Marquan. I'm Ms. Impression. Well shit! I'm damn sure impressed with what I'm seeing. Marquan opened his door and stepped out. He needed some air and wanted to make sure that he wasn't dreaming.

Impression stood 6'2 with natural blue eyes. She looked like a young Pamela Anderson, 44DD breast, 29-inch waist and a 40 inch rump shaker. Ms. Impression is the number one highest paid stripper at Club Excalibur. She was telling Marquan that she came to see her best friend strip at the club. They started to get into a deep and personal conversation. Impression told Marquan that she went both ways, but she enjoys men more than women. She told him that women hormones get too crazy for her and that, women are more jealous than men. He asked her where her man was? Impression told Marquan that he was in the federal prison for murder. Multiple murders is how she really put it. She told Marquan that she was still down for him, because when he was out, he treated her like his Queen.

Marquan said, if you don't mind me asking, what did he do for a living? "Come on now baby, I told you he got multiple bodies under his belt." He was a Hit Man. Marquan's heart almost stop beating for a minute. But don't get scared of me honey. My daddy always told me to do me. But he always tells me that he always prays that I'll never forget about him though. I'll tell you up front right now. My heart will always belong to him, and I'll never forget about my daddy. There's no man in this world that's cut out like that man! Marquan laughed. "You really think not?" "Naw!" I really don't think that there will never in life be another man like him.

Impression invited Marquan to breakfast, but he told her that he'll take a rain check on that and asked if they could meet another time. He knows that he couldn't spoil his plans with Snooty and Star, being that he had already been out of town for so long. Impression gave Marquan a business card with the address and nights that she dances there. The card also has two numbers where she can be reached at any time. Marquan tried giving Impression his number, but she refused to take it. She told him no thank you, I only pursue a man once. Impression thought that if Marquan couldn't realize the quality of a real woman, then she was more than sure that he couldn't please her or keep her attention.

Marquan saw her expression and felt that he should give her an explanation. Marquan assured her that his not accepting breakfast wasn't personal. But he already has a prior business engagement. "Impression, seeing the type of woman you are, I'd like to think that you would put business first before pleasure, right?" Impression asked Marquan, 'What makes you feel like us having breakfast together would turn into pleasure?" The fact that you approached me already told me that you already wanted me in your bed or your life. Hell, maybe even both. Impression said, "Ummmm! Maybe I was wrong about Marquan."

Maybe there is one more man, that can leave an impression on me. Impression reached over and kissed Marquan on the cheek then said, "Oh one thing that I feel is fare, I got to warn you, I can really be a bitch at times." Then she walked away and didn't even look back. Impression didn't go into the club, to Marquan's surprise. A black Limousine pulled up in front of the strip club and the driver stepped out. He opened up the back door and grabbed Impression by the hand helping her into the limousine. Marquan's mouth was left wide open, watching the limousine drive away. "Damn! Who the fuck is she?"

CHAPTER THIRTEEN
CAUGHT UP

Marquan hit the alarm on his truck and headed back into the club. It was a group of black guys going into the club and the way he looked at Marquan, it gave Marquan a funny feeling about him. But Marquan didn't pay it any attention and still went into the club. Upon entering the club, all the men went their separate ways. Marquan's normal seat was taken so he walked over to the pool tables and watched two guys play pool. One of the waitresses walked up to Marquan, so what would you like tonight? "Head, pussy or a drink:"

"Everybody Down!" I said get the fuck down now! Pow! Pow! Two shots were fired into the roof of the club. Marquan said, "damn you got to be kidding." Big Chub was being walked backwards, back into the club. He has an AK47 pointed right in his face. "Move fat ass nigga!" The D.J was now being slapped and all his music was being destroyed. All four dudes were pulling black ski masks over their faces. A female came walking in behind Big

Chub, and the dude that was holding the Ak47 on Big Chub. She unzipped two duffle bags and started pocket checking everybody. One big black dude ordered everyone to cooperate, and he assured them that nobody would die. They have everyone prone out on the floor, even the strippers. Marquan somehow managed to slip into the bathroom without them noticing him.

Marquan wanted badly to call Supreme, but how would he explain him being at the club that Snooty dance at. He could never stomach himself calling 911 to protect him. Besides that, how could a hustler call the police on another hustler? Marquan was just trapped because there was no way out of the bathroom. Marquan done the next best thing that he could do. He took the $3800 that was on him, and he stuffed it into the toilet paper holder. Then he went back into the club to be robbed with everyone else.

Marquan made sure that; he warned the other dudes that the club was being robbed. Marquan was ordered to hit the floor upon entering the room. "Get down bitch ass nigga, do you want to die?" The big black dude warned his partner, that they have two more minutes left. After the female robbed all the customers, her and another dude started robbing all the strippers. Snooty and Star were mad, because the both of them were having a good night. By the time that the police finally showed up, all five of the robbers were long gone. People were complaining about losing their money and jewelry to the cops. Marquan didn't want any interaction with no police, so he quickly retrieved his money out the bathroom and left.

BIG AND LITTLE SATAN

Snooty and Star couldn't leave. They have to stay and follow all the club rules when something like that happens. It was so much going on that Snooty and Star had no idea that Marquan was even in the club during the robbery. By the time Snooty and Star make it to Snooty house, they could hear the music playing, so they went looking for Marquan to tell him about their night. Snooty walked into her bedroom and couldn't believe what she saw. Marquan had sexy lingerie laying across the bed and it was hundred-dollar bills laying on the bed. The bills made a trail all the way to the bathroom. Marquan was singing along to Keith Sweats "Nobody" Snooty and Star stood there listening to Keith Sweat give praise to himself.

He was letting Snooty and Star know that nobody would treat them the way that he does. Tears swelled up in both of their eyes as they took in Marquan's moment of manhood. Here, Snooty and Star was having a bad day and had gotten robbed for their money, then they come home to an appreciative man that cared about them and what they do for him. Snooty and Star both got naked and joined Marquan in the shower. One washed his backside while the other one washed his front. Snooty put Marquan's back up against the wall and Star grabbed his genitals and placed them in her mouth. Then Snooty grabbed his penis and started sucking it. Marquan just closed his eyes and just let his P.Y.T's do they thing.

Right at that moment nothing in the whole world even seemed to matter to Marquan. Marquan took turns making love to them, until the bathroom was completely steamed up. Marquan stepped out of the shower and picked up Snooty and carried her to the bed. He placed her on the bed, in a doggy style position. Then went to get Star and put Star under her in the same position. Snooty breast was resting on Star's neck, they were so stacked on each other. Marquan entered Snooty vagina first and he was hitting it like that was his last time having sex. Snooty responded to every thrust that Marquan made inside of her. Just as she was about to reach her climax, Marquan pulled out. "No daddy no, please put it back in!"

Marquan pulled back and guided his hard rock penis straight into Star's vagina. Her pussy was already to explode just from enjoying him pipping down Snooty. She started busting the moment he entered her walls. "Oh, daddy yes!" Yes! But Marquan was just getting started. Star was in for the same treatment. After he saw that Star was about to cum again, he turned them over on their backs and Snooty was holding Star. Marquan wanted all legs to go up like he was about to park a new Rolls Royce in a two-story mansion. He dug them out like a man drilling to lay a new swimming pool. Marquan and Daddy almost became a number one song on the music chart. Because in sequence Snooty and Star groaned and moaned and yelled his name, until they both had cum like running bath water.

Marquan, Snooty, and Star all laid there in the bed trying to get their breaths and heart rate to go back to normal. Snooty and Star were telling Marquan about their first experience being robbed.

BIG AND LITTLE SATAN

But they were in shock when they learned that he was there also. Marquan told them to chalk it up to the game, because only two things come out of a robbery. Either you lose your valuables, or you lose your life. Marquan made them promise him that they would never try to protect anything that didn't value their lives. Snooty and Star agreed that there's nothing more precious than their lives, not even money. Snooty and Star made breakfast and it ended in them having sex all over again, but this time on top of the kitchen table and counter tops.

CHAPTER FOURTEEN
THERE'S A BLESSING IN IT

No matter how late Marquan stayed out in the streets, he always manages to go back home to his mother's house. He would have loved to stay in Snooty bed in between her and Star. But he never knew when his parole officer would pop up at their house. Marquan was always happy when he came back from out of town and his mother or sister would tell him that his P.O hadn't come by yet. When Marquan walked into the house that morning, he noticed that his mother was sleeping on the couch. He hated that she chose to work so hard and wouldn't let him help her.

Marquan remembered the tennis bracelet that he had bought her when he took his brother and sister shopping. While she was asleep on the couch, Marquan slipped the tennis bracelet onto her arm. He slipped five thousand dollars into her purse and could hear her yelling at him. "Marquan, you take this money boy, I don't want you bringing this devil money into my house!" Marquan smiled because even though his mother worked hard to get what she wanted, she still kept her faith in God, that no matter what, God would always make a way out of no way.

Marquan always parked his truck behind his mother's car, that's how she knew that he was at home and not in the streets. Marquan was more than sure that he had just closed his eyes just before his mom came banging on his bedroom door. "Boy!" Get your butt up. You ain't about to be sleeping around here all day. "Get your butt up, now Marquan!" Marquan sat up in his bed. "Ok, mama what?" Here we go with the damn devil stories. He was thinking that to himself. "What mama? Why are you bomb rushing my room?" How come you didn't just knock? Boy What? What if I was in here naked, lying next to a woman?

"Boy prison must have ruined your mind." The last time you laid naked in my house, your butt was a baby and that's the only time you'll lay naked in this house. "Hell, you use to shit so much as a baby, that shit was burning your little ass and you wanted that pamper off." Ms. Housemoore busted up laughing. Marquan was shocked to see that his mother was even laughing and was in a good mood. "Mama, why you even waking me up?" Because, before you get up and disappear to lord knows where, you and your little brother are about to cut my grass before I can't even find my car. Boy, didn't I tell you to stop blocking my car in? I'm not in prison. I can come and go as I please. "I'm the warden up in this house." So, get up now, your brother already outside taking out the lawnmower.

Ms. Housemoore started to walk out of the room, and she stopped at the door. "Oh, by the way, thanks for the tennis bracelet Marquan, it's really pretty." She turned and walked out of the room. Marquan started feeling himself because he thought that he was dreaming. Marquan came walking out of his room in a pair of sweatpants and a t-shirt. Whitney came walking out of her room. "Oh, hey bro!" I see mama must of woke your butt up too. I see you still ain't too old to get that butt kicked. Marquan started chasing her and she ran outside where Jacob was trying to start the lawnmower. "Hey Whitney, let me ask you something." What bro, stop playing so much. You just trying to hit me.

"Naw! Naw!" Come here, I'm serious. "What's done got into mama?" Marquan pulled the tailgate down on the back of his truck. They both sat down and started talking. Bro, you know that she was going to see all that stuff you bought us. She started taking Jacob's stuff and he started crying. You already know that he is a crybaby. Marquan grabbed his sister around the neck playfully.

Well, her best friend Ms. Dawson came by the house to meet you. But of course, you weren't home. "Bro, she heard momma going off about what you had bought us and saw Jacob crying. She told momma that the word of God says, "Destroy it not; for there is a blessing in it;" Child that's the devil's money and I want that stuff out of my house. So, you mean to tell me that as the God fearing woman that I know you to be, that you're throwing out a blessing from God for you kids? It may have been a sinful act that made the money, but God took what he wanted to turn into a blessing and blessed his children with it. He knew that you couldn't afford it, so he made a way for the blessing to come, girl! Girl, you better learn how your Father works.

Whitney started telling Marquan about Ms. Dawson and how she had been keeping their mother strong since he had been gone. Whitney even told Marquan how she witnessed Ms. Dawson give their mother money, when she was a little short paying some of her bills. Marquan was sitting there listening and taking in everything that she told him. Marquan wants to make sure that a big blessing was coming Ms. Dawson's way as well. Whitney told Marquan that he was going to fall in love with Ms. Dawson's daughter Krystal. I think she be in those streets like you bro, because she be rocking all the latest gear that comes out. Her clothes and car ain't cheap at all. I think Ms. Dawson be going through the same situation with her as mama do you. Marquan said, "Sis I'm proud of you. You're growing up to be an extraordinary woman." Whitney smiled and said, "Big bro I know!"

CHAPTER FIFTEEN

SHAKING WITH FEAR

Emoni was stepping out of the bathtub when she heard a knock at her door. She grabbed a towel and wrapped it around her waist. Half wet she yelled out, "Ok wait a minute I'm coming." She looked out her peep hole and didn't see nobody standing there. She turned around to go back to the shower and the knock came at the door again. Bam! Bam! Bam! Emoni looked again through the peep hole and when she saw who was standing there, piss started running down her leg. She started shaking and was acting nervous. Her ex-boyfriend was yelling through the door. Tone started yelling. "Open up the fucking door, Emoni!" I'm not trying to hurt you. I know you're in there listening to me. Emoni ran to grab her cell phone to call Marquan.

After receiving the call, Marquan was running red lights and was gripping his 40-caliber handle. Even though he still didn't have a driver's license, Marquan hadn't stopped for one light, and knew that if he got pulled over, that he would be headed straight back to prison. Marquan came burning rubber, pulling into Emoni apartments. But he had missed Tone. He had just left the apartment complex. Marquan was knocking at Emoni's door and ringing her cell phone at the same time. "Baby open the door, it's me, Emoni."

Emoni opened the door and was shaking with fear in her eyes. Marquan held her close to him until he knew that she was comfortable with him being there. Marquan closed the door and almost slipped when he stepped in Emoni's piss on the floor. She was so afraid that she forgot to mop it up before Marquan got there. Marquan started to question her. "So, what happen?" She explained her and Tone interaction and it was something that she said that made Marquan put a strange look on his face. But he didn't feel like it was the right time to question what she had said happened. He didn't know Emoni that well, so he figured that it wasn't no reason to make up a lie to put yourself in fear.

Marquan felt that he'd get to the bottom of it in his own little way. "Emoni, baby how did he get out of prison so fast?" What he do, take a plea bargain and got out early? Just hearing the word released early, made Emoni cringe up. Emoni dropped down to the floor, and she started crying. "Why me Lord?" Why me? "Not again." Marquan bent down and picked her up. He looked Emoni straight in the eyes. Hey, didn't I tell you that you were my woman? Emoni, for the first time, put a smile on her face. I don't believe that we ever talked about that before. So, are you telling me that you're my man now? Well, only you can answer that question.

Then I guess the answer is yes, if that's what you're asking me or are you telling me that I am? I'm telling you Emoni, you're my woman and nobody will never hurt you again. Never again, do you really mean that Marquan? Yep! Not even you? Not even me. Ok then, I'm all yours, then.

Marquan had stayed at Emoni's house for two days and he slept on the couch. Emoni told Marquan that she just wanted to take it slow. That when the time was right, that the both of them would know it. Marquan was starting to care about Emoni so much, that he wasn't even thinking about having sex. Marquan was just happy to be in her company, laughing, smiling, and singing LeVert songs with Emoni. Marquan told Emoni that there would be times in her life, that there won't be anyone around to protect her so he wanted to make sure that she knew how to protect herself. They wind up being a great help to each other, while spending time together. Emoni helped Marquan get his driver's license and in return, Marquan took Emoni to the gun range every day and taught her how to shoot different types of weapons.

At first, she didn't like shooting the guns, but Marquan knew just the trick to help solve her problem. Marquan asked Emoni if she had any old pictures of Tone?

Marquan took her to Kinkos and blew up a few of his pictures. Marquan took her back to the range and Emoni was shooting holes through his body and face like she was a professional. The target practice turned out to be a great asset for Marquan. Now

BIG AND LITTLE SATAN

Emoni was glad to go to the gun range, because mainly she got to spend time with Marquan. In no time Emoni and Marquan were hitting anything that they clipped up to shoot, big or small. Emoni was starting to impress Marquan with her shooting skills.

The next day Marquan took Emoni to buy her a 9mm Glock pistol. She seems to handle the weapon very well, plus it has built up her confidence to be alone. Emoni said that Tone had come by one more time, but Emoni was at work. Emoni said that he called her at work to tell her that he had been watching her. Emoni told Marquan that he said that it makes him sick to his stomach to see Marquan hug, kiss or touch her. She said that he even promised her that he'd put his hands back around her neck the same way that the police found them the day that he went to jail. But Emoni assured Marquan that she could handle herself much better now that she had a gun.

CHAPTER SIXTEEN
CHILDHOOD DREAMS DIE

M arquan was sitting at Snooty apartment counting money that Snooty and Star made while working at the strip club. He was eating Churches Chicken and drinking a strawberry soda watching tv. The news was on, "hello you're watching channel 10 news and today's stories that we're covering is." There was a riot today at the Florence State Penitentiary and there were several men seriously hurt in the riot. One of the men that we talked about earlier today was air lifted to the nearest hospital. Five men died at the prison during the riot today. Marquan grabbed the remote and turned the tv up loud as he could. Just so that he could hear what the news anchor was saying.

Snooty walked into the living room. "Damn baby, are you going death? You got that tv up loud." Snooty stopped and listened for a minute to see what has Marquan's attention. Besides, the look that he had on his face scared her more than anything. She knew something was wrong. "Baby, what's going on?" She quickly stopped asking questions when some man picture was being shown on the tv screen. "The families have been notified so we can show their pictures." They had put their photos across the screen, like they were in a police lineup for a crime they committed.

Each photo has their name under their picture. The first photo name read Christian Anderson and Marquan dropped his bottle of pop and glass flew everywhere. This inmate just died just earlier this morning. He was the one that got air lifted from the prison. A big picture came across the screen and the name read Antwan Simmons, and Marquan yelled out, "Nooooooo! Nooooooo! to the top of his lungs. "Not my nigga's!" He hugged the T.V screen and sat there crying gasping for his breath. Snooty hugged Marquan. Come on baby, go ahead, and let it all out baby! "I'm right here with you daddy."

Snooty didn't have no idea who those men are, but she knew that they must have meant a great deal to Marquan. Star was knocking at the door and Snooty went to let her in. When she entered the house and heard Marquan crying, they both couldn't believe that. He was in so much pain. The both of them held their man and him crying made them start crying. Even though they had no idea who it was they were crying for.

Marquan calmed down just long enough to tell Snooty and Star who they were and what they meant to him. Marquan told them that he had just sent Rocky and Slow Drag money to the prison. Marquan looked at Snooty and Star with tears in his eyes.

Baby I need y'all right now more than ever before. I got to send my two brothers out right. One by one Snooty and Star said, Daddy we with you. We got you. We with you.

CHAPTER SEVENTEEN

BLACK SCORPION

S upreme and Marquan have been waiting for this job to come up. They had spent months doing surveillance on Scorpion and his house. He was a sophisticated psychopath that controlled the South, East, and West drug traffic among the Mexicans in Arizona. Scorpion wasn't your normal type of drug dealer. He was very educated and collected high-end expensive cars. One of his favorites was an ultra-stretch black and white Limousine Rolls Royce that Scorpion inherited from his grandfather Black Scorpion.

Black Scorpion actually lost his life in that very same Limousine Rolls Royce. He was doing a deal for five hundred kilos with a hot head up and coming dealer out of Mexico. The dealer wanted to take over the Arizona business and become the next big player in the drug game. Scorpion mother home schooled him and at the age of ten, Scorpion was already doing High School work. He got his first degree in Sociology at the age of Seventeen. Scorpion got the taste of drug dealing and street life when he was sent to Mexico to spend a summer with his two cousins and grandfather.

It didn't take Scorpion long to realize that his grandfather controlled part of the drug trafficking in Mexico. Black Scorpion allowed his two sons and Alex, Scorpion's real birth name, to shoot his many weapons. Black Scorpion even let them help count his drug money sometimes. Black Scorpion took Alex to his favorite restaurant, and he was choking on some food. Everybody was panicking and Alex stayed calm. He knew how to do the Heimlich maneuver. Alex jumped up from the table and saved his grandfather from choking. Being that Black Scorpion was like a God to the people in Mexico, it was like Alex had just save his life.

The people in the restaurant started cheering like Alex was a hero. They started calling Alex, Little Scorpion. His grandfather was really grateful that Alex saved his life. So even he accepted the people calling him a name after him. The nickname that the people gave him made Black Scorpion proud of him. He even took Alex shopping and bought him a pair of Ostrich boots and a matching belt and a 10-gallon cowboy hat to match.

Alex treasured that gift from his grandfather in the same way that a kid gets a PlayStation for Christmas. Alex's mom use to have to wait until he fell asleep just to remove his boots that his grandpa bought him. That would be the only way that he would take the boots off. The next summer that Alex went to Mexico, it wasn't as exciting as the year before. That's when he lost his grandpa from a drug deal that went bad. After the funeral, Alex made a promise to Black Scorpion that no matter what happened to him, that he would live out his grandfather's legacy even if it killed him.

Alex's mother had much bigger plans for Alex. But he wind up breaking her heart after his grandpa funeral. Alex told his mother that he wanted to stay in Mexico with his two cousins. His mother knew that it wasn't nothing in Mexico compared to the lifestyle that her and her husband worked so hard to give him. She came in The United States illegally at first, just to provide for her son. After all her hard work, pain and suffering, Alex still wanted to return back to a place where she wanted to put behind her and never return.

Even though her dad was a big-time drug dealer, Alex's mother still didn't want anything to do with his lifestyle. In fact, the first time that she heard him call himself Scorpion, she slapped his face so hard that it looked like she left a mark on his face in the shape of a Scorpion. Well, those days are long gone and now little Alex is now Scorpion. Only he's much more powerful and richer than his grandpa.

Scorpion fell in love with a young model that he met at the Barron Davis Car Auction. Scorpion was looking at a 56 Chevy Convertible, black with red interior. Even though Scorpion loved old school classic cars, the car that he was looking at this time wasn't what has just caught his attention. It was a blue pencil dress that showed off all Lamania curves. That's what led him to the both of them. Lamania was bent over looking at the 56 Chevy when Scorpion walked up behind her and said, "Yes she is very beautiful." Even Lamania commented on the 56 Chevy. "Yes, she is beautiful, but she a little too rich for my blood." Scorpion told Lamania that it definitely looked wonderful on the outside. But of course, if it's a lot of miles on it, then it could turn into major problems later. Lamania said, "don't you think that anything this beautiful is worth putting up with a little problem?" Besides, it's an antique. Well from the looks of things, it really doesn't appear to be that old at all. But I'm not that too much concerned about the year that you were born anyways. I'm more concerned about the miles that's been put on you. "Don't you know that every man doesn't know how to take care of someone as treasurable as you?"

"Oh, my bad!" I didn't have any idea that we were referring to me instead of such a beautiful car. I was more than sure that the both of us were admiring the car. Now come on, "How could anyone look at anything with you standing in front of it?" His comment made Lamania smile. But before she walked away, she was pointing at the car. She is an antique and I'm willing to bet she doesn't have a lot of miles on her. But me honey, I haven't even been on a test ride yet, sorry! Besides that, that car you might be able to afford, but you'll have to work for the rest of your life to afford me. There's no price tag that comes on her. Lamania rubbed her hand across her vagina and walked over to the next vehicle. Under Scorpion breath he said, "Maybe nobody ain't offered you enough yet."

BIG AND LITTLE SATAN

While the bidding started, Lamania was one of the girls that were drawing more attention to the cars during the sales. When the 56 Chevy came up, Scorpion started the bid at Fifty Thousand. But another man that was into antiques also started bidding on the same car. Every time he raised his hand that only made Scorpion dick get harder. Composure is what we strive off of, even in his normal lifestyle.

The car was in great condition and the bid kept on going up. A few other guys started bidding on it and Scorpio and Lamania both locked eyes. Scorpion missed a few bids just to approach Lamania. He asked her, "Hey if I buy that car for you, will you at least take me for a ride in it?" Lamania looked Scorpion straight in the eyes and said, "Man if you buy me that car then you can ride me, in my car." Scorpion watched a man get excited because he thought that he had out bided everybody. Before the auctioneer could say sold to the gentlemen, Scorpion raised his hand and raised the bid from Sixty-Five Thousand to Seventy-Five Thousand. "Do I hear Eighty Thousand?" Everyone got quiet. Going once! Going twice! Sold to the gentlemen for Seventy-Five Thousand with the pretty lady standing next to him.

Eight months later, Lamania and Scorpion got married and a year later she was pregnant with their son. This was Scorpion first child, so he named him after his grandfather, Manuel. Lamania and Scorpion's relationship took a quick turn after his right-hand man Pico followed Lamania and some super male model that she was working with. The day that Lamania decided to go to a motel with the guy, when they exited the room Scorpion had them taken to one of his body shops and he ordered the men to remove every body part of their bodies. In the same way that his workers removed a part off a wrecked car before painting it. He didn't even have them shot or stabbed. Scorpion just ordered his men to detach every body part on their bodies. Lamania tried pleading for her life just as the man did. But the only thing that was going to please Scorpion was their blood leaking all over the floor in that shop.

To this day nobody even knows what happened to their remaining parts. Lamania's family went to the police station and insisted that they arrest Scorpion. But like they always say, Sir, Ma'am on what charges? The day that Scorpion had Lamania, and her lover killed, he made her write a letter and left it on their bed. It just said that she's unhappy and that he couldn't please her in the way that she needed to be pleased. After the Feds tested the letter and pen, it turned out that nobody's DNA was found but hers.

Manuel was only two years' old when his dad had killed his mother and her lover. So, he really didn't know his mother. The only woman that he knew was Tracy. The woman Manuel knew as his mom, she wasn't but twenty-four year's old and was going on twenty two when they got married. Even Tracy had a close call with death, after just getting married to Scorpion. Nobody knows when his temper is about to flare up. But Tracy got to experience

BIG AND LITTLE SATAN

it in front of his friends. Scorpion always spoiled his ladies with the best name brand clothing, shoes, purses, and expensive cars. Whatever they wanted to drive they got it. Tracy was pushing a 500 G. Wagon on 22inch rims with a black pearl paint job.

Scorpion always had a big crush on Salena, the singer that got killed by her assistant in a hotel. Tracy and Salena can almost pass for twins, except for the breast implants that Scorpion took Tracy to Mexico to have done. One day Scorpion and a few of his friends went to Scorpion house for lunch. Because Tracy is a great cook, and she cooked all of Scorpions favorite food for them. Tracy was wearing a short mini-Prada skirt and a half white Prada shirt tied to the side. She was showing off her flat stomach and rocking her tie up lace high heel shoes that made her ass bounce whenever she walked.

Tracy was serving him and his friends in their kitchen area. She was cutting up limes so that Scorpion and his friends could place them in the neck of their beers. While Tracy was cutting the limes, Manuel walked into the kitchen, and he loves eating limes and salt. He tried to grab one of the ones that Tracy was cutting, and she playfully slapped his hand. One of the limes flew on the floor and without thinking Tracy bent over to pick it up. When she did, it exposed her whole backside. One of the men that was drunk pointed at Tracy backside and said, "My goodness Senorita!" What a fat panocha she got. "Damn!" All the men turned to look and so did Scorpion. He jumped up from the table and charged at Tracy.

"Chooo Fuckinggg Bitchhh! He kicked her right in the vagina with his Ostrich boots, but it didn't stop there.

Tracy was being kicked like a soccer ball in a World Cup tournament. It took Manuel and all of Scorpion friends to stop him from kicking her to death. After they stopped him, he pulled out his 9mm pistol from his waistband and shot the guy that gave the comment about his wife. Pow! Pow! Pow! Scorpion pointed the gun at the rest of the guys and his son. Anymore of you fucking puntos got anything else to say? Y'all still think that my wife got a fat panocha? "Naw man! Nope not me." I didn't even look. I didn't see nothing.

Tracy was lying with her back to the kitchen sink. She was bleeding badly, but everyone knew that nobody better not go and help her. His friend Carlos lay just a few feet from Tracy, and she was trying not to look at him after it was all said and done. Also, just like Lamania, Carlos body wasn't never found nor did anyone ask about him.

$ $ $ $ $

Scorpion wasn't sleeping too well. He woke up in the middle of the night and looked at his wife Tracy. He laid there stroking her curly black hair. Scorpion was thinking that he was the luckiest man in the world to have a woman as beautiful as Tracy by his side. Scorpion had promised himself that after he dealt with the Jamaicans in the morning that he would take Tracy on a long vacation just the two of them. No guards or his right-hand man, Pico. The Jamaican's was coming to cop a hundred kilos at Twelve Thousand, Five Hundred a piece. That's One Million, Two Hundred and Fifty Thousand dollars that you couldn't trust no man word with.

Scorpion have been dealing with them for a few years and everything always went well. But this was their first time making such a large purchase at one time. Jakarta was always a good man and his word went across the world as gold. Jakarta is a real dangerous man himself and could make life very hard for you to live. If any one of them tried anything funny they both know that it would be many family and friends making the Dirty Desert Inn Cemetery a permanent home for good.

Scorpion was looking in the mirror. He was admiring the Black Scorpion that was tattooed on his neck. It was a sign of respect to his grandfather. Scorpion ran his hand across his rock-hard abs. Even though he ran the streets, he and Pico worked out six days a week. They almost look like brothers. One could easily mistake them for the U-So brothers from WWE wrestling. Scorpion looks more like Jay U-So and Pico looks like Jimmy U-So, but they're not related at all. Pico poured him a shot of Tequila and he stared at himself while swishing the liquor around in his glass.

It was times like this when Scorpion would daydream and think about Lamania. There was no woman that could ever come close to taking his heart like her. Scorpion even still have the panties that she wore the night that he had her killed. He always told

Lamania that there's no other woman's vagina that smells like hers. Scorpion removed a picture of him and Tracy and opened up the safe. He removed the panties that Lamania had on and put them up to his face. Ummmmm! He took in her scent. He sympathetically repeated her name over and over. "Lamania, Lamania!" But he got quickly snapped out of his moment of passion by his wife's voice.

"Honey what are you doing, why are you up so late?" Why don't you come back to bed? Scorpion jumped to the sound of Tracy's voice. He quickly removed Lamania panties away from his face and put them behind his back. "Ok honey yeah sure, I'll be right there." Tracy blew him a kiss and headed into the bathroom. After she left, he placed the panties back to his nose and sniffed them one last time. Ummmmm! Scorpion neatly folded Lamania panties and placed them back in his safe.

On his way back to bed, Scorpion thought that he heard a noise outside. He opened up the double doors that lead to the terrace and walked out onto the balcony that overlooked his backyard. Scorpion also inherited a mansion in Scottsdale on Frank Lloyd Wright sitting on five acres of land. Which also came with a twenty-two-year-old bomb shell of a woman. Carmena was a lot smarter than Lamania or Tracy. She was married to Scorpion's grandfather before she married Scorpion. When Black Scorpion died, Carmena didn't want to separate from her fiancé, so she married Scorpion.

BIG AND LITTLE SATAN

Whenever Scorpion got upset, Carmena could easily see that he had his grandfather's temper. The first time that Scorpion threaten to kill her, Carmena got her stuff and left the mansion. Carmena removed a Hundred Thousand dollars from one of his stacks of money and a bottle of Nivea Water and his Pit Bull C.D and left. She boarded a Greyhound to Mexico and didn't look back. Scorpion even ran into her two years later in Mexico while he was visiting family. But she was now dating some guy that have the last name Guzman, who turned out to be a drug dealer and was a killer himself. Scorpion decided to take that little Hundred-Thousand-dollar pocket change as a lost right along with the twenty-four-year-old Latino bomb shell.

Scorpion was looking around his compound and didn't seem to see anything out of order. Even though it gets extremely hot in Arizona that night the wind had a nice cool breeze that Scorpion was appreciating. He looked in every direction, even at the nice garden that Black Scorpion had put in. That's when Supreme and Marquan's heart started racing like two competitive athletes trying to cross the finish line in a race. They both gripped their weapons, even stared in the direction for a few minutes. But it was more of their consciousness that was bothering them, than Scorpion. He has just went back into a moment of making love to Lamania on their balcony. It was as if he could hear her seductive moan's and the way she screamed his name while having sex. "Scorrr! Peeee! Onnnnn! Yes Scorrrrr! Peeeeee! Onnnnn! Yes Poppie!"

Once again Scorpion was interrupted by his wife Tracy. She was still calling him back to bed. Supreme and Marquan were so grateful that she done that, because the both of them could see a rattle snake making its way over to them. But it didn't matter to Supreme, because he was ready to kill the snake on the balcony and the one in the grass. Scorpion kissed Tracy and he walked her back into the mansion. Supreme and Marquan didn't waste any time getting to their feet. They both quietly disappeared into the night air without having to kill the snake or Scorpion.

$ $ $ $ $

One by one, family members were pulling into the Dirty Desert Inn cemetery to say their last goodbyes to their love ones. Supreme, Marquan, Ecstasy, Persia, and Glory were all standing by some man's grave that said Mr. Mitchell on his plot. They were pretending to be his family while they peep the cemetery. Each one of them was packing some heavy weapons. They knew that the men that they were waiting for would definitely come prepared for any unexpected problems.

Glory kept staring at a family that wasn't too far away from where they were standing. She watched as the family hurt with so much pain inside them from losing their loved one. It even made her wonder if she would be leaving the Dirty Desert cemetery as dangerous as the men are they're waiting for. Glory dated a Jamaican drug dealer before, and she knew how they got down when it came to killing. She never told Supreme, but she wasn't blind to the type of men that they were waiting on.

Jakarta rolled deep and with plenty high-end artillery. His right-hand man is so accurate with a weapon that he shot the tip of a man's penis off just for pissing in his yard. He told the drunk man that he passed too many gas stations to come piss in hell. After serving fifteen years in prison, Bocca met a man that told him about Jakarta, and he been watching his back ever since they met.

Even though they were in a place of sad men and women, Supreme put the biggest smile on his face after he saw the trail of Rolls Royce's enter the cemetery. A white drop head led the group of cars that was coming into the cemetery. A black and white Rolls Royce Limousine trailed behind the drop head and a Blue and Gold Rolls Royce Phantom followed the Limousine. Supreme knew that his special guest had just shown up to the party. Just as soon as Scorpion and his partner exited the Limo, Supreme wanted nothing more than to leave them where they stood. But he knew that the money hadn't arrived just yet. Supreme and Marquan have a plan that they were taking lives and the money that Papa Jack wouldn't never see or know about. Supreme and Marquan had studied Scorpion very closely on this job, that's why they knew the only place that they could get close to Scorpion was his own mansion. That's the only place that Scorpion didn't need or use Pico at. Pico was sitting next to the driver in the Limousine with two gold plated 44 Magnums locked and loaded. He came in eyeballing the whole cemetery for anything that's out of place. Everything must have seemed in place because Pico didn't alert Scorpion to anything to keep an eye on.

Scorpion and Supreme looked in the same direction because they both heard the loud music before the cars can even enter the cemetery. A black 500 Mercedes Benz came turning into the cemetery with three jeeps trailing with three men in each jeep with long dreadlocks. It looked like they were sitting in an Indian sweat lodge because so much smoke was coming from each jeep. One of the jeeps was bumping Shaggy. They all had their headlights on and then they came to a complete stop at the front entrance. One of the Jamaican dudes jumped out the front jeep and ran to the Mercedes passenger side window. The men talked for a minute then they made their way through the cemetery towards the Rolls Royce's.

Supreme and Marquan were watching their every move. Supreme cell phone started ringing. "Yea, this Preme holla." After the call Supreme had a real big smile on his face then even before. Supreme whispered something in Marquan's ear and then he nodded in the direction of the front entrance. A black hurst Limousine and a Black Lincoln came rolling through the cemetery. Supreme, Marquan and the girls started making their way across the cemetery lawn.

Stigma was dressed in a black lace pants suit carrying a real big purse with a mini 14 submachine gun. Persia was wearing a short blue mini dress carrying an AK47 sub machine gun ready to do all her talking. Ecstasy was wearing a green bodysuit carrying an Uzi that separates body parts. Glory was the only one wearing a red bodysuit but had two 9mm pistols on each hip under her suit jacket. Supreme was carrying a 357 Magnum and a 44 Magnum that Marquan had the night before when they paid Scorpion a home visit.

Marquan was packing two 44 Magnums and the both of them have extended clips. Supreme told them all that if anybody made one mistake that it would be over for them. So, Supreme and Marquan planned everything perfectly. Scorpion and his men were already strapped and ready to air shit out if it wasn't right. The Jamaican's exited their vehicles with their guns out in the open like the shit was normal. It was families visiting their loved ones and burying their loved ones that didn't make it. It was a nice sunny Sunday. The weather was perfect for a funeral.

Scorpion and Pico were approaching Jakarta and Bocca, they all were acknowledging each other and sizing up the situation. "What's up star?" "Naw! That would be you, my friend." Jakarta told Scorpion, "If I had your type of money, I wouldn't be standing in this cemetery around all these dead people trying to reach your level of the game." Jakarta blew smoke in Scorpion face from the cigar that he and Bocca were smoking. The two of them started laughing at Jakarta's comment. The two of them nodded at each other which was the same thing that Scorpion and Pico just did.

"Man, what a place to do business?" Jakarta turned around and took in all the people burying their loved ones. I never thought that I'd be in a cemetery unless my people were sending me off. Well at least I'll get to see where I send people who fuck over me. Jakarta gave Scorpion a serious look. Really, he was trying to send Scorpion a silent message, that he didn't want to fuck with his money. Scorpion smiled at him and said, "My friend, don't worry about these people we're all at home here." Trust me we'll all make it here someday, by making some of the same mistakes as them. "They say that you'll return back to the same dirt that you came from." Now Scorpion gave Jakarta the same look that he had on his face just seconds ago.

Scorpion took his cigar out of his mouth and handed it to Pico. My friend let's teach our guest that pleasure and business don't mix. Pico dropped the cigar and stepped on it. The whole time he was looking Bocca in the eye's as to say don't even think about it. Because Bocca made a motion towards Scorpion after he took the cigar out of Jakarta's hand. But Jakarta put his hand up to stop Bocca from tripping , it was too much money counting on it.

"Yea, yea you right my friend, business first." Let's handle that then they'll be plenty of time for pleasure, right? "Yea right!" Scorpion nodded his head at Pico letting him know that it's okay to grab his work. Pico gave Bocca one last look as to say try me if you want to, then headed back towards the limousine. Pico removed one of the kilos and Scorpion men followed him back to their gathering. Each man had their hands on their weapons ready to handle business.

Pico came back and passed the kilo to Scorpion, and he passed it to Jakarta. Bocca was already taking out some type of drug kit just to see how pure the cocaine was that they were about to purchase. Bocca took out a sharp knife and carved a slit into the cocaine and it popped up like a white girl that was giving a blow job to a trick in a car, to learn that the police were pulling up behind them. After placing the drugs in a vial, Bocca gave Jakarta one of the biggest smiles like he was a trick relieving himself in that same white girl's mouth and she didn't miss a drop of cum. This is it boss, this that shit!

Scorpion said, "Now can I smile too." Can I see those dead presidents? See I'm nothing like you, my friend. I love the dead, them motherfucker's make me smile all the time. They all busted up laughing, knowing that Scorpion was talking about the dead presidents on money. Bocca already had a Gucci bag that was sitting next to his leg. He stepped back and waved Scorpion over to look through the bag. Just as Pico opened the bag, the same smile that Scorpion wanted came over his face. "Let's do business my friend."

Scorpion and Jakarta gave both of their men the okay to bring out the money and drugs. To Jakarta's surprise, Scorpion handed him a cigar bigger than the one that he and Bocca were smoking. "Ok! Pleasure my friend is good now." Scorpion pulled out a lighter with a Black Scorpion on the side of the lighter and gave Jakarta a light. Jakarta took one pull and started choking. While Bocca and Pico was checking over the drugs, Scorpion and Jakarta was sitting in the Limousine thumbing through the money. A Hurst Limousine and a Black Lincoln Limousine pulled up next to Scorpion's Limousine.

Scorpion and Jakarta both acknowledge the two Limousines but because of where they were the two Limousines didn't draw any suspicion to them. Jakarta and Scorpion figured that someone else fell short to the life that they were still loving. Scorpion have his men standing on one side of the Limousine and Jakarta have his men standing on the opposite side. They all have their weapons ready to pull them if anything looked out of place. It didn't take Scorpion and Jakarta long to realize that all the money was straight.

Bocca and Pico have already loaded the drugs in the Mercedes Benz 500 and the tension between the two men wasn't there anymore. They were now all walking together side by side towards Scorpion Rolls Royce Limousine. Bocca turned his attention to the beautiful attractive female that was walking towards them with the two guys. Bocca was even starting to feel sympathy for them, not really knowing who they had just lost, that he was more than sure they would miss. The back door opened up on the Rolls Royce Limousine and Scorpion and Jakarta stepped out. They were giving each other a hug and friendly handshake to say that business went well. Pow! The first shot rang out and before Bocca could even realize what happened Supreme had put a bullet right in his forehead. All the doors opened up on the Hurst and the Lincoln Limousine and gunshots ranged out. Pow! Pow! Pow! Pow! Pow! Pow! Pow! Bullets were popping off going straight into the bodies of Scorpion and Jakarta and their men. Supreme, Marquan, Stigma, Persia, Ecstasy, and Glory was shooting like the Magnificent Seven when they took over the town as Cowboys with Denzel Washington.

People started running and screaming, trying to get out of the way of the ambush that Bocca and Pico were in the middle of. All the hard work that Supreme had them put in was paying off because nobody was missing their targets. Papa Jack had sent a few trained Chinese killers to help assist Supreme on taking down Scorpion. These were men that Papa Jack call when nobody else couldn't get the job done. But it was only once that Supreme didn't get the job done, but after the Chinese left the home the man, his wife, and son was all left lying next to the family dog. Because his growl never turned into a bite after taking a bullet to the chest. Supreme and Tooki have done jobs together before Papa Jack had them pay a little visit to a fire station one day. They left the fire station on fire with a herald of bullets leaving 911 to assist them.

The Dirty Desert Inn Cemetery had more bodies lying around on the lawn than in caskets. No Pastor didn't even have to give them their final sermon to comfort their family members. The devil seems to have given the final say over every life that kept him company during their stay on earth. Just as Supreme and Marquan walked over to Tooki and his men, Scorpion was crawling towards his Limousine spitting up blood. Supreme made sure that he gave Tooki orders not to shoot to kill Scorpion. But from the looks of things, he didn't seem to have too much life left in him. Supreme, Marquan, Stigma, Persia, Ecstasy, and Glory all surrounded Scorpion. It appeared that he was trying to say something but the last words that he heard was Supreme say, "Papa Jack said Hello Mother fucker!" Pow! Pow! Pow! Pow! Pow! Pow! They all started dumping bullets into his body.

Supreme had the drugs loaded up into his Rolls Royce Limousine, then he sat the Gucci bag next to Marquan's feet and went and got behind the wheel of the white drop head Rolls Royce and drove out the Dirty Desert Inn Cemetery.

CHAPTER EIGHTEEN
CAN'T TAKE BACK
A MISTAKE

Five days had passed, and Stigma face was starting to clear up. Ms. Bergess had sent Stigma witch hazel and had told her a few old school remedies to take down the swelling. The whole time that she was there, Supreme had only spent one night with her at the suite and that had Stigma pissed. Stigma wasn't the jealous type of woman, but when she felt that her man should be by her side, right at that moment and time in her life. That's what she was expecting Supreme to do, was to be by her side. Supreme made sure that she didn't run out of Rollo's candy. That's a chocolate and caramel candy that her and little Isaiah loved to eat together.

Stigma was starting to feel sexy and pretty again. So now, she wanted to go home and be with her son. The hotel still had two days left of it and really that's what Stigma needed to completely heal. Stigma was walking around the suite in a pair of red slippers and matching red and black panties and bra set. Stigma opened her favorite cranberry drink and realized that there wasn't any ice in the room. Damn! She didn't feel like putting on any clothes just to go get ice. So, she grabbed her silk bath robe and picked up the ice bucket and headed to the ice machine.

Stigma forgot that her robe was see through, she felt like nobody else would-be getting ice at that moment. Just as she filled up her bucket and turned around to go back to her room, Bam! Stigma bumped right into someone, and it made her say, "damn." Stigma ice-bucket went flying and ice flew everywhere. "Oh Miss Lady, please excuse me." I'm so sorry. "But wow, I've never saw any sight as beautiful in Arizona yet since I've been here." My God you are beautiful. Now Stigma was realizing that the man could see her full body and shape. He leaned down to pick up her bucket and when he went to look up, his face was right at Stigma crouch. "Damn, and you smell like strawberries too."

While handing Stigma her bucket back, he asked her, "so can you please tell me who's the luckiest man in the world?" Damn you got a nose like a bloodhound. Stigma had just taken a bath in strawberry body wash. "I'm so sorry, let me replace your ice." Stigma said that it was ok because it was her fault. "That's my fault, for not paying attention to what I was doing." She grabbed her bucket and turned back towards the ice machine. Stigma knew that he was still watching her ass. "Ok sexy, I think that I better come back after you leave." So that my mind can forget what I just saw knowing I'll never get to have it. He didn't have on a shirt. So, when Stigma was walking past him, she rubbed his rock-hard abs. Wow! You really take good care of your body, don't you? Now you tell me, who's the happy woman?

"We'll I'm not a liar, sorry!" There is one, but she not out here with me. She's back in Atlanta, I'm here on business. Ok Mr. Man. "I love the fact that you didn't lie about having a woman like most men do." I'm Deshawn, he extended his hand. I'm Stigma, it's my pleasure. "I have a Dada myself." I guess we met in the right place, but at the wrong time. "Right!" So why do you say that? You're here alone and so am I. Both of our significant others left us here to be alone.

Stigma and Deshawn both felt a strong attraction to each other. Neither one of them was willing to allow their little ice spill to come in between that affection. At least, they were willing to get to know more about each other. Stigma gave in and at least was willing to talk over the phone. They both were in their own room and were conversing on the phone. Deshawn stood 5'10 with real dark skin, that made him shine like new money. He wore a low haircut and had noticeable dimples on his cheeks. His body was cut up like the actor and comedian Terry Crews.

What really attracted him to Stigma was, Deshawn didn't act like he was some baller, rapper, hustler, or a drug dealer, he was just a normal guy. He told Stigma that he was a traveling Massage Therapist. Stigma told Deshawn that she knew that God created those hands and body for a good reason. Stigma wanted so badly to invite Deshawn over to her room. Just so that she could experience for herself what type of work that he put in on bodies. But she didn't have any idea when Supreme would show up and kill them both. Stigma made up a lie and said that she works at a Law firm in Scottsdale. But she did manage to tell him the truth about little Isaiah and Ms. Bergess.

There wasn't no way that she could talk to someone so serious and not tell them about them. In fact, it was making Stigma feel scared, the fact that she even told Deshawn about her son. Deshawn asked Stigma if he could please have 30 minutes of her time just to allow her to see how well he did his job. Stigma finally agreed and told Deshawn that she couldn't stay no longer than 30 minutes.

"No! No! No!" Oh my God Deshawn stop. "Deshawn, you got to stop." Please stop, stop stop! Why are you doing this to me? Deeeee! Shaaaaa! owwww my God! "Damn man! Stigma had lost count of the many times that Deshawn have made her cum. Deshawn started out giving Stigma a massage cracking and popping different parts of her body. That she didn't know or realize that can be popped. While she laid there in ecstasy from enjoying Deshawn massage, Deshawn slipped her panties to the side so smooth, and he invaded her vagina like no man or woman have before. Stigma head was turning and moving from side to side. A few times she even tried to escape his grip. But Deshawn was much too strong for Stigma to get away. So, Stigma laid back and enjoyed what her body had never experienced before. They kissed passionately and Stigma returned the favor giving him head back. Then they got into the 69 position and took each other to a galaxy leaving each other to see stars.

Deshawn laid Stigma on her back and when he penetrated her vagina, Stigma knew that life for her would never be the same for her, Isaiah or Supreme. Deshawn finished putting down a world class performance and when he reached his climax, he and Stigma exploded at the same time, like fireworks on New Year's Eve in Time Square. Deshawn, after busting his nut, pulled out of Stigma, and laid on his back breathing hard. Stigma curled up into a little ball, and just cried her eyes out. She finally turned over and looked at Deshawn, "Man why!" Tell me, Deshawn, why did we let this happen?

After leaving the room, Stigma went to a convenience store that was across the street from the hotel. She grabbed cranberry juice and every Massengill douche that was on the shelf. Stigma was in the shower flushing a Massengill bottle in between her legs and crying the whole time. As long as she and Supreme have been together, Stigma has never cheated on Supreme. They have had many sexual encounters with them and other women. Even Stigma one on one with women. But never without Supreme being present. They always trusted and respected each other in that way. Stigma after showering had laid there and cried herself to sleep.

When Stigma was waking up to the touch that she knew oh so well, Supreme was lying next to her and kissing her in the same place that Deshawn was kissing her on earlier in the day. "Oh, hi baby." Stigma smiled happy to see Supreme. He held her face in his hand. But when she got a clear view of his body, Supreme was climbing into the bed asshole naked ready to have sex. Stigma's body shook with fear, because she knows her man and the only way, he'd get into the bed naked would only be to make her scream his name. Earlier in the day, Stigma was hoping and praying that Supreme walked in the hotel with that same sexual desire and take that horny mood away from her that she so desperately wanted.

But wanting ice and something cold to drink, Stigma got something hard and something warm to swallow. Not only did her sexual desires get fixed, but it turned out to be the best sex in her life. Supreme was now going in. "Owww! Wait, wait baby my stomach." I ate something from across the street earlier and that shit fucked my stomach up baby! It's still hurting me bad. Supreme looked over at the Styrofoam plate that sat on the nightstand. Now stigma was praying to God that Supreme didn't open that lid. Right after Stigma ordered it and they delivered it; she fell asleep, so the food hadn't been touched.

Supreme and stigma just laid there holding each other and fell asleep. The next morning Stigma woke up first and she saw the light flashing on the phone. First, she thought that maybe they overslept, and the office left a message. But she remembered that she still had another day in the suite. Stigma quietly went into the living room and retrieved the message. She picked up the card next to the phone to learn how to listen to their messages. Stigma pressed 8 you have two unheard messages to hear them press 5. Stigma press 5 and started listening to the messages.

"Hello sexy woman, this Deshawn." I was hoping to get to see you again tonight before I leave in the morning. I really enjoyed spending time with you. You are a woman that I'll never forget in my life. Hey, maybe you'll be in Atlanta someday and might want to look me up. My address is and he left his cell phone number as well. Then the call ended. You have one unheard message please press 5. Good morning stigma, I guess you decided not to call me back last night. Maybe it was just me left feeling this way when we left each other. I just really wanted to say goodbye. My cab is here and I'm leaving Arizona. You are the only one who can stop that from happening right now so call me. I could never see myself leaving you, but that's only if you're feeling the same way.

Stigma, I already told my mom that I met a special lady like her. Bye Stigma, I'll always think about you. Tears started rolling down Stigma face when the call ended. Stigma listened to the first call again to get Deshawn information and phone number. She wrote it down and just as she was about to listen to the second call again, Supreme woke up and started calling her name. Stigma quickly placed the number in her bra and jumped up wiping her tears away. Stigma! I'm right here, here I come Dada!

CHAPTER NINETEEN

PUTTING THE TEAM TOGETHER

S tigma thought that this would be a better time to ask Supreme about their future than any. She wanted to know what their future would look like after all the killings. Dada, can we talk? Supreme new them words oh so well coming from a woman. The last time that Stigma pulled the Tevin Campbell, can we talk, Stigma wanted to go into real estate school and stop living the lifestyle that they were living. Supreme had told Stigma that it was not their decision to make that call right now, until they learn who Papa Jack is. Supreme looked her in the eyes. Do you really think that this motherfucker will let us just walk away, with all that he knows about us? Don't you think that we'll die first?

Stigma finally realized that she had never stopped to even consider that thought. At times she even wondered herself many times why Papa Jack had never invited them to meet him or his family.

BIG AND LITTLE SATAN

None of them didn't even know if Papa Jack was Black, White, Mexican, or Chinese. Nobody knew shit about Papa Jack. They were in much deeper than some Charlie Angel's bullshit. Stigma met Supreme in a nightclub. That night Stigma and a few friends went out to have fun. That night Supreme kept on sending drinks over to their table.

The first time that he spoke to Stigma, Supreme told her that you're going to have my child and be my woman. Stigma clearly remembered that because Supreme never said his wife. Stigma told Supreme that she was sorry, but he picked the wrong woman in the club to say that to. Brother if that's your pickup line, you better find a new one because I don't even like kids. Besides that, one of the females that Stigma was out with they were in a relationship. Stigma got up close in Supremes' face, honey if you wouldn't have sent all those drinks to our table, you would still be smelling the pussy on my breath.

Two hours after the club let out, Supreme was in the hotel smelling Stigma and her girlfriend's vagina. Two months later, Stigma was calling Supreme to tell him that she was pregnant with his baby. Seven months later, Stigma was having little Supreme Washington junior. Supreme brought Stigma and his son to the house that they live in now. But later would move miss Bergess in to care for their son. Because he knew that Stigma needed help learning how to be a mother to their child. Supreme thought what better person that could teach her then the woman that taught her how to be a woman. Supreme always spoiled them with gifts and made sure they stayed happy. But one day Stigma told Supreme that if she was going to keep being his woman, that they couldn't keep no more secrets between them. Supreme whatever you into, then I want to be right beside you.

Supreme looked at her with a look that spoke without words. Supreme, I'm not playing with you. If you don't let me in, then I'm taking our son and leaving to be with a man that don't keep secrets from his woman. Stigma thought that Supreme was selling or running drugs. She poked her chest out, man I can handle anything that you can. I'm more man than any man that you know. Supreme walked out of the room and headed to his car. Minutes later he returned with a 357 magnum and a 9 mm Glock pistol and laid them on the bed.

OK smart ass! Can you handle them? Stigma picked up the 9mm Glock pistol. She popped the clip out and pushed all the bullets out of the clip. Then she removed the bullet that was in the chamber and popped it onto the bed. Supreme was looking surprised. "What!" How in the hell did you learn how to do that? Stigma reloaded the gun then pointed it at Supreme. Now do you want me to show you how it works, Dada?

Stigma stepdad, Ms. Burgess husband was a police officer and before he died in a traffic stop, he always taught Stigma and Ms. Burgess how to use every weapon he had. Supreme told Stigma what he does, and she didn't seem to want to walk away. All she seems to want to do was be next to her man and made sure that he came back home to her and their son. Supreme finally agreed to let Stigma prove herself.

Supreme had a job to do in Portland, OR and he took Stigma with him to do the job. Before they boarded the airplane, Supreme told Stigma that he would understand if she turned around and left him. I'd always understand if you walked away and didn't want to see me ever again, but I'll make one thing clear to you before you go, nobody is going to take my son away from me. I'll kill you and anyone that stands in my way. You'll be better off next time just pulling that trigger.

When Supreme and Stigma caught the man leaving a motel with a prostitute, to Supreme's surprise, before he could even pull his gun out, Stigma had put three bullets in his head, body, and leg. She even left a bullet in the mouth of the screaming hooker. After Stigma killed the man and his hooker, Stigma asked Supreme if there was a place that she could get a good fish and shrimp dinner.

Supreme and Persia met through Papa Jack. He had a job for Supreme in Canada. The job was going to require a woman to get to the target. Supreme and Persia met at the Spaghetti Company. That's where they received their passports and studied the family that they were going to kill. Supreme almost couldn't even believe that Persia was a professional hit man. It would be easy for her to walk into any room and not draw that type of attention to herself in any way.

Persia felt an attraction to Supreme the moment that he sat down at her table. She stood up to greet Supreme, and Supreme shocked Persia, because he kissed her on the lips then said, damn! If somebody sent someone as beautiful as you are to kill me, then my ass just might be dead. Not from what I hear about you, I don't think that I'll even be able to approach you.

Supreme and Persia worked well together, and they have never been separated from the moment they met at the restaurant. Persia has been in Supreme's life much longer than Stigma, GeeGee, and Ecstasy. Supreme was sent to handle a job in New Orleans that Ecstasy, GeeGee, and Persia were having problems with. The man was a gay man that always kept a lot of gay trained killers around him.

So, a female trying to get close to Black Diamond wasn't about to happen. Because they could do nothing but turn him off or catch a bullet. Black Diamond, which is what he called himself. He wasn't just a gay man; Black Diamond was also a rich one. He own a lot of businesses and has a lot of power in New Orleans. Even though he was a gay man, Black Diamond was still well respected in the streets of New Orleans. When GeeGee, Persia, and Ecstasy went to one of Black Diamond's business to kill him, his own personal guards returned fire back at GeeGee, Ecstasy, and Persia getting Black Diamond away. Which they successfully did.

Papa Jack sent Supreme to clean up where the girls had failed. Black diamond really has a major pet peeve when it comes to keeping his nails on point. It was once said that he had a nail tech to do his nails over 10 times in one day. The woman didn't mind because he paid her every time that she removed his nails and done them to his satisfaction.

Supreme knew that this was the perfect time to catch Black Diamond off guard. While he sat back watching Black Diamond and his guards, Supreme noticed that they were running out of patience with their boss irritating ego. Supreme watched them as they sat around eating and drinking. But now they are paying more and more less attention to Black Diamond.

Ecstasy, GeeGee and Persia were about to head to the airport when they received Supreme call. I'm on top of your hot boys and his switch men, but I'm going to need your help. The girls were so happy that Supreme called them back. Because they didn't want to let Papa Jack down. Thirty minutes later, they were all in the parking lot watching black diamond and his men.

Glory pulled up next to Supremes' vehicle and she was headed into Fly Girls nail shop. Supreme noticed a very attractive female that have parked next to him in a new black Camaro. Supreme stop everybody talking in mid-sentence. I got it! Supreme called Glory as she was walking away from her car. Excuse me baby girl, do you want to make $500 right now? Glory looked at him and turned around to walk away. Say, it will only take five minutes of your time. Supreme talked with Glory for a few minutes then he went back to his car. Two minutes later, Supreme and Glory went walking through the parking lot holding hands, looking like they were in love with each other. Supreme and Glory both are 5'9 in height, that made them look good together. Glory was so attractive and sexy that she would make a gay man think about going straight.

Supreme playfully was smacking Glory on the ass just as they planned it. They didn't want to draw attention to Black Diamond or his guards. One of the guards licked his lips at Supreme and now made him the main topic in their conversation. As Supreme entered the nail shop, Black Diamond sat up himself taking in Supremes' body. Ummmmmm! girl where did you find all of that man at? He done woke Black pussy up in here. Even Black Diamond's guard started to feel sexual attraction to Supreme, but he knew better not to say anything in front of Black Diamond.

Glory put her arm around Supreme waist. Excuse me ma'am! But can I get a manicure and a pedicure? Yes, ma'am. You can have a seat right there. Glory turned around and kissed Supreme in a way that even caught him by surprise. That made Supreme and Glory look into each other's eyes for the first time. Baby you can wait for me right over there.

Supreme smiled at Glory and thought to himself, "damn she good." Supreme took a seat and picked up a magazine. Black Diamond started ordering his guards around trying to impress Supreme, but Supreme kept his face buried into the magazine. Now the guards were sitting back and was watching Supreme closely.

BIG AND LITTLE SATAN

He noticed the magazine was a female's magazine that no straight man would have any interest in. Supreme turned around in his seat and saw Ecstasy, GeeGee, and Persia creeping. Just as he saw Persia reach for the limousine door handle, Supreme took a deep breath.

The guard was just bending over to say something in the other guard's ear. Just as he tried to stand back up, he was met with a bullet right in the face. Pow! Everybody started screaming and ducking for cover in the shop. Glory couldn't even believe what was happening in front of her. GeeGee, Ecstasy, and Persia were all holding court right outside the nail shop. Pow! Pow! Pow! Pow! Pow! Pow! Pow! Pow! Multiple bullets sounded off. Supreme calmly walked over to Black Diamond, who sat there like he knew that today would be the day that he would die.

Supreme pointed his snub nose 357 magnum right at Black Diamond's forehead. Papa Jack said hello. "Fuck you!" Pow! Pow! Black Diamond flipped backwards out of his chair and hit the floor. The nail tech started screaming and covering her head with her hands. Supreme looked at Glory, so are you coming with me? No! No! "No thank you, I'm good." I don't want your money, nor do I want to die today. Supreme said, last chance is you coming? He extended his hand out to her. It took a few long seconds, but Glory grabbed Supremes' hand and they walked out the way they came in.

Supreme rode with Glory and GeeGee drove his rental car. Ecstasy and Persia rode together in their rental. Glory was a dental assistant and was also being spoiled by her boss who was the dentist that she worked for. Glory lived by herself and had no children. But this man that have walked into her life out of nowhere have just put a different excitement into her heart and she couldn't even deny it. Even though Glory was like everyone else, had witnessed Supreme kill a man that they thought was a woman. Supreme didn't put fear in her like she thought he would. But he had just brung a sense of security into her heart and life.

Glory didn't know it, but Supreme was making plans to leave her dead in her apartment. Supreme kept his end of the deal and peeled off five $100 bills and tried to hand them to Glory. But she still refused to take his money and handed it back to him. Do you feel like that's all I'm worth to you? That even left Supreme speechless.

When they all entered Glory's apartment, they could see that she was on top of whatever lifestyle she was living. Glory closed the door and walked right up on Supreme looking him in the eyes. Man, like I told you back at that nail shop. "I don't want your money, nor do I want to die today." "I'm nobody's snitch and I'm not afraid of you or them either." I respect whatever it is that y'all stand for and would love to be a part of anything that's got something to do with you.

BIG AND LITTLE SATAN

Man, I'm not quite sure as to what all it is about you that completely turns me on about you. But if you will allow me to, I'm willing to take that chance to learn how to keep you happy. While Supreme and Glory were staring each other eye to eye, Ecstasy was putting her 9mm pistol up to Glory head and just as she was about to pull the trigger. No! No! Supreme jumped and put his hands up to stop Ecstasy from allowing her to say her last words.

Glory turned around and saw the gun in Ecstasy hand. She took a deep breath and told Ecstasy, "Baby Girl, I ain't even mad at you." I understand your position and obligation to this man. I would have done the same thing too. Right at that moment, not only had Glory won Supreme over, GeeGee, Persia, and Ecstasy had just respected and accepted Glory into their family. GeeGee said, "Bitch, I like you, what's your name?" "Glory!"

Before they left her apartment, Glory wrote a letter and left it on her bed, and as a woman GeeGee, Ecstasy, and Persia all knew what Glory was doing. Whoever the dentist was, he had been there for her when nobody else was in her life. Glory felt that she owed him that respect to say thank you and I'll always love you. Glory read the letter out loud and then kissed it. Leaving her lips on the paper and ending it with the words, You were heaven sent.

CHAPTER TWENTY

PAPA JACK'ED

S upreme, Glory, and Persia all took the plane out of New Orleans that night and Ecstasy and GeeGee left the next morning. While Supreme was on the airplane, he sat next to a woman that have her son, that felt that Supreme was his punching bag every chance that he got to hit Supreme. The woman apologized and told the little boy to stop but he wouldn't stop hitting Supreme. Persia and Glory sat together, and they were feeling sorry for Supreme. Persia looked back at Supreme and hunched her shoulders. Supreme took a deep breath, he was now wishing that he had his gun on him. He would just shoot the little boy. Supreme had to laugh out loud at his own thoughts. He just laid his seat back and closed his eyes.

Supreme closed his eyes and thought about how he got himself caught up and taking people's lives. Supreme and Marquan was at the house where they kept their drugs and Supreme had just left the house. Supreme and Marquan were feeling like they were on top of the world. They had just purchased 250 kilos of some pure cocaine. That could take a double stepping on it and would still be great for the streets. When supreme left the house, he ran off and left his cell phone on the couch and he went back for it.

When Supreme was coming down the block, he noticed an unfamiliar vehicle that was sitting on the block. Supreme and Marquan knew that block like the back of their hand. He also saw that it was a raid being pursued on their property. Supreme quickly pulled over to observe the situation but turned out that he would observe more than the raid. Supreme's heart almost jumped out of his chest when he noticed Marquan's girl pointing at their trap house.

One year and ten months later, Supreme wind up paying a crooked ass lawyer that was from New York $35,000 to get Marquan 15 years in prison because he was facing life. That left Supreme alone out there in the Dirty Desert streets to handle things on his own without Marquan. After getting raided almost twice a week, he was starting to go broke and losing a lot of good connections. Supreme from where he once was really was actually broke. Now, Supreme placed an all or nothing order with a close friend for ten kilos.

Myles knew that the drug dealing gang was an up and down game and he didn't want to turn his back on Supreme. Before all the madness hit business always was good between Supreme and Myles. Myles could remember when Supreme and Marquan bought their first quarter key. Supreme told Myles that they would take those ounces and turn them into selling him kilos someday. His words didn't go unnoticed because Supreme and Marquan started setting up major drug spots all over the valley.

Now after all that hard work of building on their childhood dreams, the closest person that Marquan let in on their family turned out to be the same one to bring them down. Marquan's girl Lulu turns state evidence on Marquan and Supreme. Supreme scarcely slipped through the cracks because after they finally arrested Supreme, Marquan took the whole case. He told Supreme that it wouldn't make no sense for them both to be down. It was my dog ass bitch that took us down hommie, so that means that I have to take one for the team.

Supreme promised to hold Marquan down and told Marquan that they'll be much bigger when he comes back home. The rest of their drug houses took major hits, but nobody treated Supreme like Lulu did and snitched him out. But like they say, when you get a taste of that good life of drinking champagne you never pour beer into your glass ever again.

So that's what made Supreme place that all or nothing order with Myles. Supreme pulled his white Corvette up to their meeting place and Myles was already sitting waiting with his parking lights on. Supreme pulled up and parked the opposite way from Myles' black Mercedes-Benz and turned off his lights on the Vet. They exited their vehicles and hugged then shook hands. Boy I hear the water been getting kind of deep on you. You know you my family, so I threw you a life raft so that your ass doesn't drown fam. So, you saving lives now Myles? Yeah OK! Lifeguard. Well, I guess you got a point there Supreme. But don't trip fam, I still got'cha right here. Hold up!

Myles headed back to his trunk and opened it up. Myles reached in and was pulling out a black gym bag and turned around. Pow! Pow! Pow! Click! Click! Click! Click! Supreme and Myles looked each other right in the eyes before his body could even hit the ground. Supreme grabbed the bag and started to stuff Myles into the trunk of his Mercedes. He opened Myles car door and removed his car keys. Before Supreme left, he checked Myles glove box and console. "Damn!" But before Supreme closed the door, he looked over the sun visor. Bam! Jackpot. Stacks of money fell down onto the seat and floor. Click! Click!, Click!, Click!, Click! Supreme stood up and looked around. Click! Click! Click! Click! Click! Supreme removed his shirt and wiped down everything that he had touched. Then he turned off Myles park lights. He jumped into his Corvette and smashed off.

Later that night, Supreme went to search Myles house. But just as soon as Supreme turned on Myles Street, it looked like a police Academy. It was so many police officers going in and out of Myles home. Supreme kept supplying his drug houses and making money. He was even starting to feel like his old self again. Until one morning he came walking out of his house. He was sticking his keys into a brand-new Cadillac XT truck. When a black van with dark tinted windows pulled up and blocked Supreme in the driveway. Three men jumped out the sliding door and was pointing AK47 semi-automatic weapons at Supreme.

Supreme just knew that this was the day that he would go join Marquan in prison. But he quickly realized that the men weren't police officers. Because he was blindfolded and being shoved into the van. Every question that the men were asking Supreme, not one of them were answered. The ride was even longer than Supreme had expected. Supreme figured that if someone wanted to kill him then they must have wanted to do it personally themselves. This was a time that he was glad that he didn't have any children, that he was leaving behind.

Supreme thought to himself, that if what preachers really said was true about good and evil. Then he definitely wouldn't be going to the same place as his mother. Because his mother was a Christian woman and was saved, she been that way her whole life until God called her home from having Sugar Diabetes. Supreme only saw his dad once, when he was six years old. So, to Supreme, his dad had really died much sooner than his mom did.

When Supreme saw light again it was brightly shining in his eyes and face. "Mr. Supreme, that is what you go by in the streets, right?" Man, what the fuck is all this kidnapping me bullshit? "What the fuck do y'all want with me?" Supreme please excuse my open invitation, by inviting you here this way. But I felt that a man who is as heartless as you, could only be a major asset to me. "Man, are you fucking crazy or something?" How in the fuck can I be an asset to you?

"Man, do you even know who you're fucking with?" Yes, I do. Your real birth name is Isaiah Supreme Washington. Yes, I do know who you are, but let's not forget that you don't know who I am Mr. Supreme. "Let me just tell you who I am Supreme, since you don't know." I'm the man that holds the key to your freedom. Just in case you really want to know what's going on. Either you work for me, or I turn this key over to the Phoenix police and Federal Government. "Man, it ain't a motherfucker in this world got the key to my life."

You might change your mind about that Supreme, after you take a good look on the table. Supreme couldn't see nothing being the light was shining so bright in his face. Click! The bright light went off and Supreme tried everything in him to see what was on the table. After a few minutes his pupils started to dilate. Mr. Supreme, remember that you brought all of this on yourself. How the hell did I do that? Well just before I stumbled across you again, I had my heart set on someone just as heartless as you, Supreme. But you took that option away from me and therefore, that job shall be yours to take on now for me. Who did I take from you, man you got the wrong person?

Just as those words left Supremes' mouth, now he could clearly see the pictures on the table. Just the sight of seeing them almost made Supreme's heart jump out of his chest. "Damn!" Supreme eyes went from picture to picture. It made him make a different face each time he looked at one of them pictures. Supreme was watching himself shoot and kill Myles. Every interaction that they had from the moment Supreme pulled up until he drove away. He was looking at himself shoot and rob Myles then dump him in his trunk. Supreme dropped his head and he now felt defeated.

That was the day that he learned to know of a man by the name of Papa Jack. But he still never saw Papa Jack or the men that brought him to that unknown location. When Supreme got dropped back off in front of his home where he got kidnapped, he was given a cell phone and fifty thousand in cash. Plus, an address to the first job that he was sent on, which he failed miserably.

Supreme was sent out to Washington D.C, to take out a whole family, but when it came time to handle his business, the husband walked into his house and Supreme didn't want to waste time allowing him to get comfortable. Supreme sat in his vehicle for hours before the man showed up. He ain't never killed nobody before and he was about to drive away, but the man pulled up and exited his car. Supreme thought shit, better him than me spending life in prison. Supreme grabbed his 357 magnum and just as soon as he opened the door, the wife came walking out the kitchen and started screaming when she saw a black man holding a gun.

Supreme always dreamed of having his own son. So, when he saw the man playing with his son, Supreme froze up and couldn't go through with it. The man didn't even know what was going on. Supreme looked him right in the face. Fuck him! If that motherfucker turns me in, then he turns me in. Supreme wasn't about to kill no kid. He turned around and ran out of the house.

Supreme was driving and his cell phone kept on ringing. He looked at the phone several times and thought that he would die at the next light. Papa Jack kept calling. Supreme got caught by a red light and the phone started ringing again. Bling, bling, bling, bling, bling. Supreme took a deep breath and answered it. "Hello!"

Mr. Supreme, in order for a man to kill and feel death, he has to be reduced to nothing. My favorite verse in the Bible is Job 3:21, which long for death but it come not; and dig for it more than for his treasure. "Supreme some of God's greatest have longed for death; however, they were not right in doing so." Job 7:5 say Supreme, so that my soul chooses strangling and death rather than my life. Supreme choose to be nothing or choose prison for the rest of your fucking life. But don't you never make that fucking mistake again. Click! Supreme phone went dead. Supreme told himself that day that he'll never make that mistake again.

CHAPTER TWENTY-ONE

BREAKING THE TENSION

Supreme and his crew had been back from New Orleans for about a week. Almost every day, he and Stigma have been at each other's throat behind Glory. Stigma really didn't care too much for her. And besides that, Glory was getting a lot of attention just about every place that they went to, because she's a very attractive woman. Supreme also was spending a lot of one-on-one time with Glory really, just schooling her. Supreme was starting to get on everyone about handling their weapons. He said that it only takes one little mistake, and somebody might not return from their trips. So, he made sure that they all spent more time at the gun range.

Supreme and Marquan were challenging the girls to see who would get better shots on their targets. Stigma was pretty much winning, and that was really stroking her ego. Glory just sat back watching them shoot and didn't say a word. Supreme loaded up one of the 40 calibers and ask Glory if she wanted to try shooting.

BIG AND LITTLE SATAN

Glory declined until Stigma made a smart remark. "Dada, I guess only good that she'll be to you is on her back." Glory gave Stigma that I'm sick of you Bitch look. "Yeah, sure," Give it to me. I don't mind trying it at all. Glory gripped her weapon tightly, just in case of any sudden strange movement towards her direction. Glory put on the earphones and let a .40 caliber sing. Pow! Pow! Pow! Pow! Pow!

Marquan hit the button to bring the target in and when it came back, he looked at Supreme strangely. Supreme said, "What the fuck, let me see that?" Marquan handed the chart to Supreme, and Glory had shot the whole center dot out of the target. Supreme with excitement in his voice, looked at Glory. "Damn baby! Why didn't you tell me that you can shoot like this?" Because you never asked me Dada. She smiled and looked at Stigma, calling him Daddy in a way all the other girls do. Supreme started passing the target around so that everyone else could see Glory art with a handgun. He tried to show Stigma, but she laid her weapon down and walked out of the room.

The attention between Stigma and Glory didn't seem like it was about to end no time soon. So Supreme knew just how to break the both of them. Supreme sent them on a job together. Supreme knew one important thing about being a police officer or hitman. No matter how much you hated your partner when it comes time to putting your life on the line, you're going to have to completely trust your partner.

The target was in North Carolina. He was a sick Iranian that owned a few expensive car lots. He loved playing poker whenever he wasn't selling you a car that he would have stolen in the middle of the night. The guy has a real bad mouth and thought that the world rested under his feet. Stigma and Glory went to the car lot that he spent the most time at. Stigma pulled into his car lot. They had rented a Burnt Orange Dodge Stratus. Stigma and Glory was wearing tight, short dresses and high heels. Just as they were walking into the car lot, all of the salesman we're trying to be the first one to approach the two beautiful women. But it was a short red head who approached them first.

"Hello ladies, how may I help y'all today?" "Are you looking to buy a car today?" "Wow, don't the two of you look stunning?" Hello and thank you. Yes, my friend is looking for something not too expensive thou. Do you mind if we just look around first? Sure. I'll show you anything that you like. Stigma made Glory laugh. "Damn! Didn't this bitch just hear me say let us look?" "Excuse me ma'am, Oh, nothing."

But if you don't mind, we'll just like to look around by ourselves, and if we find anything, we'll be sure to call you and not nobody else. OK, sure. The red head walked away but looking real sad. Another young gentleman came walking up. Well, hello Ms. Ladies, can I help y'all or is Rexha already assisting you? Sure, you can, Stigma smiled. "Oh girl! look at this one." Rexha called them ugly bitches under her breath and went to complain to her boss.

BIG AND LITTLE SATAN

Stigma and Glory was looking at a 2012 Mustang Convertible. Just as soon as the boss looked out of his office window after hearing about the red head complaint, he was out of his office and on his way towards Stigma and Glory. Well, hello ladies. What do we have here? Stigma was waiting for this rat to come and take their bait. She turned around with her legs wide open, knowing that he'd look in between her legs. Oh, hello. You guys sure have some nice cars here. Yeah, I try to keep the best cars on my lot. Oh, you must be the owner. Yes, I am. And who might you be? I'm Monte. I'm Kaylee, and this is Vanessa. She is the one looking to buy a car. Monte turned and looked at the young black salesman. Hey Chris, go and grab the keys, then find something to do.

But I'm trying to make a sale here. Grab the keys like I told you. And go make sure the bathrooms are clean. He tried to below the worker as much as he could. OK, boss. These fucking people, you try to help them, and they want to be the boss. Sorry ladies! Now let's get you in this car. Stigma gritted her teeth. She couldn't wait to put a bullet in his fucking head. "Here boss man, here you go." Monte stood back and was hoping to catch another glimpse in between Stigma's legs. Stigma closed them and slid out sideways. Girl, here you go. You're the one trying to buy it, not me.

Monte had one of his workers take the car off the showroom floor because he was about to make sure that he went on the test drive with them. It's a nice day out. Don't you want the top down? Glory was sitting at a red light and Monte was taking in now what

Glory had for him to see. Monte hit the button and the top laid down smoothly. He turned around again and tried looking in between Stigma legs again. Now ain't that much better? So how are you enjoying the car so far? It's really nice. But I really got to use the bathroom. Glory started shaking in her seat like she was about to piss in her seat. Monte looked around and didn't see any place that they could go to. Can you hold it until we make it back to my lot? Oh no, I got to find somewhere to park now.

Stigma noticed that it was a grocery store just up ahead on the right side of them. Girl, there's a grocery store right there. You better hurry up and pull behind there. Glory looked in the rearview mirror. And already peeped Stigma's vibe. Sir, do you mind? Monte answered so fast. Go right ahead and do what you gotta do. Glory found a place to park, and nobody wasn't standing around.

Glory jumped out and ran around on the passenger side. Glory raised up her dress and Monte almost had a heart attack looking at her body. Glory removed her panties and left her dress up to her waist. She walked over to Monte revealing her nude sexy body. "Here honey, will you please hold these for me?" I don't want to get them wet. Monte's mouth flew open. Yeah Sure, he grabbed her panties. Glory squatted down to pee and when she did, Monty leaned over the door to watch. Pow! Stigma put a bullet in the back of his head, blowing his brains right out of his head.

They took wet wipes and wiped down everything that they touched. Glory removed her panties out of Monte's hand. "Here sweetie, let me take those for you. You won't be getting any pussy in hell." They calmly walked away as if nothing had ever happened. Stigma and Glory got a ride back to his car lot and waited until nobody was looking and drove away. Stigma and Glory were laughing at the way Monte had just died. They both were starting to talk, and Stigma apologized for her behavior.

But she also would learn that Glory had once served in the Army, and that's how she learned to shoot so good. Stigma told her about her mom, Mrs. Bergess and her husband who was a police officer, that he taught her all about weapons and when someone was about to shoot theirs. Stigma told Glory that he told her to always be ready to shoot her gun no matter of the situation or circumstances. Glory told Stigma that he seemed like he was a good man. Glory even told Stigma a lot about the dentist that took good care of her. By the time they made it back to Phoenix they were getting along like two sisters.

CHAPTER TWENTY-TWO
BABY MAMA DRAMA

S upreme had gotten another job and it was going to require good timing and planning. They were on their way to the Country to take out five police officers in Atlanta, GA. Sergeant Hedgepeth. Officer Pechenik, Officer Shepherd, Officer Schiffman, and Officer Munclapp have all came on Supremes' list to die. They all were crooked cops, that we're setting up people in Georgia and getting away with it. They were all following Sergeant Hedgepeth. He was a really hated person in Atlanta. So, him coming up missing, the department wouldn't know who to turn to or look for. Supreme needed the whole crew on this one. So, they were all doing what they normally do before a job. They were learning all that they could about each officer and studying their pictures.

Just as supreme was about to hand Stigma a picture of Sergeant Hedgepeth, Stigma jumped up and ran to the bathroom. Urrrrr-rrr! Everyone in the room could hear Stigma throwing up. They all one by one went to go check on her. When Supreme looked through the door, Stigma was down on her knees with her face in the toilet. Urrrrrr! "Baby what's the matter, are you ok?" Yea! Yea! I'm fine Dada. I'll be alright. I think it's the pancakes and eggs we just ate. Supreme and Stigma had breakfast less than two hours ago. She was looking at it sitting in the toilet bowl. GeeGee walked up to Supreme, Dada is she ok? Yea, she says that her stomach disagreeing with the breakfast we ate this morning. But I feel fine.

Supreme started to walk towards her and she quickly flushed the toilet. Ok! See I feel better already. Dada pass me that towel right there. Stigma went to stand up and started throwing up all over again. Urrrrrr! Supreme felt her forehead. You are not running a fever baby. Maybe you need to just stay home on this one. No! No! No! Dada, I'm fine. Just give me a minute y'all. I'll be right in there. Dada, you know that you need me on this job. Yea we do, but if you're sick then what good is that gone do?

Everybody left the bathroom finally but GeeGee. She stood at the door looking at Stigma. "Girl, your ass do know what's wrong with you, don't you? Yea that food was bad. Nope, try again Stigma. Your red ass is pregnant. Stigma grabbed her stomach and just stared at GeeGee. Girl, do you want me to go get a pregnancy test from the store? Girl, for what, you need to stop playing with me, GeeGee. You'll just be wasting your money because I ain't pregnant. Bitch, if I'm pregnant then your ass is to. Because the last time I had some dick, you had it too. So, are you telling me that your ass pregnant too?

Hell, nall bitch, I ain't never having no babies. Dada releases himself in you not us. Stigma and Supreme didn't think that the girls were even paying that any attention. Girl, get your baby talking ass out of this bathroom trying to put your little hex on me. GeeGee rubbed her stomach. Ok something is cooking up in there, you can trust me on that bitch! When GeeGee left the bathroom, Stigma closed the door. She walked over to the mirror and raised her shirt up. Tears started rolling down Stigma's face. She rubbed her belly, and her mind went straight to the sex that she had with Deshawn.

"Damn bitch, look at you now, you done fucked your life up." This man gone kill me, Deshawn and this baby. Stigma was trying to remember what she had done with Deshawn phone number. Stigma felt that he should know even though she had no plans of keeping his baby. Her trying to keep Deshawn's baby would change things between her Supreme and little Isaiah for sure. Stigma pulled herself together as much as she could. Besides her already having her mind on Deshawn, here she was walking around carrying his baby without knowing.

$ $ $ $ $

Once again GeeGee walked in on Stigma throwing up, but this time they were at the Sky Harbor Airport getting ready to board the plane to head to Atlanta. Stigma jumped up and rushed to the bathroom. Urrrrrr! Stigma, girl what's wrong, are you ok? Stigma was holding the toilet bowl with one hand and have Deshawn phone number and address bald up in the other hand. Nothing I'm good. Is the plane boarding yet? No girl, but it's about to soon. Stigma stood up and flushed the toilet. She came out of the stall wiping her mouth.

GeeGee said, "so when are you going to tell Dada that you're pregnant or do you need me to tell him?" GeeGee, No! No! No! Please, pretty please, don't you tell him that. Stigma rushed over to her and started holding her hands. No don't tell him that and don't you tell nobody that shit, GeeGee. GeeGee could see the seriousness in Stigma's eyes. But why? Because if I am GeeGee, I'm getting an abortion. I don't want any more kids. Stigma didn't know it, but that's what GeeGee was hoping that she would say. Because if Stigma was pregnant, GeeGee have already contemplated leaving Supreme. GeeGee didn't want to deal with no more baby mama bullshit. GeeGee I'm serious! Promise me that you won't say anything to anybody.

"Ok bitch!" I'll promise you that on one condition. Ok whatever, what's that condition? That you turn my hands loose and go brush your damn teeth. Fuck you GeeGee, your punk ass knows that I'm going to brush my teeth. Persia came walking into the bathroom. What the hell are y'all doing in here, having a baby or something? Stigma and GeeGee superciliously looked at each other. Dada said bring y'all asses out of here, we are about to board the plane.

Supreme and everyone was checking into different hotel rooms and started getting settled into their rooms. This time they rented three Dodge Magnums. Supreme knew that those types of vehicles would keep up with the police officer's cars. Most of the time the officer's drove Dodge Magnums themselves or whatever vehicle that they confiscated and could turn into a police cruiser.

Stigma couldn't wait to be alone in her room. She picked up the phone and called Deshawn's cell phone. She sat there on the bed and was contemplating whether or not to press send. But then Stigma realized that Deshawn would have her number and would keep calling her. Even more after she called and said Hello Deshawn this is Stigma, I'm just calling you to tell you that I'm pregnant with your baby, but sorry that I called because I'm not having it. Bye! Now Stigma was just sitting there and was making up all different type of excuses. What if I call and he can't talk, because his woman sitting next to him? Stigma was trying everything that she could not to press send on her phone.

Stigma ended the call and called back, but this time she blocked her phone number. Damn girl, go ahead and be stupid. Stigma didn't give it a second thought; she pressed send and Deshawn answered on the second ring. Hello, almost out of fear, Stigma was about to hang up. Hello, who is this? This is Stigma, Deshawn, how are you? Oh no! God yes, thank you. She called me! She called me, yes! Stigma looked at the phone, she couldn't believe how excited Deshawn was to hear her voice. I'm sorry but did I dial the right number?

BIG AND LITTLE SATAN

Yea woman this me, Stigma. Naw I'm just tripping that you even called me. My mother just told me yesterday that God would answer my prayers and he did, Stigma. You called me, you called me. "Wow!" Thank you, God. Hearing Deshawn say that it made Stigma start crying. Hey what's the matter, are you ok? Yes Deshawn, I'm fine, what about you? I'm wonderful now Stigma, knowing God answered my prayers. Deshawn what's with all this, God answered your prayers stuff.

Well for starters Stigma, me and my girl Ashley are not together anymore. Stigma we broke up behind some stupid stuff. Stigma was smiling. Oh no Deshawn why? Well actually it got a lot to do with my mother talking too much. Oh no baby, don't tell me she told her about us? Stigma grabbed her mouth, because she couldn't believe that she had just comfortably had just called Deshawn baby. No that's not what happened. When I came back home, for some strange reason, I just started craving strange food's that I don't normally eat. I didn't know that Ashley had even noticed it, but I had mentioned it to my boy Devron and he said that I must have gotten somebody pregnant. Stigma grabbed her stomach.

But trip off this, that ain't what broke me and Ashley up. My mother came over to our house and kept rubbing Ashley's stomach. My girl asked her why she keeps doing that and my mother told her, because you are about to have me a grandbaby girl, don't you know that you pregnant? Child I can feel that baby in your stomach. Ashley told my mother that if a baby is in her stomach, then she is about to be rich because her tubes are tied, and she can't have no more babies. Deshawn can tell you that Camila. But your son has been having these funny little cravings lately. So, your little suspicion must be right about your son, but I'm not the bitch that he got pregnant. So, when you leave Camila, you can take his sorry ass with you, because it's over, I'm done with his ass.

Stigma, my mother kept on pressing me about who I got pregnant. But I knew that she was wrong, because besides my girl, Stigma, the only person that I've ever slept with was you, ma. I been going crazy Stigma thinking that I might have a son or daughter and they don't even know me. I asked my mother what I should do to find you and she said let's pray. Me and my mom prayed that day and I kept on praying and look what happened Stigma, you called me. My mother told me to have faith, just have faith and I did.

So, Stigma and before Deshawn could even get the word's out, Deshawn yes baby I'm pregnant. Deshawn started screaming on the phone. Yes, Yes, Yes! I'm going to be a father. I'm a father. I'm a daddy, Stigma. Stigma got quiet and didn't respond. The tears were starting to come faster down her face. Stigma, are you there? Yes, I'm still here and this is why I'm calling you baby. Deshawn, I'm pregnant but I can't have your baby. My son's father will kill me, you, and this baby Deshawn. Deshawn couldn't believe what he was hearing Stigma say. Stigma, I'll never let anybody hurt you or our baby. You can catch a plane to Atlanta now, I'll take good care of you and our baby, y'all my family.

Deshawn, Deshawn, wait, stop baby, you're not listening to me. There's not going to be no us or family. It's all my fault. I fucked up everything. But I also have to fix this Deshawn. I got to get an abortion soon. I just felt that I should call you and at least let you know that I was pregnant. I owed you that much to know you got me pregnant. Trust me, this hurts me too. It's my baby that I'm about to give up with or without you. I never wanted to do this to my child, but you don't know my Dada, he'll kill us, Deshawn.

Deshawn begged and pleaded with Stigma to just give the baby to him and his mother. We'll take good care of the baby, Stigma. I promise you that. Deshawn was crying and begging, please, pretty please Stigma. Don't do this to me, please! Wait, wait, let me call my mom, she'll tell you that herself. We'll take the baby Stigma! Deshawn I'm so sorry but I can't have this baby, Click!

CHAPTER TWENTY-THREE
FALLIN SOLDIER

Supreme and Marquan have been closely watching the Georgia Police Department in Atlanta. They watched as different police officers came and went all day out of the precinct. On the third day, they had a complete daily routine on four of the five officers. Officer Pechenik, Shephard, Munclapp and Schiffman all had been followed home for the past two days. Supreme and Marquan even got to see who their mistresses were. Officer Pechenik had gotten so comfortable with his little mistress that he moved her two streets over from his children and wife.

Sargent Hedgepeth and his brother was out on his boat enjoying his last day of vacation. They had a couple of party girls with them, and they were drinking, cutting, and frying fish. The fish that he and his brother had caught earlier.

Officer Shephard jumped out of his supped up 69 fire engine Red Dodge Charger. He walked into the liquor store and grabbed a 12 pack of cold beer. But on his way to the refrigerator cubic freezer to grab the beer, he stopped at one of the food racks like he was looking for something. But really, he was watching the blue Dodge Magnum that had been following him for some time. He couldn't clearly see the two people in the car, because the car was sitting idling across the street from the store. They were waiting to finish following him without him noticing them. He came walking out of the store and was faking like he was waving at the clerk. Bye Mark, I'll see you next time when I need more beer.

Shephard sat in his vehicle. He was adjusting his rear-view mirror, so that maybe he could get a better view of who the hell was following him. He pulled out and made his way through traffic but kept his eyes on the Dodge Magnum. Shephard started switching lanes and making sudden turns and the Dodge kept up with the Charger no matter what it did.

Shephard was sitting at the light and the Dodge was two vehicles behind. When the light turned green, Shephard pulled out into the intersection and started making donuts smoking up the whole intersection. Ecstasy said, damn! What is he drunk? Before she could get an answer from Persia, Shephard had spun out of a donut and had placed the hood of his car at Ecstasy driver's door. But when the smoke cleared there was a 357-magnum pointing at their head. They both threw their hands up in the air.

Shephard approached their vehicle. Who in the hell are you and why in the fuck are you following me? Girl, see what your ass done got me into. I told you that this was stupid, didn't I? I'm so sorry sir. But my girlfriend got a mad crush on you, and she is dying for you to ask her out. Shephard took one long look at Persia long attractive legs and quickly changed up. People were starting to blow their horns because they were blocking traffic. Shephard pulled out his badge. I'm a cop. I'm a cop. Do you know that? Hey! Ya'll almost got shot, couldn't y'all have found a better way to get my attention? He and Persia exchanged information, but while he was walking back to his car he stopped and turned around. Hey Persia, I hope you're this excited on our date. Oh, trust and believe, I will be. Shephard smiled and jumped into his car and burned rubber driving away.

Shephard is a tall cocky white dude, that stands 6'1" and look like he does commercials for steroids. He keeps his hair in a low-cut Mohawk with no facial hair. But not your baby face looking guy either. He's got a thing for old cars and weapons.

$ $ $ $ $

Schiffman and Munclapp are partners. Just about everything they do, they do it together on and off the force. The two officers' where on a domestic violence call, where a woman had poured hot grease on her husband and was threating his mistress with a bat. The woman called the police with her cell phone and was locked in their bathroom.

Atlanta police department! Atlanta police department, is there anyone home? Schiffman and Munclapp were coming through the door with both of their weapons drawn. Ma'am, drop the bat and put your hands up. Fuck that! When I drop this bat, it's gone be on this bitch head. Thinking that she can come climbing in my bed with this damn fool. She pointed the bat at someone laying on the floor moaning on the other side of the bed. Help, hep, help, somebody help me please.

Schiffman ordered the woman again to drop the bat. "Drop the bat!" Ya'll want me to drop the bat. She walked around the bed to where her husband was laying on the floor and drew the bat back, ma'am, ma'am, Noooooo! Pow! Pow! Pow! Schiffman pulled the trigger and Munclapp put three slugs into her body. They both rushed over to her and tried to revive her. But it was too late, she was already taking her last breath. Schiffman called it in and told them to send the coroners to that address. They could hear a woman's voice yelling and screaming for help in the bathroom.

It didn't take Schiffman and Munclapp long to figure out why they were on this call. The woman came out completely naked with a banging body. Damn! Both officers almost said it at the same time. She was so sexy that Munclapp kept questioning the woman with her hands still in the air. She had asked them, Sir can I put my hands down now? Oh yeah sure, I'm so sorry. Schiffman and Munclapp were talking to another officer while the ambulance was taking the husband to the hospital.

Munclapp knew that it was about to be a long night and a lot of paperwork. The lady had been questioned and was released to ride with her mistress in the ambulance. Schiffman and Munclapp headed back into the house with the dead woman that they had killed. Schiffman is only 5'8" and looks a lot like Robert Blake when he was Baretta. A lot of the officers on the force would tease him and call him Baretta. They would sing the song to him. Don't do the crime or Schiffman will make you do the time. His partner Munclapp was 5'10" slim built, but in great shape. Before he became a police officer, he was a bodyguard for high class celebrities. He's worked with people like Mariah Carey, Paris Hilton, Jennifer Lopez, and Hillary Clinton. If it was someone important, that needed to be protected Munclapp name would definitely come up as the man for the job. Besides that, Munclapp speaks four languages fluently, English, Spanish, French and Chinese. Munclapp is an ex-green beret that favored the Russian in Rocky 3. He's quiet but deadly.

Pechenik had just flipped on his lights and siren. He was doing a routine traffic stop. It was three black men riding in a brand new 2012 Infinity Q45 truck. Pechenik called in his location and have requested back up. He exited his cruiser and slowly was approaching the truck with his hand on his weapon. Hello gentlemen, may I see your driver's license and insurance please? Say man, what are you stopping me for? I didn't do anything wrong. The passenger was acting real nervous and frighten just as Pechenik was getting a call over his body radio. He was about to explain why he had stopped them. 1 Chopper 32 be careful pulling over the suspects. Backup is on its way.

BIG AND LITTLE SATAN

Pechenik knew that the men heard the call come in just as he did. Pechenik started to walk backwards while unholstering his weapon. The back window started rolling down. Pow! Pow! Pow! Pow! Pechenik returned fire at the back window and it shattered. Pow! Pow! Urrrrrrrr! The Infinity burned rubber taking off. Pechenik jumped to his feet and ran to his car, now leading the chase. Back up was just hitting the corner as Pechenik turned on his siren and chased them. Pechenik radioed in; shots fired at an officer. I'm in pursuit of a dark green in color Infinity Q45 with three black male suspects. Now there were several units in pursuit of the bank robbers. Pow! Pow! Pow! Pow! Pow! Shots fired; shots fired. "Man, I'm not going back to prison, lets serve these motherfuckers." Shut up nigga and sit back, I got this. We are about to spend this money they ain't taking shit back.

Damn! It's a helicopter following us now. "Whoop, what we gone do?" Get the bag, get the fucking bag. Pow! Pow! Pow! Pow! Pow! I can't get it man, they shooting at us. K-Lavon, get the heat man, that's the only way that we getting out this shit. The chase continued with them shooting at each other. Hold on. Urrrrrr! The driver knew the area very well, and he was keeping a nice distance between them and the police. Their only problem was the helicopter, that followed them everywhere they went.

K-Lavon finally got a chance to grab the bag with the weapons. He handed the passenger a AR15 assault rifle. That 9mm pistol that he was shooting at officer Pechenik he tossed it out the window. K-Lavon had an AK47 and Whoop was telling them what they were about to do next. K-Lavon took a few shots at the helicopter making it fall back a little. Whoop hit a few corners and came to a complete stop. All three doors popped open and when Pechenik and his fellow comrades hit the corner, Plrrrrrrrrr! Plrrrrrrrr! Plrrrrrrrrr! Boom! Boom! Boom! Pow! Pow! Pow! A rapid of bullets went through hoods and windshields of Officer Pechenik and some vehicles behind him.

They got ambushed just as soon at they turned the corner. Whoop, K-Lavon, and Lucky made them weapons sing like Gladys Knight and the Pips. Plrrrrrrrrr! Boom! Pow! Plrrrrrrrrr! Boom! Pow! Urrrrrrr! Bang! Urrrrrrr! Bang, bang, bang. The police cars were crashing into each other. Whoop, K-Lavon, and Lucky all jumped back into their truck and peeled off. Urrrrrrrrr! Whoop saw a man exiting a Ford Expedition and they carjacked him. While they were switching everything into the man's truck, they made him lay face down on the street. They hopped in his truck and did it moving. Urrrrrrr!

Whoop, Lucky, and K-Lavon, all gave each other high fives. Yea boy! Yea, what I tell y'all. They can't fuck with the Whoop nigg'aaaas! They got away with an undisclosable amount of cash. Officer Pechenik was sitting in a shot up wrecked police car. He was beating the steering wheel. He couldn't believe that he had let the bank robbers get away. A call was coming in over their radios that a man has been car jacked by three black males. Fuck! Fuck!

BIG AND LITTLE SATAN

Fuck! Fuck! Fuck! Bam Pechenik took another pound on his steering wheel.

$$\$ \; \$ \; \$ \; \$ \; \$$$

The next morning, Supreme, Marquan, and the girls were all watching their targets one by one pull into the police parking lot. They were all getting ready to start their shift for the day. They could see that officer Pechenik was taking a lot of flak from the other officers. They were giving him the blues about losing the bank robbers the day before. The officers knew that this would be the main topic in their briefing room today.

"Dada! Dada look, an older gentlemen medium build with a pot belly had just jumped out of a brand new chevy black truck. Whomever he was, Supreme knew that he has to be somebody important on the force. Supreme watched how men went out their way to be acknowledged by him. Hey Serg! One of the men yelled out loud across the parking lot. He was rushing into their department building.

Now Supreme, Stigma, and Ecstasy were putting the face to the pictures they were looking at. It's him Dada, that's Sergeant Hedgepeth right there. Supreme smiled. Welcome to the party motherfucker, now it's time to pay your dues. Officer Schiffman walked up and palmed Sergeant Hedgepeth head like a basketball and Hedgepeth drew his weapon out of his holster. Hey! Hey! Hey! He raised his hands in the air. They all busted up laughing and headed into the precinct.

Hedgepeth didn't have any hair on the top of his head just around the sides. Officer Schiffman always threatened Hedgepeth that he'd have his barber shave his head clean. Hedgepeth always told Schiffman, that he'd kill him and his barber.

It was 11:45 and GeeGee already knew that her target would be turning the corner in just about… She started counting to ten, and before she could reach ten, Officer Pechenik cruiser hit the corner. This was the time he came home most of the time to have lunch. But not at his home with his wife and children. He'd pass his block and go two streets over to his little mistress house. He jumped out of his car and ran into the house. But not before turning on the sprinklers to make sure her grass stayed looking good.

"Diana! Diana! GeeGee watched as he kissed Diana at the front door and cupped himself a handful of ass. He picked her up and entered the house, closing the door with his foot. When GeeGee walked into the house, she could hear Diana calling him by his sex name. Oh Donkey! Donkey! You make momma pussy feel so good.

GeeGee 9mm was cocked and fully loaded. Pechenik told his mistress, that he must get back to work. "All donkey no, don't leave us we miss you so much honey." Can't we try for a second round? No! No! baby I got a get back to work babydoll. He kissed Diana and slid out of bed. That's when he spotted GeeGee standing there holding her weapon to his head. Damn Donkey! That was mighty fast. She looked at her watch and it was just five minutes after twelve. Who and the fuck are you? He eyeballed his weapon that was on the nightstand in his holster. GeeGee let him know that she had acknowledged him looking at his gun. Go ahead and try it Donkey. Let's see if you are as fast as you are in bed. Oh, by the way Papa Jack said hello.

Pechenik tried to go for his gun. Pow! Pow! Pow! Diana started screaming. "Shut the hell up! You didn't do all that screaming while you were having sex with that woman husband. Next time bitch! Get you a horse. They got more stamina than a donkey. Gee-Gee turned and walked out the room.

Schiffman and Munclapp were walking into Clean Cuts barber shop. So that Schiffman can get a fresh haircut and shave. All day he has been bragging to Munclapp about the young College girl that he been banging. He told his partner that when he got a fresh haircut and shave that all the females think that he's much younger than he is. Munclapp told him so what, it doesn't help the gray hairs that's on his balls. They both were cracking up at Munclapp's comment he made about Schiffman as they were entering the barber shop.

Hey Donny, do you think that you can fit me in real quick. I'm still on the clock and don't want to get caught with a half a cut either. Yea sure my friend. You know I'll do anything for you. Oh, hey Munclapp, they both spoke to each other as he welcomed Schiffman into his chair. Another gentleman was paying for his haircut. Ok Dallas my friend, we'll see you in about two weeks. I'll see ya in two weeks Dallas, tell the family that I said hello. Ok Bobby! You and Donny take it easy. Good job, thanks. Ok Terrance, we'll see you soon.

Schiffman was now getting his hair cut and was now bragging to Bobby about his young College girl that he was sleeping with. Man, the type of job y'all got, I bet vagina be getting thrown y'all way all day. Aye Schiffman, I'm going to grab a burger, do you want one? Yea sure why not. Hey, I know already no pickles, right? Right partner, no pickles.

Supreme watched as Officer Munclapp drove away without his partner in the car. Supreme nodded to Stigma and Ecstasy to follow him. When Supreme walked into the barber shop, Bobby have office Schiffman head laid back and was applying shaving cream to his face. Schiffman eyes was closed, and he was yapping away about young vagina. Supreme walked right up on Bobby with his pistol drawn right at his face. He held his finger to his lips ordering Bobby not to make a sound.

Supreme pointed at the straight razor that Bobby was holding in his hand. Supreme was telling him to give it up. Bobby slowly handed the razor to Supreme and backed away from his station. Schiffman was asking Bobby if he ever had some young pussy before? Supreme whispered in his ear. Papa Jack said hello. Just as Schiffman tried to jump up, Supreme ran that straight razor clean across his throat. Schiffman bled out like a pig being gutted and butchered. Hey man, I ain't seen nothing. Supreme said, Yea I know Pow!

BIG AND LITTLE SATAN

$ $ $ $ $

Munclapp was standing in line at a burger shack. It was lunch time, and they were super busy with a lot of customers. Stigma had pulled her tight short's up her butt even more than they already where. She checked her weapon in her purse and made sure that it was ready to fire. She and Ecstasy started walking up towards the burger shack. Munclapp was next in line to place his order. Before he could step up Stigma bent over and put ass all in his face to see. She stood up and went in front of Munclapp to the window. Hey! Hey! Ya'll don't got no onion rings up in this joint? Munclapp couldn't help but take in a beautiful back side. Excuse me ma'am, but I do believe that I was next.

Oh, I'm sorry handsome, but did I cut or something? Yea I believe that you did. Stigma turned around and started complaining about some onion rings. Hey! Hey! Ya'll need to get some onion rings up in this Bitchhhhh! Ecstasy walked up wearing a short dress and some high heels carrying a big purse like Stigma's. Oh, excuse me officer is my drunk girlfriend causing you any problems?

Somebody in line started to complain about Stigma and Ecstasy cutting in line. Damn Officer! You gone just let them cut us? Come on here girl, before you get us thrown in jail. Girl, I don't give a fuck about no jail, and you know I love me some handcuffs. Hell, I think I got mine, shit I'll cuff his fine ass up first. Stigma started looking through her purse like she was looking for her handcuffs.

Yea ma'am I think that it's time for y'all to leave. Before I wind up putting y'all into the back of my squad car. Ok girl! If you don't want to go to jail your butt, better come on. Damn! You take a girl to jail over some funky onion rings? Ok! Ok! Stigma and Ecstasy were walking off and Stigma slapped her butt. All of y'all can kiss my ass with y'all snitching asses. Munclapp went to place his order but Stigma turned back around. Oh, Munclapp before I leave, Papa Jack said hello! Munclapp turned to grab his weapon but at the same time Stigma and Ecstasy both filled Munclapp body up with bullets. Pow! Pow! Pow! Pow! Pow! People started screaming and running as Munclapp body hit the pavement. Stigma and Ecstasy ran and jumped into their car and drove away.

$ $ $ $ $

Just as Supreme had expected. The man that they wanted more than Pechenik, Schiffman or Munclapp have just pulled up to the Clean-Cut barbershop. He was the third police officer to arrive on the scene. Sergeant Hedgepeth was exiting his vehicle and officer Kirke tried stopping him from entering the barbershop. Wait Serg! You don't want to go in there. Why is that son? Sergeant Hedgepeth pushed pass Kirke and when he saw officer Schiffman laying back with his throat cut and his blood spilled across the floor, tears started to roll down his face. Schiffman was like a son to Sergeant Hedgepeth.

That quickly drew his mind to ask about Schiffman's partner. Hey sir! Where's his partner? Oh, he said that he was running down to the burger shack. Sergeant Hedgepeth has just remembered that it was a call that came over the radio that an officer was down to the Burger Shack and Clean Cuts barbershop. Sergeant Hedgepeth told Kirke to gather as much information as he could, and I'll be right back. He quickly rushed to his car and headed down the street to the Burger Shack. Just as he saw car 211, he already knew that it was Officer Munclapp. He radioed in to dispatch and requested to have officer Pechenik come to the scene immediately.

After about two hours of learning what had happened at Clean Cuts barbershop and the Burger Shack, Sergeant Hedgepeth realized that after requesting for officer Pechenik to come to the scene, Sergeant Hedgepeth was about to call his cell phone. But another call was coming in over the radio. We have another officer down at and when the address came in from the dispatch, Sergeant Hedgepeth knows that address oh too well. He knew that whoever was taking out his officers was also coming for him too.

Sergeant Hedgepeth started looking around and surveying his surroundings. For a minute, Supreme thought that Hedgepeth was staring right at them. But Hedgepeth kept looking around as if he was confused or something.

Sergeant Hedgepeth pulled up to Diana's house and his mind went straight to all the great times that him and Schiffman, Munclapp, and Shepherd and Pechenik had experienced together. Diana couldn't help but run to Hedgepeth and hugged him in front of all the other officers. He made sure that he told her that he'll get the bitch that killed his friend. He wanted her to go down to the station so that she could help make a positive sketch on the suspect. We already have two other sketch artists there now trying to help other witnesses from two related crimes.

Diana agreed to go down to the station and help out. They have Corey from the barbershop and the cashier from the Burger Shack. Besides them, there were a few people that was standing in line who were willing to help also.

$ $ $ $ $

Sergeant Hedgepeth jumped into his black chevy truck and felt that he needed a stiff drink. He headed down to the Lazy-U bar and grill. It was a bar that a lot of officers always attended after work.

Hey Serg! Come on over and join us. Naw! I'm good! Hedgepeth walked over to the bar and he sat at the bar. Peggy, I'll have my regular. One of the other officers and his partner came and gave their condolences for the men he lost. Here Serg! That's on the house. He held the glass up as to toast to her and downed the drink in one gulp. She went to fill his glass, but the Serg declined. That'll do it for me Peggy, have a good night. Hey Serg! You, okay? I'm fine Mark, I'll see you tomorrow kid. Sergeant Hedgepeth unlocked his trunk and he sat there with it idling. He was thinking about his men, and it was hurting him badly. He beat the steering wheel. Fuck! Fuck! Fuck!

BIG AND LITTLE SATAN

How in the fuck did y'all allow this to happen to you? What the hell where you guys thinking? Hedgepeth grabbed his gun and laid it on his lap. He saw the female who was staggering and acting drunk coming his way. Hedgepeth knew that the woman couldn't have come from out the bar, nor have she been in there. When he first walked into the bar, he gave it a completely police look over. He put his truck in gear and started to leave the bar. The female stood right in front of his truck, and she stood up. Pow! Pow! Pow!

Sergeant Hedgepeth leaned to the side and a bullet barely missed his head. He returned fire. Pow! Pow! Pow! Pow! He hit the female with two of them four bullets. While at the same time he hit the gas. Bam! Knocking GeeGee straight in the air and she laid there dead in the parking lot. A few more shots rang out. Pow! Pow! Pow! Pow! But they all hit his truck. And Hedgepeth sped out of the parking lot. Urrrrrrr! Less than a minute, quite a few officers was exiting the bar with their weapons drawn.

But it was only GeeGee's body who laid lifeless in the parking lot. The officers covered each other until they reached GeeGee's body. Now the Lazy-U bar and grill looked like a policemen ball or a police award ceremony. Sergeant Hedgepeth returned to the scene after he learned it was ok. Now he was standing over the same woman who tried to take his life.

Sergeant Hedgepeth was on his way home with his hand on his weapon. He was ready for any sudden movement towards his direction. He wouldn't even pull up close to any vehicles at a traffic light. He didn't want to be trapped in no way that he couldn't escape from. He was keeping a very close eye on any vehicle that drove up behind him. Just as he turned on to his street, Hedgepeth pulled over to the side and cut his lights off. After about fifteen minutes no cars even passed by or turned on his street. Hedgepeth finally turned into his home.

The house lit up from the outside lights. His German Shepherd Duke met him as he exited his truck. He wagged his tail and playfully ran circles around Hedgepeth. That put him in a more relaxed state of mind, because if anyone was around, Duke wouldn't have been so calm and playful. His wife came to the door. Here Duke! Oh, hello honey, I thought that I heard you pull in.

$ $ $ $ $

Supreme was pacing back and forth in his hotel room, he has just got the news of GeeGee's death. Stigma, Persia, Ecstasy, and Glory were all in tears. Marquan really didn't know GeeGee all that well, but he knew that she was down and dedicated to Supreme. It was Marquan who GeeGee was with, when she got shot and ran over by Sergeant Hedgepeth. Marquan told Supreme that he tried to kill Hedgepeth after he killed GeeGee, but each bullet had penetrated Hedgepeth truck instead of his body.

Supreme held Hedgepeth picture in his hand, you dead you son-of-bitch. Do you hear me, you're dead! Awwwww! Supreme let out a loud roar. Supreme didn't know GeeGee's mother or family. He made sure that none of their family members knew anything about him like that. Just for these types of reasons, nobody could trace them back to him if something went wrong. He knew where her mother lived and where her family was from. But Supreme never made any contact with any family members. GeeGee was from California and her family grew up in Compton.

Supreme knew that this would be a bad time to try and kill Sergeant Hedgepeth. He told Marquan and the girls what his plan was and how he would get to Hedgepeth. But right now, it would be best that they returned back to Phoenix, Arizona.

The next day, Supreme, Marquan, and Persia all returned back home. Two days later Stigma, Glory, and Ecstasy caught a plane back to Arizona. Sergeant Hedgepeth was catching pure hell from the Chief and the Lieutenant. They wanted to know what the hell was going on with him and his officers that had died. Sergeant Hedgepeth swore to the Lieutenant that he had no idea as to what was going on. But he definitely was going to get to the bottom of it.

The Chief and Lieutenant's last words to Hedgepeth was, if we find out that you got anything to do with this, I personally promise you Hedgepeth, that's going to be your ass! Sergeant Hedgepeth was waiting on the fingerprints to come back on GeeGee, so that they can start serving search warrants.

CHAPTER TWENTY-FOUR
BREAKING THE BRO CODE

Even though Marquan had been through hell the last few days, he still had to prepare for what was about to occur in less than an hour. He was looking in the mirror at himself and was trying to tie his tie. Marquan was having problems with it, and so he just let it hang around his suit jacket. Before Marquan had left to go to Atlanta, he had paid thirty thousand for caskets and funeral arrangements. Plus, all the limousines and flowers for both families. Both of his friends' mothers and families were very extremely grateful for the love and respect that Marquan showed their families.

This was one time no matter how the money came, she was proud of her son as a mother. Both Rocky and Slow Drag mothers tried to thank Marquan personally, but Marquan was out of town handling business in Atlanta.

The Lincoln Limousine's pulled up in front of both families home on time just as Marquan requested. A white stretched Lincoln pulled up in front of Ms. Housemoore's house to pick up Marquan. It was a black Lincoln Limousine that was also trailing behind the ultra-stretch to pick up his mother, sister, and little brother. The back doors opened on both limousines and Supreme stepped out of the ultra-stretch.

He met Marquan halfway in the driveway. "Wow! Boy look at you, sharper than a Ginsu knife." Supreme tried cheering Marquan up, he didn't know Rocky or Slow Drag, but he had heard a lot about them while Marquan was in prison. Marquan had on an all-black Gucci suit and cream silk shirt with black Murray Gators on his feet. They hugged each other. "Man come here and let cha boy help you out." Supreme tied Marquan's tie for him. There you go, player.

"Hello Ms. Housemoore, you sure do look nice." Don't hello me boy! You can keep your charming comments to yourself. Because if anything happens to my son he better pay for your funeral too! Mama, hey hold on, there's no need for that kind of talk. Man, bro sorry about that. It's good, I understand her feelings. Ms. Housemoore gave Supreme a dirty look and grabbed Jacob hand. Come on here boy!

Marquan was still looking at Supreme. Marquan, you don't need to apologize to me bro. I understand her pain. Now let's go pay our respect to your hommies. Marquan got into the Limousine and was greeted by Glory, Stigma, Ecstasy, and Persia. They all knew that this was a time that he needed their support.

When they made it to the church, it was like some major celebrities were exiting those limousines. Everybody was checking them out at the funeral. So many people were happy to see that Marquan was home. Marquan helped Rocky and Slow Drag mothers out of their Limousine and escorted them to the church. Supreme and the girls were still standing by the Limos.

Marquan turned around and headed back towards Supreme, but he walked over to another Limousine that was last in line. The driver opened up the back door and Snooty and Star exited the Limousine. They both grabbed one of Marquan's arms and he led them into the church. Supreme mouth dropped when he realized that one of the women that was on Marquan's arm was his sister Sabrina. Stigma grabbed Supreme by the hand because she knew that he was ready to put some more bodies in a coffin.

Snooty didn't even look in Supreme's direction, she was there to support her man and little Sabrina was Snooty today, Marquan's ride or die chick. Everybody walked into Azusa World Ministry church to hear Dr. Alfred Craig give their service. Even in church Marquan and Snooty both tried their best to avoid eye contact with Supreme. Supreme even got more upset by watching his sister rub and kiss on Marquan. But after Stigma whispered in his ear several times, he knew that this wasn't the time or place to cause a scene with Marquan and Snooty.

The funeral ended and Marquan, Snooty, and Star were walking to get into the white ultra stretch limousine. Supreme was ready to leave so Marquan requested that the limousine that his girls came in take Supreme and the girls home. Supreme walked up to Marquan almost nose to nose. So how long this shit been going on Marquan? Marquan was about to respond to Supreme's question but before he could, Snooty said, daddy let me answer that for you.

Supreme it happened the moment that I first laid eyes on him but since you sent your bitch to suck my man's dick bro, we both had to stomach that one just to please your ass. But now since the both of us are grown ass adults now, that means that we don't have nobody to report our relationship to. Looks like you and the whole world is going to have to accept it. I'd appreciate it if you respect me like we respect you bro. You know we both love you, but we also love each other too.

Supreme sister's words cut him deeply but what could he truly say. Snooty was his little sister, but she wasn't a child anymore. She is a grown woman and that big brother controlling her life was about to come to an end. At least that's what Snooty and Marquan thought was about to happen. Supreme stepped back and looked at them with that, if looks could kill look. Marquan, so are you telling me that you're breaking our bro code? Do you agree with what Sabrina just said? To Supreme and Stigma surprise, Marquan said yes, I agree. But I'm hoping only with your blessing Supreme. I love your sister bro.

Supreme nodded to his girl's, and they started getting into the limousine. Supreme took one last look at Marquan, but he never gave him an answer. He got into the limo and closed the door himself. Just as Supreme gave the driver the word to leave, he rolled down the window and stared at Marquan as the limousine drove away. Stigma said, "See Dada, I told you that you should have let me handle that from day one."

Supreme knew that getting mad wouldn't solve him and Marquan's problem, unless he thought that his heart would allow him to kill Marquan. So, the only thing that Supreme knew that he could do at this point was get even. Supreme smiled at the thought of how Marquan would feel when he gives him a dose of his own medication.

Supreme rode in silence back home. He just experiencing such a beautiful funeral, took Supreme's mind on what had just happened to GeeGee. He was reminiscing on the good and bad times that they had. Plus, all the wild sexual experiences that they shared with other women and each other. That even made him realize that he has to pay his respect to her in a much better way than just saying goodbye. Just as soon as he made it home, he contacted Papa Jack to see what he could do to recover GeeGee body. Papa Jack told him that he'll look into it, but Supreme learned that they were on their way to Philadelphia, PA, the home of the great Champion Floyd Mayweather.

Marquan knew that it was major attention between him and Supreme. One of the first things that they agreed on as friends was, no family ties should ever cross on a sexual level. Supreme and Marquan agreed that they would never sleep with a mother, sister, aunt, baby mama, or any woman that was family to them. Also, no woman that they shared deep feelings for. And here he was the one to come home and break their bro code. Marquan knew that what he and Snooty had was beyond them turning their backs on each other.

When Marquan got a chance to be alone, the first thing he did was called Supreme to have a man-to-man conversation about Snooty. What Marquan didn't know was just before he called Supreme, Snooty had called her brother and was begging Supreme not to hate her or Marquan for their decision. Supreme gave Snooty his word that he wouldn't interfere or do anything to harm Marquan. Snooty knew that her brother was a man of his word. But one thing she did know was that he wouldn't completely allow it to escape his mind.

Supreme listened to how they became involved with each other. Supreme strangely could even hear the sincerity in Marquan's voice when he said he loved Snooty. To Marquan's surprise, he was shocked to hear Supreme say, well man, now I guess that I can truly say that you are family now. Marquan heard him say that, and he didn't know what feared him the most. Him accepting them or the calmness in Supreme's voice. Supreme changed the conversation by telling Marquan that they need to prepare for their job in Philadelphia.

$ $ $ $ $

Marquan was checking himself out in the mirror. He knew that they were about to leave soon, but he didn't want to leave Arizona without spending time and getting to know the woman that made him feel like women felt whenever Marquan left them after being in his presence. After Snooty grabbed Marquan's heart at the prison, it still was a woman that have left him speechless after engaging into a conversation with her. It was something mysterious to Marquan about Impression. She was the type of woman that no man could forget after meeting her.

Marquan looked at the card and knew that Impression would be at work tonight. Ms. Impression club Excalibur. Marquan kissed the card and went to jump into his truck. Marquan went and watched Snooty and star dance for a little while. He was a lot more comfortable going into the club now. He in Big Chubb really started to take to each other. Big Chubb would even allow Marquan to bring his gun into the strip club. In a way, it also gave Big Chubb some type of comfort when Marquan was in the club.

It was a little slow, so Marquan told Snooty and Star that he'll see them back at the house. Everything had been real smooth with them and their relationship. Marquan handled his business and the girls handled theirs. Marquan stopped and spoke with Big Chubb for a minute. They made a small wage on the Dallas and Miami series. Big Chubb is from Dallas and Marquan is a D Wade fan. OK, boy. Just bring my Cenote. Marquan yelled as he was driving away.

CHAPTER TWENTY-FIVE
I CAN BE A BITCH AT TIMES

Marquan walked into club Excalibur and he was impressed with the way that the club was set up. It has a few stages and plenty white girls dancing. But not too many black girls seem to work at this strip club. Marquan thought, damn! They even get racism up in this strip club. What type of bullshit is this? It didn't take long for Marquan to notice Impression. She was dancing for three gentlemen that were dressed up in suits. Marquan didn't think that a white girl could move her body like a sister. He thought, my how times have really changed. Marquan made his way over to the bar and ordered a drink.

It was Impression's time to go dance up on the stage. The DJ said, "we all know her by Impression, but I really think that she's Pamela Anderson, because she's got that Baywatch body." Let's get ready to make it rain on Ms. Impression. Three 6 mafia, hard for a pimp came on and Impression gave a new meaning to stripping to Marquan. Men were throwing fifty- and hundred-dollar bills on the stage. Like they threw dollars and twenties at Satin Doll Strip Club.

Marquan knew that the majority of the female's in the club, couldn't out dance Snooty and Star. He knew that it was the color of their skin, is what was getting Impression paid like that. Impression was through with her set and came out on the floor in a lime green two-piece booty short set. Men was pulling at her arm and holding up their money. Come over here baby, he can't afford you like I can. Marquan was now turning down a lap dance from a real sexy white female. "You want a dance?" " Naw! I'm good sexy, I'm waiting for her." He was pointing at Impression. "Yea I Know! ain't everybody?" She popped her lips and walked off.

Marquan had been in the club for three hours and still couldn't get Impression's attention. She has been watching him, but she hasn't paid him any attention yet. Marquan was about to leave, and somebody said Hey Marquan, he turned around and it was Impression. She stood there laughing holding her Gucci bag. "Damn!" You be busy up in here Ms. Lady. Yea! I told you that. They love me here. A few old men were trying to get her to dance for them. She blew them off. I'm sorry baby, but mama got to go get some rest. Impression asked Marquan what he was doing up in the club. You invited me, remember.

"I didn't think that you would even remember me." The way that these men are spoiling you up in here. Baby these are customer's, they are not no men. If they were real men, they wouldn't be in here tricking off their money. "Nor would they be hounding a bitch, just for a dance knowing they aint getting no pussy." " I see that you didn't, give none of these bitches your money." "How do you know that I didn't give them no money? You didn't even know I was here.

Impression said, "Honey you walked in the club at 12:40 and had two drink's and turned down seven lap dances." Marquan superciliously looked at Impression. "Why didn't you let me know, that you knew I was here?" "You forgot already?" Forgot what? That I can be, a bitch at times. Marquan busted up laughing.

"May I take you bag?" "See I told you, that I knew men when I saw one." Yea thank you, Impression limousine pulled up, and Marquan handed him her bag. Impression said, "Well I guess that this is it, unless you're joining me in my bed tonight?" I won't make the same mistake and offer you breakfast again. "Maybe I can offer you some of this," and she sat down in the limo and opened her legs. Marquan was looking at a clean shaved vagina with thick pink lips. "Are you hungry daddy?" What makes you think that I know how to eat pussy? "Don't trip! most men don't know how to eat pussy, but that's what my job is to teach you what you don't know."

"But you got to make up your mind, before she catches a cold out here" Then you'll have to come, and feed her some dick, that's the only way she'll get well. Marquan was following Impression's Limousine and texting Snooty and Star messages. Telling them that he was fine, and he'll see them in the morning. Marquan couldn't believe where Impression was taking him. Her home looked like most homes that he saw on T.V. when he was in prison. Impression showed Marquan around her home, then she cooked him breakfast and they ended the night, in the nude sitting back in her jacuzzi.

They were just talking and really getting to know each other that sex was the furthest thing on their minds. Plus, the both of them knew that, if they engaged into sex that their relationship would end right there. They both was starting to develop, a different type of respect for each other and they couldn't let sex blow that. One thing didn't happen that night, Marquan never did say that he was a Hit Man like her man.

CHAPTER TWENTY-SIX
MORE DEADLY THAN ME

The plane landed at Philadelphia International Airport and Marquan wanted this job to be over and done with. He wanted to get back to Impression and whatever it was they were about to start. Impression wasn't the type of woman that, you played game's with or had sex and just up and walk away. While Supreme was getting their rental car, Marquan finally called and checked on Emoni.

Truth be told Emoni was starting to win Marquan's heart. He was starting to feel a comfort with her, and no sex was even involved. She never pressed him or asked any questions that she shouldn't ask. Just like right at that moment, Emoni was always happy to hear Marquan's voice. Strangely to Marquan's surprise, Emoni asked Marquan if she could pray for him. Marquan didn't take it personally, and he allowed her to pray. "Gracious F a t h e r ! I want to thank you for sending, such a wonderful man into my life." I ask you to watch over him, in his darkest moments. Let him turn away from Satan false treasure's and that someday he turns to you lord, so that he receives a multitude of your blessing's. And keep his heart close to yours Jehovah. So that I can feel your love through him, (Amen). " Say Amen baby." Amen.

Emoni couldn't see it, but Marquan was wiping away his tears. The last time that he experienced a woman, praying over his life it was his mother. That's how she always ended their calls when he was in prison. Marquan asked about Tone, and Emoni told him that she didn't want to bother him with that. "Until you come home, focus on you baby. I'm right here." Bye! Click, Emoni hung up.

Supreme and Marquan were sitting at a restaurant in Philly. They were eating and trying to learn more about the two gentleman that was up on the big Billboard, that was posted up just outside the restaurant. The Billboard have a clear picture of the two men, that Supreme and Marquan came to pay a visit. They were the owners of Guadagnino and Sorrentino Associate's law firm. This was their first time in Philadelphia, and they were studying a map enjoying Philly Steak sandwiches. Supreme didn't feel like it was necessary to bring the girls on this trip. Being that they know just where to find the two lawyers at their firm. They were hoping to get in and out of Philly, because Supreme had left Stigma sick and Marquan have just met a woman that's got his mind racing. Supreme and Marquan just really wanted to get back as soon as possible.

Steven Sorrentino was handling a major murder case in Philly. It was some woman that have got murdered per say, by a big music promoter. His alibi was that someone had broken into their home when he was out of town promoting a show. But their next-door neighbor placed the husband there the night that his wife was found dead. The show that the promoter went to put on in Seattle was cancelled, but the plane that he took there, the ticket had been used by someone. The prosecutor had brung in two flight attendants to testify at the trial, saying that the promoter never boarded the plane.

Steven Sorrentino was asking the jury to dismiss all charges against his client. The prosecutor was up, giving the court his closing arguments. "Ladies and gentlemen of the jury, I'm well aware that I'm going up against a well-known lawyer here today." But I object your Honor. Let's make it clear to the prosecutor and the jury that I'm not the one on trial here today. "Objection accepted Mr. Sorrentino." Mr. Khaled, please stay focused on your client and this case. "Yes Sir!" I agree, my apology to Mr. Sorrentino and the jury. "Please continue."

Today we're here trying to get justice, for a mother of three and her family. She's not here to defend herself, nor was she able allegedly able to defend herself from her husband, and children's father. "I just want you, the jury to come back in here with the right verdict today." We have all heard the testimonies and saw the evidence here today. We have heard from the two flight attendants. The neighbor clearly testified to seeing Mr. Brown. You saw the pictures of the scratches on Mr. Brown at the time of his arrest, which he claims to have gotten from playing with the family dog.

Once again, Ladies and Gentlemen, Mrs. Brown and her family and friends is expecting, you the jury to not allow her husband Mr. Brown to walk away being a free man while she lay dead in some cemetery. I thank you all for taking time off your job and I know that you'll come back with a guilty verdict. Thank you.

It didn't take the jury long to come back with a verdict. The prosecutor was all smiles because normally when a jury comes back with a verdict so fast the person is guilty. The Judge read the case off. In the murder case against Mr. Phillip Anthony Brown, the jury finds you not guilty on all charges. As Steven Sorrentino and Tony Guadagnino were leaving the court room, they were being swarmed by the press.

"Mr. Sorrentino, Mr. Sorrentino!" How do you feel about having a perfect record in court in winning your thirty second murder trial? Well, it's not about my record at all. Me and my partner here, he pointed at Mr. Guadagnino. We just give our best when representing any client that puts their trust in our Law Firm. But Sir! All the evidence showed that your client was guilty. Can you be fairly honest and say that the jury got this one right? Well, I always trust and believe that the jury fairly gets the verdict right. So,

BIG AND LITTLE SATAN

is that how you felt in the Sanderson case? "Okay!" Thank y'all for your time. But Mr. Sorrentino was that officer guilty in that case or not? Wasn't he actually guilty Sir? Sorrentino and his partner pushed through the people and the photographers. They were trying to get away from the reporter.

Steven Sorrentino and his partner were back at their Law Firm. Their secretary Amirah was giving both attorneys their messages for the day. She was also gathering her things because it was the end of the day. Mr. Guadagnino asked Amirah to grab them a bottle of champaign out of his office and two glasses before she left. Amirah did as she was told. "Oh, yea by the way, congratulations on your big win today in court." Mr. Sorrentino, you looked so handsome on the television. I'll lock up, see you guys tomorrow. "Bye Amirah!" They both almost said it at the same time. Amirah was about to lock up when Supreme and Marquan walked up on her.

"Oh my! you guys startled me." If you here to see one of the Lawyers we're closed for the day and they're already gone home. Supreme smiled and said, "They just told me that you would tell us that." I just hung up on the phone with Steven, we're real close personal friends. He told me to tell you, Amirah right? To let us up before you lock the door. Supreme held up his cell phone. Here, if you'll like me to, I'll be glad to call him back. Amirah saw how well dressed they were. No! it's okay sure, I'll let you guys' in. There's no need to call him back if he's already expecting you.

Supreme knew that saying her name is what really did the job. But he could also see that Amirah wanted to personally get to know Marquan. She had given him a complete body search ending the search at his penis. "Bye! I hope to see you again, please don't be a stranger." Amirah looked Marquan straight in the eyes when she said that. On the way upstairs, Supreme asked Marquan did he want him to do the job by himself? "So, you can go fuck their secretary." Ain't you done turned into a real ladies man, my boy! Marquan smiled while checking his weapon.

Supreme and Marquan were listening at the door as the two Lawyers jerked at each other's ego. They were bragging on how great of attorney's they are and joked about the reporters comment on another case. They poured a drink and proposed a toast. Steven told Guadagnino, "I want to propose a toast to your intelligent fine ass." Mr. Guadagnino said, "Excuse me! But I do believe that you're the one with the sexy ass honey." They allowed each other to drink from each other's glass and they engaged in a passionate kiss.

Supreme and Marquan walked through the door. Man will you look at these two fags. Sorrentino and Guadagnino both jumped at the sound of Supremes' voice. Supreme and Marquan pointed their guns at each one of the Lawyers. Sorrentino stood behind Guadagnino, "Oh my goodness what do they want?"

Baby whatever it is they want, please give it to them but don't kill us please! We have wives and children, please don't kill us. Supreme couldn't do nothing but laugh at Sorrentino's comment.

BIG AND LITTLE SATAN

"Aye, take your bitch over there and have a seat." Supreme pointed at the chairs that their clients sit in when they came to see them. Thirty minutes later, Sorrentino and his partner were tied up and duck taped by their arms. Supreme tied their arms to the arms of their chairs.

Supreme went and sat in Sorrentino chair, and it has just dawned on him that the two Lawyers just might know who Papa Jack is. He knew that if he and Marquan could get to Papa Jack that he and Stigma could go on with their lives. Supreme stood up, "Ok gentlemen, since y'all like to get into shit, let's get into some deep shit!" He walked behind Guadagnino and snatched the back of his chair. Supreme pulled Guadagnino into the middle of his office. He done the same thing to Sorrentino leaving them facing each other but giving them about three feet apart from each other.

"Ok, since you two bump-it buddies like playing games with yall lives, we're going to play a little game." It's called To Tell the Truth. Y'all ready to hear the rules? Marquan slapped Sorrentino so hard that he started pissing on himself. "Yea! Yea! Yes Sir!" Supreme pulled out a 38 special and spinned the barrel. Sorrentino and Guadagnino eyes got real big. The both of them started to plead for their lives. "Don't kill us, don't kill us please!" We have got plenty of money, we'll give you any amount.

Supreme took out some pictures from his jacket pocket. Ok, I'm going to ask the both of you some questions. The first one of you tells me a lie you're getting shot. Y'all took a case three years ago, The Lagerfield case. Sorrentino and Guadagnino gave each other a real serious stare. "Ok!" Now I see that we're all on the same page here, I want to know whose idea was it to throw that fucking case?

Supreme held up the 38 special, remember what I said. "The Truth?" Sorrentino blamed Guadagnino and he blamed Sorrentino. Ok! Somebody just lied. Him! Him! It wasn't me it was him. Sorrentino was jumping around in his seat trying to tell Supreme the truth. But from being tied up and taped to the chair he couldn't move an inch. Sorrentino yelled at Guadagnino, tell him the fucking truth. Because I'm not about to die for you, cunt.

Supreme walked over to Guadagnino. Marquan went and stood behind him, then he put his gun to his head. Supreme said, "So you're the one that's lying to me?" No! No! No! "It wasn't me; it was that bitch!" Supreme spent the barrel on the 38 and he placed it in Guadagnino's right hand. Ok, so it was him. If he's lying, then shoot the bitch! Sorrentino looked at Guadagnino eye to eye.

"Click!" Sorrentino closed his eyes. He just knew that he was shot. But the 38 didn't fire. Supreme removed the gun from Guadagnino's hand and placed the gun in Sorrentino's hand. "Ok, if he lied on you then pull the trigger." Sorrentino couldn't pull the trigger. Marquan looked at Supreme as to say, should I kill him? Supreme put up one finger and went to pick up the pictures on the desk. You can't shoot your lover. I guess that you're not mad enough.

BIG AND LITTLE SATAN

"Well, did you know that he was fucking you and your wife?" While Marquan held the gun to Guadagnino's head, Supreme showed Sorrentino the pictures of him and his wife in bed. Pow! Owwwwwww! What the fuck is wrong with you? "You shot me you prick, are you crazy?" Guadagnino got shot in the leg, and Supreme removed the gun from Sorrentino. "Well, Papa Jack told me to say hello." At the same time Sorrentino and Guadagnino knew that they were about to die. Marquan already knew not to shoot. Supreme wanted to see their response and they had done just as he suspected that they would. They were begging and pleading with Supreme for their life.

"Oh! So y'all do know who Papa Jack is?" Yea! Yea! Yes, please don't kill us. "Tell him that we're sorry!" I'm so sorry that's not what was supposed to happen that day. Supreme and Marquan looked at each other almost with a sense of relief. "Okay! No more games!" How in the fuck do y'all know Papa Jack? Guadagnino answered the question even before Sorrentino could. We represented his son in a case. "What! Are you shititng me?" We tried to make every deal that we could, but the judge didn't want to give us that case.

But this was before we became Guadagnino and Sorrentino Associates. We lost that case, and his son got a life sentence. Me and Papa Jack used to golf together a lot and I promised him that Guadagnino put his head down and started crying hysterically, I tried my best, I did I really did. I promised him that I'd win Sir, but I lost. Supreme's heart was almost about to jump out of his chest.

Now Supreme and Marquan realized that they have killed all the people who have wronged Papa Jack. Supreme and Marquan knew that just as soon as they kill Papa Jack that all of this would be over. Supreme asked the main question that he had been waiting to get an answer to. "Ok, if y'all want to walk out of here alive, give me his real name and address." Sorrentino said, "we don't know his real name. All we know him by is Papa Jack." Supreme put his gun to his head ready to blow his brains out. "Wait, wait wait! We got an address and picture of him for our own safety."

Supreme and Marquan put the biggest smiles on their faces. "Where is it at?" Right there behind that picture. "Supreme started untying Sorrentino while Marquan undone the tape on his arms." "Go get it!" No! No! That's okay, I'll get it myself. Supreme removed the picture and it was a digital safe in the wall. "What's the number, what's the fucking number?" It's 22-34- and before Sorrentino could get the last number out, Pow!" A bullet came flying through the window and hit Sorrentino right in the head. His head blew open like a watermelon being tested at a gun range. His brains went all over the office floor. Supreme and Marquan hit the floor. They were pointing their guns at Guadagnino then they pointed at the window.

Supreme jumped because Sorrentino phone started ringing and it wouldn't stop ringing. Marquan said, "Supreme somebody knows that we're here." I think you better answer that. Supreme crawled over to the desk and he picked up the receiver. Hello, Papa Jack said, "That's not what you're there for to be checking up on me, Supreme." "Finish the fucking job." Click! The phone went dead.

Supreme stood up and that let Marquan know that it was ok to stand up too. Supreme looked at Sorrentino's body and walked over to Guadagnino, who already knew that he was about to die. He closed his eyes and Pow! Pow! On the way to the airport, Supreme and Marquan were wondering how in the hell did Papa Jack know that they were inquiring about him? Supreme and Marquan have just realized that Papa Jack was more dangerous than them.

CHAPTER TWENTY-SEVEN
TURNING POINT

S tigma came walking into the house carrying bags. "Boy! Stop running in this his house." "Ok mama!" "Nanna! Nanna! What Isaiah?" I'm in the kitchen baby! "Look! Look Nanna what I got!" Hello Ma. Hi baby, what have you done bought this child now? Isaiah started pulling all of his new clothes out of the bags. "Wow! Now that is nice Stigma." Isaiah was showing his Nanna a white Guess Jean suit and his Guess low cut shoes. Boy, now you about to be looking and dressing like your daddy. I know Nanna, my daddy going to love this. Child, what else you got in those bags?

"Oh! Oh! Nanna, I almost forgot my mama also let me buy you something too." She did! Okay, that was nice of her to do that Isaiah. "Nanna, she let me buy it with my own money." What baby? You thought about your old grandma? Isaiah had bought her an apron and matching hat. It said, "when I'm not being beautiful, I'm in the kitchen cooking. Ms. Bergess started crying and she hugged

BIG AND LITTLE SATAN

Isaiah, thank you baby. Nanna will you wear it all the time? She removed the apron that she had on and put on the apron that Isaiah bought her. "So how do I look?" Here put the hat on. "Owwww! Nanna you look beautiful, don't she mama?" 'Yea ma, you do." Under Ms. Burgess breath she said, shoot I look like the Pillsbury Dough Boy.

Stigma started laughing, well maybe Isaiah you can let nanna go without the hat sometimes. Stigma whispered in Ms. Bergess ear, "Ma I bought you a little something too." Here ma, turn around and let me put it on. Stigma put a diamond necklace around her neck. "Wait, wait, ma; Stigma took out a mirror from her Prada purse and held it up." Stigma! This thing cost too much money, now you take it back and get your money back. "Child, I ain't worth that much money at all baby." Stigma kissed her on the cheek. Ma, you're worth that and so much more to us. What would I and Supreme do without you around here? Stigma and Ms. Burgess stood there hugging each other and was crying. Little Isaiah looked up at them and he started hugging them and crying too.

Isaiah stopped crying and said, "Mama, I don't want to cry no more, can I go play my video games now?" Stigma and Ms. Burgess busted up laughing. They knew that Isaiah's video game was more important to him then two women in their feelings crying. Yeah, baby sure; go play your game. Isaiah dropped the bag that was in his hand, and he took off running towards his room. Stigma pointed at the floor, see ma he just like his daddy look what he thinks about my money. Ms. Burgess said, that's y'all little monster that y'all created together, child. "I know don't remind me, Mama." I try to forget that night all the time. If my fast butt haven't been there, I wouldn't have no kids. "Child, stop it! You wouldn't know what to do with yourself if you didn't have that boy."

Stigma went and put up her things and came back in her paja-mas. She walked over to the refrigerator and took out the orange juice and Ms. Bergess handed her a glass. "Here child pour me a glass to, Ms. Bergess went and sat down at the table." Here mama, "Baby what's on your mind?" "What!" "What's bothering you Stig-ma?" "Who said that something is bothering me?" Well for start-ers, that little finger of yours is just twisting your hair, and you got that sad rescue me look on your face. "Damn! you know me better than I do." "Well don't you think I should, girl who do you think raised you?" Stigma started crying. This was a time that she would have loved to sit down with her own mother. Not that she didn't love and respect Ms. Bergess in that manner because she does.

Ms. Bergess told Stigma, "Always know that when you need me, that I'm right hear baby." "I know mama." There's nothing in this world that you can't talk to me about. "You and Preme having some type of problems?" Stigma took a deep breath, Mama not yet, but we about to and I mean bad trouble. "Child you do you know how much that man love you, and that little boy in there, don't you?" "Baby if you done something wrong, I'm sure it's nothing that he won't forgive you for." "He's not about to forgive me mama." "Mama, I'm pregnant and it's not his child." Ms. Bergess took her hand and placed it over her mouth.

"Baby this is some type of joke, right?" How in the hell did that happen? No! No! I know how it happened mama. "Stigma, when did that happen and why?" Stigma told her the whole true story about her and Deshawn's little experience together at the hotel. She told Ms. Bergess that Deshawn is from Atlanta and yes, she did let him know that she was pregnant by him. Child, what did that boy say when you told him you were pregnant? "Mama he was happy, this a be his first child and he wants me to have it." Ms. Bergess put her head down on the table and then she raised it back up and just stared at Stigma. "Mama trust me, I already know what you're thinking." Supreme is going to kill me, him, and this baby.

"Stigma what made you lose control of yourself like that, baby I taught you better than that." You know how them men talk that sweet talk, to get in your pants. "You have a good man that loves you and y'all son, Stigma he will die for y'all girl." "I know mama, trust me I know that he will." But I just got weak and made the biggest mistake in my life. I didn't mean to do this to my family or to myself, mama. "I love Supreme too, mama. I just fucked up bad, real bad this time." "Mama, he gone kill me." "Child, stop saying that, that man ain't gone kill you." He go be mad as hell, but he ain't gone kill you Stigma. "Mama, you don't know Supreme like I do, he not as nice as he is in this house." 'He gone kill me and take our son, watch."

Stigma, you done went pass fucking up. Stigma looked at Ms. Bergess because she ain't never heard her cuss before. "Yea, it's that bad child, don't be looking at me, this is your mess." Ok, so what are you going to do? "What I'm going to do, what am I going to do mama is get an abortion." Ms. Bergess stopped in mid-sentence and looked at Stigma like she had just pulled a gun on her. "No baby no! You definitely can't do that!" That's not just that boy's baby inside of you, Stigma. I raised you to be a woman with or without a man, child! "You don't kill your kids; mother's give their children life not death." Good, bad, or ugly times, Stigma you do the best you can for your kids. God don't give us the opportunity to take lives Stigma, but he does grant us the will through birth to give life. It's your own self will to please your partner in a relationship and you're going about pleasing wrong. Ms. Bergess walked over to her Bible and turned the pages until she got to Luke.

"Stigma I want you to take the word of God into your heart, before you go and make a bad decision that you can't take back." Luke12:15 says, And He said to them, "Take heed and beware of covetousness, for one's life does not consist in the abundance of the things he possesses." Stigma don't be selfish for money or your own self gain. Stigma, the happy life that you're trying to desire baby! you're trying to get it the wrong way. The whole world tries to find life possessions but that's the wrong way to go about it, baby. Stigma don't you know that there is no life in these things? Life is found only in Christ and not man's happiness or pleasures.

Ms. Bergess kissed Stigma on the cheek. "Baby go pray and ask God what he wants you to do in this situation." Ms. Bergess picked up her glass of orange juice and walked out of the kitchen. Stigma wiped the tears from her face, and it was as if a light had just turned on in her head. Stigma placed her hand over her stomach and smiled. She got up and went to her bedroom and she closed the door. Stigma knew that what she was about to do was about to change her life forever. But she felt that it has to be done, for the sake of her child. Stigma went into the closet and found the box that she was looking for and removed one shoe. She looked at the shoe and made a note to herself that she needed to wear them shoes soon. Because she would be too damn fat to be wearing a three-inch-high heel shoe. Stigma removed Deshawn's phone number and put the red bottom shoe back in the box. After putting the shoes back, Stigma got out her pajamas because she wanted to get comfortable for what she was about to do. Even though she took the pajamas out, she only put on the top and kept on her purple Victoria Secret panties, she laid her bra on the bed. She picked up her cell phone and dialed Deshawn's number.

To her surprise she didn't even block her phone number from Deshawn. After about two rings Deshawn answered the phone and still didn't know who was calling him from Arizona. "Hello! Soothing Hands, this is Deshawn speaking." "Yea

Deshawn, ain't that what got us into this problem now, your hands?" Stigma! Stigma! Is this you, baby? Yea it's me, unless you done got some other female pregnant in Phoenix, or do you? Deshawn started laughing. That ain't funny Deshawn, why you laughing? No! No! Baby it ain't, but your humor sure is, Stigma. "Wow, you always make me smile or laugh." Baby, I never thought that I'd ever hear your voice again. But I'm happy that you called me sexy, are you okay? Yea I am. I never thought that I'd hear your voice either, Deshawn. "So, tell me what changed your mind and made you call me?" Well, I talked to someone that I love dearly and what she said really made me think, Deshawn. Not about me or you but about our child's life, you know.

Deshawn was on the phone smiling from ear to ear to hear Stigma say our baby. That put chills all over his body, he could see himself with Stigma and the baby. "Well right now, you just need to listen to me Deshawn and don't say nothing baby." "Just listen, okay?" I promise ma, I won't say shit. I think you be lying Deshawn, because you talking again. The both of them started laughing. But serious Deshawn, I'm thinking about having my baby now. Deshawn stopped smiling because now she said my baby this time. "Deshawn, I don't want to kill my baby so chances are here's what's about to happen." I'm going to have my baby but you're not going to be in our lives. My man still doesn't know that I'm pregnant, but when he finds out it's about to be bad for us all. To keep it real with you, me and this baby both might not be living. But from what I've been told he gone be mad as fuck. But he just might forgive me, Deshawn.

If he does Deshawn, I'm more than sure he's not going to allow you in our lives, being that this was a big mistake in the first place. Deshawn hadn't said anything until he heard her say that. "Wait hold the fuck up, so you are saying that we were a mistake, Stigma?" See Deshawn, I said listen and not talk. "Nall Stigma I can't and won't accept that shit from you woman." True enough, we both were in the wrong to hurt your dude or my girl." "Yea! Neither one of them deserved to be hurt by us, but we both are adults that made adult decisions."

Stigma it ain't nothing I did or done to you was a mistake. The only mistake that I made was leaving you and my baby in Arizona. Tears started rolling down Stigma's face. She was hoping to control the whole conversation, but hearing Deshawn say that Stigma knew that she was really feeling the same way on the inside about Deshawn too. "Man stop it, Deshawn." "Why are you making shit harder than it have to be?" "Why can't you just listen to me, Deshawn and go away, I got this man?" Deshawn, you know yourself that this is the best way for all of us.

Stigma means that there will never be no me and you without our baby being born. "Trust me Stigma, I'll never accept that, nor will I ever accept that bullshit ma." Okay Deshawn, if you can't listen to me and don't want to see me happy, then I won't even have this baby then. 'Click! Deshawn made several attempts to call Stigma back, but all he got was her voicemail.

$ $ $ $ $

Supreme and Marquan were back in Phoenix, he stopped by the house in Chandler and spent a little time with SoSo. She tried several times to have sex with Supreme, but his mind was only on seeing his son Isaiah. Plus, he knew that Stigma would be ready for him to please her in that department. It has been a while since they had any sexual encounters. The last time Supreme was in the mood, Stigma didn't feel too good back at the Hospitality Suite. They just cuddled and enjoyed holding each other.

Supreme just allowed her to give him some of her bomb ass head, even though she was horny as fuck. Supreme promised SoSo that they would make it up later. After cleaning up, he jumped into his 500 Mercedez and headed home to his family. While Supreme traveled on the highway his mind went back to when being in Philadelphia, he knew just how close he came to ending his Hit Man Lifestyle. Even though the drug game came with dealing with crackheads, thirsty niggas, bitches, snitches, and police trying to move up in the police department from making the right drug bust, so they can become Sergeant or retire.

Supreme felt that life was so much more easier, when him and Marquan were selling drugs. Even though between him and Stigma, they were headed towards being a Millionaire. They had just split a little change with Marquan, Ecstasy, Glory and Persia from the Dirty Desert Inn cemetery after killing Scorpion and Jakarta. Papa Jack gave them a nice payout for the job, like he says business is business just get the job done. All the money that was made on every hit, Papa Jack didn't deal with nobody but Supreme and nobody else. Papa Jack didn't care how he paid them; it was all on Supreme to get a job done.

Supreme split it up however he saw it best between Marquan, Ecstasy, Persia, Glory, and GeeGee who was now dead and still wasn't resting in peace. Supreme and Stigma usually walked away, with the bulk of the money from his personal relationship with the other girl's. If Marquan, Ecstasy, Glory, Persia, and GeeGee knew how much money they were cheated out of, then the next hit that they would have been going on would have been to kill Supreme and Stigma.

Supreme got interrupted in his thoughts, by his cell phone. "Talk to me, is how he always answered his phone." "Dada didn't you forget something, before you left me?" Supreme looked around his vehicle, then looked at his weapon laying in his lap. "Nope SoSo that I can think of at this moment." Dada, you forgot to leave the money for my shop. Supreme said, "When have you known me to forget about you doll?" SoSo wanted to say, "The moment that you didn't come home and beat this pussy up." But instead, she said; "Well Dada it must be today, because you know I got to give that money for the shop today," so that I can get started on my dreams and goals too Dada.

"Baby doll try looking on the nightstand and I'm more then sure you'll find twenty thousand in that envelope." "Well, Dada how was I supposed to know that, if you didn't tell me?" SoSo, it's kind of hard to talk to you, when you got my penis halfway down your throat and my nuts is following it. SoSo smiled hearing how proud Supreme was at her performance with her mouth. "Dada thank you, but don't forget that my kitty cat looking for that same attention." Real soon, I got you. Don't trip, kitty already knows who can really satisfy her. "My Dada!" Ok act like you know it then.

"I found it Dada and thanks again for supporting me with my dreams and goals." No welcomes SoSo you definitely deserve to be happy and successful. That's why I got you in my life, I know winner's when I see them. Now get that spot open so that, when I come home next time, I can be the first to get a massage. SoSo, have you thought of a name yet? "Yea! What's that?" "Relax Yo Back Massage Parlor. Supreme busted up laughing. Now that shit truly fits you SoSo, because that's just what you do baby. That's what you do! Relax a man's back, I'm proud of you Doll, get that money. Call me later Dada after you handle your business and don't be giving Stigma all that dick. Click! Their call ended with Supreme laughing.

BIG AND LITTLE SATAN

Supreme was pulling into the driveway and he put his Mercedes Benz right behind Stigma's Mercedes Coup and he grabbed his pistol. Supreme stuck his key in the door and was greeted by Isaiah's German Shepherd and chihuahua mixed puppy. Maxxi done his little tail wag and spin dance for Supreme letting him know that he knew who's boss. Maxxi jumped up on Supreme's leg and waited for his pat on his head. "Hey Prem, Oh you back?" "Yea Ms. B ain't I happy about that." "Baby, are you hungry? I got some Cabbage and Oxtail's on the stove for ya." Ms. B, tell me you made some Yam's and mixed cornbread? Child you better know it. Shall I bring it up to your room? "Naw! You just make me a plate and I'll come down for it." Where's Stigma and Isaiah? Well just follow Maxxi up them stairs and I'm sure he'll lead you to your son. "Ya girl up there in y'all room resting. Is she still getting sick? Nope, she ain't threw up since y'all been back home. That's good, fix her a plate and she can join me too.

"Ok Prem it's coming right up." "Oh, look what your son and girl bought me." Awe that's nice Ms. B, look at your apron and your bling, bling. "That's nice Ms. B, you really deserve it." Well that's the same thing ya girl said. Well look like she got it right again, see that's why she my woman. Supreme and Maxxi ran up the stairs and he peeped his head in the first room. "Dad! Isaiah threw his controller down and ran into his daddy's arms." Dad come here look how far that I got in my game. Supreme stood there and watched him kill some people in a shooting game.

"Here dad you try it." Supreme tried it and killed one man but the next guy killed him. "All Shit!" I'm sorry son, I messed up your game. No you didn't dad, I got it saved, look. Isaiah restarted the game and the man that just killed Supreme and the guy Supreme killed popped back up. "Wow! Video games, technology is a motherfucker, Supreme said under his breath.

"Hey champ! give dad a few minutes, to get settled in and eat." Then I'll be back to beat you in some N.B.A shoot out. "Naw! no way dad, you can't beat me dad." "I got the Laker's and Kobe Bryant light's out dad." Supreme started laughing walking out the room. He closed the door and made a quick pit stop at the bathroom in the hallway to take a quick piss. Supreme checked himself in the mirror then headed to his bedroom. Supreme opened the door and saw Stigma laying in that purple thung and his penis stood to attention fast. He stood at the foot of the bed and took in his woman's voluptuous ass. Stigma was laying on her stomach with her legs open wide. Her kitty was poking out in between her legs like a balloon when you first blow it up. "Damn! Supreme was thinking to himself just how lucky he was to have Stigma in his life.

Supreme walked over to the side of the bed to kiss Stigma on the neck to wake her up but he noticed a piece of paper by her hand lying next to her cell phone. He was about to place his gun on the nightstand, but he decided to look at the paper. Supreme read the name Deshawn with an Atlanta address. Supreme gave Stigma a supercilious look and he got a funny feeling in his stomach. He quietly picked up Stigma cell phone then he exited the room.

Supreme went into one of their spare bedrooms and closed the door behind him. He sat on the mink quilt that laid across the bed and he pressed send on Stigma's phone. The phone rung three times and then a voice said, "So what now? Have you finally come to your senses and decided to keep our baby or what Stigma?" Supreme said, "Nigga what the fuck did you just say?" "Keep y'all baby, what motherfucking baby is you talking about?" "Who is the fuck is this on my bitch phone?"

Never mind who I am be more concerned about why I'm on my woman phone. "I don't know who you are boy, but you're on my woman phone talking real reckless." Hold up partner, I ani't cha boy! But I take it that you're the dude that don't know how to please your woman, right? Well, you should be calling and thanking me for coming out there and smacking all that ass for ya. Boy! "Bitch ass nigga, do you know who the fuck I am?" "Your mama gave you birth but you fucking with mine, I'll be the one who take life from you."

"Well, I see you good at putting fear into women, but since you're talking to a man, I'm not impress with all your phone threats talking bullshit nigga!" I'm from the A.T.L, so I ain't the tail tucking type of dude that you use to pumping fear in. So, you can handle your business whenever you like. "Oh! and one more thing before I go, because you caught me busy rubbing on some more ass but nothing like Stigma's, I'm telling you and Stigma this Boy! If anything, happen to my child that's in her stomach, the both of y'all better come up missing with my baby." Oh! And by the way my name ain't boy sucker! It's Deshawn. Click! He hung up in Supremes' face.

Supreme looked at the address and a furious uncontrollable demeanor overcame Supreme, he wanted to kill something like never before in life. Supreme couldn't believe that a broke nothing ass nigga just tried to antagonize him on the phone about Stigma. Telling him that he has his woman and son's mother pregnant, and nothing better happen to his child.

Supreme took the safety off of his gun and he went back into their bedroom. He took one look at Stigma and pointed the gun at Stigma's head. "You dirty rotten no good ass bitch!" Pow! Stigma had never jumped up so fast in her life. She turned over to see Supreme holding his gun in his hand. It didn't take her long to see that her cell phone and DeShawn's phone number were missing. "Dada, what's wrong, what are you doing baby?" Just as she said that Ms. Bergess and little Isaiah came rushing into their bedroom. Supreme come on son put the gun down, all this ain't worth you losing your life over. Ms. Bergess could see the pain and hurt in Supremes' eyes, and she knew that she had better say something fast.

Tears started to swell up in Supreme and Stigma's eyes, neither one of them thought that they would ever come to this moment.

BIG AND LITTLE SATAN

"You got one chance to tell me what I already know, are you pregnant with another man's baby?" Stigma just started shaking and crying, she looked at her son then Ms. Bergess because she knew that after what she say, that she may never see her son again.

Ms. Burgess spoke up, "Just tell the truth baby, don't lie. God is with y'all, he not about to let y'all leave this baby by himself. After Supreme heard her say that that's when he even realized that his son and Ms. Bergess was even in the room. Come on Preme, you're smarter than this son. If you don't want her, just walk away. Just walk away Preme, she not worth you losing your son, you know how much this boy loves you. Supreme turned and looked at Isaiah for the first time, and Isaiah said, "daddy don't hurt my mommy, and tears ran down his face." "Come on Supreme listen to your baby boy, he's right. Don't kill her Preme. God will fix this for y'all, trust me, but you got to use your head."

Supreme turned back to Stigma and she already knew that look and what he wanted to do. Ms. Bergess was praying and so was Stigma. She started praying a prayer that Ms. Bergess taught her as a child. "No weapon that is formed against me shall prosper; and every tongue shall rise up against me in judgement thou shalt condemn." She kept repeating that prayer and Supreme looked at her and started emptying the bullets from his clip. He placed one bullet in his hand and tossed the bullet to Stigma. She caught the bullet and they looked into each other's eyes and had a conversation without saying a word. Supreme tucked his gun in his waistband and walked out of the bedroom. Ms. Bergess said, Amen and Stigma jumped up off the bed and said Amen also.

Stigma tried to run after Supreme, but Ms. Bergess stopped her. Child, let that man be, give him time to calm down baby, he'll be back. Stigma and Ms. Bergess hugged each other, and Ms. Bergess just kept giving praise to God by saying Amen, Amen, Amen, thank you Jesus! Little Isaiah walked over and placed his arms around them and said Amen, thank you Nesus!

CHAPTER TWENTY-EIGHT
SHAKE DOWN

The Compton California police department was standing back and was watching the big boys do their job. Detective Middleton and the F.B.I were serving a search warrant on a little house next to the Compton Swap meet on Compton Blvd. They had been watching all the drug activities that had been going on in front and inside the home. But that's not what they were looking for, they have an 8x10 photo of Regina Washington who was GeeGee. Who had just died at the hands of Sergeant Hedgepeth back in Atlanta, Georgia.

The F.B.I was ready to move in on the home, but it was a crack head female that was walking into the yard. Her hair was all over her head, she was a light skinned female that was ninety pounds' soaking wet. Someone was yelling her name out. "Aye Star, let me get a bump bitch! After you cop, you know you still owe me from last time." Star was switching up to the front door, like she still had it when she was clean back when somebody gave her that Hollywood name. Just as the door open and she stepped inside the house.

"Everybody down, everybody down now!" Detective Middleton was asking all the questions. Ma'am, whose home is this? Everybody was looking all crazy, and nobody said nothing. "Ok we can take everybody in here to jail or we can make this real easy for everybody." We already know that y'all selling drug's out of this house, I'll assure y'all that's not my problem here to deal with. "The F.B.I don't serve search warrants on petty drug dealer's home's, that's your local police jive ass job not ours." So, the next time that I ask a question and don't get an answer, I'm hauling all of your asses off to jail and I'm boarding up this fucking house. Because I can clearly see that, it's in condemned condition. Star said, "Excuse me Sir!" I just got here and really don't know what's going on, but I surely can use a blast right now, can I just cop my stuff and go?"

Detective Middleton couldn't help but laugh at Star's sense of humor. "Ma'am, I'm sorry but this is not how this works. You don't just get to go and smoke drugs in the middle of an investigation. "Well can I just go back there in the back room; I got my Whoopi?" "Your what?" My Whoopi, my pipe man. Don't you know what a Whoopi is? That's a real man to me, can't no man please me like my Whoopi can. Detective Middleton asked her why she named her pipe Whoopi. Star said, "Because I put my dope in it and hit it and it makes my Ooogie Whoopiiiii!" All the F.B.I agents started laughing. Ma'am you really have your own way with words that only you can understand. But here's what I'll do for you so that I can do my job. "Come here! You go with that agent right there and she will help you out." "Ok! Ok! Star jumped up, Aye, can I cop that first thou?" The female agent grabbed her by the arm and took her outside to search her.

Which one of you is Ms. Jean? A big fat heavy set black lady with short hair said, "That's me Sir." Detective Middleton said, "Yea I kinda figured that." It was two other females and three men; they were all sitting on the floor around a bunch of broken candles and drug paraphernalia. Detective Middleton told everybody to listen up. "Whoever don't live in this house, I'm going to give you ten seconds to leave the premises." "Don't never come back to this house ever again, I promise you if you do, the next officer that catch you, they won't be as nice as me." The whole room cleared in zero point two seconds. Leaving only Ms. Jean and some skinny man with pop bottle glasses. Ok, who are you Sir? "Aye man, that's my woman right there, I'm not about to leave here and let her go to jail by herself."

Detective Middleton said, "I don't know nothing about no Whoopi, but I do know that's a real man right there to me." The skinny man poked his chest out then he wiped his forehead because he was sweating like he was sitting in a sauna. Ms. Jean, how many kids do you have? I got three, why? "My kids are grown, ain't no kids up in this house. Why y'all running up in my crib like this? Me and Curtis ain't done nothing wrong to nobody. I'll admit that we have a drug problem but we ain't robbed nobody to get high. He get a check from SSI and so do I, man what's all this about? Do you know Regina Washington? "Yea I do, why?" "Who is she to you ma'am?" That's my oldest daughter. When was the last time that you saw Regina? "Man, I ain't saw my daughter in six years."

Detective Middleton turned and looked at the other agents that were just standing around. He knew that Ms. Jean wasn't lying to them from looking at the inside of her home. The clothing that they cut off GeeGee cost more than anything that was in the house. "Why are y'all busting up in here asking me about Regina for?" Is she in some type of trouble or something? "Ma'am I don't know how to tell you this, but your daughter tried to kill a Sergeant on the police force in Atlanta, Georgia." "What?" "Oh, my Lord No!" Not Regina, she ain't that type of girl. She will cuss you out in a heartbeat, but she ain't never tried to hurt nobody.

"Well ma'am, she fired several shots at the officer in return trying to save his life he fired shots back at her and she got hit twice." "What!" Ms. Jean jumped up. Where is my baby? "What hospital is she at?" Ma'am, ma'am, relax! "Man are you fucking crazy?" "You come running up in my house and talking about my daughter shot at some police officers, then say that she got shot, and I'm supposed to be calm?" "Man, you done lost your rabbit ass mind."

That pissed Middleton off, being as how nice he been to them, and she told him that he has a rabbit ass mind. "Ma'am she not in a hospital, I'm sorry, but she got killed in the shootout." Ms.

BIG AND LITTLE SATAN

Jean broke down and started crying, the older gentlemen went and consoled her. My Regina is dead, my baby gone. Detective Middleton quickly changed his mind as to her comment about him. He now saw a woman hurt, behind losing her child. He even went and gave Ms. Jean a hug, showing that he's still a human outside of his job. Detective Middleton asked Ms. Jean a few questions that he already knew the answer to, because it's very hard to answer any questions that you don't have an answer for. Ms. Jean had already said that she hadn't seen her daughter in six years, so it would be impossible to know anything about her. Detective Middleton switched it up and instead of asking her more questions, he just tried giving them advice. He told Ms. Jean that now would be a great time to change her life before the drugs place her in a coffin. But he also knew that those same drugs is what she was about to use to overcome her pain from losing Regina.

He gave her all the information on how to retrieve Regina's body from the police in Atlanta. Detective Middleton left and went to serve search warrants on two other addresses that they had on her. After searching those addresses, they turned out to be even worse than going to Ms. Jean's house. Both people living at the other residences didn't even know Regina Washington. But one of the apartments led to three people going to jail from being wanted for a drive by shooting at one of the high schools in Compton. After running through most of Compton neighborhood, the three men were apprehended.

CHAPTER TWENTY-NINE

NEVER HURT A WOMAN

arquan was being woke up by his sister Whitney, bro, bro, some white man is outside looking at your truck. Marquan jumped up to see who it was. "Damn! Where mama at?" She left for work already boy! Why? That's my sorry ass parole officer. "A-A-A don't be telling him nothing about me sis." If he ask who truck that is, tell him that our uncle Henry parked it there and left with his friend. "Uncle who?" "Girl, stop playing Whitney, say Henry!" Marquan who in the hell is that? Yo uncle right now, so just rock with it ok? Whitney started laughing, criminals what a life.

Mr. McKinnon knocked at the door and was looking around at the neighborhood. Marquan was brushing his teeth when he answered the door. Umm A-A Mr. McKinnon, how you doing? Good morning, come on in. "Can you excuse me for a minute?" Marquan pointed at his mouth. "Yea sure!" A few minutes later Marquan came back to his parole officer looking at the photos in the front room. He was already questioning Whitney because she walked in the living room. Good morning, Sir! "Oh, sorry about that, our little brother doesn't know how to put up his stuff." "You can have a seat; my brother should be right out."

Marquan walked in on them and extended his hand and Mr. McKinnon just left it there. "Have a seat, let's talk." Marquan looked at him like damn! This is my house and not your office punk. Damn! Do this dude got split personalities? "So, what you got for me Marquan?" His parole officer sat there twirling his handcuffs on his pointing finger. Marquan's mind told him to start beating the shit out of his parole officer and jump in his truck and take off. But Marquan thought that he better not over think the situation and see why he had his handcuffs out. Marquan already made it up in his mind that he wasn't going back to nobody's prison. "Marquan, have you been on any jobs yet?" That caught Marquan off guard, and he wasn't expecting him to say that." Um Yea! My mom be taking me when she can, and I took the bus twice. "Where did she take you and where did you go?" Whitney looked at Marquan, hell even she wanted to hear this one. I put applications in at Walmart, Fry's and he named a few other stores that Whitney took him to.

Whitney almost busted up laughing, so she told Mr. McKinnon that it was nice meeting him and she walked out the room. Whitney couldn't even look at Marquan, or she knew that she would have blown it for Marquan. Marquan told his parole officer everything that he felt he wanted to hear. Marquan even told him that the truck belonged to his uncle because Mr. McKinnon sure asked about it. Marquan was praying like hell that he didn't take down the license plate, because it damn sure was coming back to a Marquan Burton.

That would be Marquan's first time getting caught in a lie since he been home. His parole officer accepted what he had to say about the truck and his job searching and didn't say no more about it. But he did tell Marquan that he'll be checking on those applications that he put in those stores. His parole officer also told him that he'll be back to see him soon, but he didn't say when. He told Marquan to stay out of trouble and he left.

Whitney gave Marquan hell after his parole officer left their house. She told Marquan that he better go fill out those applications before his parole officer goes and checks. But before Whitney said anything, Marquan was already thinking the same thing also. After they talked about his fake jobs that they knew he didn't have, Marquan and Whitney started talking about all the women that he now has in his life. Whitney was two weeks away from having her eighteenth birthday. Marquan wanted her to know what men thought about women and how they think. He wanted to be sure that Whitney knew how to carry herself around them.

Marquan knew that she wasn't having sex because their mother had done a great job raising her. But to Marquan's surprise what he thought was an innocent little girl, she has developed into a woman right before his eyes. Whitney asked her brother, what's wrong with men that they have to have sex with a lot of women? "Marquan, does that enhance their sexuality as being a man?" Marquan was so shocked that he didn't even know how to respond to her question. Whitney told Marquan if she was a man that she would feel more comfortable just having one woman. Because at least she would know her body and who she sleeps with.

Marquan don't you know that if one of them girls give you a disease, you won't even know who burt you and you'll give it to the other ones. "Because you know Bro, you will become the one carrying the disease to affect everyone else." Women is a trip too Bro, they just want to relieve that tension just like a man and they don't care who they burn. After you lay down with the next woman, think about what I just said, it might save your life. That word pussy just sounds good, but they ain't all that good bro!

"Marquan, you are telling me that you got all these women, does that mean that you're sleeping with all of them?" "Bro, don't give me no bullshit, because I'm a woman, if you ain't pleasing them then somebody got to be." A woman gone get that love box pleased somehow, don't let no woman fool you. "Marquan looked at Whitney like who are you sis?" How do you know so much about women, men, and sex? Marquan asked Whitney was she having sex. Whitney said, "Naw Bro, I wouldn't want to call it that." But I am a woman, and my hormones flare up just like the next man or woman. Let's just say

I've allowed a few women the opportunity to tongue kiss the kitty. "What! You a dyke Sis?"

"Nope! I'm a woman and love men Bro, mainly because of you Marquan." But I haven't found or saw a man that respects himself or women to invite him to swim in a luxury pool. Right now not even you Marquan , you kinda messy to Bro and I didn't expect that from you. Because coming from where you just came from, you have had plenty of time to make responsible decisions. "I'll never be nobody's motel that they think that they can check in and out of me when they fell like it." Marquan, whenever I do decide to allow a man to sleep in this mansion trust and believe me Marquan he'll know how to keep it up and he won't put his feet on nothing. Marquan started laughing. Bro but he will know how to put his coat down so that I can walk over the puddle and not get wet." Marquan, but until that time comes remember that cat's do shed a little fur here and there. But dogs catch fleas and ticks. I'm not the one to allow somebody to suck the blood out of me. The only way that will happen is I'm on my cycle and she is into that type of shit but I won't be getting played in the process of her pleasing me Bro.

Marquan couldn't believe that Whitney had grown up so much. He didn't just hear it; he could also see it in her swag. But he guessed that it was apart of him that just couldn't see it in the way Supreme saw Snooty. They are their little sisters but when they grow up, they turn into women and that's when you got to step back. Allowing them to become the women that there already are.

BIG AND LITTLE SATAN

Whitney said, "Marquan can I ask you a question bro?" "Yea Whit you can ask me anything sis." If you had to let all your girls go right now, which one would you keep? Marquan got quiet, he never even thought about them like that. "Yea the one that I'd put my all into would be Impression." That's a cute name. I like that name Marquan. But let me tell you something that you ain't going to like or want to hear. "What's that sis?"

"Be careful Marquan! Because the one that you chose is going to be the one that hurts you." "What?" "Naw, that's crazy sis, see that's where you still got a little growing up to do." Whitney said, remember one thing in this conversation. What's that! You ain't talking to no man or woman that you're involved with. But you are talking to a woman that love you Marquan and you don't got to do nothing to win me over. "Having the same blood already done that for us." When a woman wants you Marquan, then she'll let you know. No Bro wait! You better listen, she put her hand up. "Marquan, she will let you use her, hurt, runover her, cause her pain, but it all depends on how much using, hurt, pain, and running over her that you did." Well its just one thing you need to know about a woman, Marquan. There's nobody on this earth that can hurt you Marquan worst than a woman can. Everything that you teach and show her, one day she gone put it back on your ass and if you ain't that man that you claimed to be, then Marquan you'll definitely turn into all those bitches that you ever called her.

Marquan's mind went straight to the day that he met Impression when she said I must warn you that I can be a bitch at times. Marquan jumped up and hugged Whitney. Thanks Sis, I think you just saved me. "Girl, I think that I need to talk to you more often." "Marquan did you understand anything that I just told you?" "Yea! I did Whitney." Then tell me in your own words what it is that you think I'm trying to say. I could be wrong, but it sounds like you're saying don't mistreat the women that I give my heart to because if I do in the end, she's going to hurt me, more than I ever hurt her. And the most important thing is, until a woman hurts me, I'll never truly love her until I experience my own pain. Whitney stood up and gave Marquan a high five. Bro I'm not saying not to drag them hoes, but I am saying keep your feelings out of it. Because when the feelings come in and a woman is involved with her feelings then remember Eve tricked Adam way before man did woman. "Sis I ain't got to worry about you at all." Whitney said, "I already know bro, because I'm something like a pimp." Marquan tackled her to the floor and started tickling her. Marquan knew that his sister was game tight and whatever happened to her was because she was allowing it to happen.

CHAPTER THIRTY
THANK YOU NESUS

S tigma sat on the bed and thought about the biggest mistake that she had made in her life. Besides allowing Supreme to sleep with her and her girlfriend after the club that night she got pregnant with her son Isaiah. Stigma was in a deep sleep dreaming about the wonderful sex that her and Deshawn had back in the suite. She was about to return the favor that Deshawn had just given her sending her mind into space and her body into ecstasy. But she heard a loud voice overpowering the beat that her heart was making from passionate love making with Deshawn. The last thing in her dream that she heard was, "you dirty no good bitch!" "That's when Stigma thought that all that killing that they have done was coming back to haunt her laying right there in her own bed." That quickly made her think about Isaiah and her unborn child.

That mother's instinct made her jump. Pow! When Stigma eyes opened and she could see clearly what was going on, Supreme was standing over her with bloodshot eyes and was still yelling at her. "Bitch I'll kill you; don't you know that I'll take your life?" Stigma all that I've done for you, this is how you repay me by going and getting pregnant? Stigma was about to try and lie her way out, but she looked at her bed and could see a hole put there by Supremes' gun. That's when she realized that her cell phone and Deshawn's number were missing from the bed. "Damn! How could I have been so stupid to fall asleep with that number in my hand?" Stigma started backing up the bed moving towards the headboard. "Wait! Wait! Supreme please baby, don't kill me."

"What the fuck was you thinking, Huh! You stupid bitch!" "Today you and that nigga baby gone die and then I'm going to find him so that y'all all can be one big happy family." Supreme pointed the gun at her and Stigma knew that she was about to die. She closed her eyes and started saying the first prayer that Ms. Bergess taught her. Lord, no weapon formed against me shall prosper, and every tongue that shall rise against you in judgment you shall condemn. Just as she said that prayer, Ms. Bergess and Isaiah came running into their bedroom.

"Supreme No! No! baby, please don't kill that girl." Stigma opened up her eyes and said Thank You God, Thank You. Ms. Bergess get my son out of here and Stigma started crying and to her and Supreme surprise Little Isaiah ran to his mama and hugged her. "Don't cry mommy, what's wrong mommy?" Supreme was so hurt that he wanted to blow Stigma's head right off her shoulders.

BIG AND LITTLE SATAN

But Supreme couldn't do it, not in front of their son. "Come on Preme, let's talk this out son, it's not worth losing your son; he need you and his mother." She made a mistake, but don't you make one here today. "Let me have the gun please, Preme; let me have the gun son." Supreme stared at Stigma like he was deeply, deeply thinking about still pulling the trigger.

But when he heard Little Isaiah say daddy don't kill my mommy. "Supreme looked at his son and pushed the clip out of the gun, then he ejected the bullet out the chamber." Supreme handed the clip to Ms. Bergess and then he tossed the bullet out the chamber to Stigma. Supreme placed his gun in his waist band and walked out of their bedroom. Stigma jumped up off the bed, Supreme! Supreme! Come back Dada. Ms. Bergess stepped in front of her, leave him alone child, leave him be and let him clear his head.

Stigma hugged Ms. Bergess and they both started crying and thanking God. "Thank you, Jesus! Thank you, Jesus! Little Isaiah walked over and hugged them both, and he repeated what he heard them saying. Thank you Nesus! Thank you Nesus!

CHAPTER THIRTY-ONE
I LOVE YOU

Marquan was at the carwash getting his truck washed; he always made sure that it stayed just as clean as the day Cadillac put it together. His cell phone was starting to ring but he didn't know it, because he had left his cell phone in his truck, and he was sitting in the lobby watching some old man complain about them not honoring his rain check. Marquan was cracking up laughing. When the lady behind the old man cell phone started ringing, that's when Marquan realized that he didn't have his cell phone.

"Aye big hommie this you?" "Yea that's me." "Damn! Pimpin ain't easy is it?" But I see you doing it swell big hommie. Marquan gave him a head nod; Aye make sure you take care of me, and I got you! All fo show big hommie, I gotcha! Marquan smiled at the young dude and reached into his truck for his cell phone. "Damn!" I missed eight calls. He started looking at his missed calls and six of them were from Emoni. Damn! She is blowing me up and one of the calls was from Impression, that made him smile. He looked at the last missed call and it was from Supreme. "Man, what this dude want?" Supreme hadn't said anything about another job when they came back in town. Marquan didn't think that calling him back wasn't all that important, so he pressed redial on Emoni's number. Emoni answered on the second ring, and she was breathing real hard.

"Baby what's up, are you ok?" Emoni was crying and talking so fast that Marquan could hardly understand her. "Wait! Wait! Baby slow down, I can't understand you." He, he, he tried to grab me and put me in his car. "Who? Tone, Tone did." Aye, where you at? I'm at the house, but I'm about to be late for work because he out there in the parking lot. I'm on my way. Wait! Wait! Please baby don't hang up, stay on the phone with me. Okay, I'm here! I'm right here, I'm right here Emoni, don't worry.

Marquan started running fast as he could towards his truck and the young dude was already waving for his ticket. Marquan reached into his pocket and gave the youngster a fifty-dollar bill. Aye, thanks big hommie! He started jumping up down and like he had hit the lottery.

Marquan burned rubber as he was leaving the carwash. He was running red light after red light trying to keep Emoni calm. He wasn't that concerned about the police stopping him because he has a driver's license now. "Baby, where your gun at?" Right here in my hand. "Why didn't you use it when he tried to grab you?" He caught me off guard, cause I was trying to get in my car and he popped up from nowhere. I don't know where that man came from baby. He grabbed my mouth to stop me from screaming and he was pulling me backwards. "My purse was on my arm so I used my car key to stab his hand, it must have hurt because he let me go." Then I started swinging and punching at his face. He tried to pick me up, but I put all my weight low to the ground just like you showed me baby. Marquan was smiling listening to her praise him, that's when we both fell on the ground. "Baby I started screaming, but I jumped up to my feet and tried to run." But his punk ass grabbed me again, that's when he got his car door opened and tried to put me in it.

"I knew that if I let him put me in that car, baby nobody wouldn't never see me again." He already told me when he gets out that he was going to kill me. So how did you get away? "Wait! Wait! Baby, I'm about to tell you." His face have to have a long scratch across it, because I put my Lexus key hard across his face. "He yelled awwwwe and grabbed his face and that's when I knew that I hurt him bad, so that's when I took off running." Baby I use to run track in high school and I knew that his slow ass couldn't catch me, plus some white man came out his apartment and was telling him that he about to call the police. That's when he jumped into his car and I ran into the house and tried to call you baby, you didn't answer me, that's when Emoni started crying again.

"Naw baby! When you called me, I was at the carwash getting my truck washed." Aye don't trip cause I'm turning into your complex right now; you can come outside now. "No! No! Baby he might still be out there." Trust me, if he out here I'm about to take his life. What he driving? A blue Cadillac car with four doors, it's not new like yours, baby, it's older.

"Emoni, so do you trust him or me?" "I trust you baby, why would you say that?" In an angry tone of voice Marquan said, "because I told you to come outside Emoni and your ass ain't out here!" "Ok! Ok! Baby I'm sorry Ok!" Click! Marquan hung up in her face. Emoni finally came outside looking around like she had taken a good blast of cocaine. She was looking in every direction for Tone and his car. Emoni quickly rushed over to Marquan, and she ran into his arms.

"Baby I'm so happy to see you, when did you come back?" Last night. He held her back and took in her attire. Emoni was wearing a Prada betty boop dress and Prada high heels. Her hair was pressed straight, hanging down her back. "You know your little boyfriend is really starting to piss me off." "What! He ain't my damn boyfriend, I hate that man baby and you know that." Marquan said, "Ok! Then we going to see just how much you hate him then, when I find his ass!" Marquan put an evil look in his eyes that Emoni ain't never saw before. "Baby I don't care what happen to that man and I hope that it happens soon, so that he can leave me the hell alone." His punk ass only seems to fight women, not no real man. Emoni be careful of what you ask for because that shit can come true. "Then make it come true then, fuck him!" Can you come in baby, I need to call my job, this fool about to make me lose my job. "Shit!"

Marquan grabbed his gun off the seat and locked up his truck. He started joking with Emoni. "So you mean to tell me that I go and teach you how to shoot a gun and then buy you one, then soon as somebody attack you, your crazy ass pulls out a car key and turn into a Lock Smith?" Emoni busted up laughing. "See that's why I miss you baby, your ass always making me laugh and smile." Damn, can a bitch have a kiss because you almost lost my key fighting ass? This man got my nerves up, please forgive me for cussing so much Lord? Emoni closed the door behind them and then she locked it.

When Emoni turned around, Marquan grabbed her and looked her in the eyes, "Emoni don't you trust me?" "Yea baby I trust you. You're the only person in this whole world that I trust." That's why when I was in danger, I thought to call you first, I didn't call the police, did I? Marquan kissed Emoni and she passionately kissed him back. Marquan cupped both of the cheeks of her ass and picked her up. Emoni wrapped her legs around him and grabbed his face with both of her hands. Marquan placed Emoni back on the floor but to his surprise she kept right on going down to her knees. Emoni unzipped his pants and licked the tip of his penis and that's when Marquan's manhood came alive and started to jump like it was listening to music and was trying to keep up with the beat.

BIG AND LITTLE SATAN

Emoni looked up at Marquan as she took him into her mouth, each stroke he just laid his head back and enjoyed her head game. Emoni was going from the bottom of his nut sack then back up to the tip of his shaft licking and sucking every inch of his manhood. Marquan couldn't think about nothing but the woman that was pleasing him. What Marquan wanted to experience and have dreamed about was in full effect. He grabbed a handful of her hair and ping pong her mouth moving her head from side to side. He could feel himself about to climax, but Marquan didn't want the fun to end there. He almost had to actually pry his penis away from Emoni's hand, because she was enjoying it like a Bomb Pop on a hot sunny day.

Marquan pulled her back up after reclaiming his penis out of her hand. He turned her around and started kissing her on the neck but was walking her towards the bedroom. They immediately started undressing each other removing piece by piece getting naked. Marquan walked her over to the wall in her bedroom and placed her hands on the wall like she was about to get frisked. Marquan slowly kissed her down her back and licked his tongue down the crease of her butt. Emoni started to moan to his touch, and he spread her legs and sat down on the floor backwards. Marquan spread Emoni's legs wide and he ducked under and ate her vagina like she was an all you can eat buffet. Emoni almost climbed the wall like a cat spotting a fierce dog coming her way. Ooooooo! Marrrrrquaaaan ohhhhhhh my goodness! "Baby, what are you trying to do to me?" This was a position that Emoni have never been in before with no man.

He allowed his tongue to play back and forth from her anus to her vagina and ran her body through like a car being rinsed and blown at a carwash. "Owwwww Weeeee Yeeeeees! Yeeeeeees! Ummmmm! Ummmmm! AAAAAAA! Ohhhhh! What the fuck is thisssss?" Emoni's stomach and vagina was flipping at the same time and Marquan had her by the waist and the back of her butt guiding her straight into his mouth. He cupped her butt and sucked on her clitoris and Emoni screamed and busted her juices, flushed out of her like bath water on to his chest. Ohhhhh! Owwwww! Marquan I'm cummmmminggggggg! Emoni's body got weak, and she almost fell, but Marquan wasn't about to let her fall. He licked at her berries and juices and Emoni's body jumped and jerked with every stroke of his tongue. Emoni's vagina was soaking wet, and her clitoris was the size of a baby thumb.

Marquan picked Emoni up in the air as he pushed his back up against the wall. After getting his balance, he turned her body to the wall, Marquan went back to work licking, sucking, and eating Emoni's vagina like she was the last supper. Emoni screamed Marquan name over and over again. "Mar! Mar! Mar! Marquan noooo! Noooo! Wait, wait, baby stoppppp! Owwwww Marrrrrr Quannnnn! Please baby, please stop, I can't take thisssss! Tears started rolling down Emoni's face, her body felt like never before in her life. Owwww! Weeeee! Daddy, daddy stop, daddy, I can't take it. "Yes! Yes! Yes! Daddy right there owww weee fuck daddy, yes right fucking thereeeee!

That's when Marquan heard the magic word, Daddy! And he was about to make sure that she knew he was her daddy for real. Marquan gently laid Emoni on the bed and she was already looking at him like he has robbed her of her whole adulthood. Marquan climbed in between Emoni's legs and placed her legs high up on his shoulders. Marquan wanted Emoni to feel his penis up in her back. He entered gently allowing their private parts to get to know each other by name. "Dickkkk! Pusssssssy! Hello! Emoni eyes opened up like she has just saw Tone walk into the bedroom but it was only the size of Marquan's penis. Marquan! Owwww! Daddy yessss! She closed her eyes and allowed her body to adjust to the pain and satisfaction. Emoni juices was ready to make another debut and she began to announce her arrival. "Daddy, I'm coming again damn! But this time Marquan sped up and started dog pounding her vagina. Just as she was climaxing, Marquan went deeper into her walls.

Marquan speeded up his rhythm and she opened her eyes because she wanted badly to escape the pain that yet felt so good to her body. "Daddy wait, noooo! Please stop daddy I can't take no more. I can't take it; no I can't take it stop!" Daddy, daddy, daddy, daddy! Uhhhhh! Ummmmm! Shittttt! Shitttttt! Shittttttt! Yeeeeeees! Emoni came and Marquan was just pounding away at her pussy. But now Emoni was starting to get used to the pain and suffering that Marquan was putting on her vagina. Emoni started throwing it back at him. "Come daddy beat it up, dog this pussy, it's yours ain't it?" Emoni turned over and got on her knees, come on give it to me. Marquan was giving everything that he had and Emoni started getting into his head. What's the matter daddy, you're not happy with this pussy, that's all the dick you going to give me? Marquan looked at her like what? Cum for me daddy stop playing in my pussy, what you don't want it? Ha! Ha! Is that it? Marquan grabbed Emoni by the waist and locked on her ass and pounded away until him or her couldn't breathe.

"Daddy, Daddy, Daddy, Daddy, no I'm sorry, daddy please stop!" Marquan was in a kill the pussy rhythm and that's all what was on his mind. Emoni was like the Southwest commercial, "Want to Get Away?" But she couldn't, Marquan was tearing a new section of penis into Emoni's vagina, and she had brung it on herself. "Daddddddieeee! Owwww daddddy! Here I come Babyyyyy! It was good because now Marquan was ready to meet her at the front door. The both of them was now making sounds and fuck faces. "Ohhhhhhh! Yes! Yes! Ummmmm! Ummmmm! Come on baby, cum with me, Cum with me. Marquan gave a few more strokes and they came like a volcano erupting. Emoni was letting Marquan know that the pussy was his. "It's yours daddy, it's your pussy! It's yoursssss!" The both of them exploded and Marquan fell over on top of Emoni, like he had got shot in the back. "Damn daddy! You know this your pussy man; you got my pussy over here throbbing right now." Emoni pushed Marquan up a little so she could see his face. Emoni kissed him and said, "I love you, Marquan. Please don't hurt me, ok?" "Baby I love you too, and I'll never hurt you Emoni." Emoni smiled and was happy that she chose Marquan.

Emoni was in the kitchen cooking fried chicken and french fries. The both of them were hungry, after their hot sexual performance. Emoni held her cell phone in one hand while she moved the french fries around from sticking to each other. The phone started to ring and after Emoni answered it her boss came on the line. Emoni started giving her boss some lame story that she really didn't have to because he had a crush on Emoni, and her job wasn't no way in jeopardy. But she did promise him that she would be in on time to work tomorrow. Her boss said something sexual, but Emoni just laughed and didn't respond to his comments. Marquan was sitting at the table, and she didn't want him to know that she was fucking her boss. Ok Kevin, thank you for understanding and she ended their call.

"Everything good baby?" Yea! She lied. My boss was still trying to get me to come to work. He said that I picked a busy day not to come in. Emoni started telling Marquan about the Native New Yorker restaurant. Marquan promised her that he and Supreme would come eat there one day. Marquan started telling Emoni about Supreme and how they use to deal drugs together before his own girl turned them in to the police. "What baby! Your own girl snitched on y'all?" That's why you had to serve twelve years in prison? "Yea" That bitch screwed up a good thing but that's the pass and this the future, us. She looked Marquan into the eyes, is it really Marquan? She was looking over her shoulders to hear his response. "Yea baby! Those days are long gone." Good Marquan cause' I'm cool on that lifestyle.

That's why the fool is trying to kill me know. "Why is that?" "Because I guess that he feels like that I snitched on him, but I didn't baby." Emoni went and sat across from Marquan at the table. "Marquan I'll never try to hurt nobody that I love, nor will I help no white men make money off you by watching you sit in prison." "Marquan, trust me if I wanted to snitch on him, I knew way too much about him to put him away for life then to walk in court about an ass whooping. Baby you can look my name up now. "I'm Emoni Rena Murchison born 5/21/85." Marquan my name ain't on nobody courtroom papers or snitch list. Marquan said, "Yea! They on somebody courtroom papers if he went to jail." "Yea you right baby, but you know what I mean not with me snitching on him thou."

I keep it one hundred with my man and I'm not a cheater either. "You a hustler just like Tone was Marquan and I'm a woman that know my place that's one thing my mother taught me." My daddy cheated on my mother all the time when he was in the streets. Before they became Christians, I use to ask my mother why you allow him to cheat on you and she gave it to me like this. "Emoni a dog is going to be a dog that's his nature, but there's good dogs and there's bad dogs." "Your daddy is a good dog, he protects me and his home, we don't want for nothing up in here." Whatever he gets out of those streets and women that he leaves me to go sleep with, baby I don't know if he's sleeping with, a Chow, German Shepherd, or a Collie. "Because he makes sure that they don't knock on that door at any time." He ain't never brung me anything in this house, that he ain't left here with.

Baby let me tell you one thing about that Pit Bull. "No matter what he does or where he goes Emoni, he always knew how to find his way home and home is with us baby." So let me tell you a little something about this bitch, which is also a female dog. "Those bitches out there had to wait on him to come to them or was riding around looking for your daddy." "Me baby! I left a scent on his nose that kept his nose up my ass because at all times of the night and at the end of the night that's where his nose still was up my ass baby!" Real dogs mark their territory by pissing in a spot on the floor, but me Emoni. I leave my mark on his face and penis. "So Emoni, ain't no woman's vagina or piss strong enough to stop that man from being in this house or my bed at the end of the day." Your daddy stays barking in this yard when anything gets too close to you or me. "Yea mama vagina scent did that Emoni, I'm that type of bitch that when the dog catcher catch me baby, he takes me to his house and not to the dog pound."

Emoni, even a bad dog can be trained, but you got to have that right scent for him to want to follow you and know where home is.

"Every dog can eat out of any bowl, but until you train him not to put his nose into any bowl, he'll always stay sticking his nose into trash cans and eating vaginas that a give his ass Parvo." Big dogs and smart dogs know that, when his meal is cooked his ass better be there to eat it. "Emoni, you don't know that they killed unwanted dogs at the dog pound every day, so it's best to stay wanted in a happy home." Marquan said, "Emoni your mother must have been a woman to die for?" Trust me, she was!

"Marquan I've been laced by the best, it ain't nothing that you can teach me that I don't already know." "Marquan, you thought that you pulled me daddy, but it was the other way around I pull you." You didn't talk your way into my life, or my bed trust me. I can open my front door right now and allow you to keep on going. But I see that you're a dog, that will protect your woman and home, so I had to teach you to find your way home. "Marquan said, "Emoni if I didn't think that you would be mine or that this would be my home then I wouldn't have been here either way." "I know a woman when I meet one, because I came from one, but I only saw her act like a woman and not a bitch!"

He gave Emoni a supercilious look. "Emoni, remember when we were in the store?" "Yea, how could I ever forget that day, but what about it?" "My mother had two children in that store not just one, me and Whitney." Remember, almost at the same time, me and my sister said that our mother would love you Emoni. Emoni smiled, yea the both of y'all did say that. "Emoni, I ain't never took a woman to meet my mother before, but I wouldn't hesitate to take you to meet her." In fact, she already told me to invite you to dinner. Emoni started crying, "Marquan, I'll never disappoint you or your family, just can you promise me one thing?" "Yea what's that Emoni?" Emoni went and sat on his lap, facing Marquan where she could look him straight in the eyes.

"Marquan promise me that you'll never hurt me?" Marquan said, "I promise you Emoni Rena Murchison that I'll never hurt you baby." Emoni kissed Marquan in a way that she had never kissed him before. Emoni stood up and went back to cooking their food. "Aye daddy! I'm not a jealous woman, you do know that right?" Marquan said, "nope, not that I can't speak on because I ain't never put you in that type of situation yet." Well daddy, what if I told you that I know that you're sleeping with more women than just me? Marquan started laughing. Then Emoni, I'd say that you must be a psychic or something.

"OK! so are you saying that you're not?" "Wait daddy before we go any further or you say the wrong thing because daddy, I hate liars. I can't stand them, nor can I trust them." "Daddy, you just promised me that you wouldn't never hurt me, right?" Marquan, the love and respect that I have for you, I can only expect the truth coming from you. "No lies please, Marquan!" Marquan looked at Emoni like are you trying to use some type of reverse psychology on me or something to get me to tell on myself? "Damn! Whatever she's doing the shit must be working on my ass." Because I can't lose Emoni, she a real woman, fuck! "Yea I am Emoni, so is this where you tell me that it's over between us?"

Emoni walked over to the table and sat their plates on the table. "No Marquan, why would I tell you that after just telling you that I love you?" Damn, what you think that I'm crazy or something, now? "Nope!" I just know what I just confessed to about sleeping with other women. "Naw daddy, we really good now!" I just wanted to see if you would tell me the truth or lie. "Snooty and Star!" Hearing those names Marquan almost fell out his chair. "Oh Marquan, you didn't think that I knew about your little strippers?" Marquan said, "damn Emoni are you a psychic?" Emoni busted up laughing. "No Marquan I ain't psychic, but what I ain't about to do is get hurt by nobody else." When you have feelings for someone the way that I do you, it's just important to know what you're getting yourself into. "Now, Mr. Man, can I bless our food before it gets cold?" While Emoni and Marquan ate their food, Marquan asked Emoni about Tone. He wanted to know where he hung out and the people that he knew. Emoni told him everything that she knew about Tone, plus about his family and friends.

CHAPTER THIRTY TWO

DEEPER THAN THE EYES CAN SEE

S upreme had called Marquan over a dozen times and Marquan still hasn't returned none of his calls. Supreme was so mad at Stigma that he was ready to fly to Atlanta and blow Deshawn's head off his shoulders. He was pushing his S550 Mercedes Benz down the freeway at 80 miles an hour on a 55-mile highway. Supreme tried Marquan again and got no answer and that pissed him off even more than he already was from Stigma's bullshit. What Supreme didn't know was, Marquan was at Emoni's putting down his sexual performances in the bedroom. Supreme was thinking what if it was a life and death situation and he really needed Marquan. He was replaying things in his head. Hey man I was about to die and really needed you and you didn't answer my calls.

He could hear some lame ass excuse. "Oh, Supreme I was sleep or fucking your sister, I'm sorry I missed your call bro." Supreme could see him shooting Marquan right in the face and that made him grip the steering wheel hard and bite down on his teeth. Supreme knew whatever was going on, Marquan better have a damn good excuse for not answering his calls.

Supreme decided to stop by Marquan's mother's house, just to see if his truck was parked there. When Supreme pulled up, Marquan's sister, Whitney was getting out of a Nissan Maxima wearing a Baby Phat pink and white two-piece short set suit. Her hair was pressed hanging just past her shoulders. Whitney 5'9 a hundred and thirty-five pounds 36dd with a 24-inch waist with an apple pie 38 inch rising still back side. Whitney was looking so grown and sexy, that Supreme didn't even know who she was. He just kept his eyes on the words, that said Baby Phat across her ass. "Damn! who is that?" The last time Supreme saw Whitney she was only six year's old.

Whitney really didn't know Supreme all that good, because the night that Marquan came home from prison and took them the money. Supreme stayed in the car, because he knew how Marquan's mother felt about him plus, they were in a rush. Whitney heard all the stories, about all the money that him and her brother use to have and made selling drug's. That's what caused her to grow up, without her brother in her life. Whitney's girlfriend said, "Damn Whitney! Your brother riding like that? Can you introduce me to him?" "Girl he must have just bought that car, I'm about to steal that one now that's me right there." "Ok Marquan now you are stepping your game up, yea come meet him girl." The female jumped out of her car real fast, wait!

Vicky started fixing her clothes, she was wearing a white mini-skirt and a half top Fendi shirt white and pink with white Nike's. Whitney was walking towards Supreme on the Driver's side. Supreme rolled down his window, we'll hello there, beautiful ladies. Y'all must be looking for the same person I'm looking for?

Vicky said hello! Owwwww! Girl, your brother is fine, damn! Whitney you're not going to introduce us. "Hello Marquan, I'm Vicky, your sister's best friend." "Oh! I'm sorry Ms. Lady what did you say that your name was?" Vickyyyy! "Well Vicky my bad, but I'm not Marquan, I'm his best friend Supreme." Whitney placed her hand over her mouth. "Oh my God you're Supreme!" "Yea, the last time I checked I was." Supreme, you don't know who I am do you? I'm sorry, no I don't, but who are you beautiful? Supreme, I'm Whitney, Marquan's little sister. "What! You're bullshiting me?" "Supreme opened up his car door, girl if you don't come here. When he stood up, Whitney and Vicky almost passed out, when they got to see Supreme whole body."

When Whitney hugged Supreme and took in his Cologne, Supreme had to separate them because Whitney could have stayed in his arms forever. "Girl! I mean woman I'm sorry look at you Whitney, you grew up to be so beautiful." "Thank you, Supreme!"

If Whitney was white, her cheeks would be bright red right now. Damn! Can I get a hug too. Supreme laughed and he hugged Vicky too, oh my God, man you smell so good, can I ask where you been all of my life? Supreme said, "trying to win little mama." "Well, it looks like you already won from where I'm standing." Whitney said, "Where is Marquan, Supreme, I thought that he bought him a new car." This is nice Supreme; can I drive it? Yea, sure! Can you drive Whitney? Yea man, I can drive. Aye, speaking of your brother, have you seen him today? Yea I was talking to Marquan about all his woman earlier. Supreme handsome as you are, I know you got a bunch of women too, don't you? "Naw! Too many women at one time will drive you crazy." Vicky said, "I won't drive you crazy, Supreme." Whitney looked at her watch. "Girl, you better go pick your mama up. It's 4:30 Vicky." "Oh yea, girl I'm tripping, and I don't want to hear her mouth either." I do gotta go Supreme, I hope that I see you again. Are you coming to Whitney's birthday party? Oh, it's your birthday, Whitney? Yea it is and no girl this man ain't coming to my Birthday Party. He is way too busy for that. Well, you never know, I just might show up.

"Well, I guess it would be rude if I don't at least buy you a gift." Vicky shouted out, "Forget that gift girl, take his fine ass!" "Girl bye!" "Ok I love you Whit, I'll call you later." They hugged and kissed each other on the cheek. "Girl, that man is Fo'ineeeeee! You better get him before I do." Whitney playfully hit Vicky, bye, bye, byeeeee! Vickyyyy! "Supreme nice to meet you. You can hit it later." Supreme, please, please, forgive my crazy friend, that girl ain't wrapped too tight. "Naw, it's all good, it seems like she a lot of fun." So, Ms. Lady, how about that drive now? You were serious man, you really gone let me drive this car? Yea sure, let's go and Supreme headed to the passenger side.

"So Supreme, where are we about to go?" "How about we go and buy that gift now just in case I can't make it by your birthday party." What, Supreme stop playing. Are you really serious? Whitney didn't wait to see if he was, she put the car in drive and headed towards the mall. Supreme told Whitney to buy whatever she wanted, and she bought a pair of Milsta boots black that cost $370.00. Right at that moment Whitney was the happiest woman in the mall. "Thank you, Supreme. She hugged him, are you ready to go now?"

"Wow! This is the greatest day of my life, me and Vicky been waiting on these shoes but of course we can't afford them." "Whitney, so when is your Birthday?" In two weeks. "How old are you going to be?" Well, I'm still young Supreme. I'm only about to turn 18. Whitney put her head down and turned away from Supreme and he noticed that she felt ashamed about her age. Supreme turned her to him and placed his hand under her face and lifted it up. "Whitney, don't you never in life, let me see you put your head down again. You're a woman now and you're beautiful." Whitney looked at him and smiled. Thank you Supreme, you're so sweet. You're nice and inspiring, I like you Supreme, my mother got you all wrong.

"Thank you, but do you mind, if I buy you something for your birthday?" What are you talking about, you did just buy me something for my birthday. "Nope! That's what you bought yourself." Supreme, I'm not a greedy person, this is too much already. I don't even deserve this. "Whitney come with me, let me show you what you really deserve." Whitney reaches back and took Supremes' hand because he was holding his out. He took her and bought her a pair of Chloe Gusselin pumps that cost $662.00. Then he bought Whitney a dress by Mark Jacob's that cost $800.00. Whitney, that's what I want, to see you wearing on your Birthday. Whitney, just promise me one thing, "what's that Supreme?" While you're dancing with your boyfriend on one of them slow songs, just think about me?

Whitney started crying, "Supreme you gave me the best birthday of my life, nobody has spent this much money on me since I've been living, I'll always think about you." But I don't have a boyfriend sorry, so that won't be that hard, right? "I've never in my life been with a boy before, Supreme because the type of person that I am Supreme, a boy can't please me, only a man can." Supreme started smiling, "well Whitney that makes me even more happy now to hear you say that, now I know you are a woman." Well before we go, can I at least finish giving you your Birthday Gift? "Yea sure!" Supreme took her to Victoria Secret lingerie store.

"Hello, may I help you guys?" "Yea do you mind, if we look around at a few things?" "Sure, let me know if the lady like to try on anything and I'll unlock a booth for her." Thank you, ma'am.

BIG AND LITTLE SATAN

Supreme spotted just the outfit, that he wanted her to try on; it was a hot pink two-piece panties and bra set. Whitney had even seen one that she liked and then gave the outfit to the lady, can I try these on? The lady took Whitney to a booth and told her that she picked two good ones. Supreme was standing outside the door, can you fit it? "Yea! I love it Supreme; it fits me perfect." "Ok take it off, let's go buy it." Whitney said, "Supreme I can't take it off." Why Whitney, what's the matter, you done got it stuck? "Nope! Supreme how can I take it off and you haven't saw it on me yet?" "Come here, Supreme! He was about to decline but before he could, the door on the booth opened up and Supreme couldn't believe his eyes." Whitney pulled Supreme into the booth and started kissing him and when they unlocked lips, Supreme told himself; ok Marquan, you dished it out now part'na let's see if you can take it?

Supreme stepped back and took in her body, that looked like a bag of brand new one-hundred-dollar bills after just being pressed. "Damn! Whitney why did you do that, do you even know what you're getting yourself into. Are you ready for this?" A tear ran down Whitney's face. "Baby girl what's the matter?" "Nothing Supreme, you wouldn't understand no way. Why does everybody feel like they know what's best for me?" "When is anyone going to allow me, to show them what's best for me?" Supreme can I ask you a question? "Yea sure anything Whitney."

"Have you made any mistakes before?" Yea! Supreme laughed. I've made a lot of mistakes before, but that's all a part of life Whitney. But you got to experience them, to live through them, right? Yea, Whitney you're right. Then will you stop it and let me experience mine, if you really care about me then teach me how not to make mistakes. Supreme I'm a fast learner. Whitney looked at Supreme and smiled. "Whitney I definitely care about you, so that leaves us no choice but to teach each other, right?" "Wow! Now I really know that you're a real man, because any man, if he is one know that he has to learn from a woman Supreme, that's if he wants the best to come out of him." "Whitney, how you get so wise at such a young age?"

Because like you said earlier Supreme. "I'm a woman and I know what I want out of life and who I want in life I just need to know that he wants me back?" Supreme said, here's your answer to that, and he grabbed her and kissed Whitney cupping both cheeks of her ass, he massaged them in his hands and continued to passionately kiss her. They were interrupted by the lady working in the store. She said, "well I take it that you love the outfit and it fit's just fine?"

Supreme and Whitney busted up laughing. "Yes, ma'am we'll definitely take it." Supreme told Whitney that after she turns 19 in a couple of weeks, a lot is about to change in her life. "Whitney are you ready to make that change with me?" Whitney told Supreme all of her life, that she been waiting for a change, "Yes!"

Then Supreme looked her in the eyes and asked the main question that he needed to hear and know. "Whitney, so are you ready to choose me over your brother and your mother?" Whitney gave an answer that Supreme wasn't expecting to hear. Supreme, all of my life they have been choosing people over me. At the beginning and end of the day Supreme, that will always be my mother and brother. "But I can't stay sheltered under them all of my life, I got to grow up and be my own woman just like my mother did, right?" "My mother and I was just talking about me and Vicky getting us a place together."

"Trust me Supreme, I already know how my mother and brother feel about you, now they have to learn how I feel about you too." "Yes! I'll choose you over them, and after my Birthday what can they say about it, Supreme." I'll be 19 then, and it will be two adults making adult decisions. So, that means that it's going to come with a love it or hate it experience, but if you in it then I am to baby. Supreme sat back and was feeling better about Whitney than he was before. "Yea, you're right! I couldn't have put it no better then you just have myself."

Supreme pulled back up in front of Marquan's mother's house and Marquan's truck still wasn't there but Supreme really didn't care, his anger was gone. Whitney turned to Supreme, baby I need to know one thing before I get out of this car. "Supreme are you here for me or was that just you caught up in the moment from what you saw?" "Whitney, we like Bad Boys for life baby we ain't going nowhere, you mine now sexy." "That's all I needed to know, because I feel the same way about you too." Supreme, you are the one that got me feeling the way I do, not my mother or brother so you're the only one that can take this feeling away. "If you don't feel like you can handle this, then tell me now." "Yes, you got a nice car and all, but a car can't please me nor meet my needs, but you can Supreme." I'm not Vicki; Supreme, jocking you or your money and car. "I'm grateful for the Birthday gifts baby, but you would mean more to me then those gifts back there on your seat."

"Whitney, I've never in life got myself into nothing that I can't handle, trust and believe that." Besides, why do I have to say that, I want something that's already mine anyway? Whitney smiled and reached over and kissed Supreme. "Ok! Then nobody can't speak on mine either." Supreme and Whitney exchanged phone numbers and he told her that he be busy at times. But Whitney stopped him mid-sentence. Trust me, I know what type of man you are, until you place me where you want me, I got to roll with the punches. But to Supremes' surprise Whitney put her hand on his penis and said, "Baby just don't forget that its your woman's Birthday and I want the rest of my gifts." She grabbed her gifts and kissed Supreme and walked off.

Whitney stopped and turned around and walked up to him on the driver's side. "Ok! Busy man, you call me then, I won't call you baby, be safe and you can tell my brother yourself that you were looking for him and not me." Supreme said, "Whitney, why do I feel like that I'm going to be the one learning more from you then you from me?" Whitney slung one of her bags over her shoulder and said because you is Supreme and she walked towards the house. Supreme sat there and watched the words Baby Phat until Whitney disappeared into the house, then he drove off. Whitney walked into the house and laid her back up against the door. Yesssssss!

$$\$ \ \$ \ \$ \ \$ \ \$$$

The next morning Marquan called Supreme, and he almost didn't answer his phone call. Supreme haven't been home since he and Stigma's fall out and she have been blowing his cell phone up all night. Supreme was at SoSo condominium, she had finally got her keys to her massage parlor and wanted Supreme to see it. Plus, he had promised her that he would come and scratch her itch that her kitty was having. SoSo made sure Supreme didn't leave her, she whipped it on him at the massage parlor and the condo. Supreme woke up to his phone blowing up, like the World Trade Center, Stigma was calling back-to-back.

When Supreme finally answered his phone, it was Marquan returning his call's back. When Supreme asked about him not returning his calls, Marquan lied and said that he left his phone in a restaurant and had just remembered where he left it. Supreme was still half asleep and he told Marquan to meet him at the house in Chandler at 3:00 o'clock.

When Marquan pulled up, Supreme was already there waiting for him. Supreme was on a phone call with Papa Jack, he had finally got to recover GeeGee body from the police. That made Supreme happy to know that he has GeeGee's body, now he can bury her properly. But while they were on their call, Papa Jack did request that Sergeant Hedgepeth die real soon. Supreme told Papa Jack not to worry, that this one would be on the house. Papa Jack told Supreme that, he already had money switched to an account for them and that he needed to move it soon.

Supreme had already made plans to go back to Atlanta, to take care of business. But he knew that Whitney's birthday was tomorrow, and Marquan wouldn't have wanted to leave Phoenix. So, Supreme has made plans for him, Marquan and Persia to return back to Atlanta, Georgia in three days. Supreme also had made reservations at the M.G.M Grand in Las Vegas, he rented the Presidential suite. Supreme ended the phone call with Papa Jack and started talking to Marquan.

"Hey, what's good bro!" They gave each other dap and sat down to talk. Supreme had open up to Marquan about what she did, and Marquan couldn't believe what he was hearing. Marquan thought that Stigma was the main one, who had the girl's and Supreme business in order. But Marquan quickly learned that, when the big dog is out the kitty will go out and play. "Aye, so what you want to do about this sucker in Atlanta, shouldn't we kill two birds with one stone?"

Supreme said, "naw bro! I never mix business with pleasure." This Sergeant Headgepeth ain't business no more with me. It's going to be a pleasure to split his shit, Marquan. "But this pussy ass nigga with Stigma, bro done turned into me going to handle business." You know my motto, never let'em see you coming, and right now, I'm more then sure that this nigga on alert. I want to creep up on him and fuck the shit out of him like he says he done my bitch! After Supreme told Marquan about everything that was going on, Marquan begin to tell him about Emoni and Tone. Marquan told Supreme about, a plan that he came up with. But he was going to need Supreme's help with executing his plan. Supreme told Marquan that, it was a wonderful plan and would love to help out. He told Marquan that just like before he went to prison, people need to know who they are in those streets. That nothing that belonged to them, should be looked at or tampered with.

Supreme told Marquan that he had some more money for him and that he needed to set up an offshore account real soon. Just in case he ever ran into any problems, he'd always be able to reach his money. Supreme even suggested that he make it, where Whitney or his mother could get to his money. Supreme said that the type of money that they are having, he's going to have to trust somebody.

Marquan thought about what Supreme was saying and the first person that came to mind was Emoni. Marquan and Emoni were starting to get real close, Marquan was starting to feel a sense of comfort with Emoni. He and Emoni were even starting to talk about getting a home together. He finally opened up and told her everything that he was into with Supreme and the girls and about Snooty and Star. The only part that he left out was, that when he disappeared, that he was going to take someone's life. Emoni still didn't know that the man that she was getting close to, was a Hit Man.

Marquan has gotten over that murder conscious, to let the truth be told. He was starting to get a heartless conscious towards anything or anybody. Killing to Marquan now was like taking his truck to be washed, he just had to get it done. The same way that he was sitting around to claim his vehicle, is the same way that he sat around to claim his prey.

Supreme wanted badly to talk to Marquan about Whitney, but he thought that it would be too soon to mention that they were a couple. Besides the truth to the fact was, Supreme really wanted to see that same look in Marquan's face that he put on his back at that church. Supreme was just hoping that Marquan would respond in a fucked-up way, so that he could put Marquan right where he saw his buddies laying in a coffin. "Marquan asked Supreme who was he taking with them to handle the Hedgepeth situation?" Supreme told him that he thought that Persia would be perfect for what he had planned.

Marquan said, "Yea she nice with that pistol and plus she got that look that will make any angry dog stop barking just to see her walk by." Supreme started laughing and he complimented Marquan on knocking Star. "You got yourself a little Barbie Doll there Marquan. I know she is giving Sabrina a run for her money?" "Shit! Even Stigma thought that she was sexy, you got her out of the same strip club that Sabrina work at?" "Yep! Man I can't go up in them strip clubs, it be too much pussyyyy up in them joints, that shit be driving me crazy." They busted up laughing. Marquan told Supreme, man that ain't shit! Man, I need to take you to this place called Club Excalibur. Supreme, it's so many extravagant females up in that place, and they getting major paper in that club.

"Supreme them fools is throwing $50s- and $100-dollar bills on that stage." "What! just to see some bitch shake her ass?" "Yep! But peep this, I noticed one thing thou." What's that? It's mostly white girls that's working up in that place. Supreme, damn near all of them look like Persia. Man, I bet if she worked in there, she would come home with a few thousand a night. "Supreme said, "Shit! If I sent Persia up in there, I guarantee you that she'll come out of there with more than a few thousand a night." Because Persia will go up in there and rob all of them tricks with that pistol. Marquan and Supreme started laughing. "Well shit that ain't nothing either, I saw that happen in the club Snooty and Star work at." What! Supreme really didn't care about him saying that the club got robbed. It's when Marquan said where his sister work at. "Yea, man my girls got robbed just the other day."

When Marquan said my girls, Supreme bit down on his teeth. It was like he was referring to Snooty like she was one of his Prostitutes or something. Supreme played it off, who robbed the club? "Some niggas and a female came in there and laid everybody down." "Whoever the female was I couldn't see her, because when they walked Big Chub in the club, the female was already masked up." I tucked my money in the bathroom, but they robbed my girls for their money. Supreme gritted his teeth together to stop from cursing Marquan out. "Here my sister getting robbed and this fool up here talking about losing some money, what about my sister's life?"

Supreme told himself that it was about time that he went and paid Sabrina a little visit. Their mother is dead and Supreme is all that Snooty got. He promised his mother that he would take good care of Sabrina. Now here go the same nigga that he been holding down, come home from Prison and start pimping his little sister out to trick's in a strip club. Supreme looked at Marquan and smiled. "Man looks like you done took back to the streets like a fish to water?" "Yea! It's been good, Supreme, thanks to you bro." Him and Supreme shook hands and hugged each other. Supreme was glad to hear him say that Supreme opened the front door for him. "Hey man, let's go get something to eat, I still ain't got to push that truck that I bought you yet."

Marquan didn't read the tension that was there in Supreme's voice. Life was starting to look up for Marquan and problems seemed to just start for Supreme. Marquan threw him the keys to his truck. Oh Yea! Supreme look, I got my driver's license, now we can get that paperwork straight now. "Yea! Yea! Let's do that before I kill that bitch! Marquan started laughing, Stigma damn, what was she thinking?"

CHAPTER THIRTY-THREE
HAPPY BIRTHDAY

G ood morning, Birthday girl! "Happy Birthday baby girl, you know your mama loves you?" Ms. Housemoore kissed Whitney on the cheek. "Oh, hey mama!" "Thank you, I love you too, mama" Here, open it! Ms. Housemoore handed Whitney two boxes. "All mama you didn't have to do this, you give me a gift everyday by keeping a roof over my head." Ms. Housemoore smiled, Thank you baby but it's your birthday, you're always considerate towards your mama, see that's why I love you baby. "I never have to worry about you, but your brother, child that's another story." They both started laughing. "Ok! Mama, give my brother a break at least he trying to do better."

"Oh I forgot to tell you that, his parole officer came by the house." "He did!" Where was Marquan, gone? No mama, he was here. Marquan talked to him; it seemed like it went pretty good. But he told Marquan to find a job. "Child, if he wants Marquan to get a job, hell he better give it to him himself." That boy ain't about to worry me no more. That's good mama because the more you are against him, the more resentful he's going to be. "I don't know what happened to y'all, but you should have been born first." Maybe then that boy would have gotten some sense. All mama this is nice, can you put it on for me? Ms. Housemoore bought her a diamond neckless with a diamond letter W. "Mama you sure that you can afford to give me this?" "Child I work every day and the police ain't going to come take it from you." "You know Whitney?" "Because it's paid for so don't take it off your neck." Because if you do, I might pick it up and take it down to one of the pawn shops if my money get low. Whitney and her mother busted up laughing.

Whitney opened up her other box and it was a valor sweat suit by Gucci. All mama this is nice right here. "Yea! I knew that you would like it child, since you always showing off your little body to them boys." "No, I don't mama!" Yea don't think that I don't be seeing you child. Hey if you got it then you got it and God has blessed you in that department. "I figured that you would want to have something on nice at your Birthday party." "Speaking of which girl, don't you let your wretched little friends tear up my house." "I get off at eleven o'clock and I want those people gone no later than one o'clock." Mama, I'll make sure that they leave by twelve because I know how you get. Yea because I don't want to see all that wiggling, popping, and shaking up in here.

This is God's house. Ms. Housemoore made Whitney laugh, because she tried to do the dances as she was explaining them.

BIG AND LITTLE SATAN

"Oh mama, I'm going to go stay over to Vicky's for a few days if it's, ok?" Yea child go ahead, y'all just make sure that my house is back in order. "Just like y'all found it, because if something gets broken then y'all paying for it, Whitney!" Don't worry about that because, if somebody breaks something up in here, they about to catch a beat down. Plus, my brother is going to be here too mama, to make sure that them boys respect your house. "Good! Good, I knew that boy was good for something." I'll let Jacob go stay at his little friend's house down the street so he's not up in here spoiling your party. "Oh, thank you mama, because he was the one about to catch the first beat down." "Child, y'all better not be putting your hands on my baby." Mama, Jacob is bad. He be cutting up when you are not around. "Girl, I know what he be doing, he ain't slick, hell ain't that what all of y'all be doing when I ain't around?" Whitney kissed her mother. Who loves you mama? "God! And Ms. Housemoore walked out of the room. Come eat Whitney, I made you breakfast."

$ $ $ $ $

Vicky pulled up to Whitney's house and it was packed with people. They were running in and out of the house. Vicky yelled out her car window at someone to open the gate. Whitney made sure that she had a place to park when she came.

Hey Andre! Wow! Don't you look sexy, I'll be in there in a minute. Can a brother grind on that fat ass? Man, she bad, another dude commented. "Yea! Don't you wish? Vicky gave him a, you don't stand a chance look and walked in the house." Hey Girl! Vicky was feeling herself rocking her Michael Kors mini dress with the matching purse and heels. Vicky just knew that all eyes and attention would be coming her way all night. But all that would change when she spotted Whitney in an outfit and shoes that she couldn't even afford. The last time Vicky saw that dress, it made her drop it back on the rack. Actually, it went like $800 dollars. Damn! That's a little too rich for my blood, is what Vicky and Whitney both said when they saw the $800 dollar dress at the mall.

When Vicky walked into the house, there where a lot of females admiring Whitney shoes. When Vicky approached the crowd, she overheard Whitney say that her man bought her boots. Vicky was wondering why Whitney would make up an imaginary man just to impress their friends. When Vicky walked up to them, everybody spoke but nobody even noticed Vicky's outfit, they were too busy praising Whitney's outfit and shoes. "Happy Birthday sis, here's your gift." Whitney said, "Ok! Thank you and threw the box with the rest of the gifts." That really pissed Vicky off even more, then Whitney stealing her shine.

Whitney was the one who was wearing her clothes and was on the passenger side of Vicky's car. Vicky thought the way to her shine back was to shame Whitney up in front of their friends. "Damn! Whitney, your brother went all the way out for you on your Birthday, didn't he?" He bought you a $800 dress and a pair of $200 shoes? "Naw Boo Boo! I ain't even saw my brother yet, I don't know what he bought me, and my shoes cost $872, thank you." But since you trying to front, in front of these people my man bought them.

Heyyyy! Name Me King, by The Game came on and everybody started grabbing somebody to dance with. Two dudes grabbed Whitney and Vicky and they were dancing back-to-back. Now Vicky was smiling and enjoying the party. Whitney and Vicky were shaking their asses to Young Buck 'Shorty Want a Ride With Me' when everybody in the party heard the loud horns blowing outside. Everybody went to see what all the noise was about. Whitney and Vicky went outside because they were in charge of the Birthday party, and they didn't want the neighbors complaining to Ms. Housemoore. When they walked outside it was four cars lined up in a roll with their lights flashing and blowing their horns. But it was a vehicle wrapped up in a big red bow, it was on a trailer hitched to the back of Marquan's truck. Whitney eyes lit up when she saw one vehicle in particular. It was Supreme's Mercedes Benz right behind Marquan's truck. Whitney took off running towards her brother's truck.

Marquan jumped out, "Happy Birthday Sis!" Whitney gave him a hug. "Hey bro, thank you!" Oh, you done went and bought you another car, it's nice. Nope! That's my baby sister right there. Whitney started screaming, What! Marquan don't play with me, are you serious, Marquan? Whitney grabbed the keys out of Marquan's hand, she jumped up on the trailer and opened the door. Whitney sat in the car and started blowing the horn and everybody gathered around the car.

It was a white with tan interior Nissan 300 ZX. Whitney said, "Bro what type of car is this?" "Girl, that's a Nissan 300 ZX." What, are you serious? "Yea, and if you get out, we'll take it down off the rack for you, sis." When Whitney got out the car, Supreme was holding his hand out to help her down. "Whitney that's who you need to be thanking right there." Why, who is this bro? That's my man Supreme right there, he the one picked the car out Whitney and convinced me to buy it. So, I told his ass that if he wants you to have that car then help me pay for it and he did, Whitney. "Whitney, so that's our gift to our little sister, from the both of us." Whitney looked at Supreme and started crying, she wanted so badly to just jump up in his arms and kiss him. But Whitney reminded herself to just stay cool and not draw attention to their little secret.

"Relax, relax girl, damn! But he is looking and smelling so damn good thou!" "Oh, Lord help me, not to touch this man." Whitney said, "Awe, that was so nice of you, Supreme, thank you. I've heard a lot about you." Supreme smiled and was thinking damn, she good. "Is it ok if I give you a hug too?" Supreme said, "As much money that I just left at that car lot, you better. They all laughed." Whitney gave Supreme a hug. "Preme help me take it off the rack." Everybody was patting Whitney on the back, congratulating her on her new car. There were a few, 'that's nice girl! You're lucky Whitney and I wish my family was like yours. Vicky, finally walked up to the car, wow! Look Vicky, I guess you were right, my brother did go all out for me. Whitney knew that Vicky have a big mouth, so Whitney said, "Yea Vicky him and his best friend Supreme bought it for me for my birthday." Oh, hello Marquan, Hi Supreme, she waved at him, but Marquan didn't pay any attention to her, because Whitney said Supreme name first to Vicky.

"Hey Vicky, look at y'all, don't you two look like two models tonight." Vicky smiled, thank you Marquan, your birthday gift is nice. "Marquan was the second one to comment her on her outfit." They removed the car and Whitney told her besty to jump in, they we're checking out the car together. Marquan had smelled the liquor on Whitney's breath, so he whispered in her ear. 'Sis, I know it's your birthday and you been drinking, let's put the car in the driveway and you can work on getting your license, we'll test drive it tomorrow." Whitney smiled, "Yea bro, I know you're right!" Come here Whitney, I want you to see somebody.

Snooty and Star were sitting in the Lexus 400 Burgundy with tan interior. Hey, I want you to meet my baby sister, her name is Whitney. They both got out of the car and wished her a Happy Birthday and when Whitney saw Star, she paused for a minute remembering when Marquan met her. Marquan introduced them both. This Snooty and you should remember Star? They all gave each other that, you're pretty, your hair looks nice, that outfit and them shoes girllll!, you killing them on your Birthday, Whitney smiled. Snooty said, "I told your brother to bring you by the house tomorrow, so that we can take you shopping for your B-day girl." Ok! Star and Snooty right? "Yep, you got it right." Even thou Whitney was trying to make out the face, she didn't know that Star was the same female from the Walmart when Marquan took them shopping. Star was looking so different in her stripper gear. "Ok, I got to get back to my party, she really wanted to get back to Supreme." Bye, she gave them both a hug. When she was walking away, Whitney could hear Marquan's girls say how beautiful she is. Marquan and Supreme stayed a little while then they left.

Even thou Whitney had just got a new car; she was mad as hell. Here it is her Birthday and all she got was a hug from Supreme. Now, here she was standing in the yard watching the one thing that she wanted for her birthday drive away. Vicky tried her best to control her jealousy, but it still got the best of her because she left the party without even saying goodbye to Whitney. Whitney was so upset that Vicky and Supreme left, that she ended her birthday party early.

Whitney was laying in her bed by 10:30 watching a porno movie, wishing that it was her performing those moves on Supreme. Instead of watching Ms. Blonca perform them on some ugly white man with a small penis. Whitney's cell phone started ringing and she was hoping that it was Vicky, so that she could give her a piece of her mind. Whitney paused Ms. Blonca getting pounded in the mouth, "What! She answered the phone in a real angry voice." "Wow!, I'm sorry sweetie, did I call my baby at the wrong time?" Whitney finally looked at her cell phone and it said Supreme. No! No! baby, she threw the remote on the floor. Whitney sat up. "Baby, why did you leave me on my Birthday?"

Supreme started laughing, "Woman what do you mean I left you? I didn't leave you, Whitney. I'll never leave you; don't you know that?" Whitney started smiling. "Baby, me and your brother had to go and take care of some important business." But I didn't leave you. The next words that Whitney spoke almost made Supreme drop the phone. "Then daddy, if you didn't leave me, then why am I sitting here with a vibrator in between my legs watching two white people have sex instead of me and my daddy?" Supreme almost ran into the back of the car, that he was riding behind. "Baby, wait! wait! wait!" "Why daddy!" Whitney said it in the most sexiest voice that almost made Supreme cum in his pants.

Because if you stop getting on me and go look in your glove box, you'll find an envelope and you will know that I didn't leave my baby. "What?" "Yea go look." "Wait! I got to put some panties and clothes on." Supreme grabbed his forehead and looked in the mirror, "woman what am I going to do with you?" You don't want my Poo Poo to catch a cold, do you? Supreme started laughing, "what am I going to do, Whitney?" "Hell, you better love me, daddy." That made Supreme smile. Whitney finally got dressed and opened her glove box in her car, it was a pink envelope. When she opened it, she took out a card and she read the card out loud.

"Whitney, Happy Birthday! I know that you are spending it with your family and friends, but if you could catch a taxi in the morning to the airport and meet me at 9:00 a.m., I'd love to watch you win some money in Las Vegas and don't forget to bring our gift." Whitney, I want to finish what you started in that Victoria Secret store, until then I'm sad without you.

Whitney just sat there and started crying, she was crying so much that she hadn't noticed Supreme standing right at her window. He tapped on the window, and she jumped. "Excuse me pretty lady, do you think that I can get that Birthday kiss now." Whitney hurried up and jumped out her car, man what you trying to do give me a heart attack now? She hugged Supreme, "Baby you really didn't leave me, did you?" Supreme kissed her and she was the happiest woman in the whole world right about now.

After they unlocked lips, Supreme asked her, "Now can I get an apology Ms. Lady?" "Yes, I'm sorry baby. Can you please forgive me for not believing in you?" "Ok! Just don't let it happen again, now get me that vibrator and that tape." What, you want me to give you Ike? Baby, he the only one that beat on this pussy. Supreme didn't laugh or smile, he just stood there.

Whitney disappeared into the house and came back with the DVD and vibrator. She handed it to Supreme and he slung it down the street. Whitney's mouth flew open like he had just ended her affair with a boyfriend. Supreme walked up on her with the vibrator in his hand and he licked the side of it. "Damn, I knew that pussy tasted good, but Whitney don't you never allow nothing else to penetrate that vagina never again in life." He looked her straight in the eyes because I might want to kill it. Supreme turned and walked away and she kept calling him. "Baby! Baby! Man, I know you hear me?" Supreme opened his car door, I'll see you at the airport 9:00 a.m., don't be late. He jumped in his car and drove off. "Damn! He makes me sick!" Whitney smiled and locked up her car and walked into the house.

At 10:05a.m., Supreme and Whitney were boarding flight 147 to Las Vegas Nevada. Upon arriving, Supreme rented a 2012 D.T.S Cadillac, black with tan interior. Before going to the hotel, he took Whitney to a Soul Food restaurant over on Washington street. He and Whitney ate smothered steaks, yams, mac and cheese, and corn on the cob. Then they shared some peach cobbler and ice cream. Supreme took her to the mall and let her shop. Supreme even bought a few things for himself. Whitney went and bought more lingerie but wouldn't allow Supreme to see it. What she bought she knew would turn Supreme on, she even bought him some boxers and Gucci cologne. Supreme and Whitney met back up and they drove to the M.G.M Grand hotel. On the ride up on the elevator, they were kissing like a newlywed couple. Always looking into each other's eyes.

"Baby, what you do, bring my vibrator with you?" Whitney could feel Supreme cell phone going off every two minutes. Supreme knew that it was Stigma calling him. but just like he has been doing for the past few days, he ignored her calls. "Naw, that's my cell phone, but I'm with the woman that I want to talk to." Whitney smiled, "Well at least I see you, always know what to say to keep a woman thinking." Whitney slapped him on the arm and Supreme returned the favor because he slapped her on the ass. "OK! man keep it up as hot as I am I'll get naked on this elevator or this hallway, keep it up."

Supreme was smiling and when he opens the hotel door Whitney went, "Oh my God! baby this room is beautiful." They were overlooking the Las Vegas strip. Whitney ran around checking out the suite, now baby I can seriously get used to living like this. "Supreme tested her just as he have, every woman that he took to a hotel." So, Whitney you mean that if I gave you a home like this with a maid, then you would be happy? Yea I'd be happy after you got rid of the maid because I don't need no bitch to do my job for me and my man.

Supreme stopped and looked at Whitney. "What! What! Baby, why are you looking at me like that? Supreme didn't want to call her young no more, he couldn't believe that out of all the women that he asked that question, here is an 19-year-old woman responding better than any female have." Not even did Stigma say what Whitney had said. Stigma had chosen to have the maid, now he understood why Ms. Bergess lived in their home. "No reason Whitney, other than to say that you're a remarkable woman." Now, I'm even more happy that I'm here right now with you. Supreme couldn't believe it, but here he was sitting in this exotic suite with Whitney actually having a mature adult conversation. Whitney asked Supreme, besides spoiling me because you obviously have some type of good or bad intentions for me to receive this type of attention from you and Supreme I don't even want you to tell me what they are. "I'm woman enough to wait and figure it out myself', "If it's good then we'll be just fine, but if it's bad and it hurts me, Supreme just be ready to receive it back in a much worser way." "Wow! Is that a threat? No baby that's a promise."

"Don't think that you got some, young dumb ass female in this room with you." "To keep it 100 with you, Supreme, you about to take my virginity, so that means that I'm about to give myself away to you." I'm doing that only, because I trust you and believe in you. But if your intentions are to hurt me, Supreme, you only saw my panties, but please don't take them off of me and rob me of my woman hood?

Supreme walked up to Whitney, "I take it that you didn't hear me in your mother's yard." I did hear you, very we'll, you're a man and I won't forget that. But to be clear as to what you told me baby; you told me to never allow anything other than you to penetrate your pussy. "Would that be right, Supreme?" "Yep! so was that a threat or a promise?" Supreme kissed her lips, that was a promise. Whitney walked away. "That's right, you better not threatened me, because I'll kick your butt right now." Supreme went to grab her and she grabbed her bag and ran into the bathroom baby stop!

SHAWN L. BAILEY

CHAPTER THIRTY-FOUR
BIG PAY BACK

Marquan and Emoni was at the shooting range, going through all type of bullet shells. Marquan always made sure that she got target sheets with Tone's picture on them. So that when he took her to the shooting range, she could take out all of her frustrations on him. Emoni was feeling really relaxed in her Guess capri jeans and cross back lace white cotton shirt. She has on custom diamond sparkled Jordan's and white shoe laces with her hair tied back in a pony tail. Marquan kept on telling Emoni how beautiful she looked to him. Emoni was telling Marquan that she has never loved a man or had feelings for one the way she does him.

That made Marquan start talking about making her his wife. "He told Emoni that, if she keeps melting his heart, like she been doing that he about to take her to a alter and make her wifey." "Boy stop it! You know your ass ain't about to leave all of them stripper's." "Marquan said, whoever said that I have to leave them to make you, my wife?" I got them and you too, so what's the difference Emoni? I'll never try to stop your shine, I ain't that type of woman. "See baby that's why I love you, you know your place and always stay in it." Most women see a man grinding out in those street's and all they do is cause him problems about nothing. It's females that's in the winning chair and it seems like they rather be the side chick."

"Baby, that's because most woman love that attention, more then they will ever love that man." "Like I told you before Marquan, home is home whenever he gets there; me, I want to be wherever home is baby." Me being wifey, that means that you're coming home to me. I'm never concerned about where my man goes. My concern is where he goes after he goes where he's going. Emoni started to put it on real thick, she kissed Marquan and grabbed his penis and squeezed it in her hand. "Baby! All I care about is, that you're coming home to me."

Marquan said, "Then let me show you, where I'm coming home to." You can go and find a nice home, that the both of us can come home to then. Emoni stepped back and looked at him. "Baby stop playing with me." Marquan, you know how much I care about you, baby please don't play with my feelings right now? Marquan reached into his back pocket and took out an envelope, he sat it down where their weapons were. There's $50,000 dollars in that envelope, that should start the paperwork on something nice and if you need any more I got you. "Emoni screamed, it drew attention to them, Marquan put his hands up Naw! Naw! she good." I'm sorry Sir, my baby just made me a happy woman that's all.

Marquan hugged her, see girl you about to get us kicked out of this place. Emoni grabbed the money and placed it in her purse. "Emoni, wherever you find a place at, just make sure that its got a couple of garages for these new whips that I'm about to buy." "Oh, and it's hot so make sure we got a swimming pool. I want to see that fat ass shaking in some of them bikini bathing suit's when I come home." Marquan started slapping her ass with both of his hand's. "Stop! Stop baby before I shoot you." "Girl, I'm not afraid of you with no gun, but if you got your car key's then I'm scared as fuck." Emoni slapped his arm, "Damn! baby you gone, go there on me for real Marquan?"

Emoni reached for her gun. Ok! Ok! Ok! Baby I'm just playing. They hugged and kissed each other, come on let's get out of here. Before were not welcomed back in here, because you about to be screaming way more then you just were in here. Emoni grabbed his penis again. "Ok! don't start nothing that you can't finish, I'll get that pussy right here, gun and all."

On the way to Emoni's apartment, she asked Marquan to stop at the grocery store so she could grab a few groceries. Marquan told her Ok, but he was taking Emoni to meet his mother first. "Marquan no! baby please don't take me over there looking like this please!" "Looking like what Emoni, you're beautiful." "Dang baby! at least I wanted to be looking better than this, she gone think that I'm some thug or something." Marquan started laughing. Emoni poked out her lips and crossed her arm's looking mad. "Ok! now that ain't what the Bible say, it says come as you are Emoni."

"That's to church, crazy man." Well, if you can go to God looking any way, then you definitely can go to my mama looking any type of way. "She a God-fearing woman and she not about to be judgmental like that." Any way's if we about to be living together, I'd love for you to meet my family, you already met my sister, remember? "Oh yea! I did, and she pretty Marquan." "Thank you, baby, the only ones you ain't met yet is my little brother and mother." "OK! well it ain't like I have a choice right!?" Marquan smiled and turned up the music, he was bumping that Jim Jones' Ballin'.

Marquan and Emoni walked into the house and Ms. housemoore was in the kitchen cooking Oxtails, greens, potato salad, and hot water cornbread. She has the music up loud, listening to her gospel music. Marvin Sapp, 'Never Would Have Made It' was playing and that song touched Emoni real hard. It was the song that got her through after she lost her parents. Marquan walked up behind his mother, and he kissed her on the neck. "Oh! Hey Son." But when they turned around, Emoni was down on her knees crying and praying.

Marquan was about to tell his mother who Emoni was, but before he could she went and joined her on the floor. Ms. Housemoore started praying over her and was asking God to take her pain away. "Lord complete your unfinish work in her, finish what you started give her a strength to turn away from that sinful lifestyle, don't let the devil trap her." "He trying to trap her Lord, in Jesus' name set her free. Keep your Angels around her, let her know that she'll see her parent's again, but she got to keep her focus on you and your word." Emoni started crying even harder.

Marquan stood there wondering, what the hell had just happened in front of him with his mother and girl.

After they finished praying, Ms. Housemoore told Emoni that she would see her mother again. "Don't give up baby God is your protector and your provider, don't settle for less then what God is trying to offer you." His gifts are greater than mans, you run baby; run, don't be afraid to run God will protect you. OK! Mama I won't, I'll do just that. I'll run fast as I can. Ms. Housemoore grabbed a napkin and wiped away Emoni tears. Thank you, Jesus! Yes! thank you Jesus! Marquan said, "Are y'all done?"

"Ok mama that's, and before he could even get out another word, Ms. Housemoore said, I know who she is, "That's my future daughter in law right there, Marquan." "That's who that is, that's God's child right there trust me." Emoni smiled. Thank you, mama. I'm so sorry for coming into your house like this. I'm Emoni! All baby, don't you worry about that, she wiped her face, you're just as pretty as your name. "Emoni! I love that name; I heard your name before from my son and daughter Whitney." "I change my mind child, I'll braid your hair anytime that you need me to."

Ms. Housemoore turned and looked at Marquan. "Boy! I'm going to steal this child from you, she going to church with me, ain't you baby?" "Yea I'll go to church with you anytime mama." I'm sorry! You don't mind if I call you mama, do you? "Child call me mama anytime you want to, and you're welcome in my house anytime with or without Marquan." Marquan said Ok then, I'll just leave since I'm not wanted in this family no more. "Stop it baby! you know that we love you too." Emoni grabbed Marquan by the arm, and he gave her a kiss. See what I told you?

The Lord said come as you are Emoni. Emoni punched Marquan in the chest. "Mama, she didn't even want to come and see you." "Owwwwww! Marquan, stop lying to mama, I just wanted to look nice for her that's all, she a woman I'm sure she understands that right mama?"

"Yea! but you look good to me, just like you're looking right now. You're a very beautiful woman." "See Emoni! Mama, I tell her that all the time, but she don't want to listen to me." Emoni smiled. He do always tell me that mama. Y'all hungry? No ma'am. She not, but I am mama. "Boy! I know you gone eat and Emoni is to. You ain't got to be coming up in here acting shame around me." You invite me to your house and cook; child, I'm going to eat and tell you if your food is good or bad. "Won't I Boy!" "Yea! she sure will."

BIG AND LITTLE SATAN

Emoni said, "I love your mother she real." Baby you know I like people that tell the truth. Ms. Housemoore said, "Child what are you doing with him for, then?" "Naw baby I'm just playing, that's my little man when he listens which ain't much, ain't that right, Marquan?" He kissed her on the cheek, I love you too mom.

Marquan, I was wondering who car was in the driveway when I came home. "Emoni, you got a nice car, what's that you pushing out there?" "Oh, I'm riding with your son, but I drive a Lexus 400." "Oh! that ain't your car in my driveway?" "Nope!" Oh, it must be one of my daughter's friend's. "Marquan, I thought that when I got off work, that I was going to have to come home and beat me some neggro's with my bat." But when I came home, Whitney had already cleaned up and everything. Marquan, how did the party go? They were having fun and Whitney looked beautiful. Did she take pictures? I don't know mama, I had to leave for a minute to go pick up her car. "Her what!" Her car mama. "Boy! that girl ain't got no car." She does now mama, I bought her one, that's her car in the driveway.

"Boy! I know that you're lying, right?" No, I'm not lying mama, that's her car outside. Why she ain't driving it then, if it's her car? Because I told her not to drive, until she gets her driver license. She can only drive it with you or me. "Yea! Ok Marquan, we'll talk about that car, at another time since you got company." Well, mama we already expected that, Whitney car already paid for. "So ain't no need to get mad, because I can't take it back old lady." That was her Birthday gift mama, she showed me what you bought her that was me and Emoni's gift to her. Marquan looked over at Emoni, for some type of help but she didn't say nothing.

They all ate, and Ms. Housemoore talked too much like most mothers do about their kid's. Emoni told them a lot about her and her mother and father when they were living. She even told Ms. Housemoore that her parent's, died on their way to church by a drunk driver. "All baby! I'm so sorry to hear that." "Well baby I can't take her place, but you got me now and I'm hear anytime that you need me." "Ok mama, thank you." You and your son have been so loving and kind to me. The feeling is mutual mama, if you ever need me, I'm here for you too, ok!

Emoni and Ms. Housemoore sat and talked about different churches and pastors. They both have been to each other's church and knew each other's pastors. After they ate Ms. Housemoore fell asleep and Marquan and Emoni kissed her then they left and headed back to Emoni house. Emoni was talking to Marquan about his mother, and he asked her, Emoni how did my mother know that you lost your mom and you or me didn't tell her? "Baby that's the Holly Spirit that spoke to your mother." Marquan turned and looked at Emoni, "Emoni do you really believe that? Yea, sure I do Marquan, that's how the Holly Spirit work through people." Marquan sat back and got quiet. Baby don't forget to stop at the store Ok!

Marquan decided to stay in the truck, while Emoni went to shop. Just as Emoni walked into the store, Marquan sat up and

BIG AND LITTLE SATAN

he gripped his gun. Marquan couldn't believe who he was seeing. It has been twelve years and seven months, that he dreamed to see her. There she was just a few feet away, loading her groceries into a black 740 il B.M.W, then she put what appeared to be a two-year-old boy into the back seat. Marquan shook his head. The B.M.W was backing up and was driving away. Marquan looked at the store. "Damn! what do I do. Man, you been waiting twelve year's and seven months to see Lulu." "Fuck it! Marquan started the truck and followed her. Here I am sitting in prison and this bitch out here having babies." "Fuck you and your kid's bitch!"

After about three miles Lulu turned into an apartment complex, Marquan slowed down and waited until she pulled into her covered parking spot. Marquan parked his truck a little way from where Lulu was parked. He exited his truck with his pistol in his hand. Just as Lulu jumped out of her car and went to unbuckle her son out of the back seat, Marquan hit the corner carrying his pistol behind his back. "Hello Lulu! Her mouth flew open. Marquan, baby I'm sorry they made me snitch on y'all."

"Bitch! they gave me 15 years, I done 12 years and seven months for your punk ass and you're out here having babies' while I sit and rot in prison." "You robbed me of my life, I sat up hours in drug house's just to make you happy and this is how you repay me by snitching on me and Supreme?" Bitch I could see If you got him caught up but your stupid ass sent me to prison. I hope that you enjoyed the last past 12 years, because my life been a living hell."

Lulu's baby started crying. "Marquan wait, please let me get my son, it's hot in the car baby." "Baby! Baby! Bitch, I wasn't your baby when you took that stand on me, was I?" "Yea baby! You don't understand Marquan. They made me take the stand on y'all. I didn't want to do that." They said, "that they were going to take my kids. What would you have done Marquan?" You can't ask me that question because I ain't no snitch bitch! He pulled the gun out from behind his back and Lulu saw it. "Marquan, please baby, no. Don't do this to me. What about my kids? Who gone take care of my kids, Marquan?" You ain't, you punk ass snitching bitch! Pow! Pow! Marquan slowly walked away and jumped in his truck and drove away.

When Emoni came walking out the grocery store, Marquan was laying back in his seat in the truck like nothing had ever happened. Emoni said, "Oh I'm sorry baby, I didn't mean to take so long in the store." "It's ok! What did you buy good, did you buy me some grapes?" Yea baby, I got your grapes, seeing how you ate up all of mine. They pulled into the apartment complex and Marquan helped take the groceries in the apartment. Marquan made love to Emoni again and when they finished, he told Emoni that she needed to get an offshore account. Because he got a lot of money that he needed to send to it real soon. "Ok baby, I will. I'll take care of that right away." Marquan gave her all the information that she needed to switch his money into the offshore account and reminded her again to go find them a home, in which she agreed to doing right away.

CHAPTER THIRTY-FIVE
BROKEN PROMISES

I mpression stood in the doorway watching her daddy exit his $400,000 dollar Bugatti. This the only man has more of her heart then Kevin, who everybody calls Body Count in the Federal penitentiary. "Hi daddy!" "We'll hello Peanut!" Hey! It looks like somebody putting on some weight. Her daddy patted his stomach, yea I think your mother is trying to kill me Peanut, so she can spend all my money. "Daddy! I'm serious!" Daddy, I don't think that my mother could live long enough to spend all your money. I think that she'll get sick from handing it out first, daddy.

"Hell, not that woman, I bet she somewhere swiping that damn black card right now as we speak." "Oh daddy! You know that my mother loves you just like I do." "Shit! Don't you mean that she happy that I'm a rich old man?" Impression's dad is 74 years old, and her mother is 57. So, daddy how long am I going to get to spoil you this time? "Well, I guess long enough for me to feel like my wife done gave up enough pussy, then I guess I'll go back and just watch her pussy like I always do." Impression started laughing and said daddy you are a mess. Come on and get into this house.

Her dad walked in the house and went and sat in his favorite chair that he had sent to her home from Italy. "Daddy give me your keys, so that I can grab your suitcase." He gave her the keys. "Hey Peanut!" "Yea daddy." Hey, make sure you grab my black bag too, I need to show you something. "Ok daddy!" Impression came back with both of his bags, and she helped her dad out of his hand made Italian shoe's and placed on his favorite slippers.

"Wow! something sure does smell good Peanut." "Yes daddy! I made you some chicken and Dumpling's, would you like me to make you a salad first?" "Nope, not right now but you can bring me the remote control?" It's a golf tournament that I wouldn't mind watching. Impression turned on her 70-inch T.V screen and her dad flipped through the channel's until he found what he was looking for. Impression's home phone and the T.V program were interrupted, because it said, "you have an incoming call from a Federal prison from a Kevin, if you wish to accept the call, please press five."

Impression and her dad already knew who was calling. Impression pressed five and the T.V went back to its normal programming that her dad was watching. Impression always got butterflies in her stomach, every time that she knew he was calling or heard his voice. Each time she always promised herself that she wouldn't cry when they talked. But no matter how much she tried to contain her emotions, they always seem to get the best of her. Before Kevin hung up, he asked Impression to speak to her dad. "Here daddy! He wants to talk to you."

Impression handed her dad the phone. "Hello son. Yea sure, yea, yea!" "So, how are you holding up in there, son?" Yes, ok great. I'm working on something right now. You should be receiving a visit from a great friend of mine next week. "He tells me that he'll be able to get you out of there real soon." "Yea me too!" I heard about that lawyer; they say that they found him dead in a jacuzzi with two young boys. Well God bless him son, may he rest in peace. He was telling him that the last lawyer didn't do as he was told, so they found him dead with two boys humiliating the lawyer. "Son that's why its not good to screw people out of their hard-earned money."

Yea she is sitting here looking like a million bucks, just like her mom and trying every day to figure out how to spend up a few Billion. Impression said. "Hey! somebody got to spoil me, my man not here to do it daddy, anymore." "Ok son, keep your eyes open and your head up, we'll be seeing you soon." "Don't worry you know me; everything will work out just fine trust me." Here's Peanut, I'll see ya soon Kevin.

Impression ended their call, and her dad could see that she was in a lot of pain from losing Kevin. Her losing Kevin had caused her to find happiness in a sleezy strip club. Impression thought that her dad didn't know that she stripped in club Excalibur. Her dad wanted so many times to have the whole club blown right off the corner. He could remember when he first learned that Impression was stripping. A man that worked for him called him and said that his Little Peanut was working in a strip club. He was ready to order the man, to take the head off of the man who hired her. But after he secretly went and watched her dance, that she was only seeking the attention that she wasn't getting from Kevin. Her dad sent the man back to the club and made it rain with nothing but 100-dollar bills.

He wanted to make sure all the other dancers knew who the Queen was when Impression was in the building. He gave her that nick name, because when she was a little girl, her dad would place a stack of 100-dollar bills in one hand and a bag of Planter Peanut's in the other hand. Every time he told her to pick the one that would make her happy. Impression would always choose the peanuts over the money. That's when he learned that money didn't mean everything to every woman. Because it was the taste of them peanut's that would make her smile every time. Ever since that day, he gave her that name Peanut. Impression was setting the table, so that they could enjoy the meal that she prepared for him.

Every time that he came to visit, which wasn't that much lately because he was starting to get up in age. He was almost about to turn 75 years old, but he wouldn't allow anybody to drive him around. He doesn't care what it is, he'll tell you to get the fuck out of his way, I can take care of myself. Like he was doing, in Impression's kitchen right now. He wasn't allowing her to fix his plate, he told her that after he fixed it then she can taste it first. Because women have a bad habit to place things into your food that you might not want.

He fixed their plates and allowed her to say a prayer, then he let her taste his first before he ate it. Impression was so used to him and his stubborn ways', that she didn't even pay any attention to him switching their plates.

While they were eating, he told Impression that he had something very important that he needed her to handle for him. Without even looking up. Impression told her dad that he knew that she'd handle anything for him no question asked.

"Well, do you promise me that you'll take care of this problem for me real soon?" "Yea daddy! I promise you that I'll handle it real soon daddy, what is it?" He pushed his plate to the side and got up to retrieve his black bag.

Impression was enjoying her Chicken and Dumpling's so much that she was working on a second bowl when he returned.

He opened the bag and laid out what he wanted her to handle on the table. Then her dad slid it over in front of her bowl. When Impression saw what it was, she dropped her spoon back into her bowl. She just stared at her dad, no way are you serious? He placed his hand over his chest, as a heart attack. "Impression placed her hand over her face and said, "Daddy damn! damn you, what the fuck?"

CHAPTER THIRTY-SIX

AGE AIN'T NOTHING
BUT A NUMBER

S upreme laid back in the bed wearing a pair of red silk boxers, that Whitney had bought him when they went shopping at the mall. In all of his years of giving woman money, Supreme have never had anyone of them think to buy him something. But Whitney was turning out to be something more than he could even imagine her to be. He laid there thinking back over his life. Supreme was starting to feel like he wanted something different for himself. Maybe even a new life, but there was just one problem. He was feeling like how can you capture a ghost when you can't even see the ghost?

Supreme laid there in that train of thought, until he was quickly taken out of that mood when he saw Whitney exit the bathroom. Damn! She was wearing a three-piece Teddy that made Supreme sit up in the bed. He couldn't believe how sexy and beautiful she looked. The pink bra gripped her breast, like it had called first dibs on her body. Her breast sat up so firm that, it clearly appeared that her breast was supporting the bra more than the bra supporting her breast. The Diamonds on her bra caught the lighting in the room making her look like she was about to approach a stage to perform for a crowd of people.

But right now, Whitney only has one fan, waiting for her performance. Her panties were covered in the same Diamond studs as her bra. But when Whitney turned around to model her outfit, Supreme was wondering how her panties was, even holding up on her body cause her ass cheeks had completely made that G. string disappear between her butt. All thirty-eight backed beef was making Supreme's penis rise to his manly potential. Her three-inch-high heels even gave her ass much more bounce when she walked over to Supreme. Whitney hair was blowing backwards, like it was blowing in the wind. "Damn baby!" "This is all for you daddy, come and get it." Supreme went to get up off the bed, but Whitney stopped him and took control. She pushed him back onto the bed and climbed on top of him. Whitney kissed Supreme and bit his bottom lip after she removed her tongue. She gently kissed him on the side of his neck and started working her way down to his penis. Whitney grabbed it, putting a strong grip on to it through his boxers. She kissed the tip of his penis and felt it jump like it was ready to come out and explore her young body parts.

Supreme eyes were closed, but he could feel her reach over and grab his glass of ice water. Whitney took a drink and placed the glass back on the nightstand. Her cold hands made Supreme body jerk when she touched him. Whitney went back to doing what she had first started. Whitney finally freed Supreme' man hood from his silk boxer's and took him into her mouth. Wow! the ice cube in her mouth, made Supreme penis get even harder than it was. After the ice cube melted, Supreme started to test her jaw structure. He grabbed the back of her head, and thrusted his penis deeper into her mouth. Whitney begins to choke, but Supreme didn't draw back at all.

But Whitney remembered seeing her penis teacher, in the same situation in her porno movie's. Whitney stopped breathing and she help Supreme force his penis down her throat. "Oh, damn baby! Supreme looked down to see that his penis was all the way in her mouth." That's right baby claim your dick. Supreme finally just laid back and watched Whitney make an introduction to his penis. They were becoming best friends.

Supreme turned her over on her back and took control of the whole situation. After eating and licking away, at that young philly cat, Supreme tried penetrating Whitney's love box. But her vagina was so tight that, Supreme couldn't completely enter his big Hummer into such a small parking spot. He's packing such a big, over-sized load, it was starting to make Whitney get mad feeling like she had spoil their pleasurable moment together. Supreme wasn't about to allow a beautiful moment, get away from him or Whitney. Supreme went back to bring this first-time moment back to life. He wasn't about to let her vagina die on them; he went down on her vagina giving it mouth to mouth resuscitation.

After a while Whitney's vagina started squirting like the waterfall that she pointed at when they passed Treasure Island. Owwwwww! ummmmmm! daddyyyy! Supreme went and got right in between her leg's her vagina was nice and wet and invited his penis right back into her private parking space. After a few strokes Supreme could see that pain wasn't going to stop Whitney from experiencing her first sexual encounter. Supreme thrusted his penis further into Whitney expanding her vagina more and more each time. Now she was inviting his penis more into her walls and deeper, they were like two kids riding a Sea Saw. Because now Whitney was throwing the pussy back and meeting his drive.

Supreme turned her over and placed her in a doggy style position. That's when Supreme knew that he was in a young wild vagina that hadn't been touched before. Whitney was screaming and yelling, Owwwwwww! Weeeeeeee! Yes! Yes daddy! yessssss! fuck me harder daddyyyyyy! She was serving him pussy back, like a wild bull in a rodeo, only she was the bull that saw red. Supreme was riding her pussy and holding on to the back of her hair for dear life. Whitney was taking Supreme penis, like they been having sex for years. Now she was begging him to sit on his penis. Supreme was about to experience every sex porno that Whitney have saw and Supreme gratefully accepted her invitation and tried to leave his penis in her chest.

This is where the momentum changed in Supreme's favor, because it didn't take Whitney long to learn that she needed to ride a few more stallions before she rode on a black stallion. Supreme watched Whitney as she climbed on top of his black stallion, and she tried to jump off but Supreme had locked on her like a red nose pit bull. He pushed that thang up in her and grabbed her waist to meet every thrust. Ohhhhhhh! No! No! No! Baby let me offffff! Owwwwwww! Awwwwwww! Owwwwww! Ummmmmmmm! Whitney was making more scary faces then you see at Halloween trying to escape Supremes penis. Ummmmmm! Ummmmmm! Dadddyyyy! Daddddyyyy! Dadddy It hurts. It hurts, please stop, stop! Owwwwwww! Yes! yes! Yes! No! No! No! Whitney didn't know if she wanted it or not. But the way Supreme was feeling Whitney really didn't have a say in the matter. Supreme closed his eyes and pretended like he was on a roller coaster ride at the fair.

He started to take all deep strokes, alllllllll! alllllll! daddddddyyyy! daddddddyyyy! it, it, it's hurtinggggg! Dadddddddyyy! no, no, wait, wait, pleaseeee! daddddddyyyy! Waitttttt! Whitney didn't know what had just happened, but she felt something inside of her like her vagina snapped. Supreme had just popped the cork on her champagne bottle. But a little of her champagne started to run down his shaft and that's when Whitney knew that she was no longer a virgin that her woman hood has just set in. Supreme and Whitney both exploded together. Ummmm! ohhhhh! Awwwww! Yes! Yes! Yes! ummmmm! "Yea baby! That was greatttttt! Ummmmmm! Yes, Daddy it was, so is that what I've been missing all of my life?" They smiled at each other, and Whitney flopped over Supremes' shoulder trying to catch her breath. Supreme rolled Whitney over onto her back and he was about to go back in for round two, but as he was climbing back on top of her, that's when Supreme realized that he was sleeping with a younger female. He could see that he had popped her cork. Even Whitney could feel that something was wrong. She reached in between her legs and came back up with a handful of blood. Ohhh! Noooo! daddy! Something is wrong baby I'm bleeding.

Whitney started getting excited when she allowed, the two females to give her oral. She experienced a great feeling then but nothing like sex. Nor did she end her experience with blood coming from her vagina and Whitney started to panic. "Come on baby, you got to take me to the hospital, I think you tore something up inside me. Whitney started jumping up and Supreme started laughing, because he knew that she didn't understand what had just happened to her.

Come on baby I got you, you'll be just fine let's get you in some water. After showering together, Supreme ran Whitney some bath water and he bathed her and explained her experience that she had just encountered. Whitney felt so embarrassed that her and her mom haven't had that conversation about sex.

Ms. Housemoore was so busy telling her about being saved and not living a sinful life that she forgot to share life experiences with Whitney. Supreme done such a great job explaining, that Whitney didn't feel like she has just gotten a man. But she also was starting to feel like, she have a father figure in her life which she never had.

Whitney fears went away so fast that, she was bent over in the shower begging Supreme to make her beg him to stop dogging her vagina out. "Come on daddy, fuck the shit out of me this time, make me beg you to stop, slap my ass daddy!" Supreme was enjoying the sex, but he made a note in his mind to have a conversation with Whitney about her porno fantasies. Ohhhh! Yea Daddy, keep it right there, keep that dick right there, yessssss!

After trying to go a third time, Supreme wind up being the one to tap out. Supreme told Whitney that her young pussy, would definitely be the cause of his death when he go. That made the both of them, share a good moment of laughter together. Supreme ordered room service and that allowed them time to get into a more mature conversation. Whitney said, "Baby I don't mean to pry into your personal life, but do you have any kid's?" Supreme turned over on his side and placed his hand on Whitney's stomach. He gently ran his hand across her body as they talked. "Yea Whitney, baby I have a son."

"Oh, how old is he baby, Whitney seemed to get excited for Supreme." He's nine years old and he's the reason that I make sacrifices for Whitney. I want him to be able to have things that my parents never gave to me. "Which wasn't what, Supreme?" "Just about everything that you can name." Like never walking in a shoe or clothing store with my parents and being the first person to wear the shoes or clothes first. Whitney, the first time that I put a pair of name brand shoes on my feet, I was taking on someone else athletic foot problem.

Whitney, I can remember as a kid, running to see what Santa Clause had left me for Christmas, and when I walked into the living room, my dad and mom was sitting there drinking beer and sharing a marijuana joint. I said, "Merry Christmas mom and dad, what did Santa Clause leave me for Christmas?" My dad said that Santa Clause doesn't come around our neighborhood. "But shit boy! since it's Christmas, you can finish off the rest of this joint I'm sure your mama won't mind." Do you baby? Naw! But let me hit it one more time, before his little ass kill it. "Tears started running down Whitney face, but Supreme haven't noticed it yet."

Whitney told Supreme that life wasn't great for her either growing up. "All my life I've been told, wait for my blessing from God, Supreme." But it seemed that if God did try to give us a blessing, my mother's pride always seems to block our blessings that God sent us. Just yesterday meeting you Supreme, it seemed that God got me to that age, where I can accept or deny my own blessings.

It took my brother to come home after serving twelve years in prison, for me to have my first name brand of clothing and shoes.

"Supreme and before that, the only way that I'd have on something name brand was when, my friend Vicky would invite me to go somewhere with her and she would loan me her clothes just so that she doesn't feel embarrassed being with me." I guess my mother was right Supreme. Why you say that? Because after all these years of going to bed without eating, just so that my little brother didn't go to bed hungry, I'd starve myself for him Supreme, in the same way that I know you would for your son.

"Materialistic things I can go without Supreme but love, that's kind of hard to grow up without for anybody." "Me, the only time that I felt what real love was, when I got to spend those six hours in visiting with my brother in prison." Supreme when we would go visit my brother, not knowing if we were going to run out of gas or not on the way back, which we did a couple of times." The roll of quarters that my mom borrowed from her church friend until payday, my mother would always tell me and my brother Jacob not to ask for anything out of the machines at the prison. She just wanted to allow Marquan a chance to enjoy a moment out of that place.

Funny thing that would happen baby was, "What's That Whitney?" Every time that my mother gave the quarters to my brother, he would go to the vending machine and buy everything for me and Jacob nothing for himself baby. Supreme didn't want Whitney to see it, but he was starting to tear up himself. Whitney flipped the whole conversation. "See baby that's why I brung up this conversation, it's more important that you show your son love then anything in life."

"If you keep putting money and materialistic thing's in front of him Supreme, before you show him love baby as a child, that's what he'll always expect from you and he'll grow up thinking the same way for his kids." Supreme take your money and plan a future for your son, so that if anything happens to you, baby he'll be ok on his own, without having to depend on anybody.

This lifestyle that you and my brother live got y'all shinning now, but like New Edition say baby in the end, "Can you stand the rain?" Baby that day going to come, you just experienced that with my brother. Supreme from what I hear, you experienced it too. "Yea! You a real one and you bounced back, but hey only you know, Supreme at what cost did that take?" Baby, if you want to really experience what real love is look into my eyes. Whitney got up, turned to Supreme, tears swelled up in her eyes. "Supreme do you see my tears? Supreme went to wipe them away and Whitney blocked his hand."

"Please don't wipe them away baby because I've waited too long to have this type of tears rolling down my face. Supreme these are happy tears and you put them there. I pray before you to God, that you never take them away. Supreme couldn't believe what he had just heard Whitney say to him. "Supreme let me show you how you know that I'm telling you the truth." Supreme said, "how is that, Whitney?" I'm a young woman that ain't never had anything before in my life. I got a brand-new car sitting in the driveway at my mother's house. Baby, I didn't get my happiness' parading around town, trying to impress my so-called friends. I got my happiness right here in this room, just being here with you Supreme.

Supreme kissed Whitney and picked her up, and he walked her back into the bathroom and he gently bathed every inch of her body. Supreme got dressed and told Whitney that he had something very important that he must do. "Baby make yourself comfortable and call room service and order anything that you want." Supreme kissed Whitney passionately and left their suite.

$ $ $ $ $

Three hours later Supreme came back to the hotel and Whitney was sound asleep. All that love making, had finally caught up to her body. She was laying in the bed in a red pair of panties and bra with her hair up in a bonnet. Supreme poured them both a glass of Champagne and he held the glasses in his hand. Supreme called her name. "Whitney! Whitney baby wake up!" Just as soon as Whitney saw Supreme's face, a smile came across hers to see that he was back.

"Hi! Baby, I missed you." Not as much as I missed you, beautiful. "What's all this?" Supreme gave Whitney a glass of Champagne. "Baby I'd love for you to join me in a toast baby." "Sure Supreme, I'd join you in anything baby." So, what are we toasting to? We're toasting to us! "To us." "Yes! I want to toast to the most, intelligent, sexy, phenomenal, and caring woman that I've ever met in my life." Whitney smiled, well can I join you and make a toast too? "Sure!" "To the most handsome, smart, attractive, comforting, and love making man in the whole world." To Supremes' surprise , Whitney said, "daddy I love you so much." Supreme just stopped and just stared at Whitney but he didn't return her words. "She was waiting to hear Supreme say, I love you back."

Supreme put his glass of Champagne in the air to meet hers, until he heard that clinging sound. They both put their heads back to clear their glasses. Whitney looked into her glass after drinking the Champagne, she knew that she felt something hit her lip.

Whitney removed the diamond ring. "Baby what! is this mine, Supreme?" Supreme took the ring out of her hand and kneeled down in front of Whitney. "Baby right now I can't think of anybody in this whole world who completes me like you do." Tears started falling from Whitney's eyes. "Baby will you make me the happiest man in the whole world and be my wife?" "Yes! Yes! Yes! Supreme of course I'll marry you daddy, in a heartbeat, yes!" Supreme placed the ring on Whitney's finger and to her surprise it fitted perfectly on her finger. "Wow! She was looking at the ring, baby how did you know my ring size?"

Supreme smiled and said, "Whitney I studied your hand, when you held my penis in your hand." Whitney placed her hand over her mouth. "Ohhhh! weeee! Baby. You better not ever tell nobody that story but me and I'm not playing either daddy." Whitney put her hand out and looked at her ring finger. "Baby this is so beautiful." That's' three carat's worth of diamonds, you can go to a car lot and buy a new car with that ring. What? "Man are you crazy, someday I'm about to become your wife."

Supreme said, "no baby that ain't true." The smile that was on Whitney's face quickly disappeared and turned into sadness. Supreme said wait baby, why the sad face all of a sudden? I'm sorry baby, I thought that you had just asked me to marry you. "Whitney, I did what are you talking about? After you go get dressed, we about to go get married right now baby." When you leave Las Vegas baby, you're going to leave here Mrs. Whitney Washington. What! Man, please don't play with me right now, Supreme? "Whitney, I'm not playing." Supreme was walking up to her. "I love you baby, and I don't want to spend another day without you." Whitney jumped up on Supreme and wrapped her legs around his waist. Supreme cupped her butt and they kissed for a long time.

A hour later they were getting married by Elvis Presly down on Las Vegas boulevard. Whitney was now Mrs. Whitney Mila Washington. Supreme and Whitney posed with their marriage license. Whitney looked beautiful. She have a half part down the middle of her hair, with her hair hanging straight down. She was wearing a white channel laced dress with a pair of Virgil Abloh earrings. Her Kenneth Cole open toe high heels, white and silver accommodated her French tip manicure and pedicure. Her fashion fair eye shadow was light, but popping with a seduction to her eyes.

BIG AND LITTLE SATAN

Supremes' cell phone started ringing and that's when reality sat back in. That he has a woman that's pregnant with another mans baby and they have a son that's still waiting on him back at home in Phoenix.

But Supreme and Stigma know that any feelings that Supreme had for Stigma was left back in their bedroom, where he tossed her that bullet. Before Supreme even left their home, him and Stigma both knew just what that meant, that she was dead to Supreme.

Supreme even knew that Ms. Bergess, had some type of idea as to what Supreme was saying when he tossed that bullet to Stigma. Ms. Burgess just was praying that, if Stigma had to receive that bullet that it was in her hand and not in her body. The conversation that Supreme and Whitney had before they left The M.G.M was starting to tug at him also. Whitney asked Supreme, "baby how and when are we going to tell my mother and brother we're married?"

Supreme was riding in the car, playing Whitney's question back to himself over and over again in his mind. "Oh yea, Marquan by the way, I forgot to tell you bro, that we brother in laws now. Me and Whitney went to Las Vegas and got married. Supreme could easily see him and Marquan drawing down on each other, but this time Pow! Pow! Pow! Pow! Bullet shells ejecting out of both of their weapons. That's the same way that Supreme felt that day at the church when Sabrina exited that Limousine and went and stood by his best friend's side. Supreme couldn't believe that Marquan and Sabrina could stoop so low and betray him and what he and Marquan stood for.

Here all this time Supreme had been holding Marquan down waiting for him to return back home so they could finish what they started. But Marquan come home and get his dick sucked by Supreme's girl and then turn his little sister out like she some prostitute on the streets. Supreme was snapped out of the little trans that he was in by another phone call, except this time when he saw the name Supreme took the call.

Hello! "Yes, is this Mr. Washington?" "Yea this is, how may I help you?" Um Sir I'm just calling you to inform you that your car is ready Sir. A big smile came across Supreme face, this was a call that he has been waiting to receive beside the man that made Whitney old enough to get married in the state of Nevada. "Sir it's ready to be picked up any time that you're ready." "Ok! Thank you for the call, and you have a good day." You to Sir and we'll see you when you get here. Supreme picked up Whitney's hand and kissed it making them smile at each other.

After getting married and going back to the room for newlywed sex. Supreme went and dropped off the rental car that he was driving and went and picked up a new Rolls Royce Phantom drop head, white with tan interior. Supreme and his wife Whitney Washington were rolling around Las Vegas, in a brand new Rolls Royce drop head and was spending money in all of the Casino's. Now Supreme was telling Whitney, wifey let's go win some of these

people money. After winning seventy-six thousand on the crap table, Supreme and Whitney was on the highway pushing that White
drop head back to the Dirty Desert as Mr. and Mrs. Washington.

CHAPTER THIRTY-SEVEN
WHO CAN YOU TRUST

Emoni started smiling when she saw her baby daddy walk into the nail shop. Him and his homeboys came walking in the shop being real loud and telling jokes ranking on each other. "What up Ma!" "Hey Emoni!" "What's up Fresh!" Headache, Money Dough, Oh hi baby, Emoni leaned over and gave her baby daddy a kiss on the lips. "Hello! how you doing ma'am, he was speaking to the nail tech that was doing Emoni nail's. He pulled a chair up next to Emoni."

"What's up baby what you got for me?" Grab my purse right there and look inside, my nails are wet baby. Her baby daddy grabbed her purse and took out the envelope that Emoni was giving him. "What our son doing and why you didn't bring my baby?" He is getting on my damn nerves acting just like his mama. I didn't bring him because he still gone out of town with my mama. When is she bringing my baby back, mama Ruby be just kidnapping my son. I think she said that they be back in three weeks. She told me that he been asking about you thou.

"Why your ass ain't at work?" I don't go in until three o'clock, that's why I came and got my nails done first. "Can you take some money out of there, and pay the lady and give her a nice tip?" The Chinese woman smiled, she understood tip if she didn't understand nothing else. "Money Dough, leave that woman alone, baby please get you friend. I like this nail shop, leave that woman alone boy!" All sis you be tripping, you know I ain't had me no, me love you long timeeee! Fresh and Headache started laughing. "Aye you coming by the house or you going somewhere with your little dude?" "Baby I don't know what I'm doing yet." I don't know how late I'm going to be at work, baby it's Friday.

You know how Fridays be up there. You know I always get home late. "Do you want me to come by there and tap that ass for ya?" "That sounds nice but no, because I don't know if Marquan coming by or not, but I'll call you at work and let you know something." "Boy, look at you baby all high." "Come on now, you know I'm a stay smoking on something, he popped Emoni upside the head." "Oh yea! Your ass didn't want to talk to me the other day, when your little dude was at the house." I couldn't baby he was standing right there in my face. What was I supposed to do other than what I did? You know you didn't hang your phone up and I heard you tell him that I was your boss at your job.

Emoni slapped his leg, you ain't my boss crazy man, you my sons' father. I am your boss; don't you and that sucker get it twisted. "Oh, excuse me then!" "Aye, did you see that black girl on the news today?" Naw, why? What happened to her? I don't know baby, but that shit was crazy because she stay not too far from you, that just made me concerned about you. Some fool shot her Emoni, while her baby was in the car. "What! Baby that's so sad, why would somebody do that, why she got her baby?" Did she die? "Yep! And they got away on some smooth criminal type of shit?" He started dancing like M.J and everybody started laughing. Y'all stupid baby, that ain't funny.

"Somebody shoots and kill you in front of your child, you know that's got to be a heartless motherfucker right there to do something like that." "Shit! She black, they ain't about to do shit, but take her baby or kid's and place them in some foster home." Just so that their asses can make money off them kid's, hell she lucky they even put her on the news." Headache said. "Shit they don't mind putting us on the news just as long as the nigga dead thou, that's the only way you gone see us." Emoni said, "Yea! you sure got that right." "Aye dog you ready yet, that nail shit is giving me a headache and I don't mean like that black ass nigga right there either." Aye don't be rushing my baby, take y'all high ass outside and wait. "Yea I can do that. I don't know how y'all females take smelling that shit just to look pretty." A nigga don't give a damn about no nails, we just want y'all to drop them panties.

BIG AND LITTLE SATAN

Emoni started getting on his head. "See boy, that's why you don't have a woman now Fresh, because you think like that." A headache! "What!" Man have you ever heard of any player tell a female, I can't be hitting that pussy you ain't got your nails done? "Hell n'all, because if she let me hit the pussy, I'm trying to pop her nails, wig, hair piece, and eye lashes off." Even Emoni had to laugh. "Her eye lashes Headache?" "Yep!" Man don't y'all want the woman to look sexy and attractive?

"Emoni I ain't even trippin! Hell, if she letting me ride that kitty cat, her ass ain't even got to look at me at all." Sis, if she look back and see all the ugly faces that I'm making, shit her ass might not want to give me the kitty no more. She a be like hell n'all, my baby ain't going to be coming out looking like this fool. "Baby get that damn nut out of here, before he make me pee on myself." "Ok! beautiful I'll holla, at you later." They kissed on the lips. "Bye crazy ass man, bye Headache!" Ok sis we a holla. Come on Tone, that nail polish shit stinks.

$ $ $ $ $

Supreme and Whitney were back in Phoenix. Together they had come up with a wonderful mind-blowing plan, to introduce themselves as a married couple to their family and friends. At first, Supreme had a problem, convincing Whitney to go along with the plan. Whitney promised Supreme while they shared their vows, that she would be loyal to him and their marriage. So, what she had a problem with was taking off her wedding ring to please any-body. Whitney knew that there was no way that she could fool her mom or her brother from seeing such a large diamond ring. Whenever the sun or light hit her ring, it was like you have a police flash light in your face. Supreme already have a realtor looking for them a seven-bedroom home with a swimming pool and a three-car garage.

Supreme already had a home in mind, that was a few miles from where he and Stigma lived together. Whitney didn't want to leave her husband, so Supreme rented a suite at a nice resort in Scottsdale for a whole month. The realtor told Supreme that; it shouldn't take long for her to close the deal on the house he wanted. Supreme promised Whitney that, after they got settled that they would have a nice big wedding with their families and friends, in the way that she so much deserved. Whitney prom-ised Supreme that, she wouldn't ever enter fear or ask any question about his business. That whenever he was gone, that she would just wait for him to return back to her. Supreme told Whitney that, no matter how long that he was gone that he would call, and she wouldn't want for nothing. Whitney said, "baby you can't give me nothing, that I don't have already, that all she wanted was him." Whitney told Supreme her last name, tell her who he belongs to. Supreme put their wedding rings in a safe and he made sure that Whitney has plenty of money to provide for her and Jacob until he came back from out of town.

BIG AND LITTLE SATAN

Whitney has her own key to the resort, so that whatever she bought, she could take it there and not be questioned by anybody. They both promised not to mention anything about being married, until they told whoever together as husband and wife. Supreme and Whitney have already built a strong bond and trust in each other. Supreme made love to his wife again, before he sent her back home to her mother and brother's. Supreme gave Whitney ten thousand in cash and told her that he'll take care of her credit card real soon so she don't have to carry so much cash, just as soon as him and Marquan return back to Phoenix.

CHAPTER THIRTY-EIGHT
PIGS BLOOD

Supreme, Marquan and Persia were all at the airport, waiting to make a flight back to Atlanta, Georgia. They were going to go handle some unfinished business with Sergeant Hedgepeth. The last time Marquan was there, he watched GeeGee get shot and run over like a dog crossing a busy street. Marquan tried his best to take out Sergeant Hedgepeth, but half of the bar which were cops came out with their pistol's drawn. Marquan barely escaped from having a shootout with over a dozen police officers. After Supreme checked into the hotel, they begin to right away put a plan in motion to take out Sergeant Hedgepeth.

Papa Jack had sent Supreme a little more sufficient evidence, as to where they could find Sergeant Hedgepeth. They all wanted to go and have a good meal, so they all chose the Atlanta Silver Skillet restaurant because they all had different taste buds. Supreme wants so badly to tell Marquan that him and Whitney got married. But every time that he found himself, trying to get it out the words just wouldn't come out of his mouth. Supreme excused himself from the table and went to the bathroom. Supreme really just wanted to go call and check on his wife. But just as he went to make the call, he decided not to, that it would be best that he stayed focused on the job.

Supreme told himself that he'd make a little stop by Stigma's little boyfriend house before they left Georgia. Supreme smiled because he really has something special planned for his tuff ass. Supreme promised himself that, after he gets finished with De-shawn's ass, he won't be putting his little happy dick in nobody else's woman. Marquan walked in the bathroom and that took Supreme right out of his little killing daydream moment. Aye dog, they are putting our food on the table. It seemed like Marquan was starting to read Supremes' mind. "Hey Prem! You think that after we take care of Papa Jack business, that we should stop by and pay old boy a visit that knocked your girl up?"

Supreme tried to act like that wasn't even bothering him at all. "Oh yea! I almost let that shit slip my mind. I want to watch the blood leak out of that pig so bad that I almost forgot that we got another piece a meat to put on the grill." Thanks Marquan! They dapped each other's hand and Marquan said, "man let's go get something in our stomach, so we can go hunt this pig."

This time Supreme had rented a Camaro Super Sport and a Dodge Ranger. If everything goes to plan, they could be back in Phoenix by tomorrow night. When they left the restaurant, Supreme put an address in the G.P.S system and they were already two streets over from the address that he put in the G.P.S system. Supreme was driving slow down the street and when it came to the address he just stopped surprisingly right in front of the house. This was a person that couldn't wait to lay eyes on for the last week or so it made him lay awake in bed. He kept replaying himself squeezing the trigger and emptying the clip in Deshawn's body.

The house that Supreme stopped in front of, is where two vehicles 'sitting in the driveway. Clearly letting Supreme know that somebody was in that house. The adrenaline in his body made Supreme want to exit that vehicle and go kill everybody in the house, while he sat there the front door opened and two men walked out the house. That's when Supreme and Marquan drove away before anyone could notice their presence.

Supreme pulled down a few houses and Marquan stopped right behind him. Persia asked Marquan, "what is he doing?" Marquan didn't say anything, he was just waiting to follow Supremes' lead. A red B.M.W passed by while they sat there, and after they passed Supreme slowly drove behind the two men. The next time that the B.M.W stopped, it was pulling into a liquor store. The two men were walking into the liquor store, and Supreme found a place to park. Supreme looked at Marquan and they exited their vehicles and walked into the store behind them. When Supreme got into the store, the two men was grabbing beer and was headed towards the cash register.

BIG AND LITTLE SATAN

Supreme deliberately bumped into one of the men on purpose, Supreme and the man both said excuse me. Marquan was walking down the aisle, just waiting on Supremes' cue. They were beginning to know each other so well, that their body language done all the talking for them. Persia had no clue as to what was going on, but she had already backed both vehicles up and left them running with the driver doors ajar. Supreme was about to give him the signal when the gentleman that Supreme bumped said, "Aye Deshawn!" "Yea! Man, grab us a bag of them B.B.Q chips."

It was good that the dude spoke up, because he had just saved his own life. Supreme waved Marquan off and he looked at the dude that looked like he been eating boxes of steroids. That's when Supreme decided to allow Deshawn to live just a little while longer without purchasing anything, Supreme and Marquan exited the liquor store. They both jumped into their rental cars and drove away.

Marquan saw that Persia held her pistol in her hand, ready to make it sing to anything that didn't move right. Seeing Supreme and Marquan walk out the store so calmly, she knew whatever have just happened nobody didn't die in the store. Persia didn't hear any gun shots and she had looked through the rearview mirror and witness the two men walk out the store. Persia didn't know who the men were, but she did know that God was with them in that Liquor store.

Supreme was starting to feel much better, because he was riding four cars back in the next lane following Hedgepeth. Marquan was driving in the same lane as Hedgepeth, but he was three cars behind him. The adrenaline came over probably more than it have just came over Sergeant Hedgepeth. When Supreme saw the officer turn on 'his siren, and speed off to another call, Supreme and Marquan was starting to see what it was like, to see what a day of being a police officer was like. They had already been on three calls, following Sergeant Hedgepeth.

His day started off by being called to a grocery store. They have a woman purchasing almost six hundred dollars' worth of groceries, with fake twenty-dollar bills. She stood there bragging to the cashier about all the homeless people that, she was feeding out on the streets. The cashier was having a problem with an item not pricing right, it was showing a lesser price. The lady called a worker to do a price check. While talking to the woman and looking at a 5x8 photo of her behind the checkout line, when the worker came to check the price, the woman told him to bring her back two. That was just the time that the cashier needed. After shouting over the intercom to tell the worker, to bring back two bags of shrimps. That gave the cashier enough time, to notify her boss that the counterfeiter woman was back in their store. The lady had already burned them, for thousands of dollars of merchandise, but a call had already been made to the police.

While the lady talked loud on her Black Berry cell phone, Sergeant Hedgepeth and another officer approached the woman and took her out of line and into custody. The next call that Supreme followed Hedgepeth to was two roommates had got into a fight. One roommate was tired of his roommate trying to pick up on his girlfriend. It took Hedgepeth and two other officers to separate the two roommates, and when they did both roommates wind up going to jail.

The one roommate that they were about to release, when the officer went to search him, he had a little methamphetamine in his smaller jean pocket. The call that Hedgepeth was now leaving from, was a man acting up on a local bus transportation, the city bus. Some man had got on the bus with a black backpack. He told everyone on the bus that he was sent by a higher calling to destroy all bad people and if anyone try to exit the bus that he was going to blow it up.

Supreme luckily spotted a Mcdonalds across the street, him, Marquan and Persia all went and ate burgers and watch the show just like everyone else. Until Atlanta's finest pulled the nut case off the bus. Marquan told Supreme, "man watching all of this shit, being a criminal ain't all that bad." Supreme and Persia busted up laughing at Marquan's comment. Supreme watched as the swat team took the man off the bus and turned him over to Sergeant Hedgepeth and his men. Turned out the only thing that the man had was an old alarm click and three Penthouse magazines that the officers had passing around looking at themselves. Supreme figured that Hedgepeth was content with the situation, because they were back following him on another call,

Sergeant Hedgepeth surprisingly turned into a Fitness center, and he exited his squad car and headed into the Fitness center. Supreme drove and signaled Marquan to follow behind him, they parked side by side and started talking. It was a lady getting in her car and she was carrying a Nike gym bag across her shoulder. Supreme quickly exited his rental car and went to approach the lady. Less than two minutes, Supreme and the lady were waving bye to each other as if they were old friends.

But Supreme came back carrying the gym bag in his hand. Marquan and Persia smiled as Supreme walked up to the truck. Supreme jumped in the back seat and told them what he has planned. When Hedgepeth came walking out of the Fitness center, he was walking down the same aisle that he parked on. Persia was walking towards him, like she was on her way into the Fitness center. Persia had her hand in the gym bag, acting like she was searching for something in her bag. Just as Persia and Sergeant Hedgepeth passed each other, Persia yelled out loud. "Damn! I left my gym shoes in my locker." Hedgepeth turned around to take a look at the attractive woman that passed him up. Persia stopped and turned to him, excuse me officer. "Yes! Can I help you with something?" Persia started walking up on Hedgepeth, "Yes you can Sir. "Papa Jack said hello!"

Sergeant Hedgepeth tried to pull his weapon from his holster, but it was too late. He was taking slugs into his body from Supreme and Persia 40 cal and 9mm Glock. POW! POW! POW! POW!

BIG AND LITTLE SATAN

POW! POW! POW! Supreme and Persia rushed back to their cars while Hedgepeth was hitting the ground. While Supreme was running he could hear a woman yelling. "Daddy! Daddy! Daddy! Noooooo!

Supreme saw a woman kneeling, next to Sergeant Hedgepeth's body as they exited the parking lot. Supreme didn't know it, but the woman that he saw running up to Hedgepeth it was his daughter's twenty first Birthday, her job was giving her a Birthday party. Sergeant had stopped in to give his daughter a Birthday gift. His daughter had just forced her dad to take a bite of her Birthday cake. But what they didn't know was that would be their last time eating anything together.

Supreme, Marquan, and Persia didn't waste no time heading to the airport. This was their first time that they had purchased plane tickets for themselves after a job. When they made it to the airport it was a crowd of people, that took away their presence of being there away.

The rapper T.I was in the airport and people was asking for his autograph. So, it drew a lot of attention while Persia, Supreme, and Marquan purchased tickets for a flight back to Phoenix. They still have an hour and ten minutes before they could even board their plane.

Supreme suggested that they go and have drinks at the bar. He knew they always have T.V's playing at the bar. Persia wanted to go take a picture with the rapper T.I but decided not to. Because that definitely place her in Atlanta, around the time of Sergeant Hedgepeth's death. They were all talking and having drinks at the bar, trying to look normal like anyone else taking a flight out of Atlanta. Marquan was looking around and noticed a familiar face walking past the bar. Marquan tapped Supreme to show him what he was looking at.

They both walked to get a better look at where Deshawn was going in the airport. They didn't have to go too far, because either he was boarding a plane, or he was picking someone up from the airport. Supreme and Marquan didn't have to wait too long to see who Deshawn was picking up from the airport. Deshawn stood at the gate and waited like everyone else until their loved ones exited their flight. The door opened and people started unboarding the plane. Persia walked up to see what it was, that had Supreme and Marquan's attention. Just as she was about to ask, Persia didn't even have to ask any questions, because Stigma was running into the arms of Deshawn. Supreme, Marquan, and Persia all watched as they entered into a passionate kiss while Deshawn hands explored Stigma's body. Marquan could feel the hurt and pain that Supreme was feeling right at that moment and the fact that they saw it to, is what hurt him the most.

When Deshawn and Stigma started to walk out of the airport, Supreme, Marquan, and Persia all walked back into the bar. Stigma and Deshawn were so into each other that neither one of them even noticed Supreme standing there with gritted teeth. Supreme

BIG AND LITTLE SATAN

and Marquan looked at each other and Marquan knew Deshawn
and maybe even Stigma would be dying real soon.

CHAPTER THIRTY-NINE

TAKING CARE OF BUSINESS

Marquan woke Whitney up early. He was back in Arizona and had a few important things to do that he been putting off. So, he felt that today would be better than any, plus it would give him some more time to spend with his sister and baby brother. Marquan has a soap bar on a string and was watching Whitney slap herself across the face, because he was rubbing it on her nose. Whitney slapped herself so hard that she woke herself up and saw Marquan standing over her. Marquan started laughing until she got him back with a face full of water that she had in a cup by the bed.

"Owwww! It's on now." Whitney jumped up running, headed towards her mother's bedroom. Mama! Mama! She busted up in Ms. Housemoore's bedroom, Mama! Mama! Mama! get your son, get Marquan. Her mother woke up. "Whitney what the hell is wrong with you child?" "Mama! Marquan is trying to get me." Marquan came walking into his mother's room holding a cup of water. Marquan stop! stop! Whitney hugged her mother. "Ok! Boy I know you ain't going to wet up mama because she gone beat your butt, Marquan."

"Boy! What is you and this girl doing waking me up this early with all of this nonsense?" "Mom! What do you mean, look at me your daughter done this." Marquan's whole tee shirt was wet, and Ms. Housemoore started getting on Whitney. "Girl, why you wet that boy up, like that Whitney!" "Y'all better not be messing my house up with that water girl!" "Mama, I was sleep and he came in my room rubbing things across my nose and made me slap myself." Marquan! No, I didn't mama. I was asleep and she poured that water on me. "Oh, Marquan! Mama he just lied; boy stop lying. Mama go touch his bed, I bet it don't got one wet spot on it, mama." Unless he peed in the bed. Marquan let me find out you pissing on them girls. Marquan acted like he was going to pour the water still on Whitney. Whitney and Ms. Housemoore both jumped. "Stop Marquan! They both shouted in sequence."

Ok! Marquan don't make me beat your butt boy! "What! What! You gone beat my butt?" "Yea boy! You throw that water on me." Before she could finish her sentence, Marquan threw the water and wet both of them up. "Marquan! I'm going to kill you boy! They about to take me to prison when I get up." Marquan closed the door and took off running. Ms. Housemoore and Whitney both have a cup of water walking through the house looking for Marquan. He was in Jacob's room hiding in the closet. They had searched the whole house and couldn't find Marquan. It was one place that they hadn't looked, and Whitney pointed at Jacob's room and Ms. Housemoore opened up the door slowly.

When they walked into the room, Jacob was in his room snoring and sleeping peacefully. Ms. Housemoore looked around Jacob's bedroom and didn't see nothing out of place. She was about to close the door, but Whitney whispered. He is in the closet, mama. He's in the closet. The both of them stepped into the room and closed the door like they left the room. Marquan didn't hear nothing and he opened the door. Swoosh! Swoosh! They both dashed him with their cup of water.

All man! Y'all got me that's messed up, mama. Jacob didn't know what was going on. He just saw Marquan standing there soaking wet and his mother and sister were laughing. "Man! Jacob, you didn't even warn me bro." Jacob sat there looking at all of them like all of them were crazy. Ms. Housemoore really enjoyed laughing and playing with her kids for the first time. This was something that she had dreamed about for years to do. She was really happy to have Marquan home and out of prison. This was part of her that she only knew about in the back of her mind.

Ms. Housemoore prayed that things would stay that way and that nothing bad would happen no time soon. She had even stopped worrying herself about the things that Marquan was giving them. Ms. Housemoore just came to the reality that Marquan was going to be who he is. Until God decided to stop him and want to use him for a much better purpose. Ms. Housemoore thought about 1 John 4:15 , "Whosoever Shall confess that Jesus is the son of God, God dwells in him and he in God." That made her ask Marquan, while she was cooking them breakfast, "Marquan, son do you believe in God?" Marquan looked at his mother and said, "Yes! Mama, I believe in God." I wouldn't have made it home to you if I didn't believe in God. "Going to prison ain't nothing mom, it's making it out of prison is what count." Ms. Housemoore turned around and smiled, her mind went back to the scripture that she knew well. Luke 12: 8-9, Also I say unto you, whosoever shall confess me before men, him shall the Son of man also confess before the angels of God. 9. But he that denies me before men shall be denied before the Angels of God.

Ms. Housemoore told Marquan that, you really gave your sister a nice Birthday gift, that was alright Marquan. I have been trying to help her study the driver's license manual, why don't you take my car and see if she can pass her license test. She use to driving that car, I bet she do pretty good! Marquan said, "Wow! mama you over there reading my mind. Whitney got excited, bro you gone take me today?" "Yea girl! That's why I woke up." "Marquan! Yea! Yea! mama I know, the truth will set you free right?" They all started laughing.

All of their lives Ms. Housemoore tried to raise her children, to tell the truth. That's a verse all of her kids know, because she embedded in their hearts and minds. "Somebody tell me what verse that is?" In sequence Marquan, Whitney, and Jacob said. John 8: 32 Mama. Ms. Housemoore said, "Hallelujah! thank you Jesus!" "Ok! now y'all let me know, that y'all know who in control." They all laughed at their mother's Spiritual moment.

Marquan and Whitney were at the D.M.V trying to get her driver's license, and Marquan was asking her questions about their mother best friend. Marquan was trying to get a feel as to, what type of woman she was. He wanted to do something real special for Ms. Dawson. He told Whitney about it and Whitney said that she heard her complaining that her washer machine had just gone out on her. Marquan smiled Ok! They continue to talk about their mother and all that she has been through, since he has been locked up in prison.

Whitney started telling Marquan about all those times that they had come to visit him. When Whitney got finish talking, tears were rolling down Marquan's face. He couldn't believe that even though his mother was having all them problem's, that no matter what happened she still kept coming to visit him. Whitney told Marquan that their mother doesn't mean to be hard on him, but it would kill her if he went back to prison. Bro, I know that whatever you're doing to get your money to buy and give us gift's... Whitney turned and looked at Marquan eye to eye. "Bro! there's nothing that you can buy us, that makes us more happier Marquan then you just being home with us, Marquan." You mean more to us than any money that you can print, steal, or hustle for. Whitney's words' shot through Marquan, like a thirty odd six bullet shell. He stood up and walked out of the D.M.V, Whitney knew to just leave him alone to give him time to think. Marquan watched as Whitney and the man drove away, on her test drive.

The next time Marquan saw Whitney, she was holding her driver's license in her hand. "Yea Boy! They can't stop me now bro!" "Bro now can I have my keys, to my car?" Marquan hugged Whitney and gave her the keys to her 300 ZX. Marquan was on the phone with Supreme, he was telling Supreme to meet them at his friend's car lot. Just as soon as Marquan mentions Whitney's name, Supreme told him that he'll meet him in one hour at the car lot. Supreme also told Marquan that he has something to run by him when they see each other. Marquan already knew that him saying that meant somebody was about to die.

After Marquan met up with Supreme, he bought his mother a 2012 Lexus GS'400 Champagne with tan interior. Whitney was at the car lot crying uncontrollably and that was the first time that Supreme got to hug his wife since he been home. Marquan knew that Whitney was crying, because she was happy for their mother. God was sending her a blessing her way but through her own child that she looked down on through his lifestyle. Whitney truly believed what Ms. Dawson said that day to their mother at the house.

Don't worry about how it's going to come or where it's going to come from just accept it from God when it gets there. But most of all give thanks for your blessing because it's through his love and concern that they come. Supreme didn't want to turn and walk away from Whitney but Marquan was right there watching the whole time that they were all together. Marquan left His mother's old car there; he told Hason that he'll be back to pick it up later sometime during the week. Hasan told Marquan that the car was in good hands and safe.

Supreme was about to leave and Whitney said baby guess what? "Supreme and Marquan gave each other a supercilious look. "I'm sorry, Supreme I'm so happy, that I just called you baby, Marquan did you hear me?" "Aye yes I did Whit, that's why I looked at you crazy." "Supreme cut them off, just to loosen the attention." Supreme said, Why you so happy sis? That sounded a lot better to Marquan's ears. Oh Supreme, I got my driver's license today, Whitney pulled them out of her back pocket. "All that's great sis, now you can go push that 300ZX." "Yep! you better know it boy!"

Whitney went and sat in her mother's new Lexus. She and Supreme didn't even say goodbye to each other. Whitney was just hoping that, Supreme wasn't mad at her for almost giving up their secret. Supreme and Marquan talked for a few minutes, he was telling Marquan that he got a little info on the dude Tone. Hey whenever you are ready, we can go pay him a little visit. Marquan thanked Supreme, they dapped hands and headed to their vehicles.

Marquan and Whitney wind up going by Star's house. Marquan wanted Star to go online and purchase Ms. Dawson a new washer and dryer. Whitney couldn't believe that Star was the same female that she called thirsty. Star have herself together and as a woman Whitney have to respect her hustle. After spending time at Stars house, Whitney left there with mad respect for her, and she also learned that Star really loves Marquan and have his best interest.

They found Ms. Dawson a nice set and had it delivered to her house. Marquan asked the company if they could attach a little note to her washer and dryer? It read, "Ms. Dawson I want to thank you for being a blessing to my family while I was away. Just knowing as family that's what we should always do for each other, is to be there when we need each other's help. Ms. Dawson, God is always watching and know when to provide for his children. Love Marquan and Sheila." Marquan paid extra to have it delivered today to her home, the man told him that he was just in luck. Because he has a truck being loaded up now and he'll put her order on that truck.

$ $ $ $ $

Supreme had just left his Lawyers office. He met with Shadajah to discuss getting custody of him and Stigma son Isaiah. She told Supreme that she could make it happen, but it will look better if he has a few businesses or a good job. "She wanted Supreme to show that, he could support Isaiah because Stigma have nothing to show that." Supreme told his Lawyer no worries, that he could easily take care of that problem. Ms. Shadajah told Supreme that she already knew, that was the reason she mentioned it.

Supreme kissed her and then smacked her on the ass, that thing feels like, I need to pay you a little home visit. She smiled and asked Supreme can he make that happen real soon? Supreme winked his eye and walked out of her office. Supreme pulled into his driveway. This was his first time going home since he left home. He knew that his blood pressure didn't have to go up, because Stigma was still in Atlanta with her new baby daddy. Which was a good thing, because this would give him time to remove all of his things that he wanted to leave at the resort with Whitney. Supreme saw that she hadn't bought anything with the money he left her.

That's one of the main things that Supreme loved about Whitney, that she wasn't a materialistic person. Whitney loved and respected Supreme for who he was as a person and not a provider. Supreme thought that his wife, could teach every woman in his life a little something. Supreme knew that when it came to sex, that Stigma was the one to meet all of his needs but that was only because of her experience. Stigma was running circles around Whitney, right now when it came time to put Supreme in the bed. But Supreme could see that, Whitney was a fast learner and in time sex with his wife would be unforgettable.

Not that Supreme wasn't enjoying having sex with Whitney, but it was a part of his mind and body that was craving Stigma's touch. But he was starting to get used to the fact that there may never be him and Stigma never again in life. When you cross the line that him and Stigma have crossed, truth be told ain't no putting them pieces back together. Supreme walked into the house and it seemed to be peaceful and quiet.

Supreme walked into the kitchen and didn't even find Ms. Bergess, her favorite place in the house. The house just has that clean smell to it, but not that smell of good cooking that Supreme was used to. He saw Stigma's Mercedes Benz in the driveway, so he figured that she had to be picked up by some car service. Supreme knew that Stigma has a few different credit cards because she got her own money. Plus, Stigma ain't the type of woman, to depend on nobody not even a man. That was Supreme's main attraction to Stigma, besides sex he knew that she was great at what she does. Supreme would always choose Stigma over anybody to go on a job with.

Supreme smiled for the first time. "Hello Ms. Bergess! where is Isaiah?" Probably in his room, he mad at nanna right now. Because he thinks that, he supposed to eat ice cream before breakfast. "All that boy wants to do is eat sweets, sweets, sweets!" I told him that he going to grow up and be a handsome young man but with no teeth. Supreme and Ms. Bergess both laughed. "Yea! When I was his age, I use to have to be told the same thing." "Yea! I know that's his sweet tooth, had to have come from you because I didn't allow his mother to eat that stuff like that Preme."

Being that Ms. Bergess opened up the door by talking about Stigma, Supreme figured that he'd see what type of answer that Ms.

Bergess would give him about Stigma. He knew that Ms. Bergess wouldn't lie for nobody, she would always tell him and Stigma the truth. She would tell them, "If you don't want me to tell the truth, then don't be putting me in the middle of your lies." "Where's Stigma?" Supreme made sure that he looked her right in the face. Child, all I know is that she packed a suitcase and said Ma watch Isaiah for me for a couple of days, I'll be back.

I asked her Preme where she was going, and she just left out the door. She left in a Toyota, Camry with some white man, his license plate number is she reached into her bra and gave Supreme the plate number. Supreme couldn't do nothing but, kiss Ms. Bergess on the cheek. Because even to that moment, her word was still good with Supreme. Supreme climbed the stairs two at a time, to go make things right with their son Isaiah.

Little Isaiah was sleeping laying across the bed holding on to one of his joysticks. Supreme woke Isaiah up and he jumped right into his arms. "Dad!" He and his son hugged each other. "Where you been dad, me and mom been calling you?" "Dad why my mom keeps crying?" Supreme told his son that not only do kids do bad things, adults do bad things too and mama done something really bad Isaiah. He said, "Dad! are you still going to kill my mama?"

Supreme sat down on the bed and he told Isaiah. "Son I'll never kill or hurt you or your mother, I love both of y'all son. You don't understand right now, and I don't expect you to." But, when you get older and learn what mama did, then you'll understand why you saw daddy do what you shouldn't have seen me do to you or your mom. I was wrong for that son; I pray that the both of y'all can forgive me for that son. For what I've done, I'm so, so, so, sorry champ, can you please forgive me?

Little Isaiah said, "I know that mama cheated on you dad. I forgive you dad." It's mama who messed up our family dad not you. Supreme looked at him and asked, "Champ how do you know that?" Because I watch them Tyler Perry movies with Nanna and that man cheated on that lady with that white woman dad and his wife beat him with that bat like mine, dad. "That old lady told her to beat him with a frying pan dad, like the one Nanna cook with." Madea said that she would kill'em if he cheated on her, ain't that what you told mama dad?

So that's why I thought that you wanted to kill mama cause she cheated too dad. Supreme smiled and hugged his son. "Naw champ! I'm not going to kill your mama! "Hey dad, can we go buy me some new games?" Supreme was about to say ok, but he remembered the conversation that him and Whitney had. "No champ! how about you teach me how to play the one's you already got?" Ok Dad! Look this my favorite game right here. Supreme reached and grabbed the other remote control. He had Ms. Bergess make them breakfast and then Supreme and Isaiah ate ice cream together.

$ $ $ $ $

Marquan and Whitney walked into the house, playing the same way that they left home. But Ms. Housemoore was in her room praying, Marquan and Whitney barged into her room breaking up her prayer time. "Mama! Mama! look what I got!" Whitney was holding her driver's license in her hand. "Oops, I'm so sorry mama!" Marquan came in right behind Whitney. Ms. Housemoore was getting up. "It's ok baby, I was just getting up now." Ms. Housemoore grabbed the license out of Whitney's hand. "Ok now! I knew that you could do it, child, anything that y'all put y'all mind to, child y'all can accomplish it and don't let nobody tell y'all anything different baby."

"Guess what mama?" Whitney was about to tell her mama about the new car that Marquan has bought her, but she got interrupted by the telephone, it started ringing. Ms. Housemoore went and answered the call. "Hello!" "Oh, hey girl, I was just trying to do the same thing, until these kids came barging into my room." "What! you are calling me thanking me for what?" Ms. Housemoore sat on the phone and listened to her friend read the letter that Marquan had sent with the washing machine and dryer. Ms. Dawson read the letter. "Ms. Dawson, I want to thank you, for being a blessing to me and my family while I was away. Just know as family, that's what we should always do for each other. Is to be there for each other, when we need some help. God is always watching and know when to provide for his children." Love Marquan and Sheila. Girl, I told you, that you raised that young man well.

BIG AND LITTLE SATAN

"Well, I just wanted to call and thank the both of you for the washer and dryer, that was a kind thing your son did." "I didn't know girl, when I was going to be able to replace mine." But God did it. I told you Sheila that you don't know when or where the blessing is coming from, but it's definitely coming. "Girl, all the greatest things that have happened to me, happened just like now from the unseen." Baby, again tell your son I said thank you and God bless him! Ms. Housemoore was shaking and crying so badly that Whitney had to remove the receiver from her mother's hand. She hugged her son and said, "Marquan that's the nicest thing that anyone has ever done for me in my life." That woman really has been a blessing to this family. Marquan said, "Mama I already know."

"Whitney told me everything, I'm grateful for Ms. Dawson in my absence mama." But before you say that that's the nicest thing anybody has done for you, come here mom I want you to see something. Marquan grabbed his mother by the hand and led her down the hall. Ms. Housemoore was telling Marquan and Whitney, boy I hope y'all aint ran all of my gas out of my car. "Y'all know that I got to make it to work the rest of this week?" Marquan took her outside and the first thing that she wanted to know was where's my car at Son? "Which one mama?" Ms. Housemoore had put her hands on her hips and was getting mad because she didn't see her car.

Whitney, you and this boy play too much, what y'all do with my car? Marquan handed her both set of keys. "Here boy! you gave me your keys to your truck too Son." "No, I didn't mama, that's your car right there, it's paid for mama." I'll go pick your other car up, later on this week, I left it at the car lot. I love you mama, that's your car too, right there. Ms. Housemoore dropped down to her knees and said, Thank you, Jesus! But I don't deserve it Lord, I don't deserve it. "Oh my God are you serious, Marquan?"

Ms. Housemoore cried like a baby; her, Marquan, and Whitney, they were all down on their knees in the yard with their mother crying with her. Mama, you do deserve it mama, Whitney was telling her mom that it was time for them to be happy too. It's time, it's time mama. They all stood in the yard, hugging and crying with each other. Marquan picked up his mother and walked her over to the Lexus. He opened the door and sat her in the driver's seat.

Ms. Housemoore just looked around the car and then she just laid her face on the steering wheel and started back crying all over again. While Whitney stood there and watched her mom, her cell phone started ringing. "Hello! and that's when she heard the voice that she needed to here." Supreme said, Well hello wifey, I miss you. Whitney wanted so badly to just run and jump in his arms when she saw Supreme earlier. The Ralph Lauren silk body shirt and Guess jeans that he had on was fitting him to a tee. It made Whitney want to undress him at that car lot. All she said was, Ok daddy. click!

Marquan had a long day and the person that he wanted to see, would kill two birds with one stone right about now. He needs to have Emoni move some money around and make sure that his money was secured. Before anything bad happens or just to be sure that when it rained that it didn't rain on him. Emoni opened the door wearing a pair of pink booty shorts and a short half top. "Hi baby I was just thinking about you." "What was you thinking?"

Emoni kissed him and opened up the door so that he could come inside. Then she turned and walked away, letting him get a good glimpse of her in them booty shorts. "Damn baby! what you trying to do to me?" Emoni smiled and licked her lips, now you know what I was thinking about. Marquan closed the door and grabbed both of her ass cheeks. Well, I'm glad that I read your mind. "He walked her into the bedroom and after they finished having sex, Emoni told Marquan that, she wanted to show him a few homes that she was about to go and see." He said, "before you go and do that baby, I need you to move some money around for me first." "Ok daddy! what do you need me to do?" When Emoni was done Marquan had her put a half of million in one account and another one point five million in another account. Emoni looked at him, ok baby it's done. Emoni showed Marquan both of the new balances in both accounts. Marquan put in work one more time, leaving Emoni in a deep sleep. He kissed her and headed to end his day at Snooty's apartment.

After Whitney received Supreme call, she jumped into her 300 ZX and went to meet him at the resort. Supreme had good news and wanted to share it with her over a bottle of Champagne. Whitney didn't really care what the news was, she just wanted to be in his arms. She slid her key in the door and the light lit up green. Whitney took a deep breath and turned the knob. Before she could enter the room, Supreme yelled wait! You don't have to come in, I'm already ready. Supreme grabbed the bottle of Champagne off the table and his car keys and headed out the door. He gave Whitney a little peck on the lips and kept walking towards the parking lot.

On the ride to where Supreme was taking Whitney, he told her about going to see his lawyer. He told Whitney that he wanted them to have little Isaiah. Whitney seems more happier then Supreme, about him trying to get custody of his son. Whitney promised Supreme that she'll take good care of them both. Supreme said, "I already knew that Whitney, that's why I married you baby." That made Whitney feel really good inside to know that Supreme would place that much trust in her. She was feeling like she was Beyonce and Supreme was Jay Z. The way people were riding next to them and pointing at Supremes' Rolls Royce drop head, Whitney was feeling like a Star.

Supreme was driving through a beautiful neighborhood, in Scottsdale, Arizona. Whitney was admiring the extravagant homes that they kept passing. Each home that they passed, each home

BIG AND LITTLE SATAN

was just extravagant as the next home. Finally, Supreme came to a home with a for sale sign in the front yard, Whitney's mouth flew open. "Baby please nall, don't tell me that you bought this house." Supreme smiled and said, "Baby only you can answer that question for us." Whitney, if you like it, then it's ours. "What!" "Baby are you serious?" Look at it baby, it's beautiful. Supreme responded by saying, "How do you even know that baby, you ain't even saw the inside yet?"

Supreme pulled in the driveway and they located the key in the gold box that was on the door handle. Supreme done just as the Realtor told him to do; he put in the address of the house and the box opened right up. Supreme and Whitney walked into the house, and she instantly fell in love with the house. The high voltage ceilings and two staircases reminded Whitney of the houses that they show on televisions, Of the lifestyle of the Rich and Famous.

The home has a wet bar, five bathrooms and two fireplaces, a swimming pool and a jacuzzi with a waterfall, two story home with seven bedrooms and three car garage in a gated community. It was only three homes that were in a cul-de-sac. One out of the three was one of the houses that Supreme and Whitney were looking at. They even walked outside to see what type of neighbors that they would have.

It didn't take Supreme long to notice the blue and white Bugatti sitting in the driveway of one of the homes. It also has a Black

Lincoln Limousine, parked off to the side where you can fit an R.V trailer. The other home has a Jaguar, Cadillac truck and a seven series B.M.W. Supreme didn't know who his neighbors would be; he could see that they were doing well for themselves. Supreme already knew that more than likely, it has to be some white folks because it ain't to many blacks that could afford a home in their neighborhood. Supreme thought perhaps maybe a Lawyer or a Doctor, by seeing the Bugatti sitting at the house.

Supreme and Whitney inspected the home from head to toe, trying to remember anything that they might want to have the realtor fix before they even buy the home and get stuck with fixing themselves. Supreme was told that they would get a nice deal on the house. Because it had been a while since they even had someone consider looking at the place. The last family that lived in the house was a jeweler and they had a bad experience in the home.

One day the jeweler was followed home by five guys, and they done a home invasion robbery at that house. Which caused the man to lose his wife, because he didn't give up the combination to the safes at the store and home. The jeweler thought that the men were bluffing by threating to kill his family. When the man denied giving up the combinations, the first person that they killed was his wife. Before they could even turn the gun on his two children, the man gave in and gave up the combinations to both safes. They almost got away with the murder and the robbery. But the jeweler had a double alarm that go straight to the police department and the robbers didn't even know it.

When the police surrounded the Jewelry store, the robbers didn't have the proper information to make the police leave the jewelry store. The Sergeant who approached the store with another officer, sensed that something was wrong with the owner. When the men tied up the owner and tried to leave the jewelry store, they were all apprehended and taken to jail. They were all charged with robbery, kidnapping and first-degree murder. The jeweler moved out the house and the home been up for sale ever since. So, baby give me your honest opinion, the realtor told me that she'll have it ready in two months. By then, we should have broken the news to Marquan and your mother. "Whitney gave Supreme a look like two countries about to go to war. Baby it's gone kill me to be away from you for another two months." But baby, if that's what it's going to take to make this our home together then husband, yes ok! "Yes baby, I want this house!"

Whitney and Supreme were standing on the stairs and they hugged and kissed for a long time. Supreme laid Whitney back on the stairs and he removed her Chanel panties. Supreme allowed his tongue to find her vagina and he licked and sucked at her vagina until her body showed him satisfaction. Impression was looking out the window. "See daddy! I told you to buy that house across the street, some people about to buy it probably."

CHAPTER FORTY

MONEY, POWER, OR RESPECT

Supreme pulled up in his Rolls Royce drop head; he knew that he was about to see Stigma for the first time. He was really wishing that he could have had his wife on his arm. But he was also expecting Marquan to pull up any minute. One by one the whole crew was pulling up; they were all there to support SoSo. She was opening her massage parlor. Ecstasy, Glory and Persia were exiting their vehicles. Ecstasy was pushing a Black Infinity on chrome rims; Glory was driving a red convertible B.M.W with peanut butter interior on chrome 21-inch rims; Persia was driving a Porshe 911 convertible, white with a custom ground effect kit on it.

The lady of the evening was pulling in the massage parlor and was already eye balling Supreme Rolls Royce drop head. Hey ladies! They all started hugging and kissing each other. Stigma didn't waste no time asking, "Damn bitch! who pushing big daddy right there?" All in sequence, they all said that's Dada car. The smile that was on her face, it quickly disappeared. "Ain't that a bitch! Here I am up here crying and missing this man and he out here living it up." "Hello Dada! I said Hi Dada!" Supreme walked pass Stigma and walked into SoSo parlor and watched all his girls admire his Rolls Royce drop head.

Supreme saw Stigma was about to open up his car door and he chirped the alarm and locked the doors. Chirp! Chirp! Stigma laughed and said, This mother fucker! I can't stand his black ass. Persia said, "Come on girl! we here for SoSo, don't spoil it for her this her big day." They all headed into the parlor. SoSo has Erica Badu playing softly over the parlor speakers, there were also other people there welcoming the new parlor. SoSo had even already hired three other females to work in her shop.

Frosty, Ximines, and Shalaya, they were all being introduced to each other. Stigma couldn't help but notice how Ximines was staring at Supreme. So, she made sure that their introduction was cut real short. The other two girls Stigma embraced and made their introduction welcome she even gave them compliments. Frosty was on her Jada Pickett Smith look, with a short haircut dyed red. She a light bright with chubby cheeks 5'8, 38-26-34 with that sexy baby accent.

Ximines look like Alicia Keys with designer braids and a butt like Nicki Minaj surgery backside. She had gotten some surgery done before somewhere, because she has an ass that only a surgeon can create. It was big, juicy and perfectly round, her breast seemed natural, but they all knew in another ten years from now,

Ximines would be on her K. Michell and would be reconstructing that more bounce to the ounce. But right now, she was stealing the show. Pretty face with long black silky hair, that was naturelle that stopped in the middle of her back. Smooth chocolate black skin with her long track star legs, 38dd and a 26-inch waist with an ass that would easily loose measurement trying to figure it out.

Shaylaya looks like Snookie from the Jersey Shore, but just a few inches taller. She got burgundy curly hair, with a blond streak on the left side. They were all about to pop bottles of Champagne to welcome in the shop. When they felt the windows rattling, it was Marquan pulling into the parking lot bumping D.M.X and Sisqó, 'What These Bitches Want' that made everybody take the party to the parking lot.

Marquan was dressed in all Nike gear, and he was riding with Snooty and Star. Snooty and Star were rocking Gucci booty shorts outfits in different colors with Gucci lace strap high heels. Both of their hairstyles were on point, they jumped out of the truck twerking and wiggling to the music. It even made Supreme put a smile on his face. Everybody started dancing with each other and just having fun and was enjoying the day for SoSo. Supreme and Marquan walked to the side and took a look at his Rolls Royce drop head.

BIG AND LITTLE SATAN

Oh boy! now we got to go grab me one of these Preme, Marquan was smiling from ear to ear. Marquan almost stopped breathing, when he saw Stigma walked out the massage parlor. She and SoSo were bringing everybody Champagne glasses, so that Supreme could perform a toast and bring in the massage parlor. Here Dada, let's get her ribbon put up, so I can take pictures of her shop opening.

SoSo held her big scissors while Glory took pictures of everybody. Supreme asked everybody to put their glasses in the air. "I want to pose a toast to my new massage therapist, may 'Relax Yo Back' be a major success and turn into many more to come." In sequence everyone yelled, 'Relax Yo Back'! SoSo, Frosty, Ximines, and Shaylaya all posed for a picture and then SoSo cut the ribbon. Everybody was clapping and was really happy for SoSo. They all knew how bad she wanted to open her shop. SoSo and Frosty took Supreme and Marquan into one of the massage rooms to give them their first business massages. But instead of a massage SoSo was getting, her mouth and back blown out by Supreme. Stigma and the other girls knew that it was coming soon anyway, besides that, nobody showed jealousy in that way when it came to their Dada. They have all seen each other naked and have been with Supreme together many times before. But Snooty and Star wouldn't have approved of that square bitch riding Marquans' shaft like she was doing right now. But everybody was too busy smoking and drinking and having too much fun to even notice.

Marquan introduced Star to Supreme girls, and they all hit it off right away. After Supreme and Marquan got through relaxing their back, Supreme knew that he was going to have to interact with Stigma. Because they have some important jobs coming up in Chicago, Denver, and Cincinnati besides they would be leaving in a few days.

Next up they were headed to the windy city, they were going to take out a whole family. Supreme asked SoSo to use her private room. He took his crew in there and was giving them the rundown on their upcoming trip to Chicago.

They talked and Supreme was showing them pictures of their main target. His name was Swabon Foly, a store owner on the south side of Chicago, but he lives on the outskirts of town. Swabon, his wife, mom, dad, and five kids all stay in one house up front. But Swabon parents stay in a bungalow that's in the back. It was either full payment or his whole family life was due to cover the payment. Either way it goes, it's time for Swabon to pay his dues, time was up.

After they ended their meeting, Marquan told Supreme that after he dropped the girls off, that he would meet him in two hours to handle that business. Supreme told Marquan that he'll be ready to just give him a call when he ready to head that way. Supreme already knew that he was talking about the business that they talked about yesterday. Stigma was patiently waiting, hoping that she would get a moment to talk with Supreme.

BIG AND LITTLE SATAN

When Supreme was headed to his Rolls Royce, Stigma stood in front of his car door blocking him from getting in his car. "Ok! Stigma, I'm not going to tell you to move but once, I'm not in the mood for no more of your bullshit!" Stigma started crying. "Dada please, please, just hear me out for five minutes." Then I promise that I'll move out of your way and let you go Dada. Dada please! "Supreme told Stigma that she has just wasted one of her five minutes."

Stigma said, "Dada, I know that I fucked up badly, and I don't expect you to easily forgive me. But Dada, I went and made everything better, I broke off everything that I have going with Deshawn." When she said that, Supreme was ready to move her out of his way. Because he knew that he had just seen her kissing Deshawn at the airport in Atlanta. What stopped him from physically removing her was Stigma said, "Dada I just left Atlanta and went there to explain to him and his mother why I couldn't have this baby inside me." I needed to have his mother to help me explain to him that I have a family because he is young and doesn't understand. I made a mistake, but there's nothing more important to me than you and our son, Supreme.

When Stigma said his name, that made him look at her for the first time. "Dada! I made an appointment, to have an abortion yesterday, I'm not having this baby I'm sorry." I made a mistake, but it's still my baby that's inside of me. But I love you and my son more than I love this baby or him Dada. "Dada! just give me another chance to make things better between us, Ok?"

Supreme looked Stigma right in the eyes. Stigma, the only way that I can forgive you and your baby daddy is that you go and take his life for y'all disrespecting me and Isaiah. Stigma's throat lumped up. If it would have been anybody else, then Stigma would have asked him was he crazy. But the man that was standing in front of her, she knew that Supreme meant every word that he just said.

Dada ain't it already bad enough, that I'm killing my baby. It was my fault that this happened. Stigma stood there with tears in her eyes. "Dada, I just met that man's mother, how am I going to go and kill her only son?" Supreme said, "You're running out of time, he looked at his Rolex watch." So, do I need to add your child's grandmother to that list too, Stigma? Stigma dropped down to her knees in front of Supreme. Dada! please don't do this to me pleaseeeee?

Supreme looked at his Presidential Rolex once again, Stigma I do believe that your five minutes is up. Supreme stepped around Stigma and opened up his car door. Chirp! Chirp! She was slightly still blocking his door, so Supreme pushed her over on the ground moving her out the way and got in his car. Supreme started it up and started backing out, leaving Stigma laying on the pavement.

Supreme blew the horn once and drove away. He watched Stigma laying there through his rearview mirror as he drove off. Supreme for the first time felt that whatever he and Stigma had together, it was all left right in the Hospitality hotel suites, the day that she cheated on him.

Supreme and Marquan were following a black Cadillac and the gentleman was so into his music. He was bouncing up and down smoking a blunt swerving in and out of traffic that he didn't even notice that he was being followed by a black Tahoe with tinted windows. Tone flipped off a dude that crossed over in front of him in traffic. They both blew their horns and pretended to crash into each other's car. "Fuck you, Negro! Fuck you Mexican, punk ass bitch!"

Tone was happy that he wasn't riding with his two homeboys Money Dough and Fresh, they would for sure follow the dude and stomp him out. Tone knew that all the drama that was going on right now would fuck up his high over some stupid road rage. Tone knew that he had to be in a much better mood, headed towards his baby mama, Emoni's house. Tone and Emoni might even be trying to give their son a little brother or sister. He had already picked up a bottle of that, break your baby mama back drink. Tone stopped at a Liquor store by his mother's house and bought a bottle of Hennessy and a coke for Emoni's drink. He got a big bag of that Cali High Dro, and it had been a few months since him and Emoni had sex.

Ever since she had met Marquan in the grocery store, Tone had to back off and let her butter up their Turkey before Tone come and carve it up to eat off of it. Tone and Emoni had set up so many ballers in that apartment that it wasn't even funny. Ever since Tone had gotten out of jail, after serving six months for domestic violence on Emoni, is where he met Money Dough and Fresh.

Tone was in jail bragging about all the money that he was making selling drugs. Money Dough and Fresh were in jail on a home invasion and just before their trial started, they learned that the people had moved and weren't willing to come and testify against them. So, all charges were dropped on them, and Fresh and Money Dough told Tone how they rob people like him. They all had got really cool in jail and they were waiting for Tone to be released.

Ever since then, Tone, Emoni, Fresh, Money Dough and Headache have been pulling off jobs together. Emoni called Tone and told him about the mark that she met and had just hooked at the grocery store. So, they just been waiting for Marquan to take the bait. Emoni told Tone that if they ever were going to get ahead in the game, that she might have to sleep with a few of the ballers. At first Tone was really against it, but after he started seeing the type of money that they were giving Emoni, Tone only said that he would agree if Emoni made sure that she wore a condom. The two of them live in a house with their son little Tone and the apartment Emoni be at is only to set up ballers.

To Marquan's surprise, Tone was turning up into Emoni's apartment complex. Now Marquan got the answer that he wanted. He knew that Emoni wasn't lying about Tone coming by her apartment and harassing her and would take off before Marquan could get there.

Marquan drove past Tone just as he was parking his Cadillac in a parking spot. They parked the Tahoe a few parking spots over from Tone. Supreme have on black gloves, that have brass knuckles under each glove. Tone jumped out the car smokin a blunt, holding the Hennessy bottle in one hand and his cell phone in the other one. Just as he was about to pass Supreme, Tone nodded his head at Supreme, as to say what's up to seeing a brother in Emoni's complex.

Bang! Bang! Bang! Supreme hit'em with a clean, three-piece combination, two head shots and an upper cut. Tone's cell phone flew one way and the bottle of Hennessy exploded just as soon as it hit the ground. Bam! Tone was knock out cold. Marquan backed up the Tahoe and they quickly put him into the back of the truck. Supreme grabbed his keys to hide his Cadillac and he followed Marquan out of the complex. urrrrrrrr!

$ $ $ $ $

Emoni was lotioning her body with some Peach lotion, listening to Gerald Levert waiting on her baby daddy. Even thou she was having to sleep with other men to set them up, none of them never made Emoni feel like Tone did when they had sex. Emoni guessed it was just that baby daddy thing is what got her hooked on Tone lovin. Emoni looked at the clock, she already knew that Tone ain't on time for nothing. She always joked telling Tone that, he would be late for his own funeral when the time came. Everybody would be at the church waiting to see him off, only to learn that they were still waiting for his body to arrive.

Emoni thought that maybe she should just start their dinner. Tone's favorite meal was steak and potatoes with corn on the cob, so Emoni started cooking their dinner. A few minutes into cooking Emoni's cell phone started ringing. It came up My daddy. Funny thing about Emoni calling herself, trying to set Marquan up to be robbed, Emoni was starting to get mixed feelings about Marquan. The day that she told Marquan that she loved him, Emoni actually meant every word that she said. The reason that she was inviting Tone to the apartment, it wasn't for them to have sex. Emoni really wanted to tell Tone, that she fell in love with Marquan and want to be with him.

Hello! Emoni answered the phone in her most sexiest voice. She was actually happy that Marquan was calling her, so that she could make-up some lame excuse to Marquan, so that he doesn't come by while Tone was there, but Marquan caught Emoni off guard. "Emoni baby! I need you to meet me at and he gave her the address where to go." But before he hung up, Marquan said, "I need you to get here ASAP and bring your gun." Click!

Emoni was standing there, like damn what just happened? "What do I do? She was contemplating her next move." Tone is on his way and what about our food? Emoni stood there puzzled about what she should do. But she knew that, no matter what, she has to go meet Marquan, he was expecting her. She couldn't just blow off the fact that he had just called her and said to meet him now.

Emoni cut the food off and stuck it in the oven. She walked into her room and grabbed a white and blue Fendi dress out the closet and wiggled into it. Emoni grabbed her cell phone and car keys. She was looking for a pair of shoes to match, while she was calling Tone to make up some excuse as to why she had to leave and not stay to fuck and feed him. The call went to voicemail, and she tried it again. The same thing happened, so she left Tone a voicemail. "Baby I had to go check on Shenna she got sick, and they rushed her to the hospital." I'll call you later, I love you. Beep! Emoni pressed the pound button and sent the message. Emoni didn't want to look too crazy, so she grabbed her Louis Vuitton purse and matching shoes. She switched everything out of her Donna Karan bag and put her gun into her purse and headed out the door.

On her way to her car Emoni noticed all the glass that was busted up on the ground where someone must have dropped it getting in or out of their car. Emoni jumped into her Lexus and headed to where Marquan told her to meet him. Emoni turned down the street the address was on, and she called Marquan just as he told her to do. When she got to the house, the garage door opened and he signaled her to pull inside. Emoni wasn't concerned about what he was having her do. Because she has done the same thing with Tone too many times before.

Emoni jump out looking all sexy fitting her Fendi dress to a tee. "Hi baby! I didn't take long, did I?" Naw you good. They hugged and kissed each other. Marquan asked Emoni, "Did she bring that thang?" He was inquiring about her gun. "Yea baby! I got it right here, is everything Ok?" Marquan grabbed the gun and said, "yes baby it sure will be in just a few minutes, come on follow me this way." Emoni followed behind Marquan, like a puppy following its mother across the yard.

When they walked into the house, it was empty and Emoni's human instincts kicked in. Emoni was starting to wonder why Marquan called her to an empty house and asked her to bring a gun. Emoni's pace started to slow up a little, he walked her into one of the bedrooms, and it was a man sitting in a chair with a black cloth bag over his head. It was another man standing there Emoni saw holding a gun to the man's head. Emoni heart started beating fast, she thought to herself. "Damn! Did Marquan find out that, she was trying to set him up to be robbed?"

Fear quickly came over her whole body. "Marquan what's going on baby and who are these people?" Naw baby chill! there's no need for you to be afraid, Emoni baby it's all good. That's my man Supreme right there and I told you that you can trust in me, right? Emoni shook her head slowly but was still nervous and still wasn't too excited to meet Supreme right now. Supreme took in

BIG AND LITTLE SATAN

Emoni's features and could easily see why Marquan was feeling babygirl. In Supremes' mind, he said damn! just as soon as Emoni walked into the bedroom. Supreme said wow! This boy sure knows how to pick'em, little mama a fox. Marquan walked up to Emoni and kissed her trying to calm her nerves. "Damn! baby what you thought, I called you here to kill you or something?"

Supreme and Marquan started laughing, but Emoni didn't join in on the joke. Emoni was now studying the body of the man that was sitting in that chair. Her heart started racing much faster now, now her chest was heaving up. "No! No! No! it can't be him?" Emoni mind went straight to her baby daddy Tone.

Lord please no, don't let that be him under there. Because if that's Tone then, we both are about to die when they find out we are together. Marquan is playing me right now; he knows who I am. Emoni started thinking about their son, little Tone. "Oh my God! my baby ain't never going to ever see his parents again."

Tone what have we done, what have we done to our son? Emoni kept repeating them words over and over in her head. Supreme emptied Emoni clip and put one bullet back in the chamber. He let Emoni see him place the one bullet back in her gun and he cocked it. Click! And he handed the gun to Emoni. Her mind was going wild. "Oh Lord! Oh Lord! no, no, no, what do I do? What do I do?" Marquan wasn't saying anything. Like he was thinking, you and your man tried to play me bitch! didn't think I'd tie y'all together? So Emoni decided to wait and play things out, Marquan really didn't seem angry towards her or Supreme. Maybe I'm just tripping and that ain't even Tone at all. "But why did he hand me a gun?" Emoni mind was all over the place.

Marquan finally spoke, "Baby are you ready to put an end to your problems? I finally caught this pussy going into your apartments. Me and my bro was following his bitch ass and he led us right to your apartment complex. Now you can put an end to all the fear and pain that he caused you baby. Tone was listening and was wiggling in the chair like a stripper on stage. He was trying to say something, but Marquan had him blindfolded and gagged with his tube socks and tape covering his mouth.

"Baby I want this pussy see you blow his fucking head off." Remember, you said, hurry up and handle it, right? Marquan removed his gun from his waist band then he pulled off his blindfold. Tears started rolling down Emoni face, now seeing how badly that Supreme and Marquan have beat Tone. "Emoni shoot this punk ass nigga!"

Tone was trying to see out of the one eye that wasn't completely closed shut. "Shoot him Emoni, before I leave both of y'all ass right here for wasting our time with this bullshit!" Marquan was screaming to the top of his lungs, "Shoot him Emoni, shoot his ass now!" Emoni raised the gun, and looked at Tone she was crying badly. Marquan was removing the tape from his mouth and Emoni knew that Tone was about to get the both of them killed.

Emoni's mind started racing and she began to think. "Who's going to take care of our son, if the both of us die right now?"

BIG AND LITTLE SATAN

Emoni was thinking that Tone was the one to bring them in all of this so why should she lose her life behind his hustle? Marquan removed the tape and Tone said, "Man, what the fuck is going on? Emoni, tell these fools that I'm••*Pow!

Emoni put a bullet right in Tone head and Marquan finished him off. Pow! Pow! Pow! Tone flipped backwards in the chair and on to the floor. Emoni dropped the gun and ran out of the room. Supreme nodded his head at Marquan and told him to get Emoni head right. Marquan knew that Supreme wouldn't hesitate to leave Emoni lying next to Tone.

"Emoni! Emoni!" Marquan grabbed her by the arm, hey is everything good here? First you tell me to get rid of o'boy and just as soon as I do, you up here acting like you fucking this fool or something.

Emoni noticed Supreme coming down the hallway with his gun still in his hand, but not with a comforting look in his eyes. Emoni knew that she had better change something up about her character and fast. Emoni put a smile on her face and hugged Marquan. "Thank you, baby! Thank you, it's all over that punk ass nigga got what he deserved." "I just wished that I could have beat his ass first, the same way he used to beat my ass." I'm sorry daddy, it just all caught me off guard and I ain't never killed no body before. But killing him, it made me feel better daddy then I thought that I would feel.

Supreme hearing her say, that she was the one that killed Tone made him feel a lot more comfortable with letting her live. Supreme turned around and headed back towards the room where Tone was dead in. That also gave Marquan a little assurance that they weren't about to leave Emoni behind.

Supreme had already told Marquan that, if Emoni show him any weakness that he was going to leave her next to Tone. Supreme was already making a call to have Tone body removed and disposed of. Even thou he took care of business, he never got sloppy and left something to trace back to him.

Before they all separated, Supreme asked Emoni a few questions and Emoni responded in the right way. Emoni told Marquan and Supreme that they have nothing to be concerned about. That they done her a favor and besides that, she the only person that killed anybody. Emoni asked them both, the question that really saved her life. "Hey! Y'all tell me who can survive being shot in the head and live to tell on anybody?" She was making it very clear to them that, it was her gunshot that killed Tone.

Supreme hugged Emoni and welcomed her into their family. He told Emoni we're family now and you shouldn't never fear nobody ever again in life. Emoni hugged Supreme and said thank you Supreme I do feel safer. On the way out the door, Emoni took the same deep breath that she took going out as she did coming in, because that was a door that she thought that she would ever cross again.

$ $ $ $

BIG AND LITTLE SATAN

Whitney and her best friend Vicky were walking through the Arizona Mills Mall, and they were turning heads. Whitney was wearing a Gucci one-piece short set, black and pink with the Gucci ankle boots that matched her outfit. Her outfit has Gucci printed all over the suit, her hair was in a ponytail in a pink hair tie. She had bought the outfit at the mall, when she and Supreme went shopping in Las Vegas. Her best friend Vicky always stays fly. She was wearing black lace see through two-piece short set. Vicky wore a black bra with diamonds on the bra and no shirt covering the bra and a diamond belly earring. She had on a pair of open toed half leather to the ankle and the rest of the boot was all black lace. They both were carrying their big designer purses and flopping their straight perm hair styles. It was a few guys walking through the mall and had taken their best shots at the both of them but they quickly got turned down by Whitney and Vicky. Vicky kept telling guys that they couldn't match her N.B.A boyfriend's salary. While Whitney politely told everyone, that she was a happily married woman. Two dudes tried to clown them and asked Whitney, "where was her wedding ring if she married?" Whitney really didn't know what to say, so she said I accidentally left it in the shower. One dude said yea! with that dildo that you were fantasizing with. The dudes slapped hands and walked away laughing. Vicky hated being embarrassed, so she told Whitney damn girl! why did you come up with that lie, for you couldn't have thought up nothing else to say?

What made you think that they were that stupid and wouldn't notice that you weren't wearing a wedding ring? You know these dudes, be trying to look up a bitch ass hole checking them out. Whitney said damn! "Who lied to them, I am married?" Vicky started laughing in Whitney face. Damn bitch! snap out of it, it's me Whitney, your best friend. Girl them dudes is gone now, you ain't got to lie to me. Whitney calmly said again, best friend or not, I am married, Vicky. Vicky flicked her hand and was walking away, you ain't about to trick me into telling you what N.B.A player I'm dating. I know what you're doing, I told you girl he married and I ain't about to cut my money off running my mouth. "Whitney, I told you to give me a little time and I'll tell you who he is but not right now."

Whitney said, "child I ain't thinking about you cheating with some other woman's husband." He's not my husband and that's you, her, and his problem, not mine. Vicky, That's the difference between you and me Vicky, I wouldn't settle for being somebody else mistress. You might as well go and eat pussy because you are tasting it afterwards any way. That really pissed Vicky off, and they had just barely made back up. Vicky had finally called Whitney and apologize for leaving Whitney's Birthday party. Vickey promised Whitney that she would make it up by buying them an outfit and some shoes. Vicky was secretly sneaking around and dating one of the Phoenix Suns basketball players. But she never would

BIG AND LITTLE SATAN

tell Whitney which one of the players it was. Vicky always flashed her little money on Whitney and their friends.

Vicky told Whitney that she wasn't saying all of that when she was just buying their outfits and shoes. Whitney told Vicky that she didn't need her money, or that woman's husband money. Whitney dropped the bags at Vicky feet and started walking back in the store. "Girl, take theses bag's, you know that you want this outfit and shoes." Whitney went to the rack and grabbed the same outfit and told the lady to go get her the same shoes she picked before. It was an outfit that Vicky wanted but said that she couldn't afford it. Whitney went and grabbed that outfit too and set it up on the counter. The cashier said, "ma'am that will be twenty-two fifty, will that be cash or credit?

Whitney went into her purse and pulled out a hand full of hundred-dollar bills. Vicky mouth flew open seeing the bank roll that Whitney just pulled out, and that's where she left her mouth open on that store floor. On Whitney's way out the store, she threw a hundred-dollar bill at Vicky feet like she was a stripper, "Here that's for that dry ass Pizza, that you just bought me bitch! My husband takes good care of me." Vicky, you need to get you a life and find your own man. Whitney walked out of the store and left her standing there, with the cashier holding her hand over her mouth. It was good that Vicky drove her own car, or she would be using that hundred dollars to catch a cab home.

$ $ $ $ $

It was Impression night off and her and Marquan had made plans to spend time together. It had been a long week for Impression sitting around catering to her daddy all week. Even thou she loved her father; she had actually been ready for her daddy to go back home an hour after he got there. He had asked Impression to do something that almost made her heart jump out of her chest. But he was her father and how could Impression tell him no to anything that he asked or expected of her to do?

There was nothing that he wouldn't ever do for his daughter if she asked of him. He treasured the ground that Impression walked on. It was through her dad, is how Impression knew everybody that was somebody being her daddy daughter. He was respected by everybody, and Impression and her mother always felt safe living in the house with her dad. He always kept four men that always kept a close eye on her and her mother for safety reasons. The same men that worked for her dad used to protect the 1st Black President Barack Obama, when he first served as the president.

Now here her dad was calling on her and asking Impression to do him a personal favor that she wanted to say no to so badly. Ding Dong! Impression was interrupted and taken out of her thought, of her father and his drama. When she heard the doorbell ring and saw Marquan face through the peep hole. Her thoughts of her father vanished quickly.

BIG AND LITTLE SATAN

Impression opened the door and her and Marquan just engaged into each other's eyes for a moment. That made the both of them, put the biggest smile on their faces. Impression was wearing a red Banana Republic off the shoulder mini dress and a pair of Marc Jacobs open toe platforms. Marquan had on a two-piece Pelle Pell white cotton button down suit and a pair of soft leather patent loafers. Marquan was holding a medium size bear that was dressed in a black suit and wearing a black bow tie.

Marquan handed the bear to Impression and when she hugged the bear it said. Hello beautiful, you're special. Impression couldn't believe what she had just heard the bear say. She almost couldn't hold back the tears that were forming up in her eyes. But she managed to get a grip and hold her composure together. Impression turned the bear around and saw how handsome the bear was dressed. "Awe! ain't you just the cutest, little bear I've ever seen." Marquan where did you find him, he almost made me cry?" "Thank you, baby please come in."

Baby you look just as handsome as your gift, they hugged each other and gently kissed on the lips. Marquan returned the compliment. "Damn baby! are you ever not beautiful?" Impression told Marquan that she bet that he wouldn't be saying that after he saw her wake up in the morning. Well once again baby, welcome to my little home. Marquan looked around the house and thought that he could put his mother's house inside hers and not fill up a quarter of Impressions house.

Impression invited Marquan into her game room, which he didn't even know that she had. Impression's game room almost looked like they were inside of a night club. She has a bar, pool table, dart board and flat screen T. V's that were connected to surround sound that accommodated her stripper stage and pole. Marquan was blown away. He could easily see himself living in a house like that, but with Snooty and Star. Impression walked behind the bar and asked Marquan what he would like to drink. Marquan asked her, "What all do she have to drink?" UM! just about any drink that you'll find in a bar or night club. She turned up the corner of her lip, as to say man what you thought, I'm a boss bitch? Marquan said, "Hey, just surprise me baby, I'm your guest." Impression said, "Wait! Wait! and she walked from behind the bar, will you please excuse me baby for a moment?" Yea sure!

Impression came back holding her bear. Marquan smiled. I'm sorry but I wanted him to join us, you guys make a good team at melting my heart. Impression placed the bear in one of the bar stool chairs. The bear said, "Hello beautiful, your special." Impression kissed the bear and said, Y'all special to me too. She walked up to Marquan and gave him a much passionate kiss and he returned her affection. Impression fixed Marquan a drink and handed it to him. Here baby! What's this sexy? Just drink it baby, you told me to impress you. No, I said surprise me. Then that's an impression and surprise that you won't forget handsome man.

BIG AND LITTLE SATAN

To us! They tapped glasses. To us, Marquan joined her in the toast. Marquan spotted a picture of an older man that was putting on a golf course. "Baby, who's this your man?" "Yea! that's definitely the man of my life." Oh Ok! Marquan that's my father, can't you see the resemblance? "He just went back home to my mother, he been here all week driving me crazy baby." Yea! trust me, I know how stressful parents can be. I got a mother that, drives me crazy too.

Marquan and Impression were playing strip pool, and all he'd gotten Impression out of was her platform heels. Marquan was standing there in his boxers and Impression was on the eight ball. After she made the shot, Marquan placed his boxers in the middle of the pool table. He walked over to Impression; well you took off everything that I'm wearing so what are we about to play for now? Impression dropped down to her knees, and she looked up into Marquan eyes. Marquan now it's time for us, to start playing for keeps she grabbed his penis and kissed the tip of his penis. Then Impression took the rest of him into her mouth and started deep throating right away. Marquan leaned up against the pool table and watched his penis disappear in and out of her mouth. Marquan knew that he was in the hands of a different type of woman because Impression was allowing Marquan, to invade her mouth and throat and didn't even gag once.

Marquan wanted to show off his tongue technique, so he picked Impression up and removed her clothing on the pool table.

Marquan pushed all the balls into one of the holes. He spreaded Impression legs wide open and he started teasing her whole body with his tongue. Then he started licking around her vagina. Ummmmm! Impression started enjoying her tongue company in her pussy. She pressed back and was asking for more of his tongue.

Marquan invaded her love box and made Impression vagina talk to him in a foreign tongue. Impression only knew one man that could make her body cringe in the way Marquan was doing it. That was her man Body Count but right now Marquan was doing things to her vagina that Body Count haven't even done. "Urnmmm! Ugh! Owwwwww! Ayeeeee! Mmmmmm! Impression was making every type of sound that was in the Webster dictionary. Oh, daddy yes, yes, yes, Mmmmmm!

That was Impression second time exploding into Marquan's mouth. He didn't let her experience one climax alone, his tongue and two fingers equally shared pleasure with her vagina. Marquan knew that he had her, right where he wanted her. Marquan climbed up on top of the pool table and Impression opened her legs wider. But Marquan wanted to take her vagina to another world. He turned Impression over on her stomach and laid her halfway off the pool table leaving nothing, but her ass booted up in the air. Marquan balanced himself on the pool table and wood railing and the side pocket definitely belonged to him. Ouchhh! Ouch! Oh no, no, no, let me up baby; wait, wait, oh my God! No! Marquan wait, wait, stop please! Daddy, you killing my pussy wait a minute. Marquan, why are you doing this to me? Wait baby, oh no! aggh, aggh! umumrn, umrnmmm! Daddy wait stop! Whyyyy, Why, Why, Why, Whyyyyy! Daddyyy ! Urnmmmm! daddyyyy! yes! yes! yessssss! Oh, my goodness shittttt!

Just as Impression cums, Marquan pulled her up and laid her on her back. He placed her legs up high on his shoulders and went right back to work beating her vagina like he was a dog and found a female dog in heat. Impression thought that he was trying to push his penis through to the top of her head. Impression didn't know how much longer could her body take this type of punishment. But she knew that this was the type of sex that her heart could enjoy forever. "Damn daddy, a bitch ain't going to be able to walk for days."

While Impression was trying to catch her breath, Marquan stood up on the pool table looking down at Impression with his penis covered with her juices. Impression looked up at Marquan like he was her superhero and had just saved her and her pussycat, but Marquan jumped down off the table and picked Impression up carrying her away from the pool table in his arms. Marquan laid her on top of her bar like someone had ordered her in a drink. Marquan took two bar stools and put one on each side of his body. He turned Impression's body towards him and pulled Impression's vagina towards the edge of the bar. He placed each one of her legs on top of the back of the bar stools. Marquan climbed up and put a knee in each bar stool. He grabbed his penis and looked into Impression eyes as he slid into her vagina.

Mmmmmmmmmmm! Impression welcomed them both into her warm soaking wet pussy. Ohhhhhhhh! Daddy, Daddy! Marquan knew that she didn't have no place to run, it was only oakwood and his penis that all Impression's body was about to feel. Marquan gripped his hands on the bar right up under Impression's ass cheeks. He started off taking slow strokes Ooooooh! Ooooooh! Ooooooh! Baby yes, keep it right there, daddy.

Marquan and Impression were enjoying her exchange of their sexual chemistry together, until Marquan's mind went to everything that had happened to him from the time leaving Florence prison. The only problem was good or bad, Impression's vagina was about to experience the consequences from his experiences. Impression went from enjoying the most sexual experience two bodies could offer each other to complete sexual torture. Ohhhhhhh baby! baby wait! wait! wait Maquan Nooooooo. Marquan's eyes was closed and he had turned into a mad rage.

Every stroke he took into Impression's vagina was like he wanted her pussy dead. Mmmmmm! Mmmmmmmmm! Mmmmmmmm! Mmmmmmmm constant moaning. Impression tried her best to take the pain, but she had no idea as to where Marquan's mind was at. Wham! Wham! Wham! The thrust from the pain caused Impression to grab her stomach. Now moaning and screaming for Marquan to stop, tears started rolling down her face but not so much from the pain but because Marquan was stealing her heart with every stroke he took. Ahhhhh! Ahhhhhh! Ahhhhhh! Daddy, Daddy wait! Daddy wait, wait, noooooo! no please stop. Marquan was just about to cum, but Impression's body was starting to jerk ready to explode and meet his erection. Almost at the same time they made their most ugliest fuck faces, and boom! Sperm erupted from both of their bodies.

Marquan finally opened his eyes to see Impression in tears but with the biggest smile on her face. Marquan jumped down and laid his head on Impression stomach. She gripped his head and they both fought to catch their breath. Impression just allowed her head to lay back on the bar and said daddy damn!

CHAPTER FORTY-ONE
BODY COUNT

S upreme, Marquan, Stigma, Glory, Ecstasy, and Persia were all exiting the plane at Ohara airport in Chicago, Illinois. Supreme rented two Chrysler 300 with the Hemi engines in them. One was white and the other one was charco gray on gray interior. They didn't have to check into a hotel on this job, because Papa Jack has a home there that he gets away to every few years. Supreme put the address in after he hooked up his G.P.S system in the white Chrysler 300, and they were headed towards the house.

Supreme pulled up in front of a house, that seemed to appear in a real nice upscale neighborhood. Everything seemed to be pretty quiet and from where Supreme parked he could see the house they were looking for pretty clearly. Marquan and Stigma drove the gray 300 Chrysler and headed to the store on the south side of Chicago to get a clear view of the store and to see who was working in it. They pulled up on 79th and Throop and realized that it was one of them neighborhood stores that everyone shopped at that lived a few miles from the store. They would either go there to by small groceries or liquor.

After Marquan and Stigma took a look at Swabon's store, Marquan could tell that a lot of people from the neighborhood shopped at his store. Because there were nonstop customers coming and going all day. Marquan told Stigma, that it might be a problem trying to take Swabon out at his own store. Also being that the type of neighborhood, that the south side is, they knew they have to be careful. Marquan didn't know if Swabon had cameras or what type of agreement that he had with the gang members in the neighborhood. A lot of places like Chicago, because the owners have the store running, that didn't mean that their spots didn't belong to them, and they could be watching the store for the owner.

Stigma has the heat on high, she was so happy that she brung her Ralph Lauren over coat. Plus, she had gloves on and boots and was drinking hot chocolate. Her and Marquan was sitting there debating, on rather if they should enter the store or not. It wasn't the few gang bangers that lingered in front of the store whom was bothering everybody that went in there. It was the cold weather that Marquan and Stigma wasn't used to. It was 32 degrees outside, at least that's what the temperature on the dashboard read.

Marquan was wearing a nice leather double breasted coat, that has a nice warm lining on the inside of the coat. But as cold as it was in Chicago, it didn't appear that the coat was doing him any justice because he was still shaking and shivering in the car. They both took a sip of their hot chocolates and decided that it might be best to take a look inside the store.

Before they exited the vehicle, they both checked their weapons, because if they could end the job now, they can be headed back to the airport to shake the cold weather. Marquan knew a guy that was from Chicago and used to brag a lot about Chi Raq. Right about now Marquan was thinking that he was crazy, Marquan couldn't understand how anybody there could stay outside long enough to even commit a crime. "Damn it's cold here!" Marquan and Stigma were ready to leave Chicago and not even handle the job that they were sent to do. Marquan drove down the street a little while and turned around in the famous White Castle parking lot. He drove back down 79th and pulled in front of the store. Him and Stigma exited the car and were walking into the store. "Damn! ma got Donk back there! what's good sexy woman can I go?"

Marquan and Stigma paid no mind to any of the guy's comments. Marquan just gripped his pistol just in case anyone of them tried anything crazy. Marquan opened the door for Stigma, and he closely followed right behind her. It was a big black dude, sitting in a chair at the front door. Marquan sized him up and knew that he would eat up bullets like a bag of M & Ms. It didn't take Stigma long to learn that the man running the cash register was definitely the man in the pictures. He was a fat medium built older man with gray and black hair. They took it that the woman who was eye balling them, from the moment they walked into the store was his wife.

BIG AND LITTLE SATAN

Stigma looked at Marquan, "Damn! This bitch is worser than Chinese people, she on us like we about to steal they shit! Marquan started laughing. He was grabbing a soda out of the freezer, yes, she on her shit!" Marquan knew that trying to get to them in their store, it wasn't happening. They have a thick bullet proof shield, separating them from their customers. They were passing their customers their merchandise through a small, covered area that they spined back to them after bagging up your stuff. Marquan and Stigma bought a bunch of munchies, because they knew that it was about to turn into one of them police stakeouts.

Marquan grabbed another bottle of pop, a susie Q, a bag of chips, and some Oreo's. Stigma grabbed two bags of Sunflower seeds, some cupcakes and a bag of plain chips. She didn't want to mix the soda with the hot chocolate she had already been drinking. So, she grabbed two bottles of water and a Cranberry juice. While Swabon was ringing up their munchies, Marquan looked at him like you better kill yourself before I do, making me sit in this cold weather. Swabon gave Marquan his change and they walked out of the store.

On their way back to the car, four of the dudes that saw them go into the store started following them. "Aye, say home boy! what you ride?" Marquan and Stigma kept on walking and Marquan hit the alarm. Chirp! Chirp! Marquan walked with Stigma to her side and was opening up the door for her. Say baby! I bet I can make that ass shake harder than that with me riding that donkey. One of the guys ran up in front of them and stood in front of the door before Marquan could open it. "Naw, Baby girl, let me show you what I'm working with." I'll eat the lining out of that and before he could get his words out good, Stigma was putting her 9mm automatic pistol down his throat.

"What! What you say, excuse me did you say something, what you say that you want to suck the gun powder out of one of these bullets, you punk ass lame nigga?" Marquan was pointing his 40 cal at the other three dudes, and they all held their hands up. Come on man, we just were playing around let my brother go? Old boy was pissing on himself, and Stigma looked down at his pants. Stigma removed her gun, get the fuck out the way. He ran over to where his brother and friends were.

Marquan and Stigma got into their rental car. While pulling off Stigma told Marquan to stop right in front of them. She rolled down her window. "Hey man! If I would have taken you home to ride this Donkey, what was you gone do, piss in my bed after I rocked your ass to sleep?" All of his friends started laughing and pointing at his pissy pants. Marquan drove away laughing himself at the young dude. Fuck you stupid bitch! Fuck you, should have killed me, wait till I see you again. The one that pissed on himself flipped Stigma off as they passed by.

Marquan was on a burner phone telling Supreme about their little encounter and what he thought about handling their little problem with Mr. Swabon. Supreme already knew who all was in the house. He had even learned that Swabon parents lived in a little house out back, behind the main house. He watched the old lady and old man go in and out of the front house, along with five kids ranging from the ages of two to fourteen which was an older female who looks just like Mr. Swabon's wife. They have three boys and two girls that were being watched by their grandparents.

While riding in the car to meet Supreme, Stigma and Marquan were starting to get to know each other on a different level. Supreme didn't want to be around Stigma, so he placed her with Marquan. Supreme knew that Stigma could handle herself well in any situation.

Marquan opened up a conversation between them, by telling Stigma that she handled herself very well back there. Stigma smiled and they started engaging into a conversation from that point. Stigma asked about Snooty and Marquan talked about her and Supreme problems. Marquan told her that he hopes that everything works out for them, and that made Stigma have much more respect for Marquan. She even sincerely apologized to Marquan for pulling that gun on him the day he got released. Marquan told Stigma that he understood that it wasn't her call, that it was Supremes. That he would have done the same thing if the shoe was on the other foot.

Marquan and Stigma were laughing and smiling, while sharing their munchies with each other. "They even asked each other what their plans were, after all the killing come to an end?" Really in all reality, they both knew that there may never be an ending unless it was prison or the cemetery. But Stigma told Marquan that she wanted to enroll in Real estate school and sale homes. Marquan truly hadn't thought about it. But he told Stigma that he wouldn't mind opening a strip club with Supreme and his girls. Stigma told Marquan no matter what you do, to be sure to be saving his money. She told Marqun make sure you put some away for the bad times or at least to keep the good times going. "Marquan told Stigma that Supreme have already taught him how to do that." Again, that made Stigma smile because she knew that Supreme was looking out for his friend and giving Marquan great advice.

Marquan and Stigma watched as the black S.U.V Volvo pulled away from the store. Mr. Swabon was driving his wife home and she was lying back resting her eyes. Mr. Swabon bobbed his head gently to some type of music. Supreme was even wondering what it was, that Mr. Swabon was listening to. He knew that if he didn't have that money, that whatever he was listening to, that it would be the last time that he'd enjoy any type of music. Marquan already knew where he was going, so he just allowed him to go home and spend a little time with his family.

$ $ $ $ $

Supreme watched as the little girl helped her grandpa into the house, the Foly family was all just about to sit down and have dinner as a family. The doorbell rang and Mr. Swabon told his daughter to stay at the dinner table, that he'd answer the door. He drew the curtains back and saw the two females standing there. Mr. Swabon opened the door and Persia jumped into his arms. "Help! Help! Please help us! He's trying to kill us. Mr. Swabon saw that Stigma's shirt was ripped and she was trying to hold it closed. He didn't know what to do, other than invite them into his home and lock the door. Mr. Swabon looked out the window again, to make sure that whoever was after them wasn't still following them.

When Mr. Swabon turned around to ask the girls who was trying to kill them. The pressure from Stigma 9mm pistol almost made Mr. Swabon have a heart attack. He grabbed his heart while Stigma was telling him to shut up. Stigma placed her hand up to his mouth and pointed her gun and Mr. Swabon eyes got big. Persia moved him out of the way and unlocked the door. His wife was on her way walking down the hall. "Honey is everything ok?" Persia grabbed her and put her gun to her face. Ohhh!"

The door opened and Supreme and Marquan came walking into the house. That's when Mr. Swabon said. "Please! Please! go ahead take whatever it is that you want, but don't kill us please!" Supreme went into the kitchen and walked the whole family back into their living room and made them all take a seat. He walked over to Mr. Swabon, "I'm here to collect what you owe." "Wait! Wait! I paid your guys the other day." He turned to his wife. "Didn't we honey?" She quickly joined in, "I gave the money to the same big black guy as always, call him he'll tell you that we paid."

Supreme quickly picked up on, that they must be paying taxes to one of the gangs in Chicago. Supreme laughed, just knowing that them youngsters was putting it down in their neighborhood. "Well, I'm not here about no change, Mr. Swabon." Papa jack told me to say hello! Mr. Swabon was about to explain, but Supreme, Marquan, Stigma, Glory, and Persia let their guns do the rest of their talking. Pow! Pow! Pow! Pow! Pow! Pow! Boom! Boom! Boom! Pow! Pow! Boom! Powl Pow!

When Supreme opened the door and walked out the house. The whole Foly family was on their way in heaven; wherever a whole family lays. Supreme, Marquan, Stigma, Glory, and Persia calmly walked out of The Folys home and went to their cars and left.

Marquan was laying back with his eyes closed thinking about Impression. The sex that they enjoyed together was something different and special from all the other woman that Marquan encountered since being released from prison. After having sex with Impression in her bedroom again, after their pool table romance, Marquan fell asleep holding Impression in his arms. She slept comfortably on top of Marquan, and he woke up the next morning to her running in the nude on her treadmill. Marquan carried Impression back to her bed and they finished off from where they left off the night before.

Impression wind up telling Marquan that she loved him and forced him into saying the same words back. Marquan didn't know Impression as much as he knew, that he was going to get to know her after sex. But he did know one thing, about a woman of her caliber saying I love you to a man. Marquan knew that it came with so much more than just those three words. It wasn't so much of her words that bothered Marquan, but it was the look that brung concern to Marquan. It was a look that in his whole life of living, he has never saw before in a woman's eyes. It wasn't lust, desperation, curiosity, or an overpowering joy, but a definite assurance and confidence in picking him to say I love you too.

Marquan already knew that he had picked a diamond out of the ruff to grow and shine with. But after just experiencing what he just had with Impression, he knew that Emoni didn't stand a chance. Emoni's walk was sexy, attractive, she was motherly approved, but Impression was the type of woman that walked down a runway and steal the show. Marquan was distracted by the flight attendant, asking him if he wanted a drink.

Marquan sat up quickly, because the woman that was standing in front of him looked so flawless that Marquan felt like he has to be dreaming. There was no way that this woman could be so beautiful and so perfectly put together. Marquan said, "Did I die and go to heaven or are you really real?" Ummmm! "Yes, I am, even more then you could imagine if you knew me." She smiled at Marquan's comment. Sir are you going to order something or not. "Yes, I'll have Jewl's. Maybe we'll see about that. But what will you have to drink for now?"

Jewl's wasn't the type of woman that you could even compare to another woman. She has her own unique look about herself. Her 38DD, 24-36 5'10 in height with a bronze color complexion, with long black straight hair which was in a bonnet for her job purposes. She looks like she from India; her skin was smooth as butter with not a pimple, scratch, or anything out of place on her body. Jewl's got long model legs, pretty face, hands and feet with the brightest smile. Her make-up was so perfect, it looked like she was going to take a glamour photo shoot. Marquan smiled. "Ok! Beautiful woman I'll have a water and your phone number." "Ok Sir!" No Sir, my name is Marquan. Ok Marquan, I'll be back with your water and my number. Jewls returned a minute later with Marquan water and her number. She winked and said, "Ok! now you can dream Marquan, until I see you again." Jewls turned and walked away.

Marquan and Jewl's gave each other a warm smile when they were exiting the plane in Cincinnati. She politely put her hand up to her face, as if to say call me Marquan. Supreme rented a Cadillac truck and a D.T.S Cadillac car, both of them was black. Supreme drove the car and Marquan drove the truck. They left the airport and went and checked into their suite that was already quipped with a few handguns and high power assault weapons. AR15 and a 30 odd six assault rifle.

Supreme was about to take on a serious family of killers. They were a biker gang that, hated anything with black skin. They call themselves W.G.K which stands for White Gorilla Killers. Danny and his little brother Bobby started the white biker group in Cincinnati. Everybody called Bobby Scum Fuck and his brother Danny. Most of the woman that slept with Bobby said, that he was the most sickest human being walking the face of this earth.

The W.G.K family was deep with loyal riders and two prospects.; White Boy and Hitch Hiker. I guess it ain't too hard, trying to figure out how he got his name. Hitch Hiker use to go cross country, until he met Scum Fuck. They hit it off right away and that's how he became a prospect in W.G.K. Hitch Hiker loved Scum Fuck and would die for him without thinking twice. Hitch Hiker loved Scum Fuck so much that Skull asked Scum Fuck was they fuck buddies, when they served time together in jail before he brought him to join their bike club.

$ $ $ $ $

Supreme and Marquan were looking over the weapons that Papa Jack had sent them. It was a variety of guns and high-power automatic weapons that lay under the mattress of the bed in Supreme suite. A 9mm, 40 cal, .44 magnum, 357 magnum, A-K47 assault machine gun, AR15, and a 30 odd six riffle. Just by seeing all those weapons, Supreme, Marquan, Stigma, Glory, Ecstasy, and Persia knew that the W.G.K must have some heavy artillery in their club house and homes. Papa Jack ordered a hit out for the whole W.G.K bike gang. Papa Jack told Supreme no matter what happens in Cincinnati, don't leave until the two brothers Skull and Scum Fuck was taken out. The hit would pay Supreme one Million- and six-months' vacation anywhere in the world that him and his crew want to vacation to.

Like always Supreme, Marquan and the girls were eating chicken and watching a C.D on the W.G.K biker gang. It was of all their home and club parties and park outings with other biker gangs. Marquan said, "damn he really done his homework on these crackers, this must be something personal?" Supreme was pointing out something on the television and Ecstasy was telling Glory to pass her a wing out of the chicken box. Supreme said, "hold up on that chicken right now because if y'all ain't careful playing with these boy's, that chicken is going to be the last thing that you eat." Ecstasy rolled her eyes at Supreme and got her own chicken wing out the box.

Supreme started going over the plan that he had put together. He planned on sending Persia up in the biker club, to try and get her close to Skull or his brother Scum Fuck. They had brought her all types of cutoff jeans and short sexy tops.

Supreme had Papa Jack put Persia up in some cheap sleezy motel for a week to make it look like she had just caught a bus to Cincinnati. At first Supreme didn't want to use Persia as bait. But she was the only one that, could just walk up in their bike club and not get killed in their establishment. Persia took a taxi from the Pink Pony motel, she had the taxi driver take her straight to the W.G.K biker club.

BIG AND LITTLE SATAN

When she walked in the biker bar all heads turned Persia's way. Some blonde was kissing a red head and when they finish kissing, they both went and kissed Skull. But when Persia walked into the club, she went straight to the bar. Skull quickly pushed the two ladies away, so that he could get a better look at Persia. Persia was wearing some cowboy boots, tight Daisy Duke shorts and a half halter top. She wore a red lumber Jack shirt tied up over her shirt. Persia tied a red, white and blue confederated scarf on her head. Her hair was now blond and hung straight back in a ponytail.

All the men in the bar stopped whatever it was they were doing and put all their attention on Persia. They wanted to get a look at the pretty, little bomb shell that had just dropped out of heaven and landed in their club. "Hello! You think a girl can get a beer around here?" The fat bartender hurried up and placed a beer in front of Persia. She grabbed the beer and acted like she had been drinking beer all the time. The blond that was kissing Skull, walked over and slapped Persia on the back, and allowed her hands to find Persia butt. Persia turn around and punched the woman right in the face and she hit the ground. Bam! Persia poured the rest of her beer in the woman's face, waking her back up from being knocked out.

Three of the bikers went to attack Persia, but Skull stopped them. "Whoa! Whoa! wait! He put his hand up and Persia walked back over to the bar. I'm sorry! I been waiting all day for that, and I had to waste the best part of the beer… The woman was jumping up and finally got her balance right from getting off the floor. She was going back for round two, but Skull saved her from another beat down cause Persia stood up and was ready.

"Well! Well! Well! Hello pretty lady." Persia didn't even look in Skull's direction. Skull grabbed her chair and hand and spent her around to face him. Skull took Persia beer and downed it. "Damn! what do you got to do, to drink a whole beer in this joint?" Skull said, "well maybe you can start off by, showing me and my brothers here some respect." Skull have about nine of his biker brothers and the woman that got knocked out standing behind him. You come into my bar and assault one of my girls and we welcomed you in here with a nice cold beer? Persia said, "Well so far, the welcome been real shitty and this man looking broad come and rub my ass." Sorry honey! but if I wanted a man, I would have picked one of them with a penis. Not somebody that look like a man, with the same thing I got between my legs. I don't swing that way honey, yo bad.

"Oh! and I still haven't got a chance to drink a nice cold beer yet!" Skull put up two fingers and the bartender placed two cold beers on the bar. Skull grabbed both beers and he gave Persia one. "Thanks! Now that's more like it, she took a long drink and placed the mug on the bar." She looked at all of the bikers and Skull, so tell me, does this mean that I'm not welcome? Skull put his hand up and everyone went back to what they were doing. The blonde and the red head tried to hug Skull, but he turned them over to two of his other biker brothers.

BIG AND LITTLE SATAN

"Hello, I'm Skull, and this is my club and my brothers, we're all family here." "Hi! I'm Dutches and I'm new in town as you can see that." So where are you from? "Texas." "Texas! And what brings you to Cincinnati?" Just looking for a change of pace. So, do you have family here? I guess not, right? Looks like I've already worn out my welcome here. Skull smiled, he was happy to hear her say that this was the type of chick that he started riding bikes for. Skull wanted to meet a down ass chick to ride on the back of his Harley.

"Well, I tell you what Dutches, consider my home your home now." Skull turned and looked her right in the eyes. "Dutches whatever you do, just make sure that you don't shit on me in my own house." "Ok! Yea sure Ok! I'll never do that, but just make sure you don't treat a girl like you're welcomed into your house." They both laughed. Persia was on her third beer, and she was ready to throw up on the first beer. Persia knew that she would be up pissing the rest of the night. She figured hell what the fuck! If this is what it's going to take to get to the W.G.K bikers, then so be it. Persia thought about Skull's little comment, so she told herself if Skull don't want me to shit on him in his house, then he won't be so mad if I just piss on him.

Supreme and Marquan clapped hands when they saw Persia getting on the back of Skull Harley Davison. Supreme thought that he got the main target already in less than a few hours. But that thought quickly changed, when about eighteen other bikers started warming up their bikes and took off behind Skull with pistols on their hips. They stayed behind them but at a nice distance. Supreme quickly learned that they were taking Persia back to the Pink Pony Motel.

Skull done just as Supreme expected him to do. They were going to check out where Persia was staying and Supreme already had everything sitting at just the right place. He watched as Persia walked Skull back to his bike and kissed him. Skull and his brothers started their bikes. Pluuuuuuuur! Pluuuuuuur! PluuuuuuR! and they all road out of the Pink Pony motel in a line. Supreme followed them a nice distance, before they turned back around and headed back to the motel.

Persia was brushing her teeth like a mad woman, trying to get the taste of beer and Skull out of her mouth. When Supreme walked in the room, Persia said I'm in Dada. He's coming to get me tomorrow. He invited me to a pool party at his brothers Scum Fuck house. They all laughed at hearing the name Scum Fuck. Supreme told them let's go to work, because a few of them ain't going to be at the pool, party. Stigma and Ecstasy were messing with Persia's butt in her Daisy Duke shorts. Supreme said, "let's get out of here, this room smells like piss and cigarettes." Persia said, "Oh Dada, please don't say that word, because I got to release about a bladder full of beer, but not in that bathroom let's go."

$ $ $ $ $

BIG AND LITTLE SATAN

Supreme was driving through Cincinnati following one of Skulls main biker brothers. They call him Oggie because he ate everything on his plate and everyone else's whenever they have a cookout. Oggie put you in the mind of Tom Arnold from Rosann. Oggie pulled his Harley into his garage and killed the motor on his bike. Just as he was getting off of his bike, "Oggie! Papa Jack said hello." Pow! Pow! Marquan rushed back to the Cadillac and Supreme drove away. Stigma, Persia, Ecstasy, and Glory was following another biker that were roommates. Debauchee and Dinky. Debauchee live up to his name because whenever, Skull needed you to disappear these are the main two that he sends at you.

Dinky was smaller than Debauchee, but he the one who has a very bad temper and would kill you fast. The two of them together would put you in the mind of Penn and Teller the comics, except the magic that they do to the body never comes back. They had stopped at a Liquor store, before they went home because the both of them drink beer like water. The both of them got off their bikes and walked into the Liquor store. Stigma, Glory, and Ecstasy walked into the store minutes after they did.

Dabauchee saw Stigma and immediately started calling her racist names, because her hair was blond and that really pissed him off to see that. "Hey Dinky! look at this monkey wanting and wishing that she was white." "Come here nigga! maybe if I piss on your black ass, then maybe the rest of your skin will turn colors to." Stigma smiled at Debauchee and kept on walking through the store. The cashier told Debauchee that he can't be harassing their customers.

"Hey man! what are you sticking up for this nigga for?" They need to go back to Africa or the zoo with the rest of the monkeys. "Dinky laughed and told Debauchee come on man let's just go I got our beer." Yea! You're right they stink up the store. Debauchee grabbed a few bars of soap off the shelf and toss them by Stigma feet. I'm sure that it will be hard but try washing some of that black off of you. A black blond! Debauchee started laughing, Dinky who in the hell, have ever heard of a black blond? "Do your mama know that you don't want to be a monkey anymore?"

The bikers finally walked out of the Liquor store and headed back to their motorcycles. Glory was more madder then Stigma was, hearing the racist white boy disrespect Stigma like that. Glory opened a big bag of chips and dumped them out on the store floor. She stuck her 9mm in the bag and acted like she was eating chips while walking out of the store. Stigma saw what she had done and followed suit because she grabbed a bag of BBQ chips and done the same thing as Glory. She acted like she was eating chips out of her bag as well walking out of the store.

Ecstasy walked over to the cashier and paid for her stuff and the chips that Glory and Stigma walked out of the store with. Just as soon as they came walking out of the store, "hey black, blond!" say do your daddy think that he was sleeping with a white woman to make a skunk? Don't you know black and white don't mix?

BIG AND LITTLE SATAN

Glory said, "hey pig! do your mama know, that she got to make funeral arrangements for you today?"

They were about to get off of their bikes, but before they could, Stigma and Glory raised those chip bags and Pow! Pow! Pow! Pow! Pow! Pow! Pow! They hit the ground, but Stigma wasn't done. Pow! Pow! Pow! Pow! They ran and jumped into the Cadillac truck and burned rubber. Urrrrrrrr!

Stigma, Ecstasy, and Glory met back up with Supreme. They took those rental cars back and rented more cars with a different company. Supreme rented a Ford F250 and a black Camaro then they headed back to their suite. Supreme had counted eighteen bikers, that was three down and fifteen more to go, along with Scum Fuck and his brother.

$ $ $ $ $

Scum Fuck was hugging his brothers and the females that they invited to accompany them at their pool party. There were already a lot of people there enjoying themselves. Scum Fuck have two kegs of beer and all type of Liquor. They were rocking out and having plenty of fun. There were females screaming from getting thrown into the swimming pool. Marty and Kilo were dunking all the girls underwater. "Hey Mongo catch!" He threw a slim blond in the air to one of his biker brothers.

The blond that Persia punched and knocked out in their biker club, was walking into the pool party with three more other girls.

"Hi Tap Out! These are my girlfriends, that's Kristen, Mandy, and Daisy and they all love to party!" Tap Out grabbed Daisy and ran and jumped in the pool with her in his arms. They started kissing each other just like they were a couple. They were all wearing Walmart hottest swimming suits and was looking to impress anyone of the guys that's in W.G.K biker group. Mike and Jimmy Lee was going around the party and was passing out drinks of shots and giving out bong hits. One female with orange and blond hair was stripping and swinging her top around over her head. She had already come to the swimming party on some type of heavy drugs. The W.G.K bikers cheered her on. "Shake it, Shake it, Shake it!"

She was spinning around, not even keeping up with the music or beat. Lea, the blond from the club was the head female from the W.G.K biker gang. She had been passed around to all the bikers that's in the club except for the prospects. Buckie was the one that brought Lea into the club. But when Skull decided that he wanted her, Buckie knew that he had to turn her over to the President of the club. Now, she is only there to please Skull, unless he passes her off to one of his other biker brothers.

Scooby and Little Bobby were walking through the gate with twenty pizzas each, and everyone started getting out of the pool. "Hell, Yea Scooby! it's about fucking time you pricks showed up with the pizza." Which one is Pepperoni? Cody grabbed a whole pizza and went and sat up against the fence.

BIG AND LITTLE SATAN

Look at that fat fuck. Tommy Boy was telling Scum fuck while grabbing him a few pieces. "Hey where's fucking Hitch Hiker? Somebody let me use their cell phone." Danny Boy took his off of his clip and handed it to Scum fuck. "Hey! don't you shit heads eat up all the pizza you white boys save me some." All heads turned when Skull came walking through the gate with his new piece of pussy. Skull, Persia, Kenny, and White Boy all came together.

That really pissed off Lea, seeing Persia walk through the gate with Skull. Any other time that would be her, getting the attention that Persia was receiving right about now. "Hey Pres!" one of the prospects was greeting Skull as they walked in the gate. Skull and Scum Fuck didn't waste no time hugging and greeting each other. "Hey come here! I want you to meet somebody." This my girl Dutches, she out here from Texas bro. Scum Fuck walked around Persia and checked her out. Nice! Nice! Nice! Nice! So, "what do it ride like bro?" Persia stepped closer to Skull and wrapped her arms around him, then she gave him a kiss. "Oh! it's that type of party?" Skull looked at Scum Fuck, "nope it ain't that type of party, this one is all mine bro." Scum Fuck told his brother, "That's good that it's all yours, because anything that belong to you it's mine too." Scum Fuck slapped Persia hard on the ass and went and jumped in the pool. Wooooooo! He screamed as he jumped in. "Let's Fucking Partyyyyy!" Someone cranked the music up louder.

Lea tried to walk up and kiss Skull but he turned away. "Oh, you gone diss me for this stray cat?" Persia told Lea, "At least I have a collar and tag, Bitch! Who do you belong too?" Lea was about to jump but Kenny grabbed her, come on Lea, let's dance. Yeaaaaaaaa! W.G.K, W.G.K, W.G.K! Everybody started yelling it, W.G.K, W.G.K, W.G.K. Skull told Persia not to worry about Lea, she just jealous.

$ $ $ $ $

Supreme, Marquan, Ecstasy, and Stigma sat and watched Persia as she walked through the gate with Skull and his biker brothers. They were checking their weapons making sure that they were ready to handle business. Supreme has a Ak-47 and a 44 Magnum; Ecstasy has a AK-47 and a 9mm; Marquan has an AR15 and a 45 Glock; and Glory got a 40 cal and 357 Magnum. Supreme said, anybody try to come out that front door or show up during the mayhem, Supreme told Ecstasy to lay their asses down on sight.

Tap Out was walking out the gate as Supreme and his crew was about to enter. Pow! Pow! Pow! He caught the first two bullets in the stomach and chest. The music was so loud that Skull or Scum Fuck didn't even know that it was gun shots being fired at the gate. Supreme, Marquan, and Stigma led the way. Pow! Pow! Pow! Pow! Pow! Boom! Boom! Boom! Pow! Pow! Pow! Boom! Pow!

Scum Fuck scrambled over to his brother and Persia, now he was dumping back trying to get them into the house. Pow! Pow! Pow! Boom! Boom! Pow! Buckie, Scooby, Kenny, and Cody were all laying in the yard shot up. Even one of the blond headed females got caught in the crossfire. She was lying in the swimming pool next to Mongo. Supreme, Marquan, Stigma, Ecstasy, and Glory were all driving off. Urrrrrrr! Pow! Pow! Pow! Boom! Boom! Pow! Boom! Boom! Pow! Pow! Urrrrrrr! Ecstasy hit a parked car, then swiped a mirror off a truck before she got control of the F250 burning rubber trying to get out of there.

Skull was so fucking mad seeing his brothers, laying out across his brothers back yard. Scum Fuck was pointing his gun at everybody, trying to wonder how they biker brothers allowed that to happen. "Where the fuck was you? He hollered at White Boy." The blond girl that was drunk, she tried to hug Scum Fuck. "Hey! don't worry, everything will be Ok!" Ok! Ok! Pow! Pow! Scum Fuck shot her and kicked her into the swimming pool.

Scum Fuck house was crawling with police officers and detectives, trying to piece together that blood bath that they arrived at. Skull, Persia, and White Boy had left in just enough time before the police arrived. Scum Fuck, Little Bobby, Kilo, Tommy Boy, Danny, Marty, And Milky, were all being questioned by police officers. Now the F.B I had pulled up to take over the case, being that so many bodies were involved, and it was gang related. Plus, they knew now that they were at the home of a well-known biker gangs' home. The W.G.K bikers is what one of the detectives was repeating to the lead detective on the case. "I'm telling you Dough; we've had many of problems out of these guys before here in Cincinnati." We been trying to bust their ass here for the longest.

One of the head leaders of this gang is that peace of shit right there. I'm surprised that his brother is not here now, they're like a bag of M&Ms and they both are nuts. Here are some photos of the whole bike gang. The first two pictures were Skull and Scum Fuck. The other Photo's were of different guys that were guys still in the club or use to be. Most of them were either in the county jail or in prison.

The lead detectives Dough and Fox were looking at the pictures, and headed back to where the bodies were laying. They were wondering what other biker gang that they could have gotten themselves in trouble with. Whomever it was that came and hit them in broad daylight and took all these lives, the detectives knew that it had to be behind something serious and he definitely was about to get to the bottom of it. Fox told Dough., somebody owes me some time behind bars, you can't shit in my backyard, and it doesn't get cleaned up. Fox looked at the biker whose brains were splattered on the wall lying next to a pizza box. "Well, at least he ate good, before he took his last breath, they got great pizza."

Supreme and Marquan had ditched the rental truck, that was rented by a Alexis Kimball. Supreme poured five gallons of gas into the inside and set the truck on fire. He jumped into the new rental truck with Marquan, a Burgundy and Beige Excursion, and they went to pay W.G.K another visit. Kilo was tired of all the fucking same questions over and over again. He was just happy to see his house again, after a few beers he went and took a shower so that he could get back to the club. He jumped in the water and closed his eyes; he was replaying back the whole morning at the club. "Who in the hell would have the balls to do something like that?" He got his answer when he heard a voice say, "Papa Jack said hello!" What! Pow! Pow! His body flopped in the shower, and his blood just kept going down the drain. Marquan turned off the lights in the bathroom and walked out.

$ $ $ $ $

Stigma pulled up to the red light and she could see the motorcycles coming up behind her. She had passed them, then they would pass her. Ecstasy, Stigma, Glory, and Persia were all riding in the Excursion with the music up loud, Stigma made sure that she stayed in the right lane, just in case any of the W.G.K bikers looked up in the truck and spotted Persia. They were up higher than the bikers, so that helped them a lot not to spot her. The next red light that they came to, the biker was sitting right behind their truck.

Tommy Boy, Marty, Danny, and Jimmy Lee were just sitting there, and all four doors opened up on the Excursion. Pow! Pow! Pow! Pow! Boom, Boom, Pow! Pow! Stigma, Ecstasy, Glory, and Persia, all jumped back into the Excursion, made a right turn, and drove away calmly like nothing had ever happened. Marty tried to drive his motorcycle but ran straight into a speeding car that was crossing the light. Urrrrr! Bam! If Marty wasn't dead from those bullets that were in his body, that old school Lincoln that was speeding definitely finished the job that they didn't do.

Hitch Hiker came walking into the club, Skull, Scum Fuck, Little Bobby, White Boy, and Milky, were all standing around the pool table, they were waiting on the other biker members to show up. "Hey what's up brothers."

Skull and Scum Fuck looked at each other, Scum Fuck walked over to the wall and removed a pool stick. Skull said, get that piece of shit! Little Bobby, White Boy, and Milky grabbed him, "Hey fellas what's wrong? What did I do? Skull walked up to him, what did you do, what did you do! are you fucking serious?"

"Where was you at today?" "All man, I met this hot chick, she wanted to ride on my bike, and she gave me some pussy bro. I was going to invite her here, so y'a'll can fuck too but her pussy was so good that I couldn't share her." You went to go get some pussy! You fucking pussy, you let your brothers die over some pussy? Hitch Hiker has no idea or clue as to what Skull was talking about. "What! Who in the fuck died?" "You, you piece of shit!" Scum Fuck raised that pool stick in the air, Wham! Wham! Wham! Wham! Wham! Whamrnrnmm! The bikers let him go, because blood was splashing all over their faces and on their clothes. Bam! Bam! Bam! Bam! Bam! Who died you fucking cunt? Bam! Bam! Bam!

Skull grabbed his brother because he had spazzed out and was still beating Hitch Hiker. "Clean this shit up and get this piece of shit out of here!" Skull was barking at all of his members, like one of them was next. Skull took his brother to the bathroom, so that he could get him cleaned up. They were talking and trying to figure out what was going on. To their surprise, Little Bobby walked into the bathroom. "Pres! I don't know what's going on, but it seems like ever since that girl Dutches walked in here it's been nothing but trouble." "Skull, placed his hands on the wall to think and moments later he said let's ride!" They grabbed a few weapons and headed out the door. As W.G.K was pulling in the Pink Pony Motel, Supreme, Marquan, Stigma, Ecstasy, Glory, and Persia were walking out of the room.

Skull spotted Persia and all hell broke out. Pow! Pow! Pow! Pow! Pow! Scum Fuck was still on his bike. He removed his weapon and started shooting. Supreme, Marquan, Stigma, and Persia all ducked behind the Excursion, while Ecstasy had no choice but to run back into the room and close the door. Pow! Pow! Pow! Boom! Boom! Pow! Pow! Milky caught a bullet in the stomach and when Scum Fuck tried to pull him back, Stigma opened the door and started firing her weapon. Pow! Pow! Pow! Scum Fuck got shot right in the temple and he fell over one of their bikes.

Marquan saw Little Bobby try to run in the motel office. Pow! Pow! Pow! Marquan dropped him with the second bullet. Persia stepped around the Excursion and got a clear shot at Skull but met a bullet right in the forehead. Pow! Pow! She hit the pavement. Bam! Supreme saw her hit the ground and completely lost it, Pow! Pow! Pow! Pow! Pow! Pow! Pow! hitting White Boy and Skull. Supreme ran over to him and stood over his body. Papa Jack said hello motherfucker! Pow!

SLEEPING WITH THE ENEMY

Ms. Housemoore was locking up the house when she heard a horn blowing. Bomp! Bomp! Bomp! As she was walking to her new Lexus 400 GS, Vicky pulled up on her. "Hello mama is Whitney home?" "Oh, hey baby! I ain't saw you in a while Vicky, where have you been? How's your mother? Tell her that I said hello." "Ok! She has been doing ok. I'll tell her that you said hi." "Ok baby but I don't know where that girl at. Ever since she got her driver's License child, I ain't seen that girl! She stays gone."

"Oh, I was just coming by so that I can apologize to her." "Apologize for what child, y'all sisters I know you two ain't acting crazy?" We got into it the other day at the mall, and I was in the wrong, the way I acted. I thought that she was lying to me when she said that she got married. Married, child is you crazy? "Whitney ain't got married to nobody." Married to who? Whitney don't even got a boyfriend, child. Vicky smiled; oh well, she claimed that she got married, she is flashing a lot of money around now day's maybe she is married, and you don't know it. Ms. Housemoore stood there taking in everything that Vicky just said. "Ok mama, tell her to call me later." "Ok child bye!"

Whitney was at the resort trying on a Versace bathing suit, she had passed the swimming pool and promised herself that she would lay out in the sun. It was a nice day, so she grabbed a towel and headed out to the pool. There weren't too many people at the pool, so Whitney swam a little while, then she laid back in the sun and relaxed. Whitney was gathering her thoughts and thinking about being married to Supreme. She was mainly wishing that he would come back home soon and fix her kitty cat itch for her.

Whitney was laying on her stomach when she heard, "Damn shorty! I didn't know that Phoenix got beautiful women like this out here" Whitney was about to turn over and give whoever it was a piece of her mind. But when she turned around and saw the man standing over her all that quickly changed.

$ $ $ $ $

Supreme, Marquan, Stigma, Glory, and Ecstasy all boarded the plane, but this time everyone was completely silent. Leaving Persia dead back there in that parking lot at the Pink Pony motel, it was eating away at all of them and not just Supreme, they all was taking her death hard. Tears were rolling down everybody's faces, even Marquan found himself shedding a tear. The seven of them were starting to get real close and here another one of them have taken a fall.

Supreme had taken the whole trip back wondering how he could get next to Papa Jack. "Even thou he knew that a million dollars, was about to pop up in his account. To Supreme having to lose Persia for that money, it wasn't even worth it to him anymore. He was just starting to get his head clear about losing GeeGee and now here he has to deal with Persia dying now. Here he stood and witnessed that bullet penetrate right through Persia's forehead and his heart almost stopped at the same moment that hers did.

This time instead of everyone going their separate ways, Supreme have everyone going to the house in Chandler. Supreme gave Stigma, Glory, Ecstasy, and Marquan a Hundred and fifty thousand dollars apiece and kept the rest of the one million for himself.

None of them knew that Supreme was cheating them, that's something that he even kept quiet from Stigma on every job that they went on, they have no connection to Papa Jack. So, none of them even knew what their take on the money was, only Supreme. Besides, Supreme had told everybody that they wouldn't be taking any more jobs for the next six months. That they all needed to agree on a place to vacation to, that it was all Papa Jacks treat.

Everybody was excited about that, Stigma more than anybody. She figured that by the time their vacation was over that she should have had her baby. The last time that she and Supreme talked, Stigma told him that she was having an abortion. Now Stigma wanted to have her baby, she had set an appointment before they went to Cincinnati. But it wasn't to kill the baby, it was to find out how far along she was and to know what she was having.

They ended their meeting, but before they left, they had gotten a call from Papa Jack, and they learned that they had gotten Gee-Gee's body. It was being sent to her family, but Papa Jack had paid for her funeral after learning that her parents were drug addicts and had no money. Papa Jack paid for the funeral and sent her mother fifty thousand dollars. He wanted them all to attend her funeral and say their proper goodbye's to GeeGee.

After receiving the great news, Supreme told Papa Jack that they had just lost Persia. Papa Jack told Supreme that he'll have to get back to him on that situation. But to Papa Jack, he was starting to think that Supreme and his crew were starting to get a little sloppy at their job. Out of all the men that he hired, Supreme was the only one who has lost so many hitters. Papa Jack told Supreme that the Denver trip wasn't necessary because he got paid in full. He told Supreme to tell everybody good job and to let him know where they decided to vacation to?

Stigma was putting on her best sad and miserable face trying to get Supreme to come back home. She knew that telling him how she felt wouldn't get her nowhere, so she used their son by saying he was crying for his dad. Which in fact, little Isaiah did cry for his dad, but not to Stigma, it was Ms. Bergess.

BIG AND LITTLE SATAN

Supreme felt that, if he was going to go spend time with Isaiah, that today would be a better time than any to go and be with his son. Even though Supreme was also missing Stigma just as much as she was missing him, Supreme was afraid to be around Stigma, only because he was married to Whitney and was having mixed emotions with Stigma. One minute he wanted to hug and kiss her and the next moment he wanted to shoot her and watch her just die.

Supreme was missing his wife so badly, that he wanted to tell Stigma to go fuck herself and go back to Atlanta to her baby daddy. But he knew that the slap wouldn't be in her face, it would be slapping Isaiah in his face. Supreme knew that Whitney wouldn't know if he was back or not, so he agreed to spend a couple of nights. Then he told Stigma that he would be back out of her house. Stigma felt that if he came home now, that she'll make sure that he would never want to leave them again. Just to drive Stigma crazy and to make her wonder if he'll ever show up. Supreme told Stigma that he had something important to do and that he'll meet her later at the house. Stigma reached up and tried to kiss Supreme, but he quickly declined her kiss and walked away.

Supreme figured he'd allow a little time to pass by, so he went by his Lawyers office and check on the status of him getting their son. After Stigma left the house, Supreme called the realtor and told her that he and Whitney would buy the house and that he would transfer the funds for the house. She promised Supreme that she'll take care of the paperwork immediately. Supreme thanked her and had the money sent to her office to close the deal on him and Whitney new house. Supreme even had the realtor to put the house in Whitney name. Supreme knew that he couldn't go to the resort and be with his wife. So, he knew that the only way that he could go relieve some stress was to go down to Relax Yo Back massage parlor and go see SoSo to relax his back. He picked up his cell phone to make sure that she wasn't busy and that was a call that she was expecting cause when it came to Supreme all doors close so hers can open.

$ $ $ $ $

Whitney was standing in the shower crying. She was so disappointed in herself; she couldn't believe how weak and immature that she had just acted. Whitney had waited all of her life, for a man like Supreme to come into her life. All the things that Whitney had dreamed for, Supreme had already given to her. Great sex, a home of her own and even had put an expensive diamond ring on her finger. She had done everything that her mother taught her to do, if she ever gave up her prize possession.

Whitney sat down in the tub and let the water run down on her head, her knees way up and her hands were over her face. "I'm so sorry Supreme, I'm sorry baby, so, so, sorry!" Whitney was hurting so bad, that she wanted to take her own life just to save Supreme the trouble of doing it himself. All Whitney could remember was hearing Supreme tell her to never allow another man to enter her vagina but him. Supreme meant that so much that, he even threw her vibrator away on her Birthday.

Whitney was mentally starting to blame Supreme for throwing her vibrator away in her weak state of mind. Whitney was beating her head with her fist. Why? Why? Why! Stupid, why did you even turn around? Whitney, why did you even go to that swimming pool, that was dumb girl shit! Your stupid ass wanted attention, and that's just what you got.

When Whitney turned around at the swimming pool to cuss out her admire, he stood over her with the greatest body that Whitney has ever saw on a man. He was so gentle, kind, and sweet not coming off with that Macho ego or nothing. That's what attracted Whitney to him, he just sat and listened to all of Whitney's problems about her family and best friend. Whitney even told the guy about Supreme. She thought that he was so nice that Whitney had left out the part that she was married to Supreme. Whitney thought that nothing would go beyond them just sitting and conversating. Supreme leaving her alone was making her feel abandoned and lonely. Whitney knew that she told Supreme, that she could handle him being away. But really, she was getting tired of waiting to see if something bad happened to Supreme.

Whitney knew hearing that would kill her inside. Now she understood those days that, her mother stayed up rocking waiting on Marquan to walk through the door. Whitney felt that a person really wouldn't understand, until they had to go through something like that bad. The guy asked Whitney to join him for a friendly lunch back in his room. While they were waiting for their food, he offered Whitney a friendly massage. He was explaining to Whitney how much stress she was under and what stress can do to you and Whitney accepted his offer.

The massage felt so good that Whitney's vagina got hot and soaking wet. Damn! This feels so good, no wonder people go and spend their money on this stuff. Before Whitney could even realize what was going on, the guy's tongue had invaded Whitney's vagina which was hot and warm. Whitney's mind was saying no stop, but her body was saying. "Oh my God! Man don't you never ever stop." Just as Whitney was about to cum, he swiftly spread her legs much wider and entered her vagina with a long hard penis. It felt like a bulldozer knocking down her walls. "Ummmmm! Ummmmmmm! Wwwwait, waitttt!" Whitney didn't even know his name; she was so busy talking about her that she never even asked his name. Right now, Whitney couldn't even remember if he said his name or not.

She always remembered hearing woman say that you should experience having sex with many men before you fall in love with the first penis come your way. The two men that Whitney have given herself to, most women would say sexually, that she would have made the wrong decision. Because she was comparing Supreme love making, to her mystery man that she just made love to.

BIG AND LITTLE SATAN

Whitney felt that marrying Supreme was a mistake if she based it off of sex. Because the other guy had just put that, crave me all day sex down on Whitney.

Even as bad as Whitney was feeling right now, she wanted to go knock on his suite door and beg him for round two. Damn! He made my vagina throb. Whitney was wondering if he has Lays in his penis, because he wasn't the type of man that you could fuck just once. "Whitney, stop crying, Ok, Ok! girl pull yourself together." "You fucked up Whitney, but we'll never ever do that again, right?" She looked down at her vagina besides I'll take that to my grave, my husband will never know!

$ $ $ $ $

Supreme walked into the house and Stigma already had her trap set for him. She had dropped Ms. Bergess and Little Isaiah at the mall, and she made sure they had plenty of money. Ms. Bergess was to take their son shopping, but not before taking in a movie first. Supreme called for Ms. Bergess and his son but he got no answer. Supreme walked into his bedroom to find Stigma asleep laying across the bed. She was ass hole naked and Supreme penis started to rise seeing her sexy attractive body lying there. Supreme wanted so badly to just turn around and leave, but his penis wanted to partake in Stigma's vagina.

Supreme was taking in her body and he wanted her so bad that he thought that he could hear her pussy call his name. Supremeeeee! Come eat and beat me upppppp! Without him thinking about it any further, Supreme started removing his clothes and he climbed into the bed next to Stigma. He looked at her ass and vagina. "Damn I miss y'all!" Stigma smiled and it gave her a warm feeling inside, just to hear him say that. Supreme kissed her butt and she wanted to respond to him so badly but decided not to blow this moment. He spread her legs and started liking and sucking on her vagina. Ummmrnmm! Stigma couldn't help but respond to the pleasure that she was receiving. Supreme turned Stigma over and started pounding away at her pussy. He was fucking Stigma like, he wanted to punish her for cheating on him.

Sigma wanted Supreme bad, but not in the way that he was treating her right now. She was starting to feel like a 20-dollar prostitute, that was allowing her pussy to take a beating for a little of nothing. The only thing that Stigma was glad about was, Supreme was dogging her vagina out and calling her bitches and whores at the same time. But she felt maybe he was just thinking it in his mind and not saying anything. Tears started rolling down her face, this told her that the love that she and Supreme had was long gone. But she didn't want to cause a problem, at least he had come to see their son. Stigma wiped her face and just went along with the flow. Supreme put her in a doggy style position and the treatment got even worser. "Ummm! Ouch! Dada, you're hurting me, Ahhhhh! Agggh! Ohhhh! Woahhh! Dada, Dada, Dada, you're hurting me baby." Please! Please! Stop!

BIG AND LITTLE SATAN

Supreme grabbed Stigma by the hips and he was pounding away inside of her like they were animals. Stigma was trying to break away, but Supreme have a mean strong grip on her waist. A part of her was starting to enjoy it, but she couldn't because she knew that he was acting out of anger for what she had done. Dada, stop this don't, and before she could get out another word, Supreme pounded at her vagina like he was drilling for oil. "Owwwwww! Ummmmmmm! Ohhhhhh! Ahhhhhhh! His body started to jerk, and Stigma was happy, but when he was done, he pushed Stigma out of the bed like she wasn't nothing to him.

Stigma laid there on the floor and started crying uncontrollably. Supreme didn't try to console her in no way at all. Supreme headed to the shower and Stigma thought that maybe, she'll give it another try. She got into the shower and was washing Supreme up, then she dropped down on her knees and started giving him head. Supreme grabbed her by the hair and treated her mouth like it was her vagina until he climaxed. Supreme showered and got out leaving Stigma in the shower by herself. After they got dressed Supreme asked about Little Isaiah figuring that's what he was there for, his son. Stigma told Supreme that they can go together and pick them up at the mall.

While they were on their way walking down the stairs, Supreme told Stigma that she can't fool him anymore. Supreme told Stigma that he knows why she asked him to come home that she could have just fucked him at the other house. You didn't have to lie to me and bring me here for that. Oh, and by the way! Supreme stopped on the stairs and looked back at her. "I hope you enjoyed that sex, because it won't never happen again." I got married and I'm moving in with my wife! Those two words hit Stigma, like someone had just punched her in the stomach. "What! Supreme! Supreme! She started yelling to the top of her lungs." "Isaiah Supreme Washington Sr., what the fuck did you just say to me?" Supreme looked her right in the face. "Stigma, I'm married." Ding Dong, Ding Dong, somebody was ringing the doorbell. Supreme and Stigma figured that Ms. Bergess ran out of patience and didn't want to wait. Stigma said Damn!

She felt that this was the wrong time for them to come home. Because either Supreme is about to kill her or she about to kill him. But either way it goes, this was an ass whipping that Stigma was ready to take. Stigma was coming down the stairs fussing, just as Supreme was opening the front door. Before Supreme could even realize what was going on, a 357 magnum was being stuck in his face. "Yea nigga! where the fucking money at?" Damn! Supreme couldn't believe that he have just got caught slipping like this. Him and Stigma were being robbed in their own home and Supreme was feeling so violated right now.

Stigma laid on her stomach looking at Supreme. She didn't know what was more painful, getting tied up in her own home or hearing Supreme say that he was married. Instead of paying attention to the three dudes and one female that was going through their house ram shacking their belongings. Supreme nor Stigma felt that death wish in their stomach. They were heartless killers and knew that, if the four clows was there to kill them, then they would already be dead not tied up on the floor.

Supreme knew that at some point, that they would be wanting him to open his safe. The jewelry and fifty thousand dollars that Supreme kept in his safe was nothing compared to the money they got in their offshore accounts.

Whoever put this little robbery together, must not really know much about him and Stigma. They were worth a few Million and here they were getting robbed for some pocket change. But Supreme still didn't want to underestimate nobody, he figured that if they had enough nerves to come into their home, then they damn sure were capable of leaving them dead in their own home.

"Where's the money mother fucker?" One of the dudes that had on a black ski mask, stood over Supreme and Stigma while the other three searched the house. "What money man, what are you talking about?" Why do y'all think that we got money because we live in a nice house? The female walked over to Supreme and kicked him right in the face. Blood shot everywhere. Supreme you think that we don't know who the fuck you are? Supreme knew that the shit had just gotten real. "Nigga you owe me, your bitch ass took a lot from me.

Now you can either tell me where the money at or I can put a bullet in you or your bitch head now, who goes first? She walked over to Stigma and put the gun to her head. "Wait, Wait! Don't hurt her if you say that I'm the one that owe you." Then why didn't y'all just let her go and kill me then? To hear Supreme say that Stigma knew that Supreme still loved her. But she had just hurted him badly. Now Stigma was looking around for a way for the both of them to come out alive.

"Hey, I know what y'all want, take me upstairs and I'll make this easy for all of us." Supreme gave Stigma a cold stare, like don't give that bitch shit. The female struggled to help Stigma up, but she finally got her to her feet. Ms. Bergess had been calling Stigma and wasn't getting an answer. After trying so many times, she called a cab and was about to enter the house. Seeing Supreme Rolls Royce and Stigma Mercedez Benz in the driveway blocked by a blue Suburban.

Ms. Bergess knew that something was definitely wrong for nobody to answer the phone. Ms. Burgess paid for the taxi, but she entered through the guest bedroom. She took Isaiah into the house and told him to sit in the closet and not come out until she came back to get him. "Shhhhh! baby be real quite." Ms. Bergess grabbed her 38 special snub nose that her husband bought for her and taught her how to shoot it.

Stigma had given them what they wanted, and they were all coming down the stairs. They laid Stigma back on the floor. "Ok! now was that so hard?" "Bam! she kicked Supreme in the face and then in the ribs." Motherfucker now I'll take you up on your offer and blow your fucking brains out. Stigma's heart stopped beating. No! No! Please don't hurt him, she started crying. Mr. Supreme! I know that you would love to see my face, don't you? Pow! Pow! Pow! Just as the female went to remove her mask, Ms. Burgess started shooting. They all broke towards the door, but also returned fire. Pow! Pow! Pow! Pow! Pow! "Let's go, let's go, lets gooooo!" Ms. Bergess! Ms. Bergess caught a bullet right in the chest before the last guy could run out the house. Pow! Pow! She also let off a couple shots. Bam, Bam, the both of them hit the floor. "No Ma! No, no, Noooooo!" Stigma yelled just as the bullet entered her chest.

$ $ $ $ $

Marquan was in the bed sleeping in between Snooty and Star when they heard a knock at the door. Being that Marquan had never brought anybody to Star condo before, he figured that the door was for her. Baby, baby, somebody knocking at your door. Star half ass asleep went and answered the door, without even looking through the peep hole. Just as soon as the door opened up, Star was quickly woken up.

A 44 magnum was being shoved in her face and she was being told to be quiet. "Bitch, where he at?" Three dudes were standing in Star front room wearing ski mask. Star knew that her and Marquan and Snooty were about to die. She started saying a prayer, "Lord please don't let them kill us. I know that I ain't been going to Church and been reading my Bible lately. But Lord if you get us out of this, I promise that I won't skip no more and I'll be in church this Sunday." Please, please, please, don't let them kill us.

They led Star back into the bedroom where Marquan and Snooty were still sleeping. The dude was watching Star ass jump in her thong, as they were walking back in the room. One of the guys hit his friend's arm. "'Damn! Hearing a man's voice, that made Marquan wake up. His gun was on the nightstand and when he went for it, one of the dudes started wrestling with Marquan for his gun. Snooty woke up and pulled the covers over her because she was completely naked. Marquan was fighting for his life, he felt that he survived prison ain't no way that he would allow them to take him out like this.

They had got the gun away from Marquan before he could even get it. But Marquan was fighting them while tussling with two of the three men. One of the guys' masks completely came off of his face and Marquan got a chance to see him real good before he could place the mask on his face. The dude that was holding the gun on Star and Snooty hit Marquan across the back of his head. "Bam! Blood gushed out and Marquan hit the floor, that's when the two guys that he was fighting cuffed Marquan." After they cuffed him with zip tie, they started punching and kicking him.

"You ready to cooperate big money?" "Fuck y'all punk asses. Y'all uncuff me and then let's see what it do, mother fucker." Bam! Bam! Bam! Bam! Uggggg! Marquan was getting stomped by the biggest one. Man cuff them whores and let's get what we came for. They cuffed Snooty and Star and took everything that they found. Which wasn't much but 36 thousand, a Rolex watch and some female jewelry that belonged to Star. "Damn maybe I can take your money and go and enjoy me two bitches tonight, Marquannnn!"

"Yea! you and these hoes keep stacking it up for me and I'll be back for it." I really don't see what they see in a weak mark like you. Stop fucking so much, don't you know pussy make you weak? "Look at you huffing and puffing all out of breath." He smacked Marquan on the ass, and they left. Fuck y'all punk ass niggas! Ha, Ha, Haaaaaaa! See you when you get some more money, Marquan. When Marquan, Snooty, and Star cut themselves free from zip ties, Marquan called Supreme to learn that he and Stigma were getting robbed at the same time. By the time Marquan, Snooty, and Star made it over to Supreme's house, he saw Glory, Ecstasy, and SoSo cars all parked at his house. Police cars were everywhere, and Marquan's heart almost stopped beating when he saw the coroners parked. They were walking a body out of Supreme's house covered in a white sheet. Daddy, who died? Snooty asked and before she could get an answer, she jumped out of Marquan's truck and ran towards her brother's house.

Snooty was quickly relieved to learn that Supreme was alive when she saw Supreme talking to a police officer. She went and hugged her brother. Bro, are you ok? "Yea! He kissed Snooty and kept answering the police questions." "Bro, who was that the coroners were taking away from here, that wasn't Stigma was it?" Supreme didn't answer her, so Snooty ran into the house. Stigma was going crazy and was crying because the woman that she knew as a mother figure was dead. Plus, Stigma didn't have any idea as to where Little Isaiah was at. She didn't know where Ms. Bergess took him. The police kept asking her questions. "Man fuck all that, I need to go find my son!" "What's his description ma'am? Do you have any pictures of Little Isaiah?" Stigma looked at the police officer like he has lost his damn mind. "Man get the hell away from me, asking me all these stupid ass questions." Ma'am, I'm just trying to do my job here. How can we know how to find your son if you don't help us. Stigma left him standing by himself, just as soon as she saw Snooty. The officer rubbed his forehead and started smacking the side of his leg. "Snooty I can't find my son?" "Girl what?" Stigma, where was my nephew? I don't know, my mother had him and now she is dead. Snooty grabbed her face and started crying.

By the time everything settled down and Stigma had given the police pictures to see if Isaiah was left at the mall. Little Isaiah came walking out of the bedroom, mom where's my dad? Everybody turned around and there stood Little Isaiah. "Baby come here, where were you at?" Little Isaiah explained to them what Ms. Bergess saw and said and that made Stigma cry even more, to learn that she died and was protecting her family, when Isaiah asked where his Nanna was, even Supreme shedded a tear but they didn't tell him that she was dead.

After all the police left, they all were there sitting around, trying to figure out who would be bold enough to try something like that? Supreme and Stigma couldn't figure out who came into their home to rob thern? They have just took a lost for a few thousand in cash and a couple hundred thousand dollars in jewelry. But none of that compared to losing Ms. Burgess. She was the one that held them together for years and raised Stigma and her son.

Stigma turned and looked at Supreme. "What's going on Dada?" "I'm losing everything in my life. My mom just died, and my man tells me, that he just married some bitch! Who is she Dada and where is she at?" I want to see the whore that took my man from me and his son. Stigma turned to their son, "Isaiah did your father tell you that he got married?" Little Isaiah shook his head no, but with a sad face. Now everyone in the house, was looking at Supreme like he had killed Ms. Bergess himself. Dada, what is Stigma talking about? Glory asked Supreme that question with a real serious look on her face.

Stigma said, "yea tell'em Dada. Go ahead and tell everybody what you told me earlier." You remember what you said, just before them faggots came into our home and violated our home. Marquan was looking at Supreme like bro when did you get married and didn't tell me. "Man, y'all know this girl is crazy, come on Stigma chill out with all that bullshit." We have enough problem's as it is; we need to just focus on finding out who did this. Stigma kept on egging it on and Supreme said, "Stigma did your punk ass baby daddy, have this bullshit done?" When, I talked to him on your phone, he threatened to kill me if you have an abortion? The whole room went silent, even she was strongly thinking about what he had just said. "Stigma, girl you pregnant?" Snooty asked Stigma that question, and now all eyes were on her.

$ $ $ $ $

Whitney came walking into her mother's house and Ms. House-moore was watching Family Feud. She was laughing her head off at Steve Harvey. He asked the two people that was standing at the buzzer competing. "What is the biggest thing on Steve Harvey?" The lady hit the buzzer and said his lips. Steve Harvey didn't like her answer and he said, "Well! the biggest thing on you is your damn head." That's why your big head ass can't fit them glasses.

Ms. Housemoore was cracking up. "Mama, what is so funny, what you laughing at?" "Oh, hey baby!" I'm laughing at Mr. Har-vey; he is so funny. Child, I don't know why people be trying to make jokes about him? He ain't going to do nothing but embarrass you. She cut the television off. Child have a seat any way's, me and you need to have a talk. All mama! Girl don't be all mommying me, what the hell is Vicky talking about you getting married.

Whitney sat up, just to hear what her mother was about to say. "What you mean mom?" That child came by here talking about how she wanted to apologize to you, what y'all done got into it for? "Yea mama, you already know how Vicky thinks, that she better then everybody?" "Yea! Yea! Child, she does think that her butt doesn't stink. But she also said that she came to congratulate you on your marriage!" Whitney's heart almost stopped. "What do you think that she meant by that, Whitney?" I don't know mama; you know that girl be making up stuff. "We'll she seemed pretty serious to me when she said it, you better not have gone and married nobody."

"Mama, don't you have to have a man first, in order to get married? I don't even got a boyfriend mama, so how am I going to go get married?" "Yea! I Know that's what I told that child! but she kept on saying that you was married." "Mama, I'm already married to you." Whitney kissed her mother and headed to her bedroom. On her way walking towards her room Whitney said, she just jealous mama because I got my own car and don't need her for rides no more.

CHAPTER FORTY-THREE
SEX CAN COST YOU A LOT

Marquan allowed Snooty and Star to take his truck back to Snooty place. Supreme told SoSo to go and pack a bag and he and Marquan would be picking her up at her house. Supreme and Marquan were telling each other, about the way that their robbery went down. The dudes face that the coroners removed from Supreme house, kept on playing over and over in Marquan's mind like he knew him. Supreme that dude Stigma mother killed, bro I've seen that punk somewhere before, but I can't remember where. I just can't put my finger on it, maybe he done time with me in jail or prison before. Preme, I'm damn near ninety percent sure, that I saw him somewhere before.

The dudes that robbed you, did they have any females with them Marquarn? Naw! I didn't see no female, even if there was any with them. Whoever robbed us, they didn't come into our crib with them other Fagots. Yea Marquan,! when I told you earlier that a bitch done this to my face that's what I really meant. Supreme grabbed his rear-view mirror and looked at his face and that made him even more madder. "Bro, you mean to tell me that, there were men there and they let the female kick you in your face?" Marquan knew that they had to hurry up and find the punks that got up enough nerves to invade their privacy. Somebody got to pay the price for that, the money didn't mean nothing, but the principle on the other hand did.

They pulled up to SoSo house and she jumped in the car. "Ok! Dada I'm ready, where we headed to again Atlanta?" Supreme didn't say anything, he just nodded his head yes. "So Preme! you really think o'boy, that got Stigma pregnant is the one sent them cats to rob us?" Marquan said really, "about now to me that's the only thing that makes since."

The plane landed in Atlanta, and this was an airport that Supreme couldn't wait to get back to. He was just as eager to go back to Atlanta now, as he was the day that they returned to pay Sergeant Headgepeth a little visit. Supreme rented a red mustang for SoSo and he rented a black hard top corvette for him and Marquan. They went and rented a hotel room at the Ramada Inn. Supreme ordered Pizza because that's SoSo favorite food. Supreme didn't have any pictures of Deshawn, but what he did bring would draw Deshawn right to them. Supreme had the address to Deshawn massage parlor and he knew just what to do.

After they ate Pizza, Supreme told Marquan and SoSo just how he was going to fix Deshawn for good. Supreme told them that after tomorrow, Deshawn won't be sticking his penis in nobody else woman. Marquan listened to Supremes' plan to fix Deshawn and he told Supreme, aye man do me one favor. "What's that Marqun?" "Hey! if I ever accidently screw one of your girl's, man please just tell me. Marquan hey, that's me right there and I can promise you that she won't never get this penis." Supreme and SoSo busted up laughing. Man, you one cold blooded dude, that made Supreme laugh even harder than he was.

Supreme and Marquan sat and listened to SoSo put on her most sexiest voice. When Deshawn answered his phone, SoSo was telling him that her friend referred her to him. "Deshawn! so are you as good, as my friend say that you are?" "Ok! fine then. I'll see you tomorrow then and don't forget it's room 222 taw, taw!"

$ $ $ $ $

The next night Deshawn came knocking at the door at 7:58 and SoSo made sure that she was nice and wet when she answered the door. "Well hello handsome, you must be Deshawn?" Deshawn smiled seeing how attractive SoSo was. He was so use to woman, calling him on the phone. But when he gets there that nice warm sexy voice usually turn into a muscular female with a thick mustache. SoSo stood off to the side behind the door, she had one of the hotel towels wrapped around her head. "Please come in."

Just as Deshawn entered the room SoSo said, you'll have to excuse me I just jumped out of the shower. "SoSo closed the door and turned and walked away." Deshawn saw the ass on SoSo, and his penis already started getting hard. Deshawn was already telling himself that, there was no way that he was leaving that room, without her experiencing all nine inches of his penis. He thought that if her vagina was as good as her ass look then she just might get ten inches of dick. SoSo turned around to see him check the door, she picked up her watch. "Oh! I see that you're also a man of your word, I see that you're on time too?"

I love that Deshawn, now if you're as good as my girlfriend says you are, then I'm sure that I won't have any problem referring you to some of my other girlfriends. SoSo grabbed another towel and started drying off. She already had a Victoria Secret Pink bra and panty set laying across the bed. She pulled the thong panties up. "You like?" "Hell yea! I love them sexy, they fit you well." SoSo put her bra on and turned her back to Deshawn. Do you mind? He closed the clamp on her bra. "Oh, thank you." So, are we ready?

SoSo laid across the bed and Deshawn went into his bag and pulled out a good smelling lotion. "Ohhh! that feels good already." Deshawn started to work his magic, while they engaged in conversation. So how long have you been doing this? Ummmm! Yea right there. Deshawn answered all of her questions, while admiring the thickness of her lips around her vagina. He has her legs spread out as far as possible. SoSo couldn't take it no more, her vagina was starting to get just as wet as her hair was under that towel.

Oooooh, weeeee Deshawn, am I supposed to be feeling like this? "Man, you got my pussy soak and wet looks like I'm going to have to call somebody to take care of her tooooo!" Deshawn started smiling, now going in much deeper into her body parts. "Ahhhh! Owwwww! Yea Shit Wait, wait." Oh, my goodness, maybe I just better pay you now. "Oh Shit! shit, shit, shit!" I can't take this, SoSo rolled over on her back and Deshawn already have his dick in his hand.

SoSo knew that this wasn't part of Supremes' plan, but she also knew that there was no way that she was about to let a fine piece of meat go to waste like this. SoSo knew that she has to work the situation, the best way that she knew how. "Is that for me?" Deshawn shook his penis, yes. SoSo pulled her thong over to the side and Deshawn tasted her juices just before he took her vagina through a living nightmare. They had sex every which way they could and at the same time Soso coached Deshawn to cum with her. "Come on big daddy, come on baby let me, "Ummmmm! Ohhhhh! Ahh-hhhh! Yeaaaaa! Yes!

Deshawn rolled over on his back, trying to catch his breath. SoSo got up and went and grabbed a towel and wiped herself. Just as she walked out of the bathroom, SoSo went and open the hotel door and Deshawns' face turned white, when he saw Supreme and Marquan enter the room. "Wait! Wait! Wait! I'm sorry man she called me here, she asked for it. I didn't want to fuck her! Supreme gave SoSo a dirty look, like I didn't say to fuck him. SoSo hunched her shoulders as to say, "man I know Supreme that you're not gay but look at his penis, Damn! She put her head down and moved out of their way.

"Well hello Mr. Deshawn! Deshawn tried to grab his clothes, but Supreme pointed his gun at him. "Naw! bitch ass nigga, you love getting naked stay naked." Deshawn just sat there shaking, come on brother don't kill me please! "Wow! you don't sound like that same hard mother fucker that I talked to on the phone." Now Deshawn knew that he was talking to the one and only Supreme, Stigma baby daddy. "Supreme right?" Supreme shook his head right, "You got it."

Say man, your wife came on to me, she was complaining to me about how you be leaving her in that suite. I would have never slept with your wife. Supreme said, "mother fucker you must think that you fucked my wife, Stigma ain't my wife." But if she was, you didn't care if she was my girl, woman, or wife; you maggot, when you were fucking her.

"Oh! you mean her, man she came on to me too brother." "Supreme looked at him like, is this pussy ass nigga mentally challenged or something?" Well, you wanted to know who I am, so I figured that I'd give you that much respect, too bad I can't say that much about you. Supreme raised his gun, man I'm sorry for fucking your wife and your... Pow! Pow! Pow!

$ $ $ $ $

A week later Stigma was happy and smiling walking to go check the mail in the box. Supreme had just finish giving her some of the best sex ever and she was feeling like things was changing between them. Her belly was starting to show, but that didn't stop Supreme from driving her vagina wild. After she removed the mail, she looked at the package from Atlanta and that made her look back at the house. She was hoping that Deshawn hadn't got her address and was starting to send her stuff for the baby. All this was going to do was take her and Supreme back in the wrong direction. Stigma couldn't help but allow a smile to cross her face thinking about Deshawn, it made her rub her stomach.

Stigma started opening the package right there at the mailbox just in case she has to throw it away before going back into the house. Stigma opened the package and pulled it out. Ohhhhhhh! Stigma started screaming to the top of her lung's, she could be heard screaming all the way down the street. Stigma fell down to her knees and started crying. She grabbed her stomach and started throwing up, even thou her baby wasn't fully at that age to be kicking. Stigma was feeling like her baby was kicking her in the stomach right now.

When Stigma saw Deshawn's mother's address on the package, she was wondering how in the hell did Deshawn know where her and Supreme lived. It almost stopped her heart from beating when she saw that package. But when she opened up the package and saw the content, Stigma knew that penis from anywhere. She had sucked it and rode it like a Cowboy. Seeing Deshawn penis in that box, she knew that Deshawn was dead, and she was going to have a baby with no father.

Stigma found enough strength to finally look up and when she did Supreme was standing there looking at her through the window holding her stomach. That was the moment that Stigma knew that she hated Supreme and that she would get even real soon. Supreme didn't just kill and take her baby daddy from her, but he did just take her baby daddy from her child. When Supreme and Stigma finally looked at each other, Stigma stopped crying and had the biggest smile on her face. On her way into the house Stigma opened the big green trash can that Supreme had set out to be picked up. Stigma still was looking at Supreme and she open the lid and tossed Deshawn penis in the trash and headed back in the house.

$ $ $ $ $

Marquan was riding Impression vagina like a race car driver, and she was really enjoying it. But in midstroke Marquan stopped and jumped up. "I got it, I got it!" Impression was wishing the same thing, that she wished that she got it too. Marquan grabbed his cell phone off her nightstand and dialed Supreme number. Marquan stood there naked, with Impression staring at him with an evil look. Supreme finally answered, "Hello! Preme I got it!" Remember I told you about that robbery at Satin Doll strip club? The dude was that nigga Tone and the female that was with them was Emoni dog.

An hour later, Marquan was picking up Suprerne, man slow down Marquan. "What's wrong with you bro, we got weapons in the car." Don't forget that you are a felon with weapons, slow down Marquan. "We about to get that bitch, don't trip she won't be expecting we know shit." Marquan didn't give a fuck about being on parole or being an ex-felon. Marquan knew that he only had seven months left on parole. Marquan even sped up faster than he was already going. Marquan turned up in Emoni complex on two wheels and Supreme just gave him a look and shook his head, but he was just as mad as Marquan.

Marquan wasn't worried about knocking on the door, because Emoni had given him a key the last time they were together. Him and Supreme grabbed their guns and was speed walking to Emoni apartment. Marquan opens the door and his heart almost jumped out of his chest. Emoni whole apartment was empty, they rushed through the apartment looking for her. But it was no Emoni or nothing, everything was gone.

When Marquan and Supreme made it to the bedroom, it was one piece of paper stuck on the mirror and it read. Marquan, I took your mother's advice and I decided to runnnn! Marquan grabbed his cell phone and started to check all of his bank accounts and they said, "you have a zero balance and he called and checked the next one. You have zero balance. Then he called the last account, you have a zero balance. No,No,No,No,No,No! Nooooooo! you fucking bitch you dead!"

$ $ $ $ $

Supreme was telling the moving truck driver just how much more room he has to back up in the driveway. Whitney was hugging Supreme anxiously waiting to start putting things in their new home together. Supreme and Whitney had been to five furniture stores, buying different things for their house. Supreme had spent over thirty thousand dollars on anything that Whitney said that she wanted to buy. "Hello! Yea, thank you Sir right this way." The movers were following Whitney into the house and were starting to place things wherever she wanted them to.

Supreme was smiling happy and excited to see that his wife was happy. That made him happy to see such a wonderful thing happen to such a beautiful person like Whitney. Whitney was about to tell the movers where to take the bedroom set that they were carrying. "Put that right in there and she took off running towards the bathroom. Supreme and the movers looked at each other, like what just happened?"

"Aye that goes upstairs in the second bedroom upstairs to your left. Supreme went to check on Whitney and when he found her, she was bent over the toilet throwing up. "Baby! Baby! what's the matter, are you ok!" Aaaaaaaaa! Aaaaaaaa! Whitney tried to talk but she kept throwing up. "Oh, my goodness, baby I feel terrible."

She was looking around the bathroom for toilet paper. But they hadn't done their shopping yet and didn't have any toilet paper. Supreme removed his t-shirt after taking off his dress shirt and handed it to Whitney. "Hear baby!" No baby, that's going to mess up your shirt. You didn't care about messing my shirt up a little while ago, did you?

Whitney tried to laugh and started throwing up again. Supreme wiped her mouth when it looked like she was finally done. Baby, do you want me to take you to the hospital? Naw bae, I should be fine. I got to get our house together so I can cook my husband a home cooked meal. Whitney stood up and wanted to kiss Supreme but decided not to because her breath wasn't right for that. "Well, I tell you what, you go lay down and I'll go get you something to make you feel better from the store." Supreme turned around and said, "Oh yea and a toothbrush for that mouth of yours." "What baby, my breath stink?" "Yep! He put his hands up and Whitney playfully punched Supreme in the arm." "Ok!!! I'll remember that when you want another kiss daddy."

After picking Whitney up and laying her in the bed to rest. Supreme went to the Super WalMart to go and buy some things for the house and Whitney. While in the store, he asked the Pharmacy, what would be best for someone feeling ill and throwing up? "Your wife?" "Yea! how did you know that." He told Supreme, here give her this, at least three times a day and she should be fine. But he also advised Supreme to maybe pick up a pregnancy test on aisle one. Maybe y'all expecting a new member to the family. Are y'all newlyweds?

Supreme smiled and handed him back the medication, he remembered how Stigma was throwing up in the mornings the same way as Whitney. Supreme grabbed three tests, toilet paper, and a toothbrush and toothpaste and headed towards the cashier. The woman smiled as she rung up his stuff. "Good lock Sir, I'm sure you'll be a great dad." Thank You.

Supreme woke Whitney up and he had toothpaste already on her new brush and a pregnancy test kit in the other hand. Whitney flipped Supreme off and grabbed the toothbrush and headed to the bathroom. Whitney didn't have any idea as to what Supreme was holding in his other hand. He walked in the bathroom while she was brushing her teeth and started setting the pregnancy tests around the sink. "What are these baby?" After she read the labels, Whitney started laughing. "Man are you crazy? I'm not pregnant baby." I just was a little sick, maybe it was something I ate yesterday but I'm feeling much better now.

Whitney turned and looked at Supreme. "Baby you can't be serious, you really want me to do this?" She was holding up one of the boxes, and Supreme shook his head yes. "Ok! Ok! If that will make you feel better." Get out, get out, she was pushing Supreme out of the bathroom. Whitney did the first test and two lines popped up on the test kit and she started crying. She opened the next box and tried it, and the same results came back. "Oh shit!

my mama is going to kill me!" Whitney opened the door, no baby I'm pregnant.

Supreme heard the door unlock and he walked in and hugged Whitney. He was so happy that his wife was pregnant. But without him knowing it, Whitney was feeling very different about it inside. Supreme turned Whitney around towards the mirror and raised up her Prada dress. He bent down and kissed her stomach. Then he bent her over the sink and pushed her panties to the side and hitched his penis inside of her vagina like a car being towed away. Whitney was looking in the mirror as Supreme enjoyed himself inside of her. Whitney's body was there but her mind was far away from where Supreme was. She thought about how she had failed her mother's upbringing and everything that she had taught her. It seemed that she had gone against everything that she and Ms. Housemoore had talked about. Here she was nineteen, married and pregnant with no type of career. All she has is Supreme to depend on with no job. Not that Supreme wasn't a good man and husband because he's making sure that she straight and comfortable. But Whitney was thinking, "Who in their family even know that they're married and that she about to have his...and when Whitney went to say Supreme baby, that's when it hit her right in the gut.

Could I be carrying the man's baby that I had sex with, when Supreme left me in that suite while he was out of town? Is this the guy's baby that left his name on a piece of paper on the nightstand that said call me Deshawn? Could this be Deshawn baby in my stomach and not my husband? Whitney thought that her life was headed in the same direction that she was in now with Supreme getting fucked!

$ $ $ $ $

Marquan sat in his truck laying on the steering wheel. He couldn't believe that 209 days ago he was being released from Florence State prison and got his life back, to less than 24 hours turn it over to the devil from getting released. All those years of serving time, he promised his mother that he wouldn't come out and live a sinful lifestyle. But Marquan knew that he had made a deal with the devil the moment he accepted that 50,000 dollars that Supreme gave him. Ms. Bergess even had taught Marquan verses out the Bible, to show him that a sinful lifestyle was going against God's plan and purpose for him.

But here I sit in the mouth of the snake, watching him squeeze the life out of me. By the same man that I bragged on to my friends, and he the one who wind up setting the deal up for me with the devil. I've taken the lives of men, women, and innocent children. Buried two dudes that where real friends and used the three women that really care about me. To turn around and put my trust in the woman, that took everything from me that the devil offered me. Just like my mother taught me, when she used to tell me all the time, "Marquan, go read John 10:10"

"The thief come not, but for to steal, and to kill, and to destroy. I am come that they might have life, and that they might have it more abundantly." Man, how can I allow myself to be misguided, after all I've been through? Well, I can't get it back or take it back, but I can stop the devil from putting me in his grave. "Supreme, it's my turn now brother, I'm ready to dance with the devil!"

$ $ $ $ $

Stigma put her clothes in the trunk of her Mercedes Benz, and she headed back into the house to grab the last of her son's things. The doorbell begins to ring. Ding Dong! Ding Dong! Stigma's heart started to beat real fast, because the last time that she heard the doorbell, men with ski mask and a female came running in their house with guns. Stigma had ran and grabbed her gun, this time she wasn't worried about Little Isaiah. Because she had left Isaiah at Ecstasy house, just in case Supreme showed up and tried to stop her from leaving with their son.

Stigma picked up her gun and cocked it, then she went to answer the door. "Hello!" "Hi! Ma'am you must be Valarie Ong?'" Yes why! How can I help you? Ma'am, I think you have already. You have just been served and he handed Stigma her letter and walked away. Stigma opened the envelope and it said that she was to appear in court for a child custody hearing, October 2nd at 9:00am in Judge Grammer courtroom. Stigma closed the door and laid upside the door.

BIG AND LITTLE SATAN

After all that she and Supreme had been through, he sent somebody to serve her papers to try and take their son from her. Stigma told herself that, Supreme would have been better off pulling that trigger in their bedroom, then to think that she'd ever allow him to take her son away from her. Stigma took the bullet out of her pocket that Supreme tossed to her the day that he was about to kill her. He also left and never did return back to her or his son.

Stigma stood there and started to reminisce over the years that she and Supreme shared together. That led her to go back to the times of her mother leaving her at home alone to go and be with men. The only person that loved and cared about her was dead because of her and Supreme lifestyle. Then, the one person that started caring about her just got up and walked away like they never had anything together. Stigma was smart to make sure that she and Little Isaiah didn't want for nothing. But she did have to admit that it was Supreme's doing. Even though he took from everybody else, he always made sure that Little Isaiah and her were fine.

Stigma was wearing red lipstick and she had the lipstick in her jacket pocket. She walked upstairs and headed to their bedroom bathroom and removed the lipstick from her pocket. She wrote, "Dada, I never thought that we would ever come to this. "Thank you for everything that you taught me, and for the love of my life that you gave me. But Dada, you can take this to heart, because that's just what will stop in your body if you ever try to take our son from me." "I guess only God know where this is going to end, so I'll leave this here for him to make that decision. Stigma placed the bullet on the counter and walked out of the bathroom.

Stigma grabbed as much as her and Little Isaiah stuff that she could. For a minute she just stopped and stared at the spot where Ms. Bergess was laying before the coroners removed her body. Tears started rolling down Stigma's face, she looked up to the same God that Ms. Bergess told her about all the time. But right now, Stigma was wondering, why God allowed Ms. Bergess to take her last breath right there on her floor, and why didn't he stop Supreme from leaving her and his son.

Apart of her wanted to go take all their stuff out of her car and just fight for her man. But this time, Supreme have taken it too far. First, he goes and get married on her, then he go to Atlanta and take her child's father from him. All of Stigma's life she promised herself that she would never leave any of her kids in the way that her mother done her. Now just thinking about her mother leaving her again, that made her put her hand on her 9mm and wished that Supreme would walk through that door.

Stigma didn't realize it, but she said out loud today won't none of my kids have a father Dada, if you walk through that door. Stigma went and removed Ms. Bergess apron that her son bought her, she thought that this would be the first thing she put up when she gets to wherever she is going. Wherever that is, she knew that she didn't have Supreme anymore...But she had the next best clos-

BIG AND LITTLE SATAN

est thing to him, and that was her son. Stigma took one last look around her house and walked out the door.

EIGHT MONTHS LATER...

CHAPTER FORTY-FOUR

RIDE OR DIE CHICK

Ms. Housemoore was walking around the house stressed out. She had lost close to twenty pounds behind Whitney. She came home from work one day, and all of Whitney's clothes were gone. Ms. Housemoore found a letter on Whitney's bed, and it said, Mama, please don't be disappointed in me, but this is a decision that I had to make on my own. "I've never lied to you before and I don't feel like the woman that you raised me to be." But mama not being able to be my own woman, mama you done a great job raising me and my brothers on your own. But now it's time for me to be that type of mother to my own child. When you asked me was I married mama, I'm sorry, but I lied to you. I didn't do it to hurt you, but I couldn't take you being disappointed in me. Mama, you raised us to fear you by disappointment from being able to come to you and tell the truth.

"No matter what the punishment was verbal or physical, mama I always took it, right?" But now I'm an adult woman and just like at birth, we have come to that point in our lives, that we have to separate from each other mama, in order for you to see me be the woman that you raised me up to be. So, yes mama, I am about to have your first grandchild because I'm also pregnant too mom. "But I'm pregnant by my husband, at least I did do that part right." Please don't be mad at me or hate me, but I didn't want to bring stress to me or my baby. I wanted to have a stress-free pregnancy. "My husband loves me and our child, so the both of us is well taken care of." I have a good man, beautiful home and the only thing to complete our happiness is the baby being born. I'm not sure of what I'm having, me and my husband just decided to surprise everybody when the baby comes.

"Mama, I'll call you regularly, but if you want to argue or put me down, I'm going to hang up and never call back." I need your motherly support but not attitude or negativity. I love you so much and you're my mother and so in that way we'll never be separated because you helped God give me life. I just asked you and Marquan because I know that he's walking around upset too mama, but the both of us is just asking for y'all to give us a chance, please! After I have the baby, we plan to have a big wedding and that's when I'm praying that y'all are there to give me away.

Mama, if you need anything, my husband told me to tell you that we got you. So, please don't be your normal prideful self and don't ask whenever you need something. Mama, I'll come home just as soon as I have my baby, because I want you to hold your first grandbaby. Mama, now you can fuss at your grandbaby and not me all the time, ok? I'll call you soon, just please don't do me like you did Marquan and push me away. "Oh, mama hug and kiss my brothers for me and tell them that their about to be uncles." Mama, I love you so much and miss y'all so much. I just pray that y'all will keep loving me too mama. Love your baby girl, Whitney.

Ms. Housemoore and Marquan read the letter together. Marquan couldn't believe that Whitney had pulled something like this. The conversation that Marquan had with Whitney had him feeling like she was going to be the smart one and do everything right. But here she is putting on three times the amount of stress than he ever did their mother. Marquan tried everything that he could to convince his mom that she had done the best that she could with him and Whiney.

Marquan even promised his mother that he would find Whitney real soon but that was the day they found her letter. Here it was eight months later, and they still hadn't found Whitney even after Him and Supreme threatened everybody that knew her. They even offered ten thousand dollars to anyone that could tell them about where Whitney was. It was killing Marquan to see his mother hurt in the way that she was hurting. The day that they called Whitney cell phone and left good, bad, and sweet messages then back to harsh ones, to only call back the next day and got a disconnected number, that's when Marquan promised his mother, that whoever went and got his baby sister pregnant and married her, that he was going to kill them.

But Ms. Housemoore told Marquan that killing them all that would do is take him away from her again and I don't need to lose the both of you. Ms. Housernoore even tried to put out a missing report on Whitney, but they said that she of age and if she keeps calling and saying she pregnant and got married, then that mean that she not kidnapped or dead anywhere. Whitney had even called the police, to assure them that she wasn't kidnaped or in danger.

Whitney knew her mother and didn't want her putting her in the news or in a newspaper. Because she told Supreme that, her mother would definitely go there if she had to. Whitney was eight months and a week; she is due to have her baby in a couple of weeks. She had gotten up to 165 pounds, so that was a sign that they were having a big baby boy.

Supreme had gone to all her doctor's appointments and was treating Whitney like a Queen. Even after going home and finding out that Stigma and Ecstasy had run off with Little Isaiah together. He kept it under control around Whitney. But he still has people out looking for them in the same way that Marquan had people out looking for Whitney. Whitney was still calling her mother, just like she had promised and as hard as it was for Ms. Housemoore, she decided to play along with Whitney and kept her cool. Ms. Housernoore would read scriptures to Whitney and sing songs to her grandbaby and that's when Whitney would cry.

BIG AND LITTLE SATAN

Whitney was missing her mother, just as much as Ms. House-moore was missing her. Whitney didn't know it, but every money that her and Supreme left her, she was giving every dime to a private investigator. Ms. Housemoore couldn't wait to see Mr. Ambrosio tomorrow; he had left a message on her phone. "Hello, hi! Ms. Housemoore, I guess that you're at work right now and can't answer this call right now.

"But we finally got a breakthrough on your case." "Looks like we got a name on a marriage license out of Las Vegas." I'm not sure if it's your daughter, but the name is definitely the same as hers. But we will see what comes up, we're still checking everything out. I'll come by at ten in the morning, I hope that it won't break your sleep. Ms. Housemoore had heard the message on her lunch break and thought that the five thousand dollars that she had given Mr. Ambrosio was the best money she had ever spent. Because she could go and get her daughter and be there whenever her grandbaby was born. She wasn't all that happy that Whitney was pregnant at nineteen, but if the baby was already here then what would be the since in complaining about it for. Ms. House-moore just wanted to be there for both of her babies. Whoever the baby daddy was, at this point really doesn't matter to Ms. House-moore anymore. Whitney had already told her that he treats her and the baby special.

Ms. Housemoore promised Whitney that she wouldn't get upset, that they could all just sit down and work it all out. Ms.

Housemoore even said that she would invite her Pastor, to assure Whitney that she wouldn't act out on her or the baby daddy. But Whitney still declined and that's what was bothering Ms. Housemoore, then Whitney being gone for eight months.

$ $ $ $ $

Impression was six months pregnant with Marquan's baby and hadn't seen him that much throughout her whole pregnancy. He went from being a perfect gentleman and well-respected man to have in your life, to being cruel, disrespectful arrogant, and a deadbeat father. The few times that Impression did contact Marquan, he just treated her like she was a piece of dog shit on his shoe. It was like, as if he had grown to hate women over night, she knew that Marquan had money, so it wasn't like he was a man concerned about how he was going to take care of their child. Besides, Marquan knew that Impression came from a wealthy family.

Her father is Jack Swanson, the billionaire Mogul from Ultra Cam pictures. In fact, the last time that Impression had even seen Marquan, her father had sent her everything that a baby could need or ever want for. It also was the same day that Impression learned that she was pregnant. Her father was notified of her pregnancy, even before she left the doctor's office. Impression got upset with her father and her doctor. But she already knew the fear and power that her dad had over people. That if the doctor didn't call him, then that would be her last time putting her feet up in his stirrups in his office. Impression was even wondering if Marquan felt like her dad had money shamed him in front of her. By making Marquan feel like he couldn't take care of his baby. Whatever it was, it caused Marquan to distant himself from her and the baby.

Impression was wearing all Vera Wang from head to toe, her hair and makeup was on point for the first time in six months. Marquan had agreed to come by and check on her because he knew that she was carrying his baby. He even apologized to Impression for his behavior and told her that he would explain everything to her when he got there. Impression promised to have breakfast/Lunch ready when he got there. Being that it was already close to 12:00 in the afternoon.

Marquan pulled up pumping that "Thank you baby' by the Dramatics, cause when he was in prison, Pimpin Worship would always wake the whole dorm up playing The Dramatics every morning. He used to tell Marquan, now youngster if you get one of them women real mad at you, slap them Dramatics in and she'll forgive you every time."

Marquan jumped out his truck singing, I want a thank you for your love'. Impression was standing there smiling, seeing how handsome he looked in his Louis Vuitton outfit. All look at my two babies, that sent a chill up Impression body to hear him say that. He was claiming her and the baby in the same sentence.

"Hi baby!" Impression hugged Marquan, and they entered into a nice romantic kiss. "Oh! wait a minute, I can't forget my baby."

He leaned over to kiss her stomach. But Impression could clearly see that something across the street really caught Marquan's attention. "Damn! Now that's what I'm talking about right there!" Baby that's nice, who pushing that ride right there? "Oh! I haven't met my neighbors yet, they just moved in a few days ago." "Yea! my man, Supreme pushing one of them too, whoever they are I ain't mad at them. He got the house and the right whip sitting in front of that joint, do that shit then."

"That's Ok! Baby, because when I buy mine, they going to be looking over here and saying the same thing about us baby." Marquan got back focused on Impression and he picked her up and carried her into the house. "Damn baby! something smelling good up in here, what are you cooking?" Come see for yourself.

Marquan walked into the kitchen and grabbed him a small piece of fish and stuck it into his mouth. Impression smacked his hand, I said come see baby, I didn't say come taste. Marquan turnd his lip up. "What's that Tilapia?" "Yep! how does it taste?" Marquan put a frown on his face. What, it doesn't taste good? Marquan said, bae I hate to be mean, but it doesn't taste nothing like your fish, and he put a plate under her butt. I want to eat some of that fish right there, Impression slapped him playfully.

"Baby go wash up, so that I can fix our plate." Marquan was headed towards the bathroom and Impression yelled and don't think that I'm not about to take you up on that offer. When he walked away, she said to herself, you can trust and believe that baby. When Marquan came back, the table was fixed, and their food was on the table. "Marquan said a prayer asking God to bless their food, but he also asked God to bless their child to come into the world safe." "Lord, I also ask that you allow your daughter to please forgive my absence, you know that I love her and my baby. Lord, please strengthen us to be as one and a much better family (Amen).

Impression started crying and said, "Marquan we love you to baby." Marquan and Impression started to eat, and he started telling her the truth about everything. Marquan grabbed his glass and started downing his water, but he started to sweat profusely. His eyes started to get real glassy and Impression just sat there and kept eating her food. Impression watched Marquan as he tried his best to pull himself together.

Marquan cell phone started to ring, and he looked at the blurry screen. But he could still see his mother's face showing up on the screen and somehow, he managed to push send. "Hellllo!" "Marquan, is this you baby?" Marquan was looking at Impression, "Yea mama!" Marquan, who is Isaiah Supreme Washington? Marquan was wobbling in his chair and Impression grabbed his cell phone and hung it up. "Bi Bii Bitchhh! Diiii Chuuuu posionnn meeeeee?" Marquan hit the floor, Bam!

Ms. Housemoore kept on trying to call Marquan, but it kept going straight to voicemail. She left a message for him to call her back A.S.A.P. Ms. Housemoore told Mr. Ambrosio that Marquan sounded like he was half asleep and that he would call her back soon. Even thou Marquan was unconscious he could hear the conversation that him and Whitney were having. Marquan, when a woman loves you, she will let you use, hurt, and run over her. "But bro, you got to know one thing about her, nobody on this earth can hurt you worser then a woman can, Marquan." When it's all said and done bro, all that you are teaching her, she is going to put it all back on your ass and if you ain't the man that you claim to be, then all those bitches that you ever called her, Marquan, she is going to let you and the world know that she sees it in you.

When Marquan finally came to, he was tied up and hand cuffed to that same chair that he fell out of. Impression held a 357 magnum to his chest. "Wait! Wait! What the fuck is this?" Man, take this shit off of me Impression. I don't think that this shit is funny at all.

When I get out of these handcuffs, Impression I'm beating your ass and I'm through fucking with you. "Damn! I didn't know that you was some psycho type of bitch!" Man, your ass needs to go see some psychotherapist, something is really wrong with your ass. Impression said, "Wow! that's funny, because Body Count used to tell me the same shit, Marquan!" She started yelling like she was crazy, but he usually would tell me that same shit, when he was fucking over me just like you're doing. "Woman, what the fuck do you mean, I ain't been fucking over you. I been going through pure hell, ever since the day that I left this house."

BIG AND LITTLE SATAN

Marquan tried to hop the chair around, so that they could be face-to-face. That's why I came back here today; Impression, to say that I'm sorry and then you pull this crazy mad woman shit on me? "Mad woman, mad woman, is that what you think of me, Marquan?" I told your ass when I first met you, that I can be a bitch at times, and you told me that you can deal with it. "So, Marquan! Does this really mean, that you lied, and you can't deal with me?'" Yea! take this shit off of me and I'll show you that I can deal with it. Marquan started jumping around in the chair and was trying to get loose.

Your ass thinks that me and my baby a piece of shit, that you think that you can just treat us any type of way? I invited you into my home, my bed and my life and you come in here and fuck my brains out and just up and leave me? Impression was now screaming and yelling, while pointing her gun in his face. To Marquan, he thought that she was acting psycho and was about to snap. He knew that he better do or say something real fast, so he decided to change up both of their moods.

Impression look baby, I know that you don't want to hurt me. How are you going to tell our baby that you're the one who killed their father? Impression started laughing. "Marquan, I see that you ain't all that bright, are you?" Hearing that made Marquan mad and now he wanted to get loose and snap Impressions neck for reals.

Yea! I see. That's because of me being stupid and getting caught up in a weak moment for sex. "Stupid ass mother fucker, I let you get me pregnant, but killing you Marquan, I'll blow your fucking brains upside that wall right there and finish eating my food." What you don't know is, I'm no different than you are Marquan. "We the same type of people working for the same person stupid fuck, don't you know who Papa Jack is?"

Marquan's heart almost jumped out of his chest. "What! Are you fucking kidding me right now?" "Oh! See you must have thought that I was just some stupid ass blond headed bitch that you was running game on?" "Marquan, remember I found you, you didn't find me." When you was in the strip club and it was getting robbed, think about it Marquan, did you see me up in that club? I do think that I'd stand out around them type of bitches.

Marquan was starting to remember that Impression did just pop up from out of no place and was tapping on his window. "Ok! Yea, now I see that we're on the same page now." I didn't come into the club because my dad's driver had peeped that the club had just got robbed. "Marquan most people don't run out of clubs, with guns in their hands and duffle bags across their shoulders." We were about to leave before the police was called, but my target came rushing out the club. When Marquan heard Impression say target, his heart started beating real fast and he knew baby or no baby. Marquan knew that he was about to die, he was already wondering how he heard Papa Jack name and was still living?

Impression started crying and Marquan knew that his time was running short, so he used psychiatry back on Impression. So, you mean to tell me that I gave up everything to come here and be with you and our child, and the whole time all I was is a target to you? Those words penetrated Impressions' heart like a shot of heroin to a junkie's veins. Marquan noticed that, not only did she lower her gun but she also lowered her head. Impression was about to say something but decided not to.

"Well, if you cared about me and this baby, all that money you been making, you ain't bought me one thing for your baby or offer to take me shopping or nothing, Marquan." That's when her temper turned back up because she was now screaming to the top of her lungs in his face. That's what I was just trying to explain to you Impression, before you decided to poison me. "I'm broke! I done something real stupid Impression, that I'm ashamed of." Broke! Broke! "How in the fuck are you broke Marquan and my father just gave Supreme one million dollars just a couple of days ago." "Don't you fucking try to play me Marquan, I know more about you then you think."

What are you talking about, your father gave Supreme a million dollars, a million dollars? For who? For what? A Million dollars, a million dollars! Impression started looking at the way Marquan kept repeating what she had just said. "Yea! Marquan, what you think that I didn't know?" The W.G.K biker gang that y'all just took out. "Yea, my father paid y'all one million dollars for those two cocky son-of-a bitches. I even hated them back when my dad brought them to our house, and I hate them the same now."

Marquan's mouth was hung open. "So, are you trying to tell me that your Papa Jacks daughter?" Papa Jack paid Supreme one million dollars and all he gave me was $150,000 dollars. That made Impression stop talking. "You mean to tell me that, you only got a $150,000 out of a million dollars?" Then shit, I guess that I should have been trying to fuck Supreme again. "What, you fucked Supreme before?" "Well, I won't call it that, I mean shit, we were only kids back then." I just laid there and he humped on top of me until my dad walked in on us and kicked him out of the house. Marquan, why do you keep repeating everything that I say? Marquan didn't know that Supreme was my foster brother, well until he tried to take my virginity. "Wow! That's crazy, so this nigga been using me all this time and I told him all about my feelings for you."

"So, he been playing me all this time? I guess Supreme done got pretty smart, since…She was about to say fucked again, but Marquan looked at her sideways." Naw! I mean yea he been cheating you sounds like out of your money. But no Marquan, Supreme didn't know who my dad was, none of them do. "Marquan, they all use to be foster kids and my parents helped them all and all they did was shit on them." Marquan, now my father is paying them all back for what they have done to him. "Who's your father Impression, that he can afford to fuck off all that type of money?" Marquan, my dad is Jack Swanson. "What! Jack Swanson the Billionaire from Ultra Cam pictures?" Yes, that's my father. Well I be God Da….and before he could get the whole cuss word out, Impression cell phone started ringing and it made the both of them jump. Impression picked it up, because she knew that she had to answer it. Impression gripped her 357 Magnum, so that Papa Jack could hear her shoot him. Impression pointed the gun back at Marquan and his heart started beating fast.

Baby, wait don't kill me, I love you Impression. We can make this work just me you and our baby. Do you love me Impression? Tears started rolling down her face and she answered the phone without giving Marquan an answer. Hello! yes daddy, yes daddy, yes daddy, yes, yes, yes, no I'm sorry daddy, but I can't do that. "Yes daddy, you heard me right, I can't kill my kids' father." "Yea Ok! I already expected you to say that. Can you just tell my mother that I love her?" Tell my mama that I love her and you can go and fuck yourself. Click

Marquan couldn't believe that Impression have just chose him and their baby over her fathers' command. "Impression looked at Marquan, I love you too baby. Just tell me that I didn't just make a mistake, Marquan? "No baby you did the right thing. I'm not going to let nobody hurt my family." Impression started unlocking Marquan handcuffs and got a knife to cut the rope that she tied him up with. "Baby, what did he say?" "That if I didn't follow his order, that he would kill you, me and our baby and I told him to go fuck himself."

Marquan jumped up and was rubbing his wrist from the hand cuffs being so tight. Marquan, you know my father just like I do. I don't know how much time we got before this house rain bullets or blow up. Marguan you know that we better get the hell out of here. Impression, I was serious when I said that I was broke. Impression just looked at Marquan with amazement. "Don't worry because I know that he's having all of my credit cards cut off right now." But I got a little money put up, Marquan. I never spend the money that I strip for. I got a few hundred thousand dollars, that we can take with us until we figure out what to do. "Wait right here, I'll be right back." Marquan looked at Impression like she was crazy again. No baby don't think like that, I'm serious I do love you and our baby Marquan. "Here, take this you're going to need it to get us the fuck out of here." Impression handed Marquan her 357 Magnum, and that released their tension. Marquan went and looked out of her window.

While Marquan held that gun in his hand, all he could think about was killing Supreme and not Impression for tieing him up. Two minutes later, Impression came back dragging a long black duffle bag. Impression placed the bag at Marquan's feet and unzipped it. Marquan eyes opened wide when he saw all the money. Marquan zipped it back up, let's get the fuck up out of here. Impression held a red and white Nike bag across her shoulder that had more guns, bullets, and her personal jewelry. Marquan and Impression came walking out of the house with guns in both hands.

Marquan hit the remote to his truck. "Baby come on what are you doing? We can't take that Cadillac truck nowhere. My father got hundreds of pictures of that thing. We can take my car baby, he's never saw this car before. I bought it the same day that, Body Count got arrested it was a gift for him." Impression hit the button on one of her garages and there sat a red Ferrari. Marquan hurried up and rushed away from his Cadillac truck. She tossed Marquan the keys and he just stood there at the door because he didn't know how to open the door. Impression shook her head and went and open the door and it went up in the air. Marquan put his hand over his mouth. "Whoa shit! let's ride."

Marquan and Impression were riding on the 10-freeway headed west toward California. He looked at Impression and started rubbing her belly, baby we got to make one stop first before I leave Arizona. Impression looked back at him and where is that Marquan, Snooty and Star house? Marquan looked at Impression. "Damn! Is there anything that you don't know about me?" Impression smiled yea! I didn't know that you really loved us and she rubbed her own belly. On the way to Snooty's house, Marquan exited the freeway and stopped at a truck stop on 99th avenue.

Marquan went to fill up the Ferrari because after they left Snootys house he didn't want to have to make another stop until they were out of Phoenix. Marquan was pumping gas and his cell phone started ringing. "Baby, baby! it's your mother." Impression saw that her face came across the screen and it said mama. Yea hello! Marquan stood there listening to what his mother was saying on the phone.

Ms. Housemoore was telling Marquan that his sister got married to somebody named Isaiah Supreme Washington. Marquan's heart for just a few seconds completely stopped beating. "Mama what did you just say?" She married to an Isaiah Supreme Washington and without realizing it. He said into the phone to his mother, "oh yea! this nigga is about to die today." What! Marquan, Marquan! He hung up in his mother's face, without saying another word.

Impression was looking at Marquan's facial expression through the passenger window and she knew that it wasn't a good phone call. Soon as Marquan sat back down in the car. "Baby is everything ok?" "I'm about to kill that nigga!" "Who?" Supreme! Marquan was about to pull out of the truck stop. "Wait! Wait!" Baby we got to get rid of theses now, she was holding up her cell phone. Marquan pulled over by a Diesel, after he saw the man exit his truck to go pay for his gas. Marquan and Impressions turned the volume down on their cell phones. Marquan jumped out of the Ferrari and climbed into the eighteen-wheeler and placed the two phones in the back of the Diesel. Marquan heard the truck driver yelling, "Hey! Hey! Hey! What the fuck are you doing in... Urrrrrr! Marquan burned rubber leaving the truck driver standing there with his hands up"

Marquan couldn't believe the power that her Ferrari had because less than seven minutes they were turning into Snooty apartment complex. Impression told Marquan to hurry up, that they needed to get going out of Phoenix. But Marquan insisted that Impression go inside with him. "But baby! ain't they going to see, that I'm pregnant with your baby?" "I don't care what they see, that's my baby and you are to, now let's go."

Marquan didn't know it, but he didn't just have a baby mama. He has just given himself, a real ride or die chick. Impression smiled and kissed Marquan on the lips, he jumped out and ran around and helped her out of the car.

On their way up the stairs, Marquan was trying to figure out what he was about to tell Snooty and Star. He didn't want to leave them behind, but right now he has no choice. Marquan just wanted to tell the both of them that he loved them and will send for them later once he makes it to wherever he's going. Marquan wanted them to take care of Ms. Housemoore until he could again. Marquan felt that out of the two women, that Snooty would be the one that might hate him for the rest of her life.

Because after learning that Supreme have been playing him like a bitch, Marquan also learned that all this time that they been looking for Whitney. Supreme knew where his little sister was the whole time, because he had impregnated her and married her without saying shit. Marquan was snapped out of his thoughts when he saw Snooty door halfway opened.

He stopped Impression and put his finger up to his lip, Marquan pulled out his 357 magnum and slowly walked through the house. When he noticed Snooty body lying on the floor, Impression made him jump. "Oh! my God nooooo!" That's when Marquan noticed Star body lying there covered in blood in the bathroom on the floor. Snooty was laying there with her eyes opened like she was watching her killer. Impression walked over to her and closed Snooty eyes. Because she wasn't afraid of death, she has saw many bodies that way with her leaving them that way. Marquan started crying like a baby.

Impression took a piece of paper out of Snooty hand, that she looked like she was holding on to for dear life. Impression opened up the paper to read it and it was a sonogram of her baby. Impression started crying herself, and she looked at Marquan and said, "My baby was going to have a little brother or sister, Marquan she was eight weeks pregnant." Marquan looked at Impression and just balled up his fist. Marquan knew that it was him, who Papa Jack sent those Hit Men to kill, instead the two women that he loved and a baby that he didn't even know that he was having took his bullet's.

$ $ $ $ $

Marquan was pulling up to Supreme house when he noticed the men storming around their property with F.B.I on their shirts. The F.B.I was serving search warrants at the same time on three houses. Marquan and Stigma home in Scottsdale. Ms. Housemoore's home and SoSo's "Relax Yo Back massage parlor." They were looking for, Supreme, Marquan, Stigma, Persia, Glory, Ecstasy, and GeeGee. Marquan didn't see any of Supreme main vehicles in the driveway nor was Stigma Mercedes Benz in the driveway either. Marquan looked at Impression and knew that it was definitely time to leave Phoenix, Arizona. Not only was Papa Jack looking for them, but the F.B.I also joined the search.

Marquan hit the gas and was heading back towards the highway to leave Arizona. Just as Impression took a deep breath, as to say well about time, we are leaving. Marquan pulled over on the side of the road and stopped the car. "What! what are you doing, baby let's get the hell up out of here." "Didn't you see all of the F.B.I agents?" Marquan! "Come on baby let's go now."

Marquan looked at Impression then at her stomach, he knew that he wouldn't be able to live with himself if he didn't. He busted a U-turn and floored it. EERRRRRRRRr! Impression was now looking at Marquan like he was crazy. But when she saw that he was pulling back into her neighborhood, that's when she knew that he was crazy for sure.

Impression said, honey have you lost your rabbit ass mind. She was sitting up in the seat looking at Marquan crazy. Marquan stopped at the beginning of Impression's cul-de-sac. He eye-balled all three houses until he spotted what he came back for. Impression was screaming at him, "what are you trying to do get us killed Marquan?" He acted like he didn't hear one word that Impression said. He punched the gas and rushed down the block, but the only thing that confused Impression was where he stopped at this time. They were sitting in front of the house, with the 300ZX and the white Rolls Royce Drop Head parked in the driveway. Marquan told Impression to get under the wheel and she did just as she was told. Marquan grabbed Impression 357 Magnum and went to the door and rang the doorbell and just waited. Soon as the door opened. Pow! Pow!

TWO MONTHS LATER...

Whitney jumped when she heard Deshawn Marquan Washington crying. She wasn't used to being woken up out of her sleep to the sound of a crying baby. But like Ms. Housemoore had told her the first time that she wanted to sleep-in while having a newborn baby. Deshawn wanted a changed diaper and a warm bottle of Similac. He was crying and Whitney didn't move until Ms. Housemoore came screaming and yelling. "Girl, if you don't get your butt up out of that bed and go get that baby." "Mamaaaaa! get him I'm tired, he been keeping me up all night."

"Well, child welcome to motherhood, you laid down and had him." Then, you get your lazy self out of that bed and go take care of that baby. Ain't that right, granny Little Bookie Bookie? Ms. Housemoore went and took her grandson out of his crib. Whitney finally got up and walked over to her mother and her son. Even thou Whitney was tired, every time that she saw her baby, she always starts smiling. She knew that Little Deshawn would never get the chance to see or know his daddy.

But Whitney was happy to know that Deshawn's mother wanted to get to know her and the baby and be a part of their lives. When Whitney finally got up the nerves to call, she found out that somebody had killed Deshawn Sr. and they had found him with his penis cut off. Whitney wondered what it was that he could have done to somebody for them to be so cruel. To want to remove his body part from his body. Whitney had promised Ms. Diana that she and Deshawn Jr. would come and visit her at least once a year. So that she could get to know her grandson and be a part of his life.

Whitney was so happy that Supreme had just called 911 and had asked them to send an ambulance for her. Because her water bag had broken and Supreme was tripping out over the baby coming. After Whitney finally got Supreme to calm down, the 911 operator told Supreme to take Whitney and relax her on the stairs. She assured him that the ambulance was on its way. Whitney had just kissed Supreme and told him that she knew that the baby was going to look just like him. That's when they heard the doorbell ring. Ding Dong! Ding Dong!

"Damn! Baby they must have been right around the corner when I called?" Those were the last words that Whitney heard Supreme say as he was walking away. Supreme opened the door and Pow! Pow! Whitney's heart almost stopped beating, until she looked up and saw her brother, Marquan starring right at her.

BIG AND LITTLE SATAN

Marquan had the most evilest look in his eyes, that made Whitney feel like she had just saw the devil himself. Whitney had never seen whomever was inside of Marquan at that time they stared at each other.

Marquan just turned and walked away, and I forgot about my water bag even braking. Whitney ran downstairs and was holding herself in between the legs and picked up Supreme's cell phone. "911 what is your emergency?" This time it was Whitney who was doing the yelling and telling the dispatch lady that her husband had been shot. "She asked Whitney, wait! didn't he just call about someone water bag braking?" Whitney was still yelling at the lady, that Supreme was about to die if they don't get help soon. "Help me! help me! Please help me! Send us an ambulance fast."

When the dispatch lady started to ask Whitney a million questions, Whitney could hear the ambulance coming and Supreme was choking and spitting up blood. "Wait, wait baby, please don't die on me. I can't raise this baby by myself." Supreme don't close your eyes baby, no, no, no, nooooo! Whitney started shaking Supreme until he opened his eyes up again.

The E.M.Ts was knocking at the door, and Whitney rushed to open it and they could see Supreme laying there in a puddle of blood. They went straight to work on Supreme trying to save his life. The E.M.Ts asked, Ma'am, so where is the woman, who's water bag busted is that you? "Whitney moved her hand, yes that's me my husband was calling for." The E.M.T's wind up taking Supreme and Whitney in the same ambulance. When they got them to hospital in Scottsdale, the nurses rushed them both off in two different directions.

While Whitney was trying to have her baby, the police were asking her a million questions. The doctor finally got them out of the room, so that he could do his job that he was getting paid for. Whitney had one of the nurses go and call Ms. Housemoore. Luckily, she made it to the hospital in time to see her grandbaby being born. When, Ms. Housemoore got there, the same two officers wanted to still ask Whitney a million more question.

When the police finally left, now Whitney was wishing that they would have taken Ms. Housemoore with them. Because she was starting to ask Whitney a million and one questions herself. When Ms. Housemoore learned that Whitney was pregnant by who they thought was Supreme's, she was hot as fish grease that be in the kitchen on Hell's Kitchen on Gordon Ramsay Show. But then Whitney told her mother that her baby was by a man name Deshawn from Atlanta. But mama, "I did really get married to Supreme." Ms. Housemoore was just as confused as the two police officers, that tried to question Whitney about Supreme.

"When they asked Whitney; did she see the shooter, Whitney told them no she didn't that everything happened to fast." Even thou Ms. Housemoore hated Supreme, Whitney begged her mother to go and check on Supreme. Whitney learned from her mother that Supreme wasn't dead yet. But he was still in surgery and was fighting for his life. The doctor told Ms. Housemoore that Supreme have a fifty-fifty chance of living.

Whitney had cried herself to sleep, until the nurses brought her 9 pound and 6 ounce baby boy into her room. Just as soon as Whitney saw him all cleaned up in his Little Jordan outfit that Supreme had bought him to come home in, Whitney knew just what to name him. Deshawn Marquan Washington. She gave the baby his daddy first name, her brother's name for his middle name and Supreme last name because she was married to him already.

When Whitney went home, she was so glad that Supreme had paid cash for their house. Whitney had just learned that the house was really hers and her son because Supreme had put the house in their name. Whitney was happy to know that she didn't have to go back and live under her mother's rules. Ms. Housemoore had come to stay with Whitney for a few months just to help out with the baby. All the crying that Ms. Housemoore and Deshawn was doing was driving Whitney crazy.

Whitney was ready to put her son in his car seat and put him in the backseat of Ms. Housemoore Lexus and send them both back to her house. To Whitney it was like her son and Ms. Housemoore was taking turns waking her up. Now it was Deshawn's turn again. "Here, I was in a good deep sleep and Deshawn started crying again. Lord knows, I tried my best to ignore my son, hoping that he'll stop crying. But him crying made his grandmother start her crying."

She came running into my bedroom and started her crying. "Girl! If you don't get your butt up out of that bed and go and feed that baby, Whitney!" Mamaaaaaa! get him he won't stop crying I'm tired, he been keeping me up all night. "Well, child welcome to motherhood you laid down and had him. You get your butt up and take care of him, ain't that right granny Little Bookie! Bookie!"

Ms. Housemoore went and took her grandbaby out of his crib. Ding Dong! Ding Dong! Whitney finally got up and walked over to her mother and son. "Here, you change him and feed that baby he hungry." I'll go and get the door. Ms. Housemoore walked downstairs and opened the door. "Yea! Can I help you?" "Yea! You can, Papa Jack said hello! Pow! Pow! Pow! Pow! Pow!"

THE END

SEE WHO TAKES THE EVIL ROAD IN

BIG AND LITTLE SATAN 2?

COMING SOON
BY: SHAWN L. BAILEY
THE ROLL'Z ROY$$ OF STORY TELLING

THE ROLL'Z ROY$$

OF STORY TELLING

GOD HAS THE FINAL SAY;
NOT THE HATERS